CONSTANT
TIDES

Angelise,
with love,
Peter Crawford
x

By the same author

CONSTANT
TIDES

PETER CRAWLEY

Matador
9 Priory Business Park,
Wistow Road, Kibworth Beauchamp,
Leicestershire. LE8 0RX
Tel: 0116 279 2299
Email: books@troubador.co.uk
Web: www.troubador.co.uk/matador
Twitter: @matadorbooks

ISBN 978 1838594 145

British Library Cataloguing in Publication Data.
A catalogue record for this book is available from the British Library.

Printed by TJ International, Padstow, Cornwall
Typeset in 12pt Centaur MT by Troubador Publishing Ltd, Leicester, UK

Matador is an imprint of Troubador Publishing Ltd

To the people of Messina

BOOK I

LILLA
1908

Chapter I

Her heart thumps in her chest, her cheeks burn and her limbs lose their substance. The young girl falters in her stride, reaches out to steady herself and clings to the rocklike root of the fig tree in the Villa Mazzini.

"Come, Lilla," she whispers, "be brave. You must. Where is your courage? Remember that time when you had to swim in the dark. That time you were playing dares with Rosario and Gaetano, and they said you were a coward and that you wouldn't swim out to the boat and back because it was night and girls were afraid of the dark. Well, you proved who had the greater courage then, so now show yourself once more that you are brave."

The sound of her own voice lifts her spirits.

That time, that time with Rosario and Gaetano, her first step into the inky–black water had been both frightening and enthralling. Was she to be swallowed beneath the waves as the sea monster sucked down the waters of the Strait? No, because like everyone else the monster was sleeping, so she had swum out and straight back without difficulty. And the boys? Well, that shut them up. They'd never again dared her do anything they hadn't done.

This time things will be the same, only they will be different. The night is chilled, the end of December not the middle of the summer; and this night Lilla is leaving home for good, for a new life, for her new life with Enzo in…

"America. Oh, it sounds so grand. And I will wear a dress that will give me breasts like a pigeon, a dress that shows off my ankles, or maybe a high collar with a necktie or a hat with bird's feathers; and Rosario and Gaetano will still be here with their baggy trousers and shirts made from heavy cloth. Oh, and Enzo will work in an office and he will be a man of distinction and we will be a couple other people want to know."

Lilla lingers beneath the boughs of the fig tree and wonders. Her mother, her sisters, Rosario and Gaetano: what will they think of her running away?

Her father is a hunter, married both to her mother and to the tides that govern the narrow waters of the Strait between Messina and the Calabrian coast; a man of principle, a tough man with a kind heart, a man some called a peasant and others a king.

The previous evening, when Lilla had crawled into the bed she shared with her grandmother and three sisters, she had lain awake and overheard her father and mother discussing the day.

Apart from it being Sunday, there was much that had been peculiar. For one, her father had not insisted on herding his family to the Chiesa di Gesù e Maria del Buon Viaggio to pay their respects and pray for benign weather and good fishing. Instead he had forsaken his obediences and taken to his smaller skiff, rowing with his friend, Pipo Sorbello, up to the shallows at Contemplazione where, in spite of the clouds hanging low and the heavy rain, they had managed a bumper catch of fish.

"I tell you, Rocca, there is something very odd going on," he'd said to Lilla's mother. "The fish were behaving in a very strange manner; I have never seen so many large shoals so close inshore. In such weather, the fish normally make for the deep as though they cannot bear the drumming of the rain on the surface. Yet no, it was like they were all competing for room among the shallows, competing to get closer to the sky. All one had to do was cast one's net and soon the baskets were overflowing. And it wasn't only the fish either: the seagulls, too, were wheeling and diving but not fighting for their share of the fish; they seemed reluctant to skim the water, as though it was in some way tainted."

Something very odd, that was what he had said, something very odd. Did her father know of her intended departure? Had she behaved in an unusual manner? In being overly helpful with the supper and putting her sisters to bed, had she, inadvertently, given her game away?

In the next room, her father had slept fitfully. She'd lain awake and heard him turning and thrashing, a curious unease lying over him like a prickly blanket, and Lilla had waited until she was sure he was soundly asleep before stealing past his door.

"Where are you going, my angel?" His voice had startled her.

"Nowhere, papà... just outside."

"Then I will come with you." And they'd stood together by the door of the small house, silent but for the barking of dogs and alone but for the comfort of the stars and each other.

Lilla had shivered nervously, aware that she could do little else other than wait and hope her father would soon return to bed.

"So, this boy, Enzo," he'd said at last. "Enzo Ruggeri, the son of Don Carmelo, the strong man of the harbour..."

"Yes, papà." She'd looked down at her feet as though, somehow, it was they who were responsible for the flight she was about to take.

"You are leaving us?"

Curiously, Lilla noted, there seemed no malice, no edge of temper in her father's voice. "Yes, papà."

"He is taking you away?"

The thought that the blame for deserting her family might be laid at Enzo's door had angered her. After all, it was not Enzo's decision that she should go; it was hers. "No, papà. He is going with or without me. He is not taking me away; I am going with him. We are not eloping."

Her denial had contained something of a white lie, for she had already been as intimate as she thought proper with Enzo and that intimacy had sealed their love for each other. However, there was no doubt her running away would cause her family considerable shame among the community of fishermen.

"It is the same, Lilla. To elope, to leave with someone, to run away with another. But you must not worry: only fools and the wealthy worry about what others say."

"I thought you would be angry with me; that is why I did not tell you."

"I know, my little angel and I understand. And if you had told me, then I could not deny knowing when your mother asks me. And if I give you my blessing and she finds out, then she will have both of us to forgive."

"Do I have your blessing, papà?"

"You will break your mother's heart if you go."

Lilla had wiped away the tears welling in her eyes. "I will break my own if I don't."

"Yes," her father had sighed. "And your sisters will break your mother's heart when they go. And go they will, one day. As sure as the Madonna provides us with fish, one day they will go." He pauses, thinking. "This Enzo, he is capable and honest, and he has taught you to read and write; that is good. And I watched him when he came to work with us on the luntro: he works hard, he has a feel for the sea and he does not shy away from challenge; that is good, too; that will make my sadness easier to bear. You will go to Naples?"

"We hope to."

"Hope," he'd said, as though hope was something he had put down and now could not remember where. "Without hope people drown."

"I must go, papà."

"Yes, my little angel, you must." And her father had hugged her so tight she thought he would crush the life out of her. He hadn't, though she'd understood that the bruises of his love would never truly heal.

Now, she is cold, cold of body and cold of mind; for the devil of her conscience snarls in her head and even the barking of dogs sounds like a rebuke.

Lilla shivers, this time so violently she almost falls over and she has to cling once more to the solid root of the tree to stand upright.

Is that her guilt whispering in her ear? Are her misgivings nothing more than the ripples from the conflict raging in her core? Is it that her flight with Enzo is ill–conceived, or is something truly wrong?

The Corso Garibaldi is tranquil, which is to be expected for the hours that labour into dawn, and because Lilla is supposed to meet Enzo by the Hotel Trinacria, she steals across the road and heads down the Amedeo to where it opens out into the long and broad esplanade, which runs down to and curves around the sickle–shaped harbour.

With sails furled on angled yards and crews snoring loudly, a man lit ghostly by his lantern stoops to check mooring lines. In the shadows, a ship's mate and his sweetheart embrace, pressing their bodies close so that each will remember the contours of the other's avidity. And outside the deserted market, a wharf–rat yawns and stretches; he has passed the night sleeping rough so that he can be first in the line for unloading the many barges which crowd, like ducklings, around the mothers of their invention.

The port, too, is stretching and yawning, the acid–sweet fragrance of roasted coffee mingling with a haze of salt–seasoned soot.

Beyond the Municipio and the marble statue of Neptune, a steam ship is berthed side—on to the marina. Hope. Lilla hopes: perhaps this is the ship of her dreams, her transport to a new life, her ticket to her destiny.

Chapter 2

Although the sun still sleeps behind the mountain of Aspromonte, stallholders are stirring in the market. Black-skinned pigs from Nebrodi, acidic capers from the Aeolian Islands, aromatic herbs and vegetables, a profusion of fruit and every size and shape of fish harvested from the bountiful waters of the coast, all brought to Messina by the tram which runs fifty kilometres from Villafranca Tirrena on the northern coast; the tram which runs on the rails Lilla now follows.

Her gait alternates between the stride of the confident and the shuffle of the uncertain. Enzo will be waiting for her. Enzo won't be waiting for her. Enzo must surely be there.

He isn't, not yet.

Lilla waits patiently beneath the tall façade of the Trinacria hotel and watches as the crew go about their business preparing the steamer for the voyage to Naples.

Footsteps behind her. She turns.

"I'm sorry I'm late," he says. "You are cold. Here, take my jersey."

"Oh, Enzo." But rather than the jersey, she takes his hand and holds it up to her face, feeling the cool of his signet ring against her cheek.

In turn, he hugs her and kisses her and whispers, "Did you think I was not coming?"

"No, my love, I knew you would come; it's just… your father, I…"

"He left us after the theatre, probably gone to see his mistress across the Torrente Portalegni. I had to stay for a while and calm my mother; she knows our intentions, but she will not let on; you mustn't worry."

"Now you are here, I have no reason to worry." Lilla stands back and studies him. She giggles. "Enzo, why are you dressed like a sailor?"

"My mother. She wanted Vittorio and me to wear this uniform to the theatre and I thought… Well, I thought I wouldn't look out of place."

"Is this our ship?" she asks, hoping.

"Yes. Come, we must be quick, they will want to leave. The captain told me he will hide us until we are out of the harbour."

They walk swiftly towards the steamer. The boilers are lit, shimmering sparks and an eerie crimson glow rising from its funnel.

Enzo takes her bundle of clothes, slings it over his shoulder and Lilla hangs onto his arm, reassured by his presence, excited by the promise of their future.

A sailor loiters by the gangplank.

"The captain is expecting us," Enzo says, his tone pleasant if assertive.

The man stamps out his cigarette and looks them up and down. "Wait here. I will fetch him."

"I said, your captain is expecting us. Please, permit us to board."

He smirks and looks down his thin nose. "And I have been told you must wait." The sailor walks slowly, the wooden gangway rattling beneath his feet.

A metal door opens, light floods out from inside and the door clangs shut.

Lilla shivers again and pulls closer to Enzo. "What if…"

"No, I said not to worry."

"But Enzo, this ship will come to Messina again; what if it comes back and your father refuses to unload it because he finds out this captain allowed us passage?"

"I have paid him handsomely, this captain. And besides paying him, I managed to get my hands on a few bottles of his favourite amaro. It will be in his better interest to keep our secret."

The door through which the sailor had entered, opens. Three dark figures emerge and head back down the gangplank. One, judging by his cap and the shiny gold buttons of his jacket, is the captain: of the other two, one is short and stocky, the other tall and rangy.

Enzo stiffens. "Ullo. And Virgilio."

When the men step down onto the quay, the captain stands square as if he is about to confront a storm. "There has been a change of plan, I'm sorry. These men would like to speak to you." And he turns about and heads back up the gangway, barking orders, pointing and cajoling his crew.

Piero Ullo is the shorter of the two and though he has to look up to address Enzo, his hard expression and the way he flicks his hand dismissively suggest he is no mood to compromise. "Leave the girl, you are coming with us."

"So," Enzo begins, "my father has sent his bootlickers to do his bidding. I must say I am saddened he lacks the courage to do his own dirty work." He stands his ground in much the same way the captain had stood his a few seconds before. "Piero, please, we have known each other how long?"

When Ullo ignores his question, he turns to the taller man. "Virgilio, how many ships have we unloaded and loaded together? And do you not remember that time I paid your bill and hauled your drunken bag of bones out of that bar before the owner handed you over to the Carabinieri?"

"Yes," he replies, frowning subtly, "and don't think I'm not grateful, but..."

"I have some money." Enzo reaches into his pocket. "Perhaps we—"

Ullo shakes his head. "Kid, listen to me: I like you; Virgilio likes you; in fact, we all like you." He sighs, haplessly, hunches his shoulders and splays his hands in appeal. "But look, you're not stupid; you're smart enough to know how this is going to play out. And don't go selling me any vows about how when you're in charge you'll have your revenge, that's just so much piss in the sea."

Lilla watches the charade, more petrified than disappointed; for she knows Ullo, everybody does, and everyone has heard the stories of men leaving on ships only for their bloated bodies to be washed ashore a week or two later. She grips Enzo's arm, her nails digging welts in his skin.

"If it makes it any easier, kid," Ullo offers, "Virgilio here will walk your young lady—friend back to the Borgo. That way she'll keep her respect for you and we won't have to drag you away screaming and kicking like a child who doesn't understand it's time to go home."

A lamplighter wanders past, takes a look at them, recognises Ullo and slips away into the security of the shadows thrown by the street lantern he is soon to extinguish.

"Please, Enzo?" Lilla asks. She slackens her grip on his arm and drops her hands, before reaching up to take her bundle of clothes from his shoulder. "There is no point. I know you are brave and they will only hurt you. Go with them for now: we will have time again soon."

"Not if his father has anything to do with it," Ullo sneers. "A fisherman's daughter? A worthless little shrimp like you for the son of Don Carmelo?"

Of course, the moment Lilla had seen Ullo she'd known it was not going to end well.

"Why you…" Enzo shouts, and leading with his right fist he lunges forward only for Ullo to step back and Virgilio to step round and cosh him over the back of his head with a blackjack.

The assault is swift and brutal, and Lilla is knocked over backwards out of the way as the two men catch the unconscious Enzo before he can drop to the ground.

Forgetting her fear, Lilla screams, "Bastards! Leave him alone," and she leaps onto Ullo's back, punching, biting and kicking him for all she is worth.

Don Carmelo's thug, though, is unimpressed and he reaches over his head, grabs her by her hair and pulls her down. "Enough," he shouts, spinning round and, without letting go, slapping her hard on the side of her face.

It is as though all the bells of all the churches ring at once and Lilla finds herself flying through the air only to land, skinning her hands and knees against the unforgiving paving of the quay.

"Bring him," Ullo mutters to his sidekick. And then, as if to add insult to injury, he spits down at Lilla and wipes his lips with the cuff of his jacket. "This is over," he adds, with the kind of stark finality that brooks no argument. "If you know what's good for you, Lilla Lunapiena, you'll go home and forget what's happened. And while you're about it, tell your father this isn't personal but if he wants to make something of it, he knows where to find me."

Chapter 3

Rubbing the spit from her cheek, Lilla knows there is nothing she can do to change the course of events.

She stands paralysed by her own pathetic impotence, shocked by the suddenness, the simplicity and the severity of the violence. One moment the map of her future had lain within her reach; the next, it had been seized from her and thrown away like a worthless scrap of paper.

Yet she owes it to Enzo not to give in. She cannot let him go quietly. He deserves more. She deserves more.

As the two bullies walk away, dragging his inert figure like a drunk fished from the harbour, Lilla raises her arms, screams and runs at them.

"You bastards! You filth! You are nothing more than the lackeys of Carmelo Ruggeri. How can you call yourself men when all you do is the bidding of a master?"

Without bothering to turn, Ullo swipes at her and knocks her back to the ground.

She gets back to her feet immediately and turns to look at the steamship: the captain is standing at the rail, puffing his pipe, a lazy witness to an abduction that would stir the soul of lesser men.

"You, Captain," Lilla shouts, "how can you stand there and do nothing? How will you live with your conscience? Look what they are doing to him."

Her calls, though, fail to draw a response and he simply turns away and fades into the bowels of his ship, a cloud of his pipe—smoke diffusing in the dawn air.

When she turns back towards the men, they have reached the corner of the buildings fronting the harbour. Enzo comes to and begins to struggle against their hold, so they stand him up, slap him once more and drag him into the shadows.

Lilla is suddenly very alone: alone before the hundreds of ships lining the harbour wall; alone before the Hotel Trinacria and the many guests asleep in their beds; alone before the outstretched hand of Neptune, who reassures the citizens of Messina that he will keep them safe from monsters.

"You hopeless God!" she screams and shakes her fists. "You promise, yet like all the rest you fail to keep your promises. You are nothing." Lilla moans and sobs. She falls to her knees, grabs at the hem of the jersey Enzo has given her and raises it to her face. She inhales his scent. She wipes at her tears. She muffles the outbursts of her frustration.

"Oh, Enzo," she mutters, "please rescue me from this nightmare. We were going to be so happy. Please, in the name of the love we share, wake me and tell me this isn't happening. Please, tell me this can't be happening."

For how long she kneels and sobs, Lilla isn't sure, and folk walk past averting their eyes as if she is nothing more than an uncomfortable apparition, a stowaway ejected from a ship, a disobedient child thrown out by exasperated parents.

And, like boiling water removed from a stove, her confusion settles to a calmer logic and Lilla realises her tears will only serve to dilute the energy of her misery. "Nothing comes to those who weep; you know this. There is hope," she mutters, "there must be. He is still alive. I am still alive. We can still be together."

As she wipes away her tears, Lilla finds herself staring at the bundle of clothes beneath her knees. Strangely a pair of polished shoes seem to have been added to the collection and it takes her a while to realise that they are nothing to do with either her or Enzo, because the shoes are occupied by a man who is now standing beside her.

"There is always hope," he says.

At first, she doesn't completely understand what he is saying. "Sorry," she replies, without looking up, "what did you say?"

"I said, there is always hope." He pauses. "It is of no consequence what challenges life throws at you; they are all nothing more than challenges you have to meet."

The man's pronunciation is unusual, which is why she is confused. In speaking the word hope, he had used the Italian speranza instead of the Sicilian spiransa, and yet the way he extends his vowels suggests to her that he is local.

Lilla looks up at him: he wears a tie and a heavy coat of smoothed wool, topped by a round hat with a curled brim; he has a broad moustache.

"I know you, young lady," he continues, as he peers down at her. "I have seen you about the marina. What are you doing out and about at this time of day? Shouldn't you be at home with your family?"

"Ah," Lilla catches on, "you speak Italian, but you are not, are you? You are English, no?"

"Yes."

"And you are staying at the Trinacria?"

"Yes."

"What are you doing out of the hotel so early in the morning?"

"Oh," he draws pince–nez from his inside pocket, shrugs his cuff and checks his watch, "it is just after five, not so early. Besides, I couldn't sleep. Like the dogs, eh?"

"The dogs have been barking all night, haven't they?"

"Yes, most curious. The concierge told me that when you are praying and you hear the dogs bark, it means something bad is going to happen. Some old Sicilian proverb, he said: a bad omen."

Lilla scoffs at the idea. "Well, you don't need to worry; something bad has already happened, so perhaps they will stop their barking now."

"And you, young lady, you must gather your things and get on home, and I have to go to the telegraph office; the one by the railway station."

"Will it be open this early?"

"Oh yes. They work through the night."

"What's your name, signor?"

"My name is Gordon. That's my surname. My Christian name is Nathaniel. And who do I have the pleasure of addressing?"

"I am Lilla, Lilla Lunapiena."

"Lilla Lunapiena," he repeats. "What a beautiful name. Well, Lilla of the full moon, I must cut along."

"What do you do, Mr Gordon? Why are you going to the telegraph office?"

"I am a representative of Lloyds of London. I am here to assess the repairs to a ship, in the dry dock. I must send some communications before the office wakes up, after which I hope to meet a lady who is coming here from Giardini Naxos." Gordon bends down, so that his face is nearly level with Lilla's. He has kindly eyes and the smooth features of one who does not worry.

"Who is coming from Giardini?"

"My," he says, "aren't we full of questions at this hour! A lady, one Mrs Robertson, a nurse. I have to help make arrangements for her to return to Britain."

"Why is she living in Giardini?"

17

"Well, she doesn't actually live in Giardini Naxos; she lives on an island called Isola Bella." With his thumb and forefinger, Gordon lifts Lilla's head slightly, gently, so that he can look directly into her eyes. "Now I don't know what calamity has befallen you this chilly night, but may I suggest that you be off home; you'll get chilblains sitting on this cold stone. Come on, here's a couple of coins. Get yourself something to eat; the bakers should be up and about by now."

"I don't need your money, Mr Gordon."

"I see, not only a beautiful young lady, a proud one, too."

"No," Lilla grasps one last, ironic smile from her depleted locker. "No, it's not that. It's just that I have a bag of freshly–baked scaniatu; my mother's. The ricotta is nice, even if she never puts enough sausage in them. Here, would you like one?"

Gordon is amused, charmingly so. "Thank you, I will. Though only if you promise me you will get off home."

"Yes, thank you. I am all right now. You are a nice man. I wish everyone was like you."

"Well..." The colour in his cheeks glows warm. "Come on, now. Let's be standing up; that is a start, at least."

He reaches for her arm and eases her up.

"Thank you, Mr Gordon."

"Thank you for the scaniatu, young Lilla. Delicious, I'm sure. Now, remember, there is always hope. Be seeing you." And with a touch of his hat brim and a salute with his doughnut, Nathaniel Gordon is off, his military stride bearing him swiftly south around the harbour.

There is hope, of course there is. And there is yet a future for her and for Enzo. What has happened is nothing more than a temporary setback, a challenge that, as Mr Gordon so rightly says, has to be met. It is a test of the bond between them and a trial of the authority and the tenacity of their love.

The kindness of a stranger, a gift of hope, and the fires of frustration and humiliation dissipate in her cheeks as the desire for vengeance dilutes in her veins. Lilla Lunapiena is no longer a stranger to herself; that nice man Mr Gordon has seen to that.

Chapter 4

The Ruggeri family have recently moved to a tall terraced house, a stone's throw below the church of San Gregorio and a short walk from the Duomo, on the other side of which, across the Garibaldi, lies the marina. Hemmed by the Strait and the Peloritan mountains, Messina has had to gain height rather than weight, and once modest dwellings now boast two, three and in some cases four stories, each level graced by tall, shuttered doors opening onto ornamental, iron–railed balconies shaded by striped awnings.

The street, like its new resident, is on the up. However, unlike the two men who drag their unwilling cargo down it, the Via dei Templari cannot vet the character of its tenants.

Carmelo Ruggeri is waiting at the door.

"Why did you think you would be able to get away with such a childish trick?" he hisses at Enzo.

Ullo and his sidekick release their prisoner. Carmelo nods. The men walk away.

"Surely," he continues, staring down, "you are not naïve enough to think I would not hear of it."

Of course Enzo had not expected his father to hear of his plans. Perhaps it was his brother, that maggot, who had spilled the beans. And Enzo had reasoned that Vittorio would have been overjoyed to see him gone! Really! This was taking his sycophancy to a whole new level.

And could not his father have intercepted him before he set foot outside the door, earlier? Perhaps or more probably not. That was just like his father, wasn't it? That was how Carmelo Ruggeri met all his challenges, wasn't it? No preamble, no pretence, no subtlety; a goat, a Girgentana buck in rut, head down, corkscrew horns to the fore. Only he hadn't fought the fight, had he? No, he had paid Ullo and Virgilio to do his dirty work, so maybe Ullo was the real buck and his father the nanny.

"Get inside, Enzo. We will discuss this in a more civilised setting."

Upstairs in the living room, Carmelo ushers his son to a chair, while he remains standing.

"Did they hurt you?" he asks.

Enzo is momentarily caught off guard by this rare display of concern. "No," he replies, all too aware that his head is unpleasantly sore.

Saverina knocks, enters the room, frowns at her husband and removes a delicate oil lamp from the dining table. As she leaves, and hiding her expression behind the lamp so that Carmelo does not see it, she winces and then purses her lips at her son: a blown kiss of sorts, a communication of her sympathy, a measure of her affection.

When the door is closed, his father continues, "Have I not told you before that this Lunapiena girl is not suitable for you?"

"Don't you mean that she is not suitable for you?" If this is to be yet another headbutting competition, Enzo knows he must front—up or be chased off the mountain.

Carmelo Ruggeri smiles; a resigned, almost warm and patronising smile that suggests the foolishness of youth is to be expected. However, when the warmth fades and his smile wanes, the new Don's demeanour is more that of a man who will not forgive easily.

"That is not the point, Enzo. I have not dragged our family out of the harbour only to see you squander your future on the daughter of that fisherman. She is not suitable for you and that is that."

"Yes, father, I know exactly how you feel about her; you constantly make your feelings all too plain to just about everyone in the harbour. Do you ever give thought to how that makes me feel, or worse, how that makes Lilla feel?" Enzo raises his right hand, as if beseeching a power greater than that which stands glowering before him. "And her name is Lilla. You insist on referring to her as the daughter of that fisherman: well, I cannot argue the point about Lilla being the daughter of a fisherman, but that fisherman? You know very well that Nino Lunapiena is, like you, as respected as any man who earns his living from the waters of the Strait. So please, out of respect for her if not me, her name is Lilla."

"You think the food on our table comes from the Strait?"

"Don't the ships come from the Strait?"

"Enzo, don't play the fool with me, I expect better of you. You would prefer to pass your life in a hovel, have your wife bear yet more fisher–sons and condemn your daughters to sit in the street and sew pretty patterns for the rest of their days?"

"Since when did my father look down on the people of his past?"

"Be careful, boy." His father's tone hardens, his eyes now as dark as the ocean at night.

"Be careful? Why, father, only a man ashamed of his past would deny those who know it."

Carmelo sits back and waits. "All right, if you want to rile me, then do so. But first, please tell me what it is that makes you think the prospect of your life with this girl, in another country, is so much more attractive than the prospect of your life here in Messina?"

He doesn't, though, wait for his son's response.

"Look, let me say this: in Messina we have the most natural harbour in the Mediterranean. Because of this and because of centuries of trade, our city is prosperous. You must understand, Enzo, that if our Sicily is the breadbasket of Italy, then Messina is the centre of its distribution. Screw Palermo! They may think they own our country, but we are much closer to the mainland. We unload and load nearly a thousand ships a week and that is two thousand reasons why our city will grow more prosperous and our business more profitable. Why, our women no longer walk barefoot and even our beggars have better manners than those in Naples. That all promises very well for the future. Our future. Our future and yours. What you should also understand is that your future is now, right here, in Messina. Stay here with me, with your family, with us, and let us grasp our future together."

"With Lilla?" Enzo asks.

"Why does it have to be with her? What about that Bartolotta girl? She is sweet and will make a man a good wife." It was exactly what his mother had suggested when she'd tried to persuade him to stay. Clearly, they have been discussing an alternative.

"That Bartolotta girl? Oh, father! I know looks aren't everything, but she runs Neptune's Scylla a close second."

"Your cynicism does not become you, Enzo."

"And please, father, I am eighteen years old and therefore old enough to know my own mind. This is how it is now. This is how it will be. Enzo and Lilla. We are going to America, a land of freedom and possibility; a land where every man will have the opportunity to make his own name; not a land where the success of the son depends on the position of the father."

Carmelo Ruggeri's complexion grows ever darker. He leans forward and, pointing menacingly at his son, shouts, "No, Enzo, you are not going anywhere. And most definitely not with that fisherman's daughter. That is the end of our discussion, I will hear no more talk of it."

"No, father, this is only the beginning of our discussion; that is if you can call trying to force your will on me a discussion. And please, I must ask you again to stop calling her that fisherman's daughter. How would you like it if you knew people at the harbour referred to mama as that Don's wife? Imagine the disrespect you would feel."

"Better the wife of a Don than a woman who guts fish."

Enzo considers his reply and, recalling the scuttlebutt he has heard about the harbour, he decides to take a chance. "At least Nino Lunapiena only kills fish so that others may eat."

Carmelo bristles with anger. "So, this is what they whisper behind my back, eh? Well, let them whisper it. Knock a few heads together to make them see sense, yes. But murder, no. Though perhaps it is better that they believe the rumour than know the truth: it serves a purpose. My purpose."

For a moment, peace breaks out; but only for a moment.

"My father, I have never believed the rumours. And, you should know, I have more than once split my knuckles against the skulls of those who have spread them." He pauses hoping his fealty will be appreciated. "What I need you to realise is that now, I am like you were then and now I have to stand up for what I believe is in my best interests, in spite of knowing this will cause you hurt. I hope you can understand that."

Carmelo rubs his face as if he has just woken from a deep sleep. He examines the table cloth for a moment, picking at a loose thread and then brushing it away. "Oh, yes, my son, I can understand that all too well."

"Then surely, please," Enzo offers, softly, "if you cannot give us your blessing, at least just let us go in peace."

"No. I have told you: you are not going."

"I am. We are."

"No, Enzo, you are not. Until we know different, this is my family and you are my son. You will show me the respect I am entitled to."

"Oh, I see." Now it is Enzo's turn to bridle and he does so as though some heavenly light has suddenly shone down, illuminating the true knot of their difficulty. "This is not about Lilla and me. It's not about us leaving to be together. This is about what other people will think of you. You are worried that they will say, "There goes Don Carmelo. He used to have what it takes, but now he can't even control his son." Does that really matter to you?" Enzo is careful not to sneer, for he knows well that distaste, like the poor flavour of a dish, might be tolerated, whereas disrespect will only serve to ruin an entire meal.

His father grimaces and shakes his head in annoyance. "Your brother has more common sense."

However, Enzo's disrespect knows no such limitations when it comes to Vittorio. "That backscratcher? He would happily stab me in the back if he thought it would gain him favour with you."

"Vittorio uses his brain: you use your brawn. For the future, it will be those who employ their thoughts wisely who succeed. Brawn will not be enough."

Enzo stands. "Then you are welcome to him, father."

"Sit down, I haven't finished."

"No. We are finished."

"Sit down, Enzo."

"No, father. We can talk all night but, like the whirlpool, we are only going to go around in circles and that will only deepen our disagreement. With respect, we have talked enough."

"Respect?" Carmelo shouts. "You talk about respect? Sit down."

As Enzo turns away towards the door, he feels rather than sees his father move towards him.

The son hesitates; he does not want to fight with his father; it is not right.

Carmelo, though, suffers no such reservation. He is right. A father is always right. He must be.

With a brute force Enzo would never have believed him capable of, Carmelo slams his son head–first into the closed door.

CHAPTER 5

Lilla shivers.

The harbour is now awake. Heads down, their hands deep in pockets, men scuttle by, and across the Strait the silver light of dawn creeps stealthily over the peaks of Aspromonte. Before her lies the steam ship she had thought to be her salvation; a great grey ship, her lanterns lit; the smoke of her coal furnace thickening the air; the chatter of her crew as they stamp their feet against the cold steel of the deck. Lilla's future was right there before her eyes, right there within her reach.

She shivers again, more violently this time. In fact, she shivers so violently she falls to the ground and bangs her elbow.

"You stupid girl!" she mutters, picking herself up. "Get a hold of yourself before your nerves get the better of you. What would Enzo think if he saw you in such a state?"

Lilla looks round, self–consciously, and is surprised to notice that several other people are picking themselves up, too.

The city seems to be talking: it is whispering and groaning about her.

Something is wrong. Something is very wrong. The sound is not that of living beings, it is the lament of those already in hell; souls screaming out for forgiveness, imploring the bowels of the earth to set them free from their torture.

The whispering and groaning escalate to a hiss and a roar and soon rises to a deafening crescendo, and Lilla realises that it is not people she can hear; rather it is the earth in some form of pandemonium beneath her feet, turning, turning over and turning around, rising up and falling back like a giant struggling in his torment.

Suddenly, oh so suddenly, her stomach falls through her torso and she finds herself looking down at the rail tracks on which she had not a moment ago been standing. The curve where they join is beautiful and smooth, like the graceful curve of the arch above the huge doors to the Duomo. But that is strange. How can she be seeing this? Why is she looking down from such a height and how did she get to this place from which she is looking down?

And as suddenly as she is up in the air, Lilla is falling, falling fast towards a ground that is now rushing up to meet her. She lands heavily, her bones jolting, her head banging, her vision blurred. But before she can gather what little sense she has to call upon, the earth trembles once more and she is flung backwards, like a doll, in the direction of the hotel. Lilla is bounced along the road, first left then right, then up and again down. The world, her world, the one in which until a moment ago she was living, has gone completely mad, and she is not altogether certain that she is still alive.

She leans against a wall that trembles like a petrified dog. She tries to get to her feet and yet every time she tries, Lilla is thrown back down. The wall? How is she beside a wall? Not ten seconds ago she was standing in the middle of the Palazatto, twenty paces, maybe more from the doors of the hotel, and now she is beside it as though the ground is a skin stretched tight and vibrating, and she has been bounced, tumbling like a bean, along its surface.

A splitting, cracking, wrenching sound cleaves between her ears and the pressure in her skull threatens to burst it wide open. She is the plaything of a vicious child whose only entertainment is to launch her from one block of stone to the next. She screams.

She screams hysterically, her eyes wide, seeing and at the same time disbelieving.

A man reels, loses his footing and is pitched over into the water. The steam ship of her dreams is picked up and hangs in mid–air. She can see its hull, all of it, its vast propeller and its long rudder. The mooring lines snap, the stone bollards fracture, break off, and are whipped away into the night.

A man is trying to run. His legs reach out as the land appears to move towards him. He makes no progress. He stumbles. He falls. He jerks upright and is catapulted down into the water. The ship is released from its extraordinary suspension and crashes down on top of him, rolling as if to iron him flat. Then, abruptly, it comes to rest, leaning against the harbour wall, the crew hanging for dear life from rails and davits.

The world has gone crazy. Crazy, like a man who shakes his head in the hope his demons will lose their purchase and fall out from his ears. The mountains, they are coming to claim their right: they are squeezing the narrow strip of land up against the Strait; they are hellbent on pushing the city into the sea; they desire only to destroy Messina and bury the souls who have sought to carve their names upon its stones.

Lilla holds on, and she holds on as tightly as she can ever remember holding on to anything. And yet, the wall does not want her; it will not permit her to hold on, it rejects her and shakes her off like a persistent flea. A crack opens up beside her, a crack large enough to swallow her whole, and she stares down into the black bowels of the once beautiful city. A burst of searing flame leaps up from the fissure, swiftly followed by a jet of foul liquid, which sprays her and slams her back against the wall to which she had been so desperately clinging.

The purgatory is unceasing; it will never end. This is the hell she had heard others tell her she would find if she left with Enzo.

"Hope," she yells. "We had so much. Where is it now?"

Lilla hangs on for her life. For his. For theirs. For the life of the city.

"Holy Mother of God, is it a sin, to hope? Is that it? Is it so wrong to wish for better? Is this why we are being punished? For hoping?"

CHAPTER 6

The blood congeals at his nose and blocks his breathing.

His father had followed up his assault with a forceful cuff to the back of his head, knocking him off–balance. And whilst Enzo had tried to recover what was left of his composure, his father had dragged him unceremoniously down the stairs, opened the trapdoor to the cellar and launched him down the wooden steps into the darkness.

"You will stay there until you come to your senses," Carmelo Ruggeri had shouted after him, as he'd slammed the trap shut and slipped the bolt.

The fall, or rather his ungainly cartwheel into the cellar had hurt: his elbows are skinned, his knees the same and the bruises on his back will take a long time to heal. They will heal; that he is sure of. What may never heal, though, is the bruising to his ego. In his futile attempt to persuade Enzo from his course, his father had invoked the promises of a bright future. Well, that future, any future, would now be tainted with the poison of contempt.

Contempt? Contempt or perhaps hatred? For though this is not the first time he has been beaten and locked in the cellar – surely, there is nothing uncommon in a father's ire: doesn't every son bear that cross? – this is the first time the energies of his father's practice have affected someone else and that is not only completely unfair, it is also totally unacceptable. After all, what misdemeanour has Lilla committed other than to fall in love with him?

If his father is guilty of a crime, though, it is that Lilla should find herself deserted in the marina at such an hour – something only he can be held responsible for – and as a result, Lilla is to be faced with one of only two equally unappealing choices: either going home with her tail between her legs or waiting around to see if Enzo can free himself from his dungeon.

For the first time in many years, sitting in the dark on the stone-hard floor of the cellar, Enzo hangs his head in his hands and begins to cry. There is no hope. There is no justice. There is no Lilla.

There is, also, no point in feeling sorry for oneself. He wipes his nose on his sleeve, forgetting for a second how much his nose already hurts.

"Madonna della Lettera," he moans, "can you see me here in this prison? Can you not free me from the cords tying me to my father? I do not wish him dead, but perhaps you could grant him a measure of humility."

And as he waits for a reply Enzo believes will never come, the cellar trembles. A jar falls from a shelf and smashes against the floor, startling him.

The trembling passes.

"So," he mutters, sarcastically, "you have heard me, that is a start. Now show me what you are going to do for me, for us." The hairs on the back of his neck stand up and his ears warm, a sure sign that he is disconcerted.

"I know that shaking," he mumbles. "I have felt it before. But where? When?" He rubs at the back of his neck to settle the hairs as he dredges his memory.

"Yes, of course, you fool. Was it a year ago? Or was it longer? No, it was last year, in October. We went to Reggio to stay with zio Giovanni and zia Margherita. There was an—"

Don Carmelo's elder son never finishes his sentence, for his thoughts are suddenly drowned by a rumbling, roaring thunder and he is without warning tossed upwards against the joists of the cellar ceiling. And as soon as he is up, he is flung back down, then against the wall, then back down on the floor. He is winded and he gasps, trying to draw some air, any air, into his lungs, as he reaches out for something to hold on to so that he might learn which way is up. But before he can get his bearings, Enzo is flung up and down once more, and once more from side to side, this time so violently that he believes he has been mistaken for a cork in a furious sea. He is beaten and thumped, and he buckles against the walls of his imprisonment. He rolls and lurches and tumbles and sprawls. He grabs at the wood of the steps as they fly past and he has almost gained a hold, when he is jerked back and away and up and down again. The turmoil seems endless and he screams in fear, his words lost to the tumult of destruction.

How long the barrage lasts he does not know, as the crashing increases in volume, louder and louder until his eardrums burst and his head explodes in a crescendo of agony. The house. The house is falling down on top of him. A beam smacks him across the side of his body, grazing his back, another sweeps him aside, jolting his spine, and a third cracks against his head, conjuring brilliant bursts of incandescent light in his eyes until, like fireworks, they die away to vanish, taking with them his sight.

CHAPTER 7

Though she cannot hear herself, Lilla is still screaming. She has her eyes hard shut, her hands stuck fast to her ears, and the panic of her heart thumps through her head.

"Oh mama. Oh Enzo, my love, make it stop." And as if he can hear her, the vibrations, the pulsations, the revolving and quivering, the trembling and the wrestling of the monster below begin to slow, and the beast of her terror falls silent and still.

Silence. Silence pure and peaceful, cool and clean, comes to her rescue and she clambers up against the wall, trying to stand up. The ground is no longer moving. The world, her world, has stopped turning.

"Thank you, mama. Thank you, Enzo. When I asked, you delivered."

Yet now there is dust, dust and a revolting, overpowering smell. And the brilliant quiet is torn by the crashing of masonry, the snapping of wood, the sharp scraping, sliding, clashing of tiles and the clanging, jangling resonance of bells falling from their campaniles. People are screaming and screaming and screaming, and hell is once more returned to the city. But at least the ground is no longer shifting. At least, Lilla can now find her feet.

"And what? What is happening now? Is the world falling around our feet? What am I to do now?" she moans.

Lilla feels blood trickling on her face and reaches up to feel the wound from which it flows. The blood is black, not red and her fingers, now mixed with the dust, are coated in a sticky emulsion.

A body, that of a man, lies naked at her feet. There had been no one near her when the tremors began and it takes her a moment to understand why he should be without his clothes when she still wears hers. Then it dawns on her: he has been thrown out of the hotel window above her, his head smashed open against the paving that has greeted his fall.

Lilla has never seen a man naked, not her father and not even Enzo.

Enzo! Enzo, of course. Why is she thinking of herself and not him? The thugs, they have taken him home: perhaps he is safe.

She stumbles and staggers across the debris towards the corner of the block: the dust is now choking and blinding, and she runs her hand against the wall to find her way. When she makes the corner and turns to peer up the street, she is confronted by a vision worse than the hell she has just survived. An eerie yellow flame shoots skywards through a miasma of dust and the street is no longer an elegant thoroughfare to the majesty of the Garibaldi; it is a mountain of rubble.

A man staggers, ghostlike, wrapped in nothing more than his bed—quilt, seemingly oblivious to the blood which streams down his legs: his hair hangs down in muddy braids, his eyes are wide and staring, and yet he is unseeing. "The Day of Wrath," he shrieks. "All is lost," and he falls backwards, disappearing into the gaping maw of a fissure. A jet of water like an urgent fountain spurts from the fissure, extinguishing the yellow flame.

Lilla inches past, clawing her way to the Piazza through the clouds of dust which ebb and flow like tides.

She glances up and catches a glimpse of the Chiesa dei Catalani. By some miracle the rounded walls of the main apse still stand and even the dome of the cupola is intact.

The same cannot be said of the properties in the Corso Garibaldi; their roofs have collapsed inward and their outsides have slid down into the street leaving their insides exposed, their beams sticking up and out like the broken bones of a half—eaten fish. On one floor she can see people, clinging to curtains and furniture, crying out for help, imploring anyone alive to help them down. In their distress, husbands and wives stand, gazing up pathetically, shocked and stunned by both their survival and their inability to save others. As they too watch, people, some naked and some in nightshirts, slip and fall, screaming in their terror as they plunge into the shattered, splintered remains of their homes.

Her senses, like the sharp, irregular fragments of a glass smashed against a marble floor, have deserted her and in a daze, Lilla wanders amongst the debris of the Garibaldi, making past the church.

"Where am I going? Where? Oh, yes, Enzo. Enzo's house." Lilla tries to remember where. "Oh, my love, your house."

She had been there twice, alone on both occasions. Her father had warned her that Signor Ruggeri would not take kindly to her and for once, or perhaps more honestly because Enzo too had warned her, she had for the first few weeks after meeting the handsome young man, taken her father's advice. However, like a dolphin cannot resist the temptation to swim beneath the bow of a boat, her curiosity had got the better of her and one day she had summoned her courage and sought out the address.

That first time, she had waited and watched, spying on his mother and his young sisters as they came and went; and she'd dreamt, fancifully if not frivolously, that one day perhaps she and Enzo would live in such a grand property and keep a cat, a domesticated, adoring cat unlike those scrawny, flea—ridden animals that had lounged on the pavement and eyed her suspiciously.

The second time, Carmelo Ruggeri had returned unexpectedly and caught her. In words she had never heard, though whose meaning she completely understood, he'd shouted at her. She'd been upset and had thought to tell her father, but on her way home she'd recalled his warning and thought better of it.

Once more, Lilla closes her eyes and tries to imagine her best route through the chaos and carnage. Enzo's house lies on the far side of the Via Cardines, a narrow street which, he'd told her when recounting the history of the city as they sat one afternoon in the Gardens of the Villa Mazzini, was originally named the Via della Giudecca, after the Jews who populated it. So, for the sake of her own safety, she decides to keep to the wider, more open Piazza dei Catalani and then take the Via Primo Settembre into the Piazza del Duomo; that way, the only narrow street she will have to risk will be the one that leads up in the direction of the Chiesa di San Gregorio. And, if she can keep the helical bell tower of the church to her left and in front, then with a little luck she should come across the Via dei Templari somewhere on her right.

Her head! Blood is streaming down her face. She reaches up to press against the wound, hoping to stem the flow. Her hair is caked in blood and dust, yet the liquid feels lighter than before. Her shoulders, too, are soaking. But not with blood.

Lilla looks up and fat rain drops sting her eyes as if they are thorns hurled from the sky.

An old man stands, staring at her, his mind closed to a horror he cannot comprehend. He raises his arms as if to petition her and is immediately, magically and shockingly buried beneath an enormous lump of falling masonry. One second, he was right there in front of her; the next he is gone, flattened, disappeared without trace.

Lilla begins to run, blindly. The Primo Settembre is no longer broad, it is now a narrow valley winding between tall hills of broken brick, bordered by jets of flame and fountains of foul liquid. And as if the debris of nature's wrath isn't sufficient to delay her progress, her way is now blocked by a horde of onrushing terror–crazed lunatics, some half–dressed, some undressed and others wearing bizarre assortments of clothing: a man in a bodice, another with his head poking out of a torn bedsheet, a starkly naked woman clutching a hat with which she vainly tries to protect her head from the falling mortar.

They are oblivious to Lilla's presence; they simply run straight through her, bumping her this way and that in their panic to reach the marina.

"Not that way!" a man shouts at her, "there is only death in the city. Make to the port. Find a ship. Get away. Save yourself."

When she doesn't reply, he waves her away as though she must be deaf or stupid, or more likely mad.

The Piazza del Duomo, too, is a sprawl of rubble. The fountain of Orion is unmolested by the tremors, yet beside it the great cathedral's roof has fallen in and only the left wall and door remain intact.

More people, their faces gaunt, their expressions hollow, are running towards the marina, clambering over the wreckage that is now strewn so haphazardly about the piazza. Those who are not running are only walking because they are either carrying or supporting a loved one who cannot stand. They seem uncaring of the sharp stones and jagged stumps of beams which shred their bare feet, and they scream and moan in panic. In the midst of the hysteria, two ear–splitting explosions to the north send vast fireballs high into the rainy sky. The gas lanterns flare brightly, then fail.

Lilla is barged roughly out of the way by a man she does not at first recognise.

It is Don Carmelo. His chest is bare and bloody; his trousers torn; his eyes wild, as though he is running from the very devil himself.

"Signor Ruggeri, it's me, Lilla."

Enzo's father hesitates at hearing his name.

38

"Where is Signora Ruggeri?" she asks. "Where are the girls and Vittorio?"

Carmelo foams at his mouth, his face a landslide of mud and tears.

"Gone!" he shouts at her. "They are all gone, I tell you. Run. Run for your life." He pushes and then tries to shove her from his path, yet Lilla stands her ground. She is not to be deterred. Her one thought is Enzo. He must be alive. He must be. If anyone deserves to be saved, it is her love.

"And what of Enzo, Signor Ruggeri? Where is Enzo?"

"That boy?" he sneers. "That fool. And you, you snivelling little harbour slut, this is all your fault. Get out of my way."

Lilla lowers her head and stares up at him. "Not until you tell me where Enzo is. Now, where is he?"

"Where do you think he is?" Carmelo replies, spraying her with spittle. "He is at home in the cellar. You put him there. If you hadn't interfered, he would be alive. Alive here with me. Now get out of my way."

Lilla stands back and is bowled over by a swarm of people. She is pushed and shoved and scratched and punched, yet her desire is stronger than that of the tide of humanity which flows before her and she gets back to her feet and watches as Carmelo Ruggeri staggers away.

The Via Oratorio San Francesco narrows towards the top, taking a small right and then left turn before the entrance to the Templari.

As Lilla reaches the bend, the ground begins to tremble again and the façades of buildings either side of her crack and slump down into the road. The rubble is slippery from the incessant rain and her legs are now ripped and bloody from her scrambling and slithering.

A woman lurches from a house to her left as its balustrade detaches and falls to the ground with a startling crash. She shrieks, turns and rushes back into the house, which crumbles and caves in, burying her in her flight.

No sooner than the ground has begun to tremble, it stills and Lilla carries on. Enzo's street is now only a few metres away. She dips into a doorway to catch her breath before one final dash. Yet the carnage she has left behind is little more than a sideshow to that being staged in the Via dei Templari. Not one building is intact, the front of the terraced houses having been ripped clean away to reveal the skeletons of their construction, pictures hanging askew, clothes hanging on stands, shadows dancing eerily on every floor.

At the foot of Enzo's house lies a mountain of rubble, on top of which Enzo's youngest sister lies peacefully asleep.

Lilla climbs up and examines her. She leans her ear against Lucrezia's small mouth, but can neither feel nor hear her breath. She pinches her arm hard and waits for a reaction. Lucrezia's smile is that of an angel Lilla has seen painted on the ceiling of the Chiesa di Gesù e Maria del Buon Viaggio. Well, that is now who or what Lucrezia is, isn't she? An angel on her way to a better place, on her way to any place so long as it is not the hell of this place. Lilla studies the lifeless form of Enzo's sister: her dark curls, the down at her cheeks, her cherubic lips, her delicate hands, the small gold ring on her finger; the gold ring her mother must have given her at her confirmation.

"Lucrezia, go forth from this world," she whispers, trying to concentrate, trying to remember the prayer. "In the name of the father who created you and… Oh please, Madonna, look after this young girl. Look after Enzo's sister as if she was your own."

"Enzo?" Lilla shouts out his name. "Enzo?" And the louder she shouts, the greater her anxiety builds: and the greater her anxiety builds, the more her tears flow. She shouts again and again, until she can no longer hear if she is still shouting. "Enzo? Oh, Enzo, don't leave me here. Take me with you. If you are dead, take me with you, I beg you. Don't leave me here."

For how long she calls for him, Lilla isn't aware. All she knows is that the rain continues to fall and the street is lit by yellowed flames.

"How can it be?" she asks Lucrezia as though they are sitting beneath the old fig tree in the Villa Mazzini on a sunny afternoon. "How can it be that the flames still burn and yet the rain still falls?"

And as Lilla tires, she grows cold and silent. Silent but for the screams of the multitudes and a curious, harrowing, whispering wind, the like of which she remembers from a storm upon the Strait. "Has God not punished us enough?"

Lilla rests her weary head on Lucrezia's stomach. "Oh, Enzo. The sea," she mutters. "The sea is coming to claim us."

Chapter 8

"Wake up now. You can't sleep there all day. Wake up, young lady."

Lilla sits up, blinks and rubs her eyes: it is daylight, still raining hard and she is cold, very cold. The man speaks in English accented Italian, much the same as the man she'd met down in the harbour. She turns and notices the still form on whose stomach her head has been resting.

"Whoa," the man reaches out to steady her. "Mustn't worry, my dear. Nothing more you can do for her, now. Best see what we can do for you, eh?"

"No, I'm fine. We must… Oh, poor Lucrezia."

"Never mind poor Lucrezia, you're in a pretty dreadful state yourself. Best see if we can't get you to one of the medical stations." The man is thickset, with bushy eyebrows and a square chin. He wears the kind of cap a ship's officer would wear. "Let's see if you can stand up for me, eh? Slowly now."

"What about Lucrezia? We can't leave her here. Not like this, she'll freeze to death."

"Now then," he replies, placing his large, warm hands on her arms, "plenty of other people in need of help; we'll get to your friend Lucrezia in good time. Up you get."

Lilla tries to stand, but finds her legs have no energy and she sinks back down, covers her eyes with her hands and begins to cry.

"Right then, I'll have to carry you. Your legs are in a bit of a state. We need to get them dressed or they'll turn bad." He picks her up and lays her gently over his shoulder.

Lilla glances between Lucrezia's pale form and the mountain of rubble as the man picks his way carefully to the bottom. Once there, a handful of other men are waiting.

"Now then, Smith," the man says, this time in English, "you take her."

"Yes, Mister Read, I've got her. Blessed rain," he mutters, "slippery as an eel, she is. As if a bloody earthquake isn't enough."

Lilla comes to and begins to struggle.

"Just you hold on there, young lady," Read says, trying to calm her.

"But Enzo... he's in there."

"I dare say he is," he replies, his tone soft, sympathetic. "And if he is, I'm afraid that's where he'll be staying for the moment. We can't go digging around in there. What with these aftershocks, the rest of the building might come down any minute. As I said, we've got to get you down to the medical station: you've been out here most of the day and you're as weak as a new-born lamb. If we leave you here any longer, you'll likely as not die of cold."

"But, the flames. What about the flames? He'll burn."

"There, there, young lady. I'm sure your Enzo will turn up. Got to believe that. No point in getting upset now, is there?"

For Lilla, the next minutes pass in a blur of bouncing and swaying as the two men pass her back and forth while they navigate their way around and over mounds of rubble. Joists have shaken out of their pockets, bringing whole floors crashing down one upon the other, trapping the residents beneath piles of bricks, stones, tiles, beams, laths and mortar. At one house, a woman screams for help and then quiets; at another a corpse is hanging upside down, pinned at the waist by a long section of cornice which leans like a bolster against the wall. Surrounded by chairs, a piano stands upright in the middle of the street and a bedstead, square on all

43

four of its iron feet, is littered with books and papers. And as if these visions aren't sufficiently bizarre, towards the bottom of the street a fishing skiff perches against a fallen statue.

On noticing the skiff, Lilla grows agitated. "My parents? What about my parents? I must go to them."

"All right, my dear. Just you settle down," soothes Read.

Lilla's energy, though, cannot match her curiosity and concern for her parents, and she sags back onto her guardian's shoulder, asking dreamily, "Where are you taking me?"

"Down to the esplanade."

"Why? I need to go home."

"Get you patched up first, then you can go home."

"You're not from Messina, are you, Mr Read? Where are you from?"

"City of Cardiff, country of Wales. Long ways from here."

"What's the name of your boat?"

"Afonwen. Coal ship."

"Why are you here?" Lilla is delirious and intrigued in equal measure.

"We are looking for Ali, Ali Hassan, one of our firemen. Came ashore last night."

She wonders whether their man Ali was the man she'd seen embracing the woman in the doorway near the Municipio. "Do you know Mr Gordon?"

"No, miss."

"My father's a fisherman," Lilla mumbles as she surrenders and slumps down on his shoulder.

"Is he now? Well, you be quiet now. I'm sure he'll be along to find you soon." He rubs her back, gently, as her mother used to when putting her to bed. "Smith?"

"Yes, Second Mate Read?"

"Passed out, she has."

Chapter 9

Enzo, too, wakes up, although waking from sleep is a gentle process far removed from that of regaining one's consciousness.

He tries to open his eyes: he can't, the sandman has sealed his eyelids with a deep crust of dirt and dust. He tries to think: he can't, the devil's blacksmith is busily engaged hammering his thoughts against an anvil. And when he tries to shift his torso, Enzo senses a stabbing, stinging pain somewhere down near his hips and realises that he cannot move the lower half of his body.

"Mama," he says. Then, more loudly, "Mama? Mama, I am here, down in the cellar, please come and help me."

He waits, listening.

Nothing. A groaning, creaking, crackling noise… nothing more.

His arms are weighed down and he struggles to lift them, finding both to his dismay and relief that they are only covered in what feels like a shale of brick fragments, wood splinters and mortar.

"Why am I covered like this?" he asks no one in particular. "Have I banged my head so hard that I have knocked the plaster from the walls?" His disorientation is multiplied when he realises he isn't sure whether he is sitting upright or hanging upside down. His nose is bloody; that, he remembers, was caused when his father banged his head against the door. Yet now, he can taste some thin, almost metallic liquid. Blood! His mouth is full of it. He spits.

"Mama, Vittorio, Angelica, Lucrezia? I am down here, in the cellar."

He doesn't call for his father, for his father is the true reason he is imprisoned so. And in thinking of his father, a scroll of unpleasantness is rolled out before him: the betrayal of the ship's captain, the intervention of Ullo and Virgilio, the blow to the back of his head, being thrown at his father's feet, his father's intransigence, his insult, his violence and worst of all his disrespect towards Lilla.

"Lilla. Oh, Lilla, where are you now?" Even the small effort of asking, tires him and he draws a deep breath to shout out in frustration.

A fog of dust still hangs in the cellar: it lines his lungs and his airways, and provokes a fit of coughing and spluttering which, in turn, pains his bruised ribs.

"Oh, Lilla."

The mere idea of her softens him; as though in thinking of her his mind has generated some anaesthetic fluid which soothes his aching head and shepherds his wits towards a placid delirium.

That first time Enzo had noticed her; he recalls the moment so easily, the memory so vivid, so colourful, so real:

A summer's day, he is helping load a consignment of oranges into the hold of a steamship and as he walks back down the gangplank, he sees her standing there, the full moon of her eyes following his every move. He pokes his tongue at her. She giggles and runs away.

The next day, and for what seemed like the whole summer, she appears and stands watching him, waiting for him to acknowledge her presence. The other stevedores soon catch on to the fact that she cannot take her eyes off him and rib him mercilessly.

She seems so much younger; she has no breasts to speak of and looks perhaps scrawny; not underfed, not tall or short, just a young girl who has some growing up to do. Her hair is hidden under a white scarf which frames her face, drawing his attention to the warmth of her round eyes; those full moons that beguile Enzo in his every waking moment.

The next summer Lilla appears again, though this summer her form has changed. No longer is she a young girl: the past winter seems to have prepared her for spring, for Lilla resembles the orange blossom and the young leaves and the fruit of the trees; still immature, yes, but she has filled out and developed pleasing curves which, unhappily, attract the attention of his colleagues, one or two of whom mutter crude suggestions about their desires for her. Enzo chastises them for their low humour and, because of his overreaction, he is made to suffer all the more.

One day, and perhaps because she seems so pleased whenever he pauses to return her attention, Enzo asks her where she lives.

"The Borgo del Ringo," she says. "My father is Lunapiena the fisherman."

Enzo knows him, or if not knows him personally, then certainly he recognises the name. Her father is well–known among the people of Messina, a king among fishermen. He is not a man who people fear, not like Enzo's own father. Rather, Nino Lunapiena is noted as a man who looks after his brethren; for if a fisherman is lost to the waters of the Strait or maimed in his work, his family are provided for; Lunapiena sees to it, personally. That is his reputation; a man upon whom others can depend.

After work and instead of going straight home for dinner, Enzo takes to walking with Lilla. In the same manner that she has blossomed in the spring, so their relationship blossoms through the summer; and soon, they become inseparable. Inseparable, that is, until his father gets to hear about his son's liaison with the daughter of that fisherman.

One evening, late September, when the swordfish have run their last through the Strait, they sit beneath the old fig tree in the Villa Mazzini and bathe in the hope of each other's love. Enzo is captivated by her and Lilla is enchanted by him: they kiss and linger, seeing in their minds an endless horizon of possibility.

Afterwards, as he walks home, Enzo knows both their futures lie together. That kiss! Such a kiss! Not the kind stolen or dared by adolescents enthusiastic to learn what the fuss of adulthood is about. No, that kiss, stolen in the dying light of evening, seals their fate for all time.

When he gets home, though, his father is waiting. A friend, or perhaps someone who had been tasked with keeping an eye on them, has reported their naïvety, their all too public display of affection.

A reprimand. Verbal, firm, though not physical.

Yet the more Enzo grows aware of his father's displeasure; the more he grows attracted to Lilla. Like a hawk moth drawn by the light of a gas lantern, Enzo cannot keep himself from her.

The second time, they are witnessed in the Piazza San Paolo. Too late, Enzo spots Piero Ullo's dead eyes turned their way and when he gets home, his father beats him, just like he did today, and locks him in the cellar, just like he did today.

Enzo hopes Lilla is somewhere down near the open spaces of the marina; somewhere where she was able to escape the collapse of the city.

Collapse! Of course. That is what has happened to their house. He is in the cellar and the rest of the house has been shaken so ferociously it has collapsed on top of him. Collapsed, not only on top of him but in all probability on top of mama, Angelica, Lucrezia and Vittorio, too. And if they did not have any warning of what was about to happen, then they wouldn't have had the time to escape the falling of the floors, which means...

"Stop it, you fool," he scolds himself. "They will have had the time to get out and because that bastard locked you in the cellar, it is only you who didn't have time. And now, now look at you!"

He rubs his eyes to clear away the dirt and dust and, when he opens them, he can see no more than when his eyes were sealed shut.

Enzo waits, hoping his senses will adjust to the darkness of his prison. He wriggles and screams in agony: something in his hips pains him. Perhaps a bone is broken. Perhaps a nail has been driven into his leg.

He feels down around his waist and his hands come into contact with a heavy beam of wood that lies across his thighs. He tries to slip his hands beneath the beam: he can. He tries to lift it: he can't. Perhaps if he flexes his fingers against his hip, he can tip it forwards and release the pressure on his legs? Searing pain rifles up through his stomach into his chest and he screams.

The measure of his distress and the understanding of his predicament scare him in a manner he has never been scared before, for it is now clear that he cannot move until someone comes to free him.

"Papà," he shouts, "please come and get me out of the cellar." Papà: Enzo has called for his father and he realises that if he thought he may have been scared before, now that he has stooped to beg for his father's assistance, he must be truly petrified.

Enzo leans his head back and scans what he believes should be the ceiling of the cellar.

He can see vague shapes and if so, how is it that the light is finding its way down to him? The luminescence is yellow, like that of a gas lantern, and yet it is not steady, not constant; it flickers like a candle, so it must be...

"Mother of God! Fire, and I cannot move."

Chapter 10

Down by what until recently had been the market on the marina, a crowd is gathered outside a makeshift medical station.

Resting on Read's shoulder, Lilla stares wide—eyed at the bodies lying untended along the Palazzato.

"Are they all dead?" she asks.

"Yes," he replies. "They all ran down here hoping to be rescued."

At his mention of people running, Lilla remembers fighting her way through the panicked throng of citizens rushing in the direction of the marina. "So, why weren't they? What happened to them?"

"The water, it came and went; one minute it was there and the next it disappeared, like when you pull the plug out of a bath. Nearly did for our ship; nearly turned us right over—"

"Which one is yours? Which ship?"

"That one." Smith points away down the quay towards what is left of the Hotel Trinacria.

"The long one, with the tall funnel?"

"Yes, that's the Afonwen. Thought we'd lost her. Jumped right up in the air, all three thousand tons, and then dropped back down against the wharf; nearly capsized us."

"Yes, I saw you," Lilla says, as if relating a dream. "I was on the quay. I thought you were all going to die."

"I don't mind telling you, so did I."

"Can you put me down now?"

"Are you sure you can stand?"

"Yes, thank you. I feel much better.

Read slips her to the ground, not letting go until he is sure her legs will take her weight. "Best get into the aid station. Nasty cut on your leg. Wouldn't want it going septic now, would we. Might be a bit of a wait though; they're awful busy in there."

Lilla stares up and down the quay. "So why? Why are all these people dead?"

"Well, it's like I said, all these people came down here hoping to escape the falling buildings, hoping to be taken off by boat. Only, the water level kept dropping, then all of a sudden it came back in one great big wave. Like a wall of water, it was; swept right in over the wall," he points across the way to the outer harbour. "Carried right on until it hit the marina. All these people standing here, well… there wasn't anywhere safe for them to go."

"So many of them have no clothes on," Lilla mumbles, and again she remembers the hysterical people rushing past her. "I guess they didn't have time to put anything on."

"Yes, miss. It all happened so quickly. We got crashed into by that Italian ship, there, and that Norwegian one over there."

A man wearing a white captain's hat, four gold rings at his cuffs, walks their way.

"Mr Read?"

"Yes, Captain Owen."

"Where is Smith?"

"Just over there, sir. He's helping that fellow with the broken arm."

"Well, best you let that young lady get to the medical station, we've got work to do. We'll need the ship's ladder and some rope: there's a couple of children trapped on a balcony in the main street and we need to get them down before another aftershock does the job for us."

"Yes, Captain. Be right with you, sir." Read bends down and wipes some of the grime off Lilla's face. "Go on now, you go and get those legs of yours seen to. Off you go, you're safe, you'll be alright."

Lilla pushes her way through the crowd milling around the medical station.

Inside, people are petitioning the few doctors to treat their loved ones, each case more urgently in need of attention than the one he is dealing with. A man sits dazed, his scalp torn from his head; another, his leg broken open at his knee, hangs on tight lest it fall off; and a woman stands, expressionless, both her shoulders dislocated, her arms hanging limp.

In the cot next to where Lilla stands, a girl of a similar age is sitting upright, waiting patiently for someone to come and remove a jagged splinter from her neck. Unable to move her head, she turns her eyes slowly to look at Lilla. "How can this be happening?" her look asks. "What have we done to deserve this?"

As Lilla watches, her wound begins to bleed profusely.

"Here. Quickly, here," Lilla shouts. "You must come or she will die."

A doctor rushes to the girl's side and tries to stem the flow of blood by pressing his hands around the wound. He grimaces, shakes his head and bends to whisper in the girl's ear.

She is still looking at Lilla, her expression confused. She had been in bed, dreaming of blue skies and blue waters, of friends and family, and a world she is yet to know. She frowns. So, how does she come to be here and why does this complete stranger hold her just like her father? How? And why? Surely, someone must be able to explain.

She is still looking at Lilla as the light fades from her eyes, and the doctor cries as he cradles her head against his chest.

A woman comes and wakes the doctor from the dream he was sharing with the girl. He wipes away his tears and gently, oh so gently, he picks the girl up in his arms and bears her away towards the back of the tent.

As the woman wipes the cot down with a piece of rag, she notices Lilla. "And what is the matter with you, young lady?"

"My legs," she says, standing back as far as she can without bumping into the man behind her. "It's nothing, really. Just a cut." There is no doubt in her mind that there are others in much greater need of treatment, so Lilla turns to leave.

"Just you hold on there a minute." The woman has a broad face and intelligent eyes, and her skin is pale, like the colour of milk. "Come, sit up here." She pats the top of the cot as though she expects Lilla to leap up onto it. When Lilla doesn't move, the woman reaches over and pulls her roughly by her arm. "Come on now. We haven't got all day and there's plenty more behind you."

"I'm all right, really."

"Yes, I'm sure you are. Best have a look, though. Can't have you getting an infection or worse, tetanus." She swabs Lilla's legs with some clear liquid that smells both sickly sweet and vinegary.

Lilla winces. "That stings."

"Yes, I'm sure it does. It's only a solution of carbolic, though. Won't hurt for long and it will clean the cut." The woman pauses, examining the wound. "Well, we probably ought to suture this, but the doctors have a lot of more serious injuries to deal with and it's stopped bleeding, so I'll put a bandage on it for now."

"Are you a nurse?"

The woman hesitates. "In a manner of speaking."

"What does that mean?"

"It means, young lady, that I used to be. I've been living here for three years. I'm from England. Do you know where that is?"

Lilla shakes her head and feels woozy.

"It's a long way away."

"Why are you living here, then?"

"I've been looking after an English lady."

"Why have you stopped looking after her?"

"Oh, she passed away. It was her time. She lived on a little island near Taormina. Liked to swim every day; thought it was good for her. I told her she would end up with pneumonia. Didn't listen to me, did she? "

Lilla thinks for a few seconds. "Did she live on Isola Bella?"

The woman's curiosity is piqued. "Yes, she did."

"Do you know Mr Gordon?"

"Nathaniel Gordon. Yes. How do you know him?"

"I met him this morning, early, before the earthquake. He was down, here, in the marina. You must be Mrs Robertson, Mr Gordon told me he was expecting to see you. Why are you here?"

"Well, we felt the earthquake, as I would imagine everyone within a thousand miles did. Just as well I was on my way here, eh? Wouldn't have had the pleasure of meeting you, would I. Besides, as I said, I used to be a nurse and I speak the language, so I thought I might be of some help."

"What about Mr Gordon? Do you know if he's all right?"

"No, not yet. The railway is not running. I came in a buggy and walked after the road became blocked with landslips. Not an easy journey: had to climb a fair bit."

"You speak very good Italian, Mrs Robertson."

She fixes Lilla with a questioning stare as she ties the bandage off in a tidy knot. "And you, young lady, speak Sicilian like the fishermen. What's your name?"

"Lilla. Lilla Lunapiena."

"And where are your..." A cloud darkens her thought. "I mean, where are you from Lilla?"

"I live in the Borgo del Ringo."

The woman's countenance very suddenly eases; no longer is she stiff and bossy. "Oh, I see. Well, I'm sure they'll be all right, even if they must be worried sick as to where you've got to. Now, I want you to keep off those legs for a while; give them a chance to recover. Why don't you stay here for a bit and later you can show me where you live?"

"But my parents, they'll need to know if I'm all right."

"Yes, yes." Her air of authority returns. "Like I said, Lilla, you stay here for a bit and I'll take you home later. Now, be a good girl and go and sit over there. Try not to get in anyone's way."

"But Enzo, I must... He must be trapped." A vision of the hill of rubble that had been his family home in the Via dei Templari, Lucrezia sleeping a sleep from which she will never wake up, the fires, the smell of the sewers...

"And who, may I ask, is Enzo?"

"He's my... my... Oh, his house is completely destroyed. I saw his sister; she's dead. His father was running to the marina; he's probably dead, too. My parents..." Lilla speaks quickly, her anxiety creeping up on her like the cool north wind her father calls Tramontana. "Enzo, we were going to be together. I don't know if he's—" She falters, her chin wobbling, tears welling in her eyes.

Mrs Robertson reaches out to hug her. "There, there, young Lilla. It's been a terrible shock to everyone. It's not just the city that's suffered from the earthquake; it's all of us, too. We must keep our faith. We must believe we will get through this." She lays Lilla down on the cot and covers her with a blanket. "I'll look after you. Don't you worry. Just you have a little sleep."

And, in spite of all the crying, moaning, and wailing, and perhaps because the realities of her predicament are too terrible to contemplate, Lilla falls asleep.

CHAPTER 11

The noxious smell of flesh burning, a dreadful pain below his chest, a horrifying apocalypse in which the earth yawns and people tumble headlong into its gaping maw.

Enzo shivers and startles awake.

"Oh, I had forgotten," he mumbles. "I was hoping this was all a bad dream." His eyes grow accustomed to the poor light in the now deconstructed cellar and the weight and shape of the beam pinning his legs confirms his worst fears: he will not be able to free himself without the help of others.

Out in the street, beyond the confines of his prison, fires still burn, the yellow light of flames flickering through the gaps between the snapped joists and cracked masonry that had not so many hours ago made up the floors of his home.

"Hello?" he shouts. "Can anyone hear me? Is there anyone there?" And again, the pressure exerted in his chest by his shouting produces an ache that multiplies and metamorphoses into agony: it is as though a demon is plucking his ribs from their purchase and wrenching them one by one out from his body.

When the spasm passes, Enzo smiles, wistfully.

"Mama," he whispers, in the hope that by speaking beneath his breath he will not induce a pain similar to the one he has just triggered, "weren't you always telling me that the moment we recognise what we want out of life, is the moment we lose it. That is our irony, isn't it?

"Here I am, mama, a prisoner to my thoughts and all I would like is not to be able to think because all my thoughts remind me of what I cannot have. Lilla, oh Lilla, my fresh–faced love, my girl with the breath of a summer breeze and lips of warm sugar; my simple yet complex, serious yet funny…"

The floor of the cellar trembles and palls of thick dust descend from the jumble of oversize matchsticks criss–crossed above his head. Fragments of brick and tile plummet from only God knows how high up; they sting and prick and graze and scratch, as though thrown by a crowd at a stoning.

Enzo cushions his face with his hands and prays, silently. He cannot slip his lines, not like the boats in the outer harbour which will cast off and escape across the Strait to Reggio Calabria. He cannot flee, not like his friends who will be far beyond the city boundary by now. He cannot break out of his dungeon.

"Please, Mother of all that is good, please make this stop."

But the trembling does not stop and Enzo fears the worst.

"If this is my time, please Mother, take care of my girl."

The house creaks and grinds, and somewhere out in the street, a water main fractures and water gushes into the cellar. Somewhere up above him in what remains of his family's home, a brace dislodges, breaks free, and sails through the void to clout him hard on the top of his head.

"It hurts, mama. It hurts too much." His hands drop. His head lolls. Is it sleep or is it a state far less desirable and far more permanent? And when it happens to us, how can we know?

CHAPTER 12

For the second time in her life Lilla wakes to the sound of a voice other than her mother's.

"Open your eyes, dear. Come along now."

"Where did all these blankets come from, Mrs Robertson?"

"From the merchantmen. Men like those who brought you in yesterday. They've stripped their beds and given over all their clothes and medicines; can't be a shred of cloth left on any of the boats. Now up—you—get; you should feel a little brighter. You've slept all through the night."

"All night? Why, what day is it?"

"It is Tuesday, St Aileran's Day, if I recall rightly. Well, it is in Ireland anyway. Saint Sapiens the Wise some call him. Died of the fever; one of those foreign diseases from overseas. Couldn't have been that wise, now could he?"

Lilla is very openly astonished. "You mean, I've been asleep since yesterday afternoon? No, I can't have been. I have to look for my—"

"Yes, you do and I'll come with you. Put some of these clothes on; you'll need them, it's still cold and rainy outside."

"Where did you get these from?"

"I borrowed them from someone who'll not miss them."

"I'd rather not have known that, Mrs Robertson."

"You asked. And it's not so much that there aren't any shops open, as there aren't any shops left. Now, hurry up, we've got business to be attending to and Dottore Roselli can't spare me for too long. How're those legs of yours?"

Lilla sits up, swings them over the side of the cot and examines them. "This one," she points to her bandaged leg, "hurts a little. It itches, too."

"That's good then; that means it's beginning to heal. Can you stand up?"

"Yes. Look. I'm fine, really I am." She recalls some of the horrors of the day before. "Is Messina still the same today?"

"It is. No sense in pondering on it, though. Mustn't get down on ourselves, otherwise others will follow suit and we can't have that. Right, now," decides Mrs Robertson, reaching into the woollen bag hanging at her elbow. "Here's a piece of bread. Not much to be going on with, but it's all that's been handed out, and there are some barrels of fresh water outside, so let's get a drink and we'll be off."

"Where are we going? Isn't there too much to do here?" Lilla looks around the tent: on almost every bed an injured child lies either staring listlessly or sobbing quietly.

"There is. There's far too much to do. So, we'll get you home and then I'll come back. I've slept a bit myself and a walk in the fresh air will clear my fuddled head. Now, hurry along." She hauls back the tarpaulin flap and ushers Lilla out.

The marina is a hive of activity and anchored in the outer harbour are two large warships, one markedly longer than the other and both with high vertical prows and tall, thick masts. The warships dwarf all the other craft busying to and fro as though they are little more than whitebait in the presence of great grey sharks.

"That's the Piemonte, the one with two funnels," Lilla says, a little absent-mindedly, "she's one of ours. I've seen her in the

Strait before. The one with four funnels I don't know; she has a British flag at her bow."

"That's right. HMS Sutlej, a cruiser; a training ship so they tell me." Mrs Robertson stands up a degree or so straighter. "How do you know the flag?"

"Enzo taught me." Lilla's face collapses. "Oh, Enzo."

The older woman wraps her arm round her young charge. "Now that's the second time you've mentioned this Enzo. Your young man, is he?"

Lilla bites her lip, hard, and digs what's left of her nails into her thumbs to distract herself from the lump rising in her throat. "Mm."

"Where does he live, then?"

"In the Via dei Templari, up towards the Chiesa di San Gregorio. It was where those sailors found me."

The hiatus of emotion is not lost on the older woman. She bends a little and peers directly into Lilla's watery eyes. "Well, young lady, I suppose the question you have to answer is do we go in search of your young man or your parents? My guess is both. So, what you have to do is decide who is first on your list."

"My parents, Mrs Robertson. We must find my parents first. They'll be worried sick. And besides, I spoke to Enzo's father just after the earthquake finished and he told me Enzo was—"

"Right then! Your parents it is. In the Borgo del Ringo, you said. Let's be going. Take a drink of water on the way and we'll see if you can't clean up your face a bit. Wouldn't want your parents thinking you'd let yourself go just because of a little earthquake."

However, when they turn from the harbour Lilla gasps. The full extent of the damage to the city is all too starkly apparent.

Along the front of the marina, the Corso Vittorio Emanuele is a rubble–laden shambles, and though the ornate façade of the once splendid Municipio still stands, it is plainly obvious from its vacant windows that the interior has collapsed. To her left, part of the front of the Hotel Trinacria has slumped down into the street, and as far as she can see to her right, the harbour front has crumbled into the water. In both directions, dead bodies covered in sheets lie at sporadic intervals and the smoke of many fires drifts in the moist air.

The destruction of the city being almost too much for her to take in, Lilla turns her attention back to the harbour. Steamers out in the roads hang by their anchor chains, some heeled over, others hard up against the quay; barges float capsized and, in the outer harbour a second vast ship clanks and bangs as it drops its anchor.

When Lilla gazes down, though, it takes her a while to realise that there are bodies floating in the water.

"Oh, Mrs Robertson, look."

"Yes, Lilla. Terrible thing. I'm told there's hundreds of them. Panic, I suppose. Nobody knew what to do: if you came to the harbour you got washed away; if you stayed where you were, chances are you were buried alive. Seems like you were one of the lucky ones. The Good Lord must have a plan for you."

Survivors loiter and stare, their expressions gaunt and gormless, their limbs paralysed for lack of instruction.

"Who's in charge, Mrs Robertson? People are standing around doing nothing. Shouldn't they be digging, helping, pulling all these bodies out of the water?"

"Of course, they should. Trouble is, there's no one in charge. They're all gone: the Mayor, the Bishop, most of the local government people, the Carabinieri, all gone. The customs and the Santelia barracks are destroyed; hundreds dead and missing. Seems the Hotel Trinacria was one of the worst affected: they tell me Angelo Gamba and his family didn't survive, although I saw the Hungarian prima donna; she got out with only her arms broken. Mr Ogston, the British consul, poor man, escaped with his niece, but the rest of his family perished." Mrs Robertson sips from a cup of fresh water and sighs. "One woman I tended to has lost eleven members of her family. Eleven! Imagine." She shakes the thoughts from her mind. "Right, Lilla. Come along now, drink up; no knowing when we'll get more water."

As another great warship anchors in the Strait, they make their way along the once beautiful esplanade.

"That's a Russian warship," Lilla notes, hesitating, wishing, hoping the host of nations responding to Messina's disaster will soon set everything right.

"Come along, now. No time for dreaming."

The Borgo del Ringo, the fisherman's quarter, lies two kilometres up the Corso Vittorio across the Torrente San Francesco di Paola, and their progress is hampered by having to pick their way around the many corpses and over the rubble, which occasionally heaps across the esplanade into the harbour.

Lilla covers her mouth with her hands. "What is that awful smell?"

"Never mind that, young lady. That'll be the carbolic they're spraying the dear departed with. That and all the broken sewers."

The harbour wall is cracked and crumbled, and zigzag fissures in the marina, often as wide as a barrel, mean they have to jump and step from one uneven level to the next. Gas lanterns lean at ridiculous angles and women wring their hands in despair, knowing that without a husband to provide, their futures are at best bleak.

At one section, they have to turn a corner and make their way up to the Garibaldi which, when they eventually get there, looks to have sheared along the middle, one side of the road shifted several metres above the other.

"It's a wonder anyone is still alive," Mrs Robertson mutters, as she clambers over a jumbled stack of smashed beams.

Near the theatre, they come across a man wearing underclothes, an opera hat and wooden sabots. His expression dazed, unwavering and apathetic, he stands in a doorway, the door behind him held at a careless angle by its top hinge. To his chest, he clutches a young child covered in a shawl.

"Please, lady," he asks, his eyes dull and stony, "have you seen my wife?"

"Where did you last see her?" Mrs Robertson replies.

"She is inside. She won't come out."

Lilla and the older woman walk over and peer in through the gap in the entrance. Inside the roof has fallen in. A woman's leg protrudes from the unruly mass of brickwork.

Mrs Robertson steps back, bends to the man and peels back the shawl covering the girl's head. She recoils, briefly. "Now you listen to me, my good man. You know where the market is? Yes? Well, take your daughter down there, to the medical station. Ask for Dottore Roselli, he'll take care of her."

"But I don't have a daughter," he replies.

"Then, who's this on your lap?"

"I don't know. I was asleep and woke up out here. I don't know how I got here and I found this girl lying on the ground. Please can you take her, I don't know what to do with her." His bottom lip quivers and he begins to cry.

Mrs Robertson stands up and glances at Lilla, her face a picture of sadness. "What's your name, sir?" she asks, in a kindly tone.

"Papali. Gianni Papali. We only came for the opera. How long have I been here?"

"Well, Gianni, there's no point in sitting here getting all upset. Just you take her where I said. Come on, set to it. No sense in sitting here, you'll die of exposure. Come on, off you go. Lilla, help the man up."

His limbs are frozen almost stiff, but with a little cajoling and a warm hand, he stands and wanders off the way they have come.

"Poor dear," she says.

"Mrs Robertson?"

"Yes, my dear— Oh, watch yourself, that's sharp. Sorry, let me give you a hand. Here, take mine. Just get down off this bit... Now, what was it you wanted?"

"Are you always this... Well, like you are. Don't you ever get frightened?"

"Naturally, my dear. Everyone gets frightened sometime or other. It's how you deal with being frightened, that's the important thing. If you let everyone see you're frightened, then they might be frightened, too. No sense in that, now is there?"

They make their way over yet more mountains of rubble, each helping the other, each warning the other of uneven ground and hazardous debris.

"That's what Mr Gordon said. Or something like that. Something about life being full of challenges and how you have to meet them whether you like it or not. You must know him very well."

"No, Lilla, I've never met the man. We've communicated in writing and by telegram. Anyway, maybe that's just the way we are, us British. Some see us as a bit stiff, a bit phlegmatic, but that's no bad thing, eh, especially when a bit of calm is called for. Now, give me a leg up, will you, this mountain of matchsticks is so high I can't see over it."

Lilla, though, waits until the woman looks back to question her lethargy. "I don't know how to repay your kindness, Mrs Robertson. I'm sure my parents will be very grateful."

"No bother. No need to thank me. Let's find your parents first, before we go thanking each other. As I said, there must be a reason why the Good Lord has seen fit to spare us both from this catastrophe." She pauses, cranes her head over the top of a pile of beams as though they are the topping to a barricade. "Ah, we're here. Oh, my! The banks have fallen in. We'll have to wade across. It's exactly as its title suggests, a torrent."

They do make it across, even though Mrs Robertson has to gather her skirt up around her waist. She shivers and looks skyward as though the freezing–cold water is little more than an inconvenience. Once on the north bank, she rubs Lilla down with her own scarf, ensuring she doesn't dislodge the bandage at her leg.

The Borgo del Ringo is almost a village in its own right, as it is separated from the city by not only the Torrente, but also the few remains of the old city's fortified walls. Fields stretch away towards the mountains; fields in which rudimentary shelters of bamboo and sail cloth are being hastily cobbled together with twine and fishing line; fields in which spare wood from the ruined houses is being gathered and burnt to keep the newly homeless warm.

"So, where is your parent's house?"

"It is down near the water. This way."

Lilla leads her guardian down alleys sticky with mud and littered with dead fish, whose glazed eyes seem to follow them as they pass by. The village shows less devastation than the city they have just struggled through; the smaller, basic, single–storey dwellings having withstood the shaking of their foundations far better than the tall, colonnaded structures of the city.

The dead lie twisted in the agonies of their departing, not so much crushed as battered and drowned by the huge tidal wave that has swept ashore, catching them as they huddled together in the cold night air.

Lilla's pace quickens. "It is here, just around the corner."

They turn, to be confronted by the beach and the water, and what looks on first impression to be a picture of perfect calm. Yet when they glance about, they notice that the fishermen, their wives and their children are nowhere to be seen. And, on closer examination, they also realise that the walls of the once white–washed houses are now covered in the flotsam and jetsam of the sea.

"Oh no!" Lilla screams as she starts running along the littoral. She slips and falls, regains her footing and sets off again.

"Mama? Mama?"

When she reaches her parents' house, the windows have crashed in and the front door is missing. The wreckage of the small fishing boats lies smashed against the houses, as though a giant has gathered them up, squashed them between his hands and tossed them from the roofs. More fish, as though they were part of the day's catch, lie limp and listless, slowly rotting.

Lilla is bewildered by the sight. She staggers back in shock, fortunate that Mrs Robertson has now caught up and is there to prevent her from falling.

"Hold on, my dear. Hold on." For a moment, Mrs Robertson grapples with her young charge and as gently as she can, she turns Lilla round to face her.

"Oh no, they can't be." Lilla's head slumps.

"Listen, we don't know. We simply don't know. Look at me. Come now, look at me."

Eventually, Lilla raises her head and stares back into Mrs Robertson's eyes: they speak to her of concern, of abject sorrow, of pity.

"How many brothers and sisters do you have, Lilla?"

"I– I have no brothers, only three sisters."

"And who else should be inside, apart from your mother and father?"

"Just my sisters and my grandmother. Why?"

"Because I want you to stay here while I go and look in the house. Don't follow me, do you understand? Wait here and don't move. Lilla, look at me, listen to me. Tell me you will stay here."

She nods her head slowly, twice.

Mrs Robertson relaxes her grip. "Promise?" she asks.

Lilla nods once more and waits.

For what seems to Lilla like an eternity, she stands and prays, her arms wrapped around her shoulders, her knees trembling and her eyes tight shut.

"Lilla?"

"Yes, Mrs Robertson. Your father is not here."

"Oh, wonderful! That's so wonderful. He's safe, I know he is. He must have taken them—"

"No, Lilla, I said only your father is not here. Your mother, your sisters and your grandmother are all inside." She pauses and turns to comfort her.

Lilla, though, sees the end of a journey from which there is no return etched deep in the woman's face. "It can't be true. All of them? How can it be? No, I don't believe you. My father would have saved them. He would have. I know him; he can do anything; he would never leave them." She makes to brush the older woman aside.

"I'm sorry, Lilla. You mustn't go in there. They didn't have a chance. They must have gone inside to escape the wave." She grabs the girl and pins her arms around her.

Through her sadness, Lilla's anger like a lighted match suddenly flares and she struggles to free herself. "No, it's not possible. It can't be; it mustn't be."

"There, there, my poor girl. There, there," Mrs Robertson coos. "Nothing you can do for them now. Best you stay out here."

Wrapped in their world of sorrows, neither hear the man stumbling towards them. "Lilla," he calls. "Lilla!"

He waits, watching the two women in their embrace, knowing, hurting, understanding that Lilla, in her confused state, is trying to make sense of what has happened to her family; those whose proximity has ensured her warmth all these recent winter nights, those whose mumblings and squirmings have both annoyed and reassured her, those who are now and forever more cold and fated never again to wriggle in their sleep.

"Lilla?" he asks once more, as softly as his gravelled tones will allow.

Her head is still buried in her guardian's bosom; a berth of solace and solidity from which she would happily never depart, but... She turns her head.

"Pipo. Oh, zio Pipo," she whispers, the light of hope briefly rekindled in her eyes.

"Yes," is all Pipo Sorbello can think of to say. His expression matches his tone, solicitous and at the same time apprehensive.

"Have you seen papà?"

"Yes." His eyes fill with tears. He cannot bear the weight of her gaze, so he looks down at his cap which he feeds through his hands as though its rim is a string of rosary beads.

"Oh, Pipo. My poor Pipo," she whispers.

Like an obstinate child unwanting of support, Lilla tries to shrug off the binding arms of her comforter.

Mrs Robertson, though, will not release her. She studies Lilla for a second, before sensing from her some reassurance that she will neither charge into her parent's house nor descend into unrestrained hysteria.

Lilla raises her arms and steps towards her father's old friend.

However, before she can drape the limbs of her compassion around him, Pipo steps back, holding up his hand to ward Lilla off. "No. Please. I am not deserving of your sympathy. Concettina and I, we both escaped. I don't know how. Maybe it is because we did not have children to think of. Perhaps that is why we ran when the trembling stopped. Perhaps because we ran, this is why I feel so guilty, so ashamed..."

Mrs Robertson makes to speak, but Lilla glances and shakes her head.

This time, and so that he cannot refuse her consolation without some more physical objection that might risk causing her offence, Lilla steps towards him more quickly. She places her hands gently on the corners of his shoulders and, furrowing her brow, looks Pipo deeply in his eyes.

And as her own tears trickle down her reddened cheeks, she says, "There is no shame in wanting to live, zio Pipo. We must not feel guilty because we have been spared. These decisions... They are not ours to make. Now, tell me where does my father lie?"

Pipo Sorbello nods, a tear drops from his eyes and splashes on his shoe. He half turns and points down towards the beach. "He is there, at the water's edge. He is with the young boys from next door; with Gaetano and Rosario. When the wave came, they must have been trying to move the boat and by the time it reached our house, and you know where we live, much higher up, it was unthinkable, the size: it was a wall of water taller than the doors of the Duomo. People down here, they never stood a chance." He hangs his head on her shoulder and cries.

They stand, cold in a squall of the heaven's tears, and Lilla murmurs, "Cry, zio Pipo. Cry, as the whole of Messina is crying."

CHAPTER 13

"You were fortunate not to be with your parents," Mrs Robertson says.

They are walking, or rather navigating their way deftly between the crevasses splitting the surface and the ruin of bricks and broken wood piled in the road.

"Fortunate. That is not how I would describe my situation," Lilla replies, disconsolately. "Perhaps, like zio Pipo, the Madonna della Lettera has been watching over me."

"Your uncle, eh? Here, take my hand." In the face of her exertions, Mrs Robertson blows a little. "I'll pull you up. That's it. Up you come. I mean..." she adds, before moving on to the next obstacle. "I mean, normally you would have been at home and, if you had been you would not be here with me now. Surely that is good fortune, Lilla."

"Yes, Mrs Robertson. But is it good fortune or did our Madonna lead me away from the house knowing she would save me? When our forefathers went with Saint Paul to Palestine to ask the Madonna for her blessing, didn't she send them back with a letter giving us her blessing and promising us her protection? Well," she scoffs, angrily, "where is her protection now and why has she watched over me and forgotten my family?"

"That's not ours to question, Lilla. We must not doubt our path. The Lord moves in mysterious ways His wonders to perform and if your young man hadn't told you to meet him on the front, you likely as not wouldn't be here. Just as if those sailors from that ship hadn't found you, you would have died of exposure by now. Ours is not to reason His wonders; ours is simply to do His bidding."

As they pass the wrecked houses, many of the façades torn off as though their builders had simply neglected to face them, they hear moans and groans. They stop to listen and occasionally they call out and wait for a response, but when none comes, they move on.

"There are more people about now," Mrs Robertson observes. "Some of these men, they're not from here: they're blond and look strong: northern or eastern. Not people from Sicily, I don't think."

"What language are they speaking?" Lilla asks, pausing for a moment.

"Not sure as I can hear them. Might be Russian. Didn't you say you'd seen a Russian flag on one of those enormous warships."

In what is left of the once proud Via San Camillo, men in blue jackets are busy clearing rubble. One turns and shouts in their direction, but as he does so the world begins to tremble and roar once more.

"Lilla," Mrs Robertson shouts, reaching out to grab hold of her young companion. "Quick. Come here. To the middle of the street."

However, as she takes a step, Lilla is suddenly bounced up and down, one second like the tip of a stick on a snare drum, the next as though she has been kicked by the pedal of a base. She screams and falls to the ground.

Somehow, the older lady falls in her direction and the two cling to each other.

71

Debris crashes down from the buildings and there is little they can do other than sit and wait and hope the masonry lands elsewhere other than on top of them.

Even though the aftershock lasts no more than a few seconds, the turmoil beneath them, the roaring in their ears and the crashing all around them seems interminable.

"Are we going to die?" she asks.

"Close your eyes and hold me, Lilla. Just hold me tight and wait. It will stop in a minute; it has to."

When the trembling ceases and the dust settles, Mrs Robertson gets to her feet and pulls her young charge up with her. The Via San Camillo appears the same, except that some of the piles of debris are now taller than they had been but a few moments before.

The men who had been clearing the rubble are gathered together in a huddle, patting themselves down and wiping the dirt from their eyes.

Mrs Robertson looks to Lilla like a ghost, as though she has rolled in a basin of flour; and yet apart from her altered appearance she seems relatively unperturbed by her experience.

"I beg your pardon," she shouts back at the man. "I didn't hear you. What did you say?"

The man separates himself from his party and wanders over. "I'm sorry, I don't speak Italian," he says in English.

"That's perfectly all right," Mrs Robertson replies in the same. "I do, even though I am British. What do you want?"

His face is spattered with soot, his fingers raw from tearing at the bricks and he recoils at her brusque tone. "British, eh?" he says. "Well, what the bloody hell are you doing wandering about Messina? Not exactly Sunday promenade at Brighton Pavilion is it?"

His humour lost on Mrs Robertson, she turns her nose up at him.

"Joking apart," he continues, "You shouldn't be here; these aftershocks will likely as not bring the rest of the city down. Shouldn't you be at the harbour trying to get a boat out?"

"Yes, probably we should," Mrs Robertson replies. "But no, we won't be. This young lady's friend might be buried in the ruins of a house; we're going to see if there's anything we can do."

"Well, I don't know whether that's brave or just plain foolhardy. Never mind the danger from the aftershocks bringing down the already unstable buildings, I hear the Cappuccini jail has been destroyed and all the criminals escaped. Caught a bunch of them red–handed trying to break open the vault at the depository. Just thought you ought to know, that's all. Just you be careful. Where did you say you were going?"

"I didn't. We are going to the Via dei Templari. It's up beneath the San Gregorio, two streets across from here. Can you come and help?"

The man scratches his head in thought, turns to glance at his working party and replies, "No, not while we've got our hands full here."

"What about others?" Mrs Robertson asks, as though there should by rights be a queue of workmen waiting for instruction.

"People arriving all the time, Mrs. Be better in the morning."

"Why are there so few of you? I thought there'd be more. It would appear the authorities have been rather slow to react. Or perhaps it is that they don't care what happens to the people of Messina?"

He scratches his head again, inspects his bloodied hands and sighs. "It's not that, I'm sure; it's more that nobody knew what was going on here. The telegraph office is completely destroyed and what with the signal towers either side of the Strait being down, the Marconi radio isn't working either. Turns out the rest of the world didn't find out what was going on here until an Italian torpedo boat fetched up in Naples last night."

"And you can't spare us even a little time?"

"Wish I could. Wish I could. Trouble is we're a bit taken up with searching for Captain Passino of the Piemonte. Turns out he was ashore on Sunday night and hasn't been seen since. This is his house... Or was," he adds, as an afterthought.

"How can you expect to find anyone alive in that?" Mrs Robertson asks, pointing at the tumbled remains.

"I expect the same can be said of wherever it is you're going. Look," he says, sympathetically, "it's really not safe for you to be here. Why don't you count your blessings and get out of the city? Forget Messina, the city is no more."

CHAPTER 14

If he didn't already know it is impossible, Enzo would be minded to think time is standing still. And how does he know it is impossible? For the simple reason that he has wished it before and it has never happened.

Whenever he was in Lilla's company, he would wish it. Oh, how he would wish it with all his heart! And he would imagine how fantastic it would be to have the power to halt the world in its turning so that he could preserve the joy of her.

Now, though, the world seems to have ceased both its turning and its trembling, and it is suspended in its misery just as he is suspended in his.

"Another shake like that, Enzo," he mutters to himself, "and your teeth will be jump out from your jaw. Surely, there can't be any more beams left to fall."

He opens his eyes, slowly, fearing that all he will see is more rubble cementing him in the darkness of his tomb.

But wait! Though his sight is bleary, his eyes painful and his eyelids glued gritty and shut at the corners, there is light. And, no longer is the light the threatening yellow of flame; it is the grey light of day, the light of a dawn mist on the Strait, a light which promises.

Enzo's spirits soar, bubbles of excitement and expectation coursing up through his muscles. He tries to stand and while his torso obeys his command, his legs don't.

"Oh yes," he says, "my legs. How stupid of me!"

Yet the fact that he can see a sizeable triangle of sky above fills him with hope.

"Hello," he shouts. "Is there anyone there? Please, come help me. I am down here, in the cellar."

He listens.

Nothing.

"Hello. Help me, please. Help me." Enzo shouts again and again, and he shouts until he can no longer hear himself shouting and his voice grows weak.

And still no one comes.

His mouth is dry and he is wickedly thirsty. Yet there is good news, because for the first time in as many hours as he has forgotten, Enzo realises that he now has sufficient light by which to fully appreciate his surroundings.

What he sees, though, does not fill him with any great relief.

The beam pinning down his legs is so broad and heavy that it will require more than a few strong men to shift it, and the cellar, too, is almost full of rubble. Almost, because here and there small pockets of irregularly shaped cavities have been protected by masonry and beams that have fallen and now lean against the walls at varying angles.

He twists his upper body to look behind him and immediately wishes he hadn't, as a stinging pain shoots up from his hips into his chest.

Enzo swears under his breath. However, his oath soon mutates into a fit of hysterical giggles as he also realises that though he needs water, what he has glimpsed behind him might, for the moment, suffice.

He reaches up over his head and touches the round, cold glass of a bottle.

"So, papà" he mutters, "you may have buried me, but at least you have buried me near your wine. And look here! What have we here?" Within reach to his right hangs a pair of fat salami and, on a shelf dropped at one end, two loaves of bread.

He eases the bottle from behind his neck and holds it before him, studying intently the amber liquid as if it holds within its flavours the very essence of life.

Enzo sinks his teeth into the cork and pulls the bottle. At first the stopper squeaks and resists, but after a good deal of coaxing, it slips out with an exquisite pop.

"Steady now, you fool. Remember how strong this is? Can't have you getting drunk, now can we?" And a second fit of hysterical giggles consumes him and immediately reproduces the pain in his hips.

When the pain has subsided, he raises the lip of the bottle to his own and—

"Hello? Is there anyone down there?"

Enzo is dreaming, surely? He is dehydrated, that's for sure; so perhaps now that he is so close to some relieving liquid, his mind is playing tricks on him.

He lowers the bottle and inspects it further. There is nothing strange about it; it is simply a bottle of Malvasia. He raises it again, sticking his lips out towards the bottle in pleasant anticipation.

Enzo sips. Nectar! Freshness. A spring afternoon in an orchard: he is lying on a bed of apricots and acacia blossoms, and the air is thick with the perfume of ripe fruit and honey and—

"Hello? I said, is there anyone down there?"

He splutters. He coughs. He wheezes, wipes a dribble of wine from his mouth and winces at the cost of his exertions.

"Yes. Yes, I am here. Is there anyone there?"

The man above shouts, "Of course there is someone here, you idiot. If I wasn't here, I wouldn't be calling down to see if anyone was down there." His voice is gruff, uncultured and his tone sarcastic.

"Can you help me?" Enzo asks in a polite yet insistent tone.

"Of course," comes the response. "I am not trapped like you and if you were not trapped down there, you would not need my help. Of course, I can help."

"So, help me, please. But be careful where you put your feet; if you bring any more of the house down on top of me, I'll never get out. Are you alone, or are there others with you?"

A silence extends, as though the man is either counting the number of his companions so as to be accurate in his reply or—

"There are enough here to get you out of your coffin. Tell me, young man, what is your name?"

The prospect of his rescue triggers a wave of relief, which sweeps through his mind, chasing all caution from his thinking.

"I am Enzo Ruggeri. I am the son of Don Carmelo Ruggeri. You may know him... in the harbour, he—"

"Yes, I have heard of him. Big man, eh, your father? Is he down there with you?"

"No, I don't know where he is. He's probably out there looking for me." Enzo reconsiders for a moment. "No, on second thoughts he probably isn't. Forget I said that."

"I'm going to lower you a rope," the gravel–voiced man offers. "Do you have any money down there with you? Is there a safe in the house? Is it in the cellar?"

"Money?" Enzo repeats, baffled. "What has money got to do with you helping free a man who is imprisoned?"

"Well," the man scoffs, as though humouring an audience, "a man does not get drunk on gratitude alone. Do you have any money? Come on, boy, do not play games with me; your situation is far worse than mine."

"If I have no money, if there is no safe, what will you do, leave me down here? Surely any reasonable man will not leave another to die in such circumstances."

"What?" the invisible man screams as though a heavy weight has suddenly fallen on his foot. "You expect reason in the middle of this lunacy? Ha, if you have no money, then expect to stay where you are and good luck to you."

Enzo is perplexed if not insulted by the man's lack of compassion. Yet he understands that, like those he has loaded holds with, many men are like donkeys in that they refuse to take a step forward unless offered an incentive.

"No, I have no money," he replies, "I have something far more valuable."

"Oh yes, and what might that be?"

"I have a bottle of Malvasia, a little bread and some salami. Have you not thought that perhaps food will be more valuable than money in the coming days?"

The silence suggests the man is weighing up the potential of Enzo's offer.

"It is a good point, you make, young Ruggeri, but it is not enough. Do you have a cross and chain around your neck? Perhaps a ring or two?"

Enzo looks at the silver ring on the little finger of his left hand. "Yes, I have my signet ring, though I'm not sure I can get it off."

"Then try."

His mouth is too dry to spit, so he takes a sip of wine, wets his finger and pulls. After a good deal of turning and twisting, the ring does at last slip off. "I've got it."

"Then I'll lower a rope and when you have tied the ring, the bottle of wine, the bread and salami to it, we will decide whether your payment is sufficient. If it is, then my friends and I will shift all these beams and get you out of your prison. How much wine and food do you have?"

Enzo opens his mouth to reply and then thinks better of what he had been going to say. "Just the one bottle and the one salami. That and the bread, it is all I have. I hope you are a man of your word."

"My word?" he scoffs. "My word is all I have and, perhaps more importantly, it is all you have. Besides, your ring may be worthless and I already have a pocket full of jewels. Here, here is the rope."

The rope turns out to be not much more than a rough, slender cord, which descends in stages through the triangle of light.

Enzo feeds the ring through it, presses the cork back into the neck of the bottle and ties it securely. "Ready, pull up. Be steady. It is the bottle."

The ring and the Malvasia ascend.

There is a brief pause. No doubt the ring is being inspected and the quality of the wine tested.

"Good! The ring is acceptable and the wine is good," the man decides. "Now the salami and the bread."

The rope returns and the items are similarly tied and despatched upwards.

Again, there is a pause in communication.

"It's good, eh?" Enzo prompts.

The pause extends.

Without warning, a fog of dust falls from the triangle of light and he can hear footsteps crunching on the rubble above him.

"Hey, you... you come back here," he shouts.

There is, though, no response and judging by the grunting and heavy breathing, the man is busying himself.

"Hey, you. Are you still there? What are you doing?" Enzo shouts.

"I'm collecting another ring. A small gold ring," he replies, still struggling.

"Who are you taking it from?"

"Someone else who no longer needs it."

Enzo's thoughts cartwheel in desperation. "You are robbing the dead? You bastard!" he shouts as loudly and with as much anger as he can generate.

"Shout as loud as you like, young Ruggeri. The dead will not listen. Thank you for the salami and the wine."

"You said all you had was your word. Call yourself a man? You are not even an excuse for a man. You are nothing."

Enzo strains to listen, eventually diluting his venom with the consolation that at the very least he did not lose all of his meagre provisions.

There is more scuffling of feet from above and another cloud of dust descends. Shouting. He can hear shouting, loud and urgent, and imperative.

"Hey, what's going on up there? I'm down here. Hey!" he yells.

Chapter 15

"What did that man say?" Lilla asks, as they pick their way up the Corso Cavour.

"He said, Messina is no more."

"No more?"

"Yes, that's what he said, no more." Mrs Robertson hesitates. "He is wrong though. Messina has been destroyed many times and your ancestors have always rebuilt the city. They will do the same again, I'm certain of it."

They turn right into a street nearly as broad as the Corso Cavour yet almost equally impassable. And when they look up towards the monastery, they can see that beyond it the Chiesa Sant' Agostino is completely destroyed.

"Come one, Lilla. Let's keep going. I don't want us to get caught in another of those aftershocks; there's no telling how much more these ruins can stand."

The going is interminably slow and each time Lilla slips and grazes herself her older companion wonders aloud whether the young man is worth the trouble they are being driven to.

"Yes, Enzo is everything to me. Especially now that I am alone, Mrs Robertson. You'll see. I promise you; you'll see."

Half a backbreaking hour later, as they help each other over the top of yet another mound of debris, a man is scrambling down the slope across the way. His jacket and trousers are torn, his black hair a mess of curls and his face dark and stubbled. Under his left arm he carries a bulging cloth sack; under his right, a dark–grey metal object.

When he reaches the bottom, his eyes dart this way and that as though he is looking for an escape. He looks up and spots them.

He stumbles, clutching the sack close. "You… you women, have you got any money?"

Both Mrs Robertson and Lilla are stunned by both his rudeness and his question.

"Money?" Mrs Robertson is indignant. "Money?" she repeats, this second time furious to the point of apoplexy. She squares her shoulders and breathes in deeply, the abundance of her bosom rising like a fortified wall. "We have our lives, sir. At this moment in time, that is all we can ask for."

The man, though, isn't interested in her platitude. He raises his right arm: the metal object is a revolver.

Lilla is amazed. Amazed and fascinated. It is the first handgun she has ever seen, and it has a squarish barrel as long as her hand and a folding trigger, which hangs down like a curved sewing needle. Yes, she has seen the soldiers from the barracks carrying rifles… But a handgun?

"Now, you listen to me, you pompous old windbag," he growls, "you'll pray for mercy like all the others when I've put a bullet in your belly. Hand over what you've got, before I run out of patience."

Lilla is transfixed: the revolver possesses a cold grey sinister hue, like that of the leaden sky.

Mrs Robertson stares impassively at the robber for a few seconds before the iron in her back melts and she lowers her head. However, it isn't so much surrender she has on her mind, it is sympathy: "And why, you poor fellow," she says, softly, "do you imagine we would have money? What possible use would it be out here in this apocalypse? Now, leave us alone and get on with your looting; we have nothing for you."

In spite of the cold and drizzle, the man is sweating profusely. He glances nervously over his shoulder, his forehead furrowed over wild eyes. "Show me your hands?" he screams. "Go on, hold them out for me so that I can see them."

Lilla finds she cannot react to his demands; she simply stands in wonder and watches him.

He points the revolver directly at her, jolting her out of her stupor.

She reaches out both hands, her bare fingers fluttering in fear.

He turns his attention to Mrs Robertson. "Now you, old woman."

She, too, holds out her hands, her fingers bare except for a plain gold band which adorns the third finger of her left hand.

"Take it off," he orders, thrusting the gun at her.

"As you can see," she says, "this is my wedding ring and I promised my husband on his deathbed that I would wear it for the rest of my life. So, if you are going to shoot me, do so. Besides, you won't get it off my finger even when I am dead; I've worn it for so long now that even I can't take it off."

He scoffs. "Don't you worry, I'll cut it off just like I cut the ring off the finger of that girl back there. Now, take it off."

"Which girl? Back where?" Lilla screams, oblivious to the fact that he might shoot her simply for making a noise.

Slowly, the man switches his attention from Mrs Robertson and leers at Lilla. "From that pretty little thing in the white dress lying on top of what's left of the Ruggeri house."

"Oh, Lucrezia," Lilla screams. "You devil, you are not a man. You are not even an excuse for a—"

"Ah, you know young Master Ruggeri, do you?" He steps towards her and looks her up and down. "Pretty girl, aren't you. Friend of the boy's, eh?"

A brief smile flicks across her face. "You've seen Enzo?"

"No, not exactly seen." He rubs his lips with the back of his hand, the butt of the revolver protruding from his fist. "No," he repeats, his lecherous expression betraying his lewd imaginings, "not exactly." And all too dreadfully soon, it occurs to him that he might be able to realise his desires. "No," he continues, drooling like a starved dog in sight of a bone, "you mustn't worry about young Enzo... He's gone. He's finished. He's never coming back. You're better off with me. Your old Tulliu knows how to treat a girl right. I'll look after you."

"Gone?" Lilla stammers. "You mean, Enzo..."

"Oh, yes. He's done for. Just like the rest." He glances over at Mrs Robertson and hisses, "Now you, old woman. Just you have that ring off by the time me and the young lady get finished or like I said, you'll be losing your finger along with your ring. Understand?"

"God will never forgive you, Tulliu." Mrs Robertson says. "And I won't forgive myself for allowing you to." She checks her footing and steps towards him.

He turns, holds the revolver out at arm's length and aims it at her face.

Lilla tries to intervene and raises her arms, pleading, "No. No, you can't. I—"

A shot is fired. The world explodes.

Chapter 16

Spitting the cork from the second bottle into his lap, Enzo takes a long, slow sip, rolling the wine around in his mouth, savouring the sweetness in the life of the liquor and again acknowledging his good fortune at being imprisoned within reach of such a ready supply.

He closes his eyes, rests his head back and allows his mind to wander.

Not long after he began to walk with Lilla on a regular basis, she invited him home to meet her father.

A man of medium height, broad of shoulder and sturdy of hip, Lilla's father welcomes him politely, if cautiously, into their small house down by the waterfront. And, after a handshake which squeezes the blood from his fingers, the fisherman looks Enzo deep in his eyes and asks him... if he would like to go hunting?

It is, in itself, a perfectly natural and simple question coming, as it does, from a man who hunts. And yet, Enzo immediately recognises the complexities of the invitation.

First, Nino Lunapiena wants to know whether Enzo understands the subtle divide that separates those who hunt swordfish from those who merely fish. Not, of course, that any hunter would ever be so patronising as to look down on a man who uses a net or a line.

Second, he wants to know whether Enzo is bold enough to want to risk his neck for the pleasure of his daughter's company; for hunting swordfish is no child's game, it is both dangerous and tough work.

Third, and perhaps most importantly, coming as Enzo does from the city, and with a father who is reputed not only to be wealthy, but also one who enjoys a certain standing in society, Nino Lunapiena wants to know whether his daughter's suitor might believe himself above such manual labour. The question is asked silently, does he?

"When can we go?" he replies, without hesitation.

Nino Lunapiena smiles, his eyes twinkling with mischief. "This Sunday. Be here soon after dawn. No later."

On his way home, Enzo floats across the Torrente San Francesco di Paola in a haze of euphoria. Now, all he has to do is impress on the fulua and the luntro and his second most intimidating obstacle will be overcome.

That Sunday...

Yes, that Sunday.

He arrives down at the littoral a few minutes before dawn, a slice of pani cunzatu to prepare him for the day. It seems appropriate, the pani. Some call it the bread of misery because if you are unfortunate and poor, you eat it plain. If you are more fortunate and not so poor, then you rub the bread with sardine or anchovy or fennel or sultanas to give it flavour. And if you are extremely fortunate and sufficiently wealthy, you have the lot. In deference and because he doesn't want to be judged, Enzo decides he will survive the day on just the one sardine.

The fulua is sturdy of hip, tall of mast and built to withstand most if not all of whatever poor weather the Gods decide to conjure. As he chews on the bread, Enzo strolls about, studying its dimensions: the length — twelve paces stem to stern, the beam — as wide as two horses are long, and the slender mast, with its steps pegged either side, several times the height of a tall man. The fulua, they tow behind smaller luntri out into the Strait and anchor it. The luntro, the smaller, faster skiff, is the boat from which the funcitta launches his lance.

A short man appears at his shoulder. "Enzo?" he asks, gazing out across the water, the rugged outline of the Calabrian hills sharpening with every second.

"Yes."

"My name is Pipo, Pipo Sorbello." He wears a flat cap, a shirt that was once both white and embellished with a collar, and a pair of black baggy trousers. "Pleased to meet you."

They do not shake hands; they simply stand and stare and bathe in the pearlescent beauty of first light.

Soon enough, other men appear and though they briefly look their new crewman up and down, they seem relatively relaxed with his presence.

Enzo observes the language of their expressions. A tall man of middle age, whose slow eyes suggest he is either bored or taciturn or both; the kind of man who will deal with every eventuality, if and when that eventuality eventually arrives. Another, a little shorter and younger, with black shaggy hair, restless eyes and eager lips; he rubs his chin in anticipation of the rewards he believes the day will gift him. The third is a thin–framed man, older, probably a good few years older than the others, though his age is difficult to estimate because his head is bald and brown as flayed goat hide; he is the man who makes the lobster traps, he is the one who makes ropes, he is the one whose mother is the sea and whose father is long lost to the horizon.

When Nino arrives, he mumbles a greeting and they stroll down to the water's edge. There, they place blocks of well–worn wood beneath the prow and drag and push the luntro down the rudimentary slipway into the sea.

To begin with, the three latecomers and Pipo row the boat out to the fulua. Three other boats join them and they tow the fulua to its anchorage out in the cool waters of the Strait.

"The fishermen of Chianalea, the village below the Castello Ruffo in Scylla; they have it easy," Nino explains. "The hills along the Calabrian coast to the north of the Strait stand very close to the water, so they post a lookout on the high ground and when he sees the swordfish, he waves a flag and directs the luntro towards it. We don't have the benefit of the high ground here, so we have to spend more time looking for the fish. On the other hand, we hunt the narrower waters here at the neck of the Strait and when the swordfish run, they are more confined and more plentiful."

With a stone he is honing the metal tip of a slender wooden lance, fully twice his height, which he then couples to a trident with three hinged barbs, the bottom ends of which curve outward.

"Here in the Strait," Nino continues, "we have the tides to deal with. Every six hours the sea from the north does battle with the waters from the south; whereas out in the open sea, in the Tyrrhenian, the waters are generally calmer and so easier for rowing."

"This battle of the tides," Enzo is keen to show that he is not a complete novice, "they call it Charybdis; it is the whirlpool that tormented the galley of the Greek Ulyxes on his journey home from the Trojan War. And the monster of many heads which devoured his sailors, it was named Scylla after the village of the rock at Castello Ruffo. I read it in the book by Homero."

"Yes," the funcitta replies, "I have heard this too. Me, I don't read and what use has a man for books if he cannot read?"

Enzo colours, embarrassed not only by his stupidity in assuming that a man of Nino Lunapiena's stature could read, but also by a sudden and tender desire to want to teach him.

By the time they are out in open water, the sun has risen and the air thickens like a broth on a stove. Nino suggests his oarsmen rest and they slump down on their oars, their heads forward, catnapping.

Nino is examining the rolling hitches where he has fastened the thin rope along the length of the long lance. If he doesn't like the look of one, he undoes the knot and rolls and re–ties it methodically, diligently checking each one by pulling and twisting the rope to ensure the line cannot slip.

"Yes, yes. We have one!" the lookout in the fulua shouts, pointing away towards the sun.

"Good eyes," Nino says to Enzo. "Now, you must row."

Enzo clambers aft and stands to his oar: the others have placed him at the stern so it will be easier to follow their stroke. The oar is long and wooden, and not sculpted like the oars he has seen in picture books of men sitting as they race on a calm river; a race watched by other men sporting trim straw hats and women dressed in lace and finery. No, Enzo's oar is rough in texture and heavy, and he has to stand and set his feet and bend his back in order to push and pull in time with the man in front.

The lookout, from his vantage point on top of the mast of the fulua, maintains a constant gabble of instruction, "To the left. To the right. Hurry. Faster. Slow. To the left. More. He's coming around behind. Wait. Now. Go. Hurry…"

Pipo climbs the small mast of the luntro and balances precariously, hoping to see the fish.

All the while the four row, Nino stands in the prow, his feet set like a wrestler, the lance held high and angled, his right hand at the back end above his head, and his left, with a few loose coils of line hanging below his fist, halfway along so that the tip points slightly down towards the water.

With Nino's encouragement and the promise of a catch, the men chatter as they urge each other's stroke: "Gio, you row like an old woman." And, "Pipo, my mother rows faster than you."

Yet Nino's stare never leaves the water. Say what they like, the oarsmen will never distract him; for he knows he will have one chance, with one lance and if he misses by so much as a finger's width, the swordfish will be gone down deep, and they may have to return to the Borgo empty–handed.

The men push and pull and roll their wrists, the boat surging forward.

Pipo swivels on his rest. He has seen the fish. "Now. She is behind us."

Enzo glances down. A silvery streak flashes alongside.

"She comes," yells Pipo. "Now. Now. You will see her."

Nino tenses, his hips jerk and twitch, his feet feeling for the boat beneath him. He raises his lance and with a force that will all but take him over the prow, he thrusts the lance down into the water, his right hand propelling it on its way.

For a split second, the lance sticks upright out of the water, then it very suddenly disappears below, taking the line with it.

The funcitta turns, and frees the line, ensuring it does not foul against the side of the boat as it runs out. That he says nothing tells the men he has struck clean and firm.

The men cheer and ship their oars, and Pipo shins down the mast. The tall one moves with surprising haste and agility; he lifts the basket of coiled rope to his chest, allowing the line to pay out, permitting the fish to run free and deep.

"Now, we must both be patient and swift," Nino says to Enzo. "If the fish is female, her mate will not leave her. Swordfish are like us, they only take one mate and if he comes, with the Madonna's blessing, we will take him too."

The line plays out at terrific pace and soon enough the first basket is empty.

This swordfish is strong and fast, and is diving deep: the second basket of line is required and the tall one lifts it up clear.

"A good fish?" Pipo asks.

"Yes," Nino replies.

Soon enough, and just as the second basket is close to empty, the line falls slack.

They wait, the tall one holding the line between two hands, feeling for the fish, every quiver reassuring him that the swordfish is still attached.

They wait, glancing amongst each other, smiling, nodding, happy.

The line tightens, then slackens, the fish turning and twisting in its flight.

"Bring the fish in," Nino says. "Enzo, you help with the line."

The boat rocks unsteadily as he steps forward, the others holding onto him as he makes his way past them.

Now aided by the tall one, he begins hand over hand to pull the line on board. Pipo sits behind them, coiling it neatly back into the basket lest one of them tangle their feet and fall.

The line is wet, thin and rough on their hands: the task of pulling it back in long and arduous.

"How much line have we paid out?" Enzo asks, as his hands sting against the line.

"You are tired already?" the tall one asks.

"No, I am interested to know, that is all."

"Nearly two baskets," Nino says. "One hundred metres, a little less perhaps."

Enzo hauls and hauls, hand over hand, his back groaning in objection. He grows confused; for at first, he was aware of the help the tall one was lending him and now, as his body tires, he feels as though he is hauling all on his own, especially when the fish rebels against the tension of the rope and tries to drag him overboard. He glances behind him.

All of the crew are watching him; no one is helping. They collapse in a fit of laughing which, ordinarily, might draw Enzo's anger. However, on this occasion he is not unhappy to be the butt of their humour; for if they thought they would rile him, they probably wouldn't play him so and he takes their ribbing as a sign that they are happy to enjoy his company.

"You bastards," he says and sets himself back to his hauling.

"Oh, now he calls us bastards," one says, in a tone which suggests he is properly offended.

Enzo hesitates in his hauling. In defining their status as the children of unmarried parents, perhaps he has overstepped the mark; after all, he is a guest on their luntro, and considering his vulnerable position, standing as he is at the very edge of the gunwale and holding on tight to the line, one smart kick in his backside and he will be joining the fish in the waters of the Strait.

He turns, a little nervously.

To a man, and including Nino, they guffaw and slap their chests in appreciation.

Soon enough, though, they settle down and get back to helping him and they haul the long silver–grey fish up to the side. First, its long, serrated bill pierces the surface, like a rapier through a dark mirror. Next its dorsal fin carves a wedge, threatening like that of a shark. And finally, its crescent–shaped tail swishes, spraying the men with cool, salty water.

They murmur their appreciation.

The swordfish stills and Pipo leans over the side and ties a slip–knot over its tail.

Suddenly, the fish understands that now is its last chance to object before she is lifted clear of her natural habitat. If the men manage to land her, her life is over, for there will be no more opportunities to escape. She thrashes and wriggles and rolls and tries to dive away back down to the safety of the deep; she squirms and flails, but all to no avail.

The tall one kneels down and grabs the swordfish by its tail, careful not to let his hands slip in case he cuts himself, and together the men drag their prize up over the side and into the boat.

Later, they catch the mate, a smaller fish than the female, but no less welcome. Faithfully, he had circled the luntro until all Nino had to do was wait patiently for the right moment to throw his lance. There was no great anxiety, no great stress to the second catch; the swordfish had quite simply surrendered in order to be with his mate.

"I have heard it said that the male will leap into the boat to be with his partner." Pipo's eyes had spoken of sadness, as though he felt guilty that he should have to benefit from another's blind loyalty. "But you must believe what you are comfortable believing; I have only heard this."

The others smile at their young helper. He has brought them luck! And on their row back to the Borgo, each of the crew takes his turn to question Enzo. "So, what did you think of hunting the swordfish? Did you find the work too rough?" And, "A day passed harvesting from the sea is better than a day passed counting numbers, no?"

They are right. The sea is free and it sets one's spirit free.

Now, Enzo takes another sip of his father's Malvasia and rests his head back. "Ah," he sighs, "that was a good day."

CHAPTER 17

The sound of the shot echoes through Lilla's head, as though all the cannons of the world have fired at exactly the same second. Terrified that when she opens her eyes, she might find Mrs Robertson's bloodied corpse lying before her, Lilla keeps them shut tight, her face screwed up and her hands flat against her ears. She can feel the fat drops of rain smacking her skull through her hair; they, too, echo like the gunshot.

Strong hands pull at her arms.

She shakes her shoulders, brushing them away. If that man has killed Mrs Robertson, she won't be surrendering to him without a fight; for if he thinks he is going to take her virginity, when she has preserved it so conscientiously for Enzo for when they are in America, then he had better–

The strong hands are back at her arms again.

"Lilla!"

She squeezes her hands back over her ears. Yet that was not the voice of the robber, Tulliu; that was a woman's voice. Lilla opens her eyes.

Mrs Robertson stands before her, intact and exactly in the state she had been before the gunshot. "It's all right, Lilla. I'm still here."

"But I heard the... I saw the... How can that be?"

Lilla follows the line of the older woman's sight down to the rubble strewn around her feet.

Tulliu lies dead. Completely dead. A hole, the size of a ripe blood orange, blown out of his chest. And a blood orange would be most suitable, Lilla decides as she grows used to the colour, for his upper torso is covered in fresh blood, his fresh blood.

She looks up. Men are standing at the foot of the mound of rubble across the way; one of them carries a long rifle. And whereas Tulliu was swarthy, unshaven and poorly dressed, this man is incredibly tall and broad and blond, and though his clothes are dirty, his blue uniform, and those of the others about him, lends him an ordered, secure aspect. He is smiling at Lilla; a curious reaction for one who has just taken another's life.

The men pick their way over to the two women and stand, appraising the lifeless form at their feet: judging by the way they keep glancing at the one with the rifle, they are discussing the merits of his marksmanship.

Lilla moves to her companion's side; the older woman is trembling, so Lilla slips her arm around her waist. "It's all right, Mrs Robertson. You're all right. No harm done. Except to Tulliu, of course."

"Yes, dear. You're quite right. I was just afraid he was—"

"Well, he didn't. He probably would have, but he didn't then and he won't now. So, what language are these men speaking? That tall one, the one who keeps smiling at me, the one with the gun; he's so big he's like three men all rolled into one."

Mrs Robertson wipes at the corners of her eyes, breathes deep and very quickly regains her composure. "Excuse me?" she asks, drawing the group's attention from their examination of the corpse. "Excuse me, but who are you? Where are you from?"

They look up and stand back, making way for a shorter man, an officer judging by the yellow starred epaulettes at his shoulders.

He stands to attention, bows politely and clicks his heels. "Russkiy, I am Russian. Leytenant Korsakov of the Battleship Makarov at your service. We can speak Italian, Russian, English or Latin. Which would you prefer, madame?"

"Italian will be fine, thank you, Lieutenant," Mrs Robertson warms to him. "We are most grateful for your help. And if I may say, in keeping with your manners your timing is impeccable. Another minute and this man would..."

Lieutenant Korsakov straightens and bows once more. "Madame, I must politely and respectfully interrupt to suggest that even taking into account the inclement weather and the danger from the aftershocks, this is no place for women."

"Yes, we know. Really we do."

The Russian lieutenant's complexion is pale and his full Russe moustache dwarfs his small nose. "Then permit me to ask why you should be here? The city is in danger of imminent collapse. We have already lost one of our working party."

"I am saddened to hear that, Lieutenant Korsakov."

"Yes. As are we. A brave yet foolish man, he ignored my orders and entered a building to free a woman trapped by fallen timber. There came a sudden aftershock, the rest of the building came down and by the time we reached him, he was beyond all help. May God rest his soul." Korsakov bends his head in respect and his working party follow suit.

After a brief silence, he continues. "As you have witnessed, madame, the streets are littered with felons such as this one; some have even taken to wearing the uniforms of the Carabinieri." He glances down. "He was trying to rob you?"

"And worse," Mrs Robertson confirms.

"Then we were right to shoot him." The lieutenant squares his narrow shoulders, turns and nods at the man carrying the rifle, before crouching to look over the corpse. "There are units of the Italian army on their way here from Naples, but at present we are the only functioning law in what is left of the city."

He picks up Tulliu's revolver, which he hands back to one of his men, and then he notices a folding knife sticking out from a pocket. As he removes it, he sees the sack lying by the corpse. Lieutenant Korsakov takes it and stands up.

"Ah, the ill—gotten gains of a dishonest profession," he says opening the sack to inspect its contents. Then, he drops it, his pale face very suddenly turning several shades paler.

"What is in the bag, Lieutenant?" Lilla asks.

Korsakov doesn't, though, hear her; he has his hand over his mouth and his eyes are wide with shock.

Lilla and Mrs Robertson both turn their attention to the ground, where the sack has fallen open.

The small collection of rings would be unremarkable were it not for the fact that some of them were still attached to fingers.

"Come, Lilla," Mrs Robertson commands. "Come now, look away."

Lilla cannot though, because one particular ring on one particular finger has caught her eye. "No, it can't be," she murmurs. She kneels down on the wet bricks and without reaching to touch it, she examines the ringed finger more closely.

"Come away, now," her companion demands. "That is quite the most unpleasant..."

"Young lady," says the Lieutenant, having recovered his composure.

"It's all right," Lilla replies, dreamily. "A fisherman's daughter is accustomed to dead fish. This is no worse." However, as she recognises the gold band her eyes water and tears flow.

"Oh, Lucrezia," she whispers, "even in death there is no peace for a child as beautiful as you."

Keeping his distance, the lieutenant asks, "You know this... this ring?"

"Yes. Yes, I do." Lilla wipes her tears away. "Yes, this belongs to Lucrezia Ruggeri, my Enzo's sister. Her body lies… No, her body lay on the debris before the Ruggeri family house in the Via dei Templari; it is the next street on the left." Without taking her eyes off the ringed finger, Lilla points. "Lucrezia was wearing white bedclothes. She was dead, really, perfectly dead; she wouldn't have felt anything…"

Lilla falls quiet: there is another ring that has caught her attention.

To distract her from her morbid curiosity, Mrs Robertson coughs theatrically and addresses the Russian in a stentorian tone, "It is why we are here. This young lady has lost her entire family to the earthquake and we are trying to locate her fiancée, who she hasn't seen since the minutes before. We think he is somewhere in the family house, perhaps trapped, although this criminal seemed to think he is dead." She turns her attention to the kneeling Lilla. "Gone, finished, done for. Wasn't that what he said?"

Lilla looks up, her eyes filled with yet more tears. "You can be unkind when you believe the situation calls for it, can't you Mrs Robertson? Is that what you meant when you said the British were stiff? Are you being stiff now, because you think Enzo may be dead and you think trying to find him is too dangerous?" Her tone is accusing, disparaging, and perhaps even a little mocking. "Well, I will not rest until I have seen proof that Enzo is dead. Do you understand?" Lilla's temper begins to boil. "Do you hear me, Mrs Robertson?"

"Yes. Yes, of course, my dear. Come now. It's all a bit upsetting." The older woman glances at the Russian.

He nods his head, walks over to Lilla and, putting his hand under her arm, encourages her to stand up.

"But what about these rings, these fingers?" she asks, grasping the sac. "They may belong to the dead, but even the dead have families. We must find who they belong to."

"And we will," Lieutenant Korsakov assures her. "We will. I will hand them over to the mayor's office."

Lilla, though, is not to be parted from the sack. "No, you won't. You can't." She looks over at her companion, her frustration simmering. "Didn't you tell me the mayor was dead and that there was no one in control?"

"Yes, I did—"

"Then we must take them with us," she shouts angrily. "We must hand them over to the proper authorities. There are people," she screams, "people who loved these rings and these fingers: they are all that is left of wives, of children, of loved ones. We must take all of them with us. We must find out."

Steadily, and with as much tenderness as his rainswept uniform will permit, the Russian officer lifts Lilla very slowly upright. However, he does not notice that she still has the sack grasped firmly between her white—knuckled fingers and the remaining contents all fall from the open neck of the sack and tumble to the ground.

Mrs Robertson, the lieutenant and his men all gasp, both in horror and in wonder.

Lilla's head, heavy with the weight of her sorrow, is bent to her chest in defeat and through the veil of her tears, she stares at the chaos of delicate fingers, of sparkling jewels, of hunks of white bread and black salami all spread out at her feet. At first, she can only appreciate the cold reflection of diamonds, the yellow sheen of pearls, the pigeon blood of rubies and the apple green of jade; and then, as she wipes her face, her eyes focus.

Before, when she had seen Lucrezia's finger hacked from its rightful place on her hand, her communion ring sullied by her own blood, Lilla's heart had been infected with a misery so poisonous that she wondered whether she would ever be able to forgive the world its repugnance. Now though, as she looks down, she finds her heart infected with a similar poison once more, yet this time the poison is concentrated a thousand times so that it produces an agony so visceral and painful that she doubts she will ever be able to bear its legacy; for there at her feet, surrounded by gems of unthinkable beauty, lies Enzo's signet ring.

CHAPTER 18

Enzo had come away from his hunting with her father a changed young man; for that day he'd realised he would never be truly free if he remained shackled by the expectations of his own.

"My father," he mutters to the beam that has settled like a table across his legs. On its conveniently flat surface, he has set out what's left of the salami and the bread and the now half–empty bottle of Malvasia. "My father, I wonder where he is now? Probably with his mistress in that hovel over the Portalegni."

Enzo is finding his thoughts a little ungovernable. They seem to dash about his mind like unruly children, which is perhaps no surprise considering he is exhausted by both an absence of water and a poverty of options.

"Is a man not a man unless he has both a wife and a mistress? Is it true, that one is more attractive to other women if one is known to keep a mistress?"

He shakes his head, perplexed, bemused and now enveloped in the shower of dust from his hair. "Oh, why do you put up with him, mama?"

That last night, they had been to the theatre:

Sunday 27th December and Carmelo Ruggeri must and will have his family about him. The great and the good of Messina are turning out at the Teatro di Vittorio Emanuele and best manners, and therefore best attire, are the order of the evening. Enzo's mother, Saverina, has been provided with funds for a new modern, slim—waisted dress, one which does not hang so low it collects dust from the floor; his two younger sisters have been prettified with white lace brought in from Taormina; and he and his younger brother, Vittorio, have been decked out in matching blue marinière shirts and white bell—bottomed trousers. Enzo had objected to this appalling matching uniform, but only because had he been too easily persuaded, his father might have suspected something was up.

And even though the Hungarian soprano, Paola Karalech, stands no chance of replacing Lilla in the pantheon of his affections, the evening is not without its consolations: the tenor Angelo Gamba cuts a dashing figure, his singing touches the very seat of Enzo's soul, as it does that of every man present, and the notion that Gamba's Radames would rather die imprisoned in a vault than live free without his Princess Aida appeals to Enzo; for, as he realises during the rousing chorus, what use is life without love.

At precisely the moment Ramfis, the high priest, sentences Radames to be interred alive, Enzo turns to find his mother gazing adoringly and yet perhaps a little sadly at him. Hers is a look of such intense love that Enzo is uncertain as to how he should react, so he looks away, quickly turning his attention back to the stage.

Outside the theatre, the evening is chilled but dry; perfect for a ten—minute stroll up the Corso Cavour. Yet with his new—found status, Carmelo decides a buggy is more appropriate and he hails one of the many waiting in line in the Garibaldi.

Arriving at their house in the Via dei Templari, Carmelo asks the driver to wait and informs Saverina that he has affairs to attend to and will therefore be home a little later.

"All right, children," their mother reassures, as they watch the buggy drive off, "let's not freeze out here when there's a perfectly warm stove inside."

Enzo is the last up the steps. He hangs back, taking in the gloom of the gaslit street, an unsavoury concoction of conflicting emotions pooling in his stomach; for he hates his father not simply for cheating on his mother, but also for providing his son with another reason to hate him. However, and if he is honest with himself, Enzo knows that it isn't so much his father's lack of devotion to his mother that gives him cause; it is the tight rein he keeps on his son that has fostered within him a need to break free. Maybe, after this evening, he will no longer have to put up with his tyrant of a father. Maybe, after this evening, he will never see his father again.

"Enzo, please hurry up and close the door," his mother calls.

Enzo looks up and down the street, committing every block, every cornice and balustrade to memory.

When Lucrezia and Angelica are in bed, and Vittorio has tired of his bleating about why his elder brother is permitted to stay up later, Saverina suggests she and Enzo sit together and talk.

"Yes, mama?"

Saverina has kind, reliable eyes, and their language is often subtle and gentle. It is how she is now, albeit that her smile is reserved, suggesting that rather than her having to ask, her son may like to tell whatever it is that preys on his mind.

"Yes, mama," he agrees, searching for the right place to begin. "You know, mother, that I would rather do anything than hurt you and that I will always hold you close to my heart, wherever I am. But you must also recognise that I cannot stay here and live chained to a future that is to be imposed upon me by my father." He pauses.

"Ah," his mother says, "I see it is not only Angelo Gamba who rehearses. Do go on, Enzo."

He colours, though he is by no means finished with his script. "Mama, you know all too well that we are alike and I have seen the way you look at us when we fight. You understand that our arguments are without foundation and that we use them only as an excuse to exercise our tempers. We fight not because of the differences between us; we fight because of our similarities. We are cut from the same cloth, carved from the same wood, fashioned from the same stone." Enzo is aware of mixing his metaphors, but he is more painfully aware that he has to add some clothes to the skeleton of his news; simply to lay it bare will risk shocking his mother beyond repair. "We will never be happy in each other's company."

"But, the business?" she asks. "Who will keep the business going if your father falls ill or when he no longer has the strength?"

"Vittorio. You know how good he is with figures and besides, he wants to. We've all seen the way he clings to the pages of your good books. He is desperate to be admired, desperate to please; it is what drives him." Enzo knows his mother knows this only too well: Lucrezia and Angelica are rarely subtle in trading knowing looks and sniggering every time the younger brother sucks up to his parents.

"But, Enzo, your brother is not tough like you. He might grow a head for business, but he will never grow the back required to keep the men in check. They would eat him for breakfast, bless the dear boy."

"Oh, I wouldn't worry too much about Vittorio, mama. He would give Machiavelli a run for his money." Of course, he is lying; everyone knows Vittorio couldn't fight his way into or out of a paper bag. Enzo leans forward and takes his mother's hands. "But we both know the real reason for my leaving, don't we?"

Saverina's eyes water at the mention of his imminent departure. "Lilla."

"Yes, mama, Lilla. And we both know that my father will never permit us to be together. He forgets his past and thinks only of his future. He—"

"And you, Enzo? Are you the same? Are you only thinking of your future?" His mother withdraws her hands and sits up straighter in the hope that the slight alteration in her posture will lend some authority to her words.

"No, mama, I am thinking of our future. Both Lilla's future and mine. This is not simply about me; it is about Lilla and the love we share."

Saverina slumps, a concession of sorts. "But you are both so young; how can you talk of love? And you have only known her for a few months; how can you be so confident? How can you know that she will become a good wife?"

"How can Lilla know whether I will become the man of her dreams, mama? Did you know when you were married?"

Saverina's eyes turn to the floor.

And Enzo is about to make the point that his mother had never been offered the opportunity to decide who she married; she had never had the chance Lilla has. However, he will not dare to suggest she is unhappy with her situation. He will not dare because he has too much respect for his mother and, perhaps more importantly, because his daring might cause her to examine the boundaries of her own happiness, an examination which might lead to a less than favourable conclusion.

"But Enzo," his mother beseeches, her palms pressed together, her fingertips pointing upwards as if she is praying to both him and a higher power: "Why does it have to be her? Why does it have to be a fisherman's daughter from the Borgo del Ringo? Why not the Bartolotta girl? She is sweet and... she will make a man a good wife."

"That Bartolotta girl? You mean the girl who just happens to be the daughter of the Salvatore Bartolotta who insists on telling everyone he is next in line for chief of the customs house? Whatever next? Why don't you suggest I wait and see if Princess Yolanda is available; she may only be seven, but who knows, perhaps King Vittorio will think me fit for a son–in–law."

"There is no call to speak ill of our king," Saverina snaps.

Enzo reins back the stallion of his indignation. "No, mama, you are right and I apologise, particularly to Princess Yolanda. As long as she lives, may she never be as ugly as that Bartolotta girl."

"Your cynicism does not become you, Enzo."

"No, mama, you are right again, and again I apologise."

The mutual sadness of their understanding that the path of their conversation can only lead to one end is too much for either to bear, especially in each other's company.

"Mama," he reaches out for her hands once more, "what matters most is that I love Lilla and that she loves me. What matters to my father is he believes that my love for Lilla will somehow devalue his newfound standing; that in some way he sees Lilla's people as lesser people. They are not; they are fishermen and fishermen are the very life–blood of our community. They are a proud and noble people; they have more honour than any of the fifty people my father scraped and bowed to at the opera this evening."

"Enzo!" The fire of challenge flames in Saverina's eyes. "Do not force me to choose between my respect for your father and my love for you. Youthful impertinence is acceptable, but only when unspoken and you of all people know how hard your father has worked to put the bread on our table and this roof over our heads. You know the risks he has taken; the prejudices he has had to overcome."

"Yes, mama, I know. And when I am down at the harbour helping load and unload cargo, many of the men remind me: it is a badge I have to wear. "Look, there goes Ruggeri's boy. He chose the right parents, didn't he?" "The heir to the Port of Messina," that's what they whisper. That's another reason why I have to leave: I cannot bear to be thought of as someone's son, as one who inherits. Don't you see, I have to make my own way, and America will provide me, provide us, with that chance."

In looking up at the ceiling, Saverina dismisses such a fanciful idea. "Did not your zio Pangrazio go to America? Did he not come back with Tuberculosis and die for lack of breath?"

"Mama? Zio Pangrazio left for America because he got the Garufi girl pregnant and he only came back because she married old man Mazza. He died because he never had the breath for work." Enzo could have said his uncle Pangrazio only possessed sufficient breath for idle gossip, but both he and his mother know her brother had drunk himself into an early grave.

"Mama," he begins again, this time more gently than before, "if I stay here with Lilla and my father does not give us his blessing, this can only lead to confrontation with Lilla's father and Nino Lunapiena is a king among fishermen. You know too well how such a confrontation will end ."

Saverina nods in agreement, a reluctant agreement which implies that whilst she does not accept his vision of the future, it is unarguably accurate.

Enzo holds up his left hand, the back of it towards his mother. "Do you remember what you told me when you gave me this ring?"

She nods and then, surprisingly, looks away.

"You told me that the day we moved into this house you had found it tied to the back of a side–table. How long it had been there, no one could know; but you told me the ring must have meant a great deal to someone, otherwise why would they have hidden it? Do you remember what else you told me, mama?"

She glances at her son and then away again.

"You told me that every gift carries with it a wish, and that your wish was for me to follow my heart. You also told me that as long as I wear this ring, I carry your wish with me wherever I go. With me! Wherever I go! Through good times and bad, through happy and sad. That was what you said, mama: through good times and bad, through happy and sad."

Now, trapped in the cellar, Enzo understands why his mother could not look at him: it was because she was the one who told him he must follow his heart and if she hadn't, then perhaps he might not have fallen so heavily for the young girl from the Borgo. And he remembers, too, Lilla's love for the ring; for whenever they met, she would lift his hand to her face and rub it slowly against her cheek; she used to tell him she liked the cool of the metal against the heat of her skin.

Enzo holds up his hands and in the dim light, he can just make out the clean strip of his little finger where the ring used to sit.

"Oh, mama, where are you now? Oh, Lilla, where are you?"

CHAPTER 19

"Lilla, pay attention," Mrs Robertson chides. "Do it like I showed you."

"Sorry. I was just thinking about..."

"Yes, I'm sure you were. And you would have every reason to, my girl. Trouble is, what's done is done and we have too many of the living to look after; there's nothing to be gained by dwelling on what might have been." The square–shouldered woman sets down her bloodied swab and taking the bandage from Lilla, she rolls it in a series of continuous revolutions round the leg of the young boy. "Like this, see? Twirl it, don't pack it; then split it and tie it off. We don't have enough dressings as it is, so don't waste them. Only the Good Lord knows what we would have done without the medical equipment these naval people have given out."

"Yes, I'm sorry, Mrs Robertson."

"Don't be sorry, my girl; be sensible, that's all I ask."

"It's just..."

"Of course. I understand. It's Enzo and your family you're thinking of. Well, there's plenty of others who deserve our thoughts and prayers; as many as a hundred thousand, maybe more, or so the doctor believes. He's heard that the wave swept away the university at Torre Faro. They say even as far south as Riposto there are people trapped in the ruins of the cathedral and across the Strait, Reggio Calabria has been wiped off the face of the earth. Much of Scylla and Palmi, too. We must be thankful; that's all we can be."

Lilla looks up at her guardian in disbelief. "Thankful? How can you be so... so positive at a time like this? People have lost everything they ever had. I have lost everything. Everything, Mrs Robertson. There is nothing here for me now. There is nothing left. I have no one." Tears well in her eyes.

"You have me, Lilla." She wraps her arms around her young companion, and hugs her and kisses the matted hair on top of her head. "You have me. I promise you; you'll never be alone again. Not as long as there is a breath left in me, my girl. That, I promise you."

Along with other volunteers, survivors and the few doctors left alive, they are working in a warehouse near the railway station. The high–ceilinged building has been converted into an aid station and if it doesn't quite hold the chill wind at bay, it does at least provide shelter from the incessant rain. Motherless children mill about at the entrance, watching, waiting, wondering.

"Now, remember how I showed you," Mrs Robertson murmurs. "Twirl the bandage so it wraps around the limb. Not too tight, mind, but make sure it's tied off securely."

As she wipes the tears from Lilla's cheeks, there is an ear–splitting blast, quickly followed by a succession of several further blasts.

The ground shakes, people scream and dust cascades from the ceiling. Mothers gather up their children and rush, stumbling towards the doors; doctors lean over to protect their patients.

Lilla grabs her guardian around her waist and hangs on. "Is it an aftershock? Is this the end?"

They wait. They pray. And like the motherless children, they wonder. In spite of the dust, everyone studies the ceiling for the slightest indication that it might fall.

Much to their surprise, though, the warehouse does not collapse about their ears and gradually the echoes of thunder dissipate to leave in its place an eerie, stunned silence.

Little by little, like a returning tide, conversation returns amid the horrors of amputating shattered limbs, excising infected flesh and cleaning open wounds.

Mrs Robertson giggles, nervously. "No, it's not the end, Lilla. It's a beginning. I do believe King Vittorio has arrived."

"The king?"

"Yes, the king. Though how many of the city's already unstable buildings will have fallen prey to that grand salute is anybody's guess. They say the king has cut short his shooting in the Abruzzi mountains." She tilts her head and arches a questioning eyebrow. "Now, isn't that just grand of the little man, eh?"

Mrs Robertson surveys her own handiwork and pats her patient on his head. "Right, off you go young man. And try to find somewhere to lie down for a while. Even if you have to share, get that leg of yours up off the ground."

She turns back to Lilla and breathes deeply. "As I was saying before we were so rudely interrupted: you must tie them off properly, otherwise they'll come undone and soon enough the dressings will drop off; that way we'll get the little beggars bothering us again when our time would be better spent looking after new patients. Come now, let's get back to work: if we take care of the minutes, the hours will surely take care of themselves."

And the next few hours do exactly as she has predicted. If the one–time nurse and her young helper speak to each other at all it is only to instruct and query, as a procession of children are funnelled through the crowd towards the makeshift bed on which Mrs Robertson deals with an assortment of minor injuries that require cleaning and dressing. Every now and then, the shroud of their concentration is punctured by the howl of pain or the wail of misery or grief: in the face of overwhelming numbers, the doctors are making do with the little chloroform and ether they have available.

Sometime later, though it is because of the lack of sun impossible to tell whether it is still morning, there is a commotion outside. The hubbub of conversation in the aid station dribbles into a curiously reverential silence.

A woman enters. She is, unlike the doctors who wear blood–stained whites and the patients who wear soiled rags, dressed in a lace–fringed black dress with a black fur stole covering her shoulders. Yet it isn't her glamorous attire that sets her apart from the people standing back to permit her entrance to the aid station; rather it is the glittering tiara perched on top of the perfect nest of her dark hair that leaves no one in any doubt.

"Queen Elena!" Mrs Robertson says. "With the Duca di Lantra and the Conte della Trinitá."

Men remove their hats and caps, and bow. Women lower their eyes and curtsy. A hard–faced, elderly woman wearing a drab skirt and embroidered smock, steps forward from the crowd, throws herself to the ground and kisses the queen's feet.

People gasp, astonished at such a breach of protocol.

At the queen's side stands a man in a sombre frockcoat and high collar; he steps forward.

With a gentle sweep of her white–gloved hand, the queen intercepts her courtier, beckoning him stay. She smiles generously, and her broad and strong forehead, her dark eyes, the graceful curve of her cheeks, her modest lips and her sculpted chin exude a warmth and serenity that enlightens those watching that she both understands the gesture and is not in the slightest perturbed by the sudden intrusion.

Queen Elena bends to the woman, reaches down and encourages her to stand up, speaking to her under her breath so that no one else can eavesdrop the intimacy of her message.

At first, the woman is uncertain of what she should do next. She glances up and then cowers down, lowering her gaze back to the floor.

The queen, though, is insistent and whilst others hold their breath, she lifts the woman to her feet, nods a reassurance and stares deep into her eyes.

People sigh. The awkward moment is over; the effrontery, like her gentleman—in—waiting, brushed aside.

Eyes wide with awe, Lilla is speechless. Before her stands the heroine of her favourite fairy—tale; the princess who left her family in Montenegro and gave up her religion in order to marry her Crown Prince of Naples. The account of their courtship, their marriage and her mother's disapproval had long been a favourite bedtime story, one Lilla's mother would embellish with each telling.

"She is more beautiful than I had imagined. Taller, too," Lilla murmurs to herself. "How is it possible for a mother to look so young?"

Mrs Robertson beams with pride. "I knew she wouldn't let the King come alone. He's so much like his father, a man who 'never disdained to shake our rough hands', or so the men of the Ostia Marshes proclaimed. Even after his father was shot, King Vittorio refused to blame his people. Why, in the middle of the night, a couple of days after his father's funeral, there was a train crash in the Castel Giubileo, in Rome. The Grand—duke of Russia, the Grand—duchess and other dignitaries had travelled over for the ceremony and were returning home. They were all on the train, so when the king and queen found out about it, they didn't wait for their royal carriage, they jumped in a taxi and went straight down to the scene. The king dismissed his guard, told them to get on and help in the rescue, while he and the queen helped look after the injured. They are, as we say, both for the people and of the people."

"You seem to know much about of our royal family."

"A little," she says, modestly. "Now, what did I tell you about concentrating, young lady. Finish up what you're doing and help me with this little girl. Poor thing, she's no idea how bad the cuts on her hands are and it's a wonder if her nails will ever grow back. She must have been clawing at the bricks for a lifetime."

The queen, escorted by her gentlemen and lady–in–waiting, makes her way slowly round the aid station, pausing now and again to offer the afflicted comfort and the bereaved commiseration. On more than one occasion while listening to a family's tale of woe, Queen Elena is seen to draw a handkerchief and dab at the corners of her eyes.

Lilla is wrestling with a child unwilling to have her wounds disinfected: the saline solution stings and the young girl cannot understand why she should be subjected to yet more pain when she has put up with so much already. Lilla does not notice the queen approach.

"Mrs Robertson?" Queen Elena asks, as if she is surprised to find someone she knows working in such filthy conditions.

"Your majesty."

"What are you doing here? I expected you to be at Isola Bella, minding the lady Trevelyan."

Lilla is once again struck dumb as she begins to understand that her guardian knows more than the little she suggested regarding the royal family.

"I'm sad to report, your majesty, that my lady Trevelyan died the October before last. She was buried at Castelmola; the whole town turned out for the funeral."

"I'm sorry to hear that, Mrs Robertson, and even more sorry that I did not attend." Queen Elena falls silent, a moment of contemplation, a pause for recollection and of respect.

"I believe your majesty had her hands full at the time, what with the expected arrival of the Princess Giovanna. How is the Princess Mafalda?"

"Enjoying good health, thank you."

"And the Princess Yolanda? Why, she must be nearly eight."

"She will be, this coming June. Yolanda is well and loves her swimming, much like your Miss Trevelyan, or rather Mrs Cacciola I should say. Has Mr Cacciola dispensed with your services?"

"He has, your majesty. No cause for me to stay in Taormina now that I no longer have anyone to care for. I was en route when this dreadful earthquake struck the city." Mrs Robertson sighs heavily, turning to take in the many injured lying about the aid station. "And King Vittorio? Is he enjoying good health? It is a boon that you have come. People will be so heartened to know you care."

The queen's pearly white complexion colours briefly. "The king is very naturally saddened by the suffering of his people. So much so that to the consternation of his ministers he is digging amongst the ruins with his bare hands. Also, he is humbled by the timely and generous assistance afforded by so many nations, even if he is a little vexed by the inappropriate flamboyance of their welcome." And as if she has committed some faux pas in letting slip that the king can be dismayed and is therefore mortal, the queen raises her head and asks, "So, who is this young helper you have by your side?"

"Your majesty, may I present Lilla Lunapiena."

The queen extends her hand.

Lilla stands and studies it. She knows she ought to bend her knee like others have and yet Lilla also knows that having never curtsied or tried to curtsey, there is every chance she will tie her legs in a knot and tumble inelegantly to the floor. She is also certain that the queen, however down to earth she may appear, will not want to shake a hand that is caked in the dried blood of her most recent patient, so she ignores the hand, bends her back and nods briefly towards it. "Pleased to meet you, your majesty."

"As am I, Lilla. Such a beautiful name. After the Madonna della Lettera, I understand. Let us hope she remembers to smile over the city in the coming weeks." Queen Elena lingers, her dark eyes fixed on Lilla's face, her dark eyebrows frowning in concern. "Tell me, young lady, how old are you?"

"I'm sixteen, your majesty."

"Truly?"

Lilla lowers her eyes. "Well, soon to be sixteen."

The queen waits, expecting.

"This next month, the eighth."

The queen smiles, her teeth even whiter than her skin. "I thought we had something in common; we share the same birthday. Tell me, Lilla, where are your..." She hesitates and glances at Mrs Robertson as a dull thought plays on her mind.

Mrs Robertson reads the thought and furrowing her brow, shakes her head.

"All of them?" Queen Elena asks.

Lilla, though, does not want to be side–lined from a conversation she now realises concerns her. "Yes, your majesty, they are all dead. Every single one: my mother, my father and my sisters. Even Enzo, my fiancé. All gone to rest with the Madonna."

The queen raises her head as if she has very suddenly noticed some anomaly in the ceiling of the old warehouse worthy of her regard. No one in their immediate vicinity mistakes her change in posture for anything other than what it is, namely a brave attempt to hold back the growing tide of tears rising in her eyes.

Everyone is watching. Everyone is waiting. Though for what, nobody is sure. This monarch. This matriarch. This mother to a greater family.

Standing beside her, Lilla can both see and feel the emotions brimming within the regal guise, and it is evident to her that

Queen Elena is trying her best to stifle her inner distress whilst at the same time attempting to maintain an outward calm. Lilla recognises the whirlpool and knows its overwhelming power; she reaches out to hold the queen's hand and—

Without warning, the floor of the warehouse begins to tremble, though this time there is no accompanying twenty—one—gun salute.

And as if choreographed in one expansive stage manoeuvre, people stare uncomprehending at the person nearest them. Then they look up to the ceiling as the beams begin to vibrate and the dust of ground mortar billows down on them. Once more, the doctors and nurses cover their patients.

People run. For the tenth, eleventh or perhaps thirteenth time since early Monday morning, people dash for the safety of outside. In the aid station, there must be eighty mothers, fathers, sons and daughters, grandparents and orphans. Some are too sick and too frail to move and some, because of their injuries, simply cannot move from their cots.

In their haste to leave, people stumble and fall, and the mad scramble quickly develops into a stampede, those who tumble instantly trodden underfoot. In their panic, the queen's greater family disregard her noble status. To them, suddenly, she is little more than just another obstacle placed in the path to their survival. The terror blinds them and without thinking they shove her aside.

Queen Elena falls; one beautiful woman swept aside by a wave of grotesque hysteria.

Lilla, too, is bumped and buffeted. However, she sees the queen go down and without thought for her own safety, flings herself on top, all the while shouting for the onrushing crowds to hold back. Shoes, boots and knees trample across her back. A person stumbles and falls on top of her. A hand pushes her hard against the queen's back. A foot flattens Lilla's outstretched hand.

The aftershock lasts fifteen or perhaps twenty seconds. When you cannot run, when you are trapped, Lilla learns, the shaking of the ground seems to last forever. Was this how it was for Enzo?

The world vibrates. Their bodies seem suspended. Their tongues will surely be shaken from their mouths, their eyes will surely be shaken from their sockets and their heads must surely become detached from their shoulders.

And then, as violently as the aftershock began, it ceases and the trembling calms amid a crashing of already weakened walls and cracked ceilings.

The dust settles, the medics examine each other and their traumatised patients, and Lilla is still stuck like a limpet to the queen's back.

Strong hands, like those she has imagined belonging to an omnipotent power, prise her from her berth and lift her.

Lilla is met with an owlish, kindly face, his knowing grey eyes filled with concern.

"Are you hurt?" asks the man. He is the escort who stepped forward when the woman prostrated herself at the queen's feet.

"Oh, yes, a little." She shrugs, nonchalantly. Lilla turns, remembering the feel of the fur stole that had saved her face from greater damage.

Standing beside her, the queen is being dusted off and pored over by her lady—in—waiting. Her eyes are a little glazed and her face is powdered with black dust. She ignores the fussing and summons a smile, suggesting no real harm has been done: "That was very brave of you, young lady."

Lilla rubs at her ribs and flexes the blood back into her flattened hand. "What are a few feet when I have survived falling houses? Oh, your majesty, your mouth. Your lip is cut."

"It is no more than a scratch."

However, her courtier and her lady—in—waiting are not so easily convinced and they hail a doctor.

"No," the queen says, sharply. "The doctors have enough to deal with. They should not have to waste their time on one who has come here out of choice. Mrs Robertson?"

"Yes, of course. Let me take a look at you."

"If I may say," the man with the kindly face interrupts, "we have your personal physician with us, perhaps he should—"

"No," the queen replies. "Mrs Robertson looked after Yolanda and Mafalda perfectly well when they were mere infants, I'm sure she is more than capable of attending to me. That aside, I should hope my physician is directing his energies elsewhere. Mrs Robertson?" Queen Elena asks again and glowering at her escort, perches on the edge of the cot, waiting.

Mrs Robertson bends to inspect the graze. "I'm afraid we only have a saline solution, I…"

The queen turns her head and winks at Lilla. "I see your leg is bandaged. Does it hurt?"

"A little."

"Did Mrs Robertson clean your injury with saline solution."

"Naturally," Lilla replies, puzzled.

"In that case," she decides, offering her chin, "if saline solution is good enough for you, then I see no good reason why the same should not be so for me. Please carry on."

Mrs Robertson fetches a clean swab, dips it into the bowl containing the clear solution and dabs, gently, at the wound. "Just a bit of grit, a little dust," she coos, as though she is indeed talking to an infant. "There. I don't believe that requires a dressing. One moment, let me look at your hands, your majesty." She murmurs to herself as she inspects them. "Good, not so bad; your gloves protected you. You will, though, be bruised from your fall, so perhaps you should ask your physician to check on you when he has time."

"Thank you, I will." The queen stands up and, turning to her escort and her lady—in—waiting, she fixes them with a penetrating glower. "We must find somewhere for all these children who have no one left to care for them. Please make some enquiries as to the whereabouts of the Sisters of the Poor."

Lilla straightens as if coming to attention.

"Yes, Lilla? You have something to say?"

"Yes, your majesty. I have been told that the Capuccin Convent and church have been destroyed. A Russian officer said there is nothing left standing in that area."

"I don't doubt it," Queen Elena replies. "It would seem barely a building in the city remains unaltered. Yet the Sisters are a hardy and resourceful congregation, and I am confident that if anyone can find a way to attend to the children's needs, the Poor Sisters will." She turns to address her escort. "Also, I think it would be a good idea to contact the Englishman, Mr Joseph Whitaker of Palermo."

"At the Villa Malfitano? The Marsala wine family?" the Duca di Lantra asks.

"Yes. I believe he is patron of the Palermo Home for Waifs and Strays. Let them know we will make a donation; we do not expect them to provide all the necessary funds. Perhaps they can take some of these orphans. See to it, please."

"At once, your majesty."

"Also, be so good as to furnish me with an apron," she says, removing her gloves and rolling up her sleeves. "And before I lend my assistance to these over–pressed doctors and surgeons, I would like a word with Mrs Robertson in private, so would the three of you wait elsewhere. And please be so kind as to take young Lilla with you? Provide her with some food; poor thing doesn't look as though she's eaten in days."

The escort and lady–in–waiting exchange knowing looks, bow and retire.

Obediently, Lilla follows them towards the door, the promise of food enlivening her limbs. However, as the sea of people crowding around them parts, she glances back at her guardian.

Lilla's is both a questioning look and, perhaps, an admission that she is reluctant to stray too far from the woman who has been her one constant of the last two days.

"It's all right, Lilla. You can come back as soon as Queen Elena and I have had our talk."

Chapter 20

"You didn't tell me you knew the queen."

"No," Mrs Robertson snaps, "I didn't. It doesn't do to crow about one's acquaintances, particularly when they happen to be royalty. Apart from that..." She is concentrating as she tries to peel back the dried and crusted clothing from the lacerated hip of a young boy who will not stop from crying.

"Apart from that?"

"Apart from that, you did not ask me." She grimaces and applies more solution to the bloody cloth.

"What is that smell?" Lilla asks.

"Gangrene," Mrs Robertson replies, her voice heavy with pessimism. "This poor dear must have been buried for a long time. He has pressure sores all over his upper torso, cellulitis in several places and his hips are in a shocking state. I think if he's any chance, he must go to one of the naval ships for treatment. Lilla, you know which doctor is the one called Roselli?"

She nods.

"Well, be a good girl and go and ask him to come here. If he asks why, tell him what I've just told you. Tell him also that I think this boy's hip bones may be fractured; there has to be a reason he's in so much pain. Go on, quickly now."

When she returns, she says Dottore Roselli is overloaded with patients and that he will come as soon as he has finished what he is doing.

"I wonder when that will be," Mrs Robertson grumbles.

For the first time since she has met the English nurse, Lilla notices the irritation of fatigue creeping into her tone. "I am tired, too," she says.

"In that case, Lilla, you stay here and do your best to distract this one from his discomfort while I go and press his case with the proper authorities."

Mrs Robertson is gone far too long for Lilla's comfort and whilst in her care the young boy grows delirious.

She looks around for someone to help her, but all are taken up with their own individual tales of woe.

"Forgive me, my beautiful boy," she whispers in his ear, "I don't know how to be a mother. I don't know what's right to do."

He looks up, pleading: his eyelashes long and lustrous, his perfectly round face shining pale beneath grey streaks of dried mud and ash. A sheen of sweat glistens at his brow. He shivers.

Lilla pulls him to her young breasts and tenderly kisses his mop of unruly dark curls. He is in some way familiar to her, but she cannot place him. Right now, in this cold, damp and foul-smelling warehouse, Lilla isn't confident she can recall what anyone ever looked like: not her parents, her sisters nor Enzo. All the faces she summons to mind seem either strangely obscured by woodsmoke or brick dust, or twisted unrecognisably with intense pain.

The boy shivers again, though this time his action is more convulsion than shiver. He is burning up, the infection seeping through his body the way tiredness is now seeping through hers.

She lays him down and climbs up on the cot beside him, cuddling him close, cradling his head, draping her free arm over his shallow chest, both protecting him and warming herself in the latent heat of his fever.

"Oh, please come back soon, Mrs Robertson," she mutters. "Please hurry." And with that last hope in her mind, Lilla falls helplessly and deeply asleep.

A hand squeezes her shoulder; guilt hisses in her ear, "How long have you been asleep?"

"Lilla? Wake up. Come on, Lilla, wake up now." Mrs Robertson is standing tall over her. "Quickly now. Up off that cot and go and find Dottore Roselli again. Tell him I'll be over to see him in a minute or two. Tell him he's not to interrupt what he's doing. I'll explain all when I see him."

"Why? I...You said I..."

"Yes, girl, never mind what I said, just do as I ask. Off you go. Quickly now."

Lilla doesn't question, there is an urgency to the woman's order, an obduracy in her insistence similar to that of the queen when she asked her lady—in—waiting to leave her so that she could talk with Mrs Robertson in private.

The good Dottore Roselli is a slender man, his wispy hair prematurely grey, his glasses seemingly round and small compared to his considerable nose; and his demeanour is that of a man who is exasperated by being asked so many questions for which he has no answers. When Lilla tries to speak to him, he ignores her for a full minute, so she tugs at his elbow.

"Yes? What is it you want?" he says, gruffly. His knee—length smock is stained red with the blood of his many patients. "Can't you see I'm busy."

"Of course, doctor. Everyone is busy," she replies a little rudely. "I have a message from Mrs Robertson?"

Briefly, he sucks his teeth in exasperation. "Go on, then. Deliver your message. What does Prudence Robertson want you to tell me that's so important?"

"Prudence?" Lilla repeats.

He does not turn to address her; he keeps his gaze fixed firmly on the stomach of the old woman lying supine before him. "Yes, Prudence. Now what is so important?"

"Mrs Robertson says you are not to interrupt what you are doing and that she will come in a minute or two to explain all to you."

"Ah, I see." The good and seemingly tireless doctor softens. He hesitates and turns to Lilla. Removing his glasses, he stares down either side of his broad and slightly crooked nose. His eyes, though slowed by tiredness, exude compassion in abundance rather than frustration. "In that case... What is your name, child?"

"Lilla. Lilla Lunapiena."

"And what a very beautiful picture your name paints. You must be the young lady everyone is talking about. It appears that you dress wounds as well if not better than some of the trained nurses. Can this be true?"

Lilla is quietly surprised that one supposedly so busy is setting aside the time to engage her in conversation. "Mrs Robertson is a good tutor."

"Oh yes, she is," Dottore Roselli says, smiling, his thoughts drifting. "She certainly is. However, that is only to be expected, isn't it?"

"To be expected. What do you mean to be expected?"

Oblivious to the needs of his patient, the doctor ponders for a moment, before lowering his head in a conspiratorial manner and in a hushed voice replying, "Clearly, you have no idea what or who you are dealing with, do you, young lady?"

Lilla shrugs, "No. I didn't even know until you told me that her name is Prudence. All I know is that she's been caring for an old lady who lived on Isola Bella and that the queen knows her."

He chuckles.

"What's so funny?"

"Well, Lilla, you put your words together so wisely, for that is how it is with kings and queens. It is the etiquette of the court that they are permitted to know you. You, on the other hand, are not really supposed to know them. Am I making myself clear?"

"So why? I mean, how does the queen know Mrs Robertson?"

"Because, young lady, your Mrs Robertson was governess to the Queen's first two children. You didn't know this?"

"To Princesses Yolanda and Mafalda?"

The doctor winks and raises his finger to his lips. "Precisely. But that's a secret between you and me, eh Lilla? Just between you and me, now, eh?"

"But what harm is there in people knowing?"

"Prudence is a very private person and she believes, as all of us doctors do, that the intimate details of people's personal lives are of no concern to others. Now, does this basic concept rest easily with you or are you one of those who likes to stick her nose into people's private business?"

An image of the doctor sticking his considerable beak in people's private business leaps into Lilla's mind and she chuckles.

"What is so amusing?"

Lilla is, though, embarrassed by her vulgar imagining and in order to avoid answering asks, "Why was Mrs Robertson not governess for Prince Umberto?"

The doctor considers for a moment, no doubt weighing whether he will be breaking his oath to Hippocrates by replying. "When the Prince of Piedmont was born, Queen Elena asked King Vittorio for permission to nurse the infant; something of a departure from the manner in which previous royal siblings had been brought up. The king believed, quite correctly, that his successor would be stronger and healthier if he was nursed by his own mother, and that the young Prince Umberto would be more inclined to take on some of his mother's gentler qualities. Mrs

Robertson was not one to disagree, and whether she disagreed or not, it was correct for her to find employment elsewhere."

Lilla is hypnotised by the doctor's account and her eyelids grow heavy, as they would when her mother told her stories at bedtime. "Does she not have a family of her own?"

His smile is warm and delightfully paternal. "No and yet yes. Mrs Robertson has no children to call her own and yet she is a mother of sorts. From what I have seen of her and from all that I have heard, I am sure she would, given the opportunity, make a wonderful mother."

The old woman on the cot groans, as if to suggest she is more deserving of the doctor's attention than the young girl he seems so taken with.

Dottore Roselli stands up straight and looks out over the sea of cots. When he is happy that he has located what or whoever it was he was searching for, he nods and turns back to Lilla. "Now, young lady, I must attend to my patient's needs and you must continue with your work. I am sure Prudence will be grateful for your continued and very professional assistance. Of you go, now, and remember what I said."

"Yes," Lilla says. "Thank you, doctor. And thank you for all you are doing for us."

He smiles that warm, fatherly smile once more. "This is what I am here for, Lilla, to help those who cannot help themselves. This is why I am here."

The good doctor's words hold fast in Lilla's mind as she jostles her way through the throng of sick and injured.

When Lilla arrives at the cot, the boy has disappeared and Mrs Robertson is treating a new child, a three or perhaps four—year—old girl with a badly swollen ankle. The girl breathes too rapidly, her pupils are the size of black saucers and her skin is cold, clammy and ashen in colour.

"Find me another blanket, please, this poor girl is in shock. Two if you can. And make sure they're dry."

"Yes, at once," Lilla replies, taking a quick look round and spotting a vacant cot on the other side of theirs. Quickly, naturally and without drawing attention, she collects the blankets, checks they are dry and folds them around the girl's shoulders. When she looks up for some recognition that she has done what she has been asked, she notices Mrs Robertson's cheeks are damp and her eyes watery.

Lilla hesitates, coming to realise that she doesn't need to ask about the boy because he must have died in her arms and the reason the older woman sent her away to find the Dottore was so that she wouldn't know and therefore wouldn't be upset. That, at the expense of her own emotions, Mrs Robertson should want to protect Lilla from hers, touches Lilla so profoundly that her heart threatens to burst out of her chest with love for the woman who has so readily taken her under her wing. She makes to say so until she is interrupted by a voice in her head that reminds her of the woman's down–to–earth nature and she decides that perhaps it is, for the moment, in both their better interests if she doesn't mention her growing love for her guardian.

"This ankle requires a cold compress," Mrs Robertson declares. "Lilla, take this roll of bandages outside and soak it in rainwater. I can't tell if the ankle's broken and there's not much we can do without one of those new–fangled shadowgram machines I keep reading about. We'll keep the foot elevated and let the doctors have a look at it when the swelling's reduced."

A short while later, Mrs Robertson suggests they need to take a rest and get some food.

On board the naval ships, the cooks are working overtime in their galleys baking bread and biscuits, and tenders shuttle the badly needed supplies ashore. Survivors scavenge amid the broken crates of fruit that have been tossed like unwanted children's toys along the marina, and sailors in blue jackets line the quayside doling out carefully measured rations of fresh water.

Lilla and Mrs Robertson sit sheltered from the wind and rain beneath an awning, while they see to the grumbling of their stomachs.

"Dottore Roselli said your first name is Prudence," Lilla mumbles as she munches on a chunk of white bread.

"Did he now?"

"Yes."

"It is my given name. Not that I'm inclined to thank my parents for their fancy."

"Don't you like it, then?"

"It's not that I don't like it, Lilla. It's just that it's a bit pretentious, if I'm honest." The thought makes her chuckle.

"He told me you were governess to Princess Yolanda and Princess Mafalda, and that's how you know the queen."

Mrs Robertson's laughing fades. "Well, he's right about that; though I'm not sure what business it is of his to go crowing about my place."

"He also said you were a mother of sorts." Lilla watches for her reaction to the doctor's assessment of her character.

"Well, I have too many years behind me to be a mother now. That's all done and finished with."

A silence, not unpleasantly imbued with sadness, falls between them.

"I don't mean to be rude, but what did you and the queen talk about?"

Mrs Robertson ceases her chewing and fixes Lilla with a surprised stare. "My, you're not as green as you are cabbage–looking, as we say."

"I don't know what that means."

"It means, Lilla, that you aren't as naïve as people might at first think you are. Though why I say that when I've only known you painted in mud and ash, dressed in rags and struggling like everyone else to survive in this upturned world, is anybody's guess."

The silence returns until the older woman decides it is right to break it.

"Queen Elena asked me about your family situation. The good lady was interested to know why you were with me and not with friends of your family."

"What did you tell her?"

"The truth, in your words. I repeated that you are all alone in the world, as are so many young children."

"I'm hardly a child, Mrs Robertson. I'm nearly sixteen."

"Yes, but you are alone and as we've already witnessed, this is no place for a young lady without a family to protect her. And by that I don't necessarily mean the criminals who are wandering the street. This dreadful episode will no doubt attract the more unscrupulous members of society in just the way bees are attracted to honey. It's inevitable. It's the less agreeable way of the world."

"But I have my people. Not all the fishermen will have been taken by the great wave. Zio Pipo will look after me. Remember, my father was a father to many in the same way that the queen is a mother to all. The fishermen will not forget that, however poor they are or however many mouths they have to feed."

Prudence Robertson nods, thoughtfully. "Yes, I had thought that. They are fine people; they measure wealth differently from others. Yet the queen put an idea into my head and I have given it a good deal of thought."

The silence returns until it is Lilla's turn to break it.

"Are you going to share the queen's idea with me? Or is that what Dottore Roselli described as her business and so something you would rather keep to yourself?"

"No, Lilla," Prudence turns and putting her arms around her young charge, she pulls her to her ample bosom in much the same way Lilla had the dying boy. "What Queen Elena suggested concerns you as much as it does me, and I will tell you as long as you promise me you will consider what I have to say very carefully and not jump to any conclusion. If you promise me this, then I will tell you. What do you say? You are sufficiently intelligent to be able to think for yourself; that much I have learned about you in the short time we have been together."

Lilla plays dumb for a moment, wondering if, and in her heart hoping, that what she is about to hear will be what she has wanted to hear since she both met the older woman and understood that Enzo is not coming back to rescue her from all the horror and madness.

"Yes, Mrs Robertson, I promise you I'll think about whatever you say. You've been so kind to me already, how could I not do as you ask?"

"And one more thing, I should be rewarded if you would call me Prudence when we are alone. I don't care to be too familiar, so it might be best to address me formally when we're in company. But when there's just the two of us, I think it only right and proper that you should address me by the name friends call me. After all, that is what we have become, isn't it? Friends."

"Yes, Mrs Robertson, I mean Prudence. Thank you, I will try to remember."

The older woman sighs, evidently preparing herself. "What the queen suggested was that I might like, if you agree, to adopt you; to take you back to England with me and to live with me as my daughter: to care for you, provide for you and see to your education. Lord knows there have been too many children orphaned by this dreadful earthquake."

Once again, Lilla's heart threatens to burst from the confinement of its repressed emotions, and it is all she can do to prevent herself from blurting out that she would like to — no, love to — tie herself to the apron strings of the wonderful matronly soul who sits comforting her.

"Can it really be so easy for you to adopt me?" she asks "Don't you have to have permission from the authorities?"

"Of course, I do. Fortunately for us the king and queen have brought with them Mr Orlando, the Minister of Justice, and Mr Bertolini, the Minister for Public Works. She says that between them they should be able to see to the formalities and if needs be, she will ask the Duca di Lantra to speak to Sir Rennel Rodd, the British Ambassador in Rome."

"Does she really have that much power that she can decide what happens? Is it really so simple for others to decide what happens to people like me?"

Prudence bridles her lips, contemplating. "Lilla, your parents are no longer here for you and you have not suggested that outside of your uncle Pipo there is anyone else to care for you. I am sure there will be a proper procedure to follow, some red tape that will have to be worked through. The queen," she says, with a knowing look, "can be most persuasive. Don't forget, she is a mother herself, so she understands what's best for children."

"What's best for me, you mean," Lilla mutters, dreamily. And as she speaks her mind, a thought, a feeling, a curious anxiety begins to gnaw at her initial, impulsive desire: Enzo. She has seen his signet ring. It sits, alone, in her pocket and without thinking, she reaches in and toys with it, reacquainting herself with its cool texture, its curve and its permanence.

Tears well in her eyes and very soon drip in great individual drops, which splash into her companion's lap.

"I know," Prudence Robertson whispers. "It's Enzo you are thinking of, isn't it? And quite right you are too."

Lilla nods and more and heavier tears fall. "It makes no sense. Nothing. I can't stop thinking about him. It's just that I know for sure my family are all gone. You saw them and Pipo saw them. They are gone and if they weren't, I know you and Pipo would not tell me such a lie. And while I could not be more heartbroken by their leaving me, I cannot bear to think that Enzo might still be suffering. Perhaps that terrible man was lying; he was the sort who would do that, if only to gain some pleasure from seeing someone else suffer. But I feel sure Enzo is still alive somewhere. I feel it in my heart. Please tell me I am right. Please."

"There, there." Prudence caresses her head and hugs her tight, hoping to banish the sorrow from her. "I know this is difficult. I know it's not easy. We have to make do with what we know. It's all we can do." She quiets for a while, absorbing Lilla's tears, rocking her gently to calm her fear, wishing she had the power to mend her broken heart. "I tell you what, why don't we ask some of these marines if they'll go by your Enzo's house and have a look for him. What do you say?"

Lilla sits up, wiping the tears with her soiled and shabby cuff. "No, I would have to go with them. I would have to see for myself. I won't believe he's dead until I have seen his body."

"Now, Lilla, you recall what that Russian officer said: the buildings are not safe, never mind the streets. I don't think that's a sensible idea."

"Ah, yes," she replies, defiantly. "Sensible. You are so sensible. Always so practical, so prudent."

"It is true, Lilla. I am sensible and sometimes I am a fool unto myself as a result. Yet I understand your distress and I am not going to forbid you to go lest you forever hold it against me. That would not be a sensible manner in which to start our… our kinship."

"Does that mean you'll let me go with them?"

Prudence smiles. "Lilla, I am not yet your official guardian, so I could not stop you if I wanted to. I could, I suppose, ask for you to be detained so that you couldn't go, but that wouldn't get us off on the right foot, now would it?"

Her smile changes from wistful reflection to one of begrudging admiration. "There's something else I've noticed about you, Lilla, you're headstrong, if not remarkably self—willed and, like me, in no little way stubborn. Perhaps that is why you have survived where so many others have not. However, if I'm right and you are as stubborn as I am, then I know only too well that whatever I say, you will find a way of doing exactly what you want." She pauses, turning Lilla's face to hers. "So, yes, in the morning we'll ask one of these angels in blue jackets if they'll help us."

"Not now? Not tonight?"

"No, Lilla, not now. It will be dark soon and if Enzo has managed to survive these past thirty–six hours, I'm sure he'll manage another twelve.

Chapter 21

The bottle of Malvasia is empty, the salami is gone and what's left of the bread is so dry it is impossible to swallow in a mouth devoid of saliva.

"How's that for irony, eh, Ramfis?" Enzo chuckles. "Radames interred after all."

His legs no longer hurt; that is good; that is a positive. But he cannot feel them, so does that mean they have died? Surely that can't be good; that must be a negative. And the cold? He has stopped shivering; that can't be good either.

Weighing the good against the bad! What else is there to do?

Enzo is sleepy. Oh—so sleepy. Yet the thought of closing his eyes and surrendering to his fatigue frightens the devil out of him. "What if I never wake up?"

He does though, fall asleep and quite naturally his subconscious turns to Lilla for comfort.

They lie beneath a furry animal hide on the floor of a wood–panelled room, a fire flaming in the grate casting dancing shadows against the ceiling; they are warm, warm and close.

The dream, a much–needed distraction, pursues a pleasingly erotic course, along which he imagines all manner of carnal possibility, thus restoring some warmth to his core in the process. They kiss, they touch, they caress and even though neither has yet seen the other without clothes, the confidence of their intimacy suggests they know the other's form as well as they know their own.

In the dark, the young man's body glows with a carnal fervour. Nerves, previously crushed, come to life. Muscles regain their substance. A tremor ripples through his torso. His limbs tremble; his mind quivers with ideas.

Enzo wants to see Lilla; he needs to see her. He can see her face but not her form: she is laughing at his blue marinière shirt and white bell–bottomed trousers; she is telling him he looks ridiculous and that he should take them off. Hurriedly, he drops his trousers and stands on one leg as he tries to free the other from the trouser leg. He is shaking in anticipation: shaking so violently that he finds standing upright impossible. Enzo trips, he staggers, he loses the battle and falls. His hands bang against a hard surface: pain. His back bangs against the same: more pain.

"No," he shouts, "one doesn't feel pain in a dream." Reluctantly, because he knows that in doing so he will have to surrender his fantasy, Enzo opens his eyes.

There is fire, his world is lit and everything is shaking: the beams, the blocks, the bricks, the walls: everything is shaking.

From above, there comes a great creaking, a raw tearing.

He looks up.

The sky! He can see the night sky: an aftershock must have disturbed the debris. He watches, mesmerised, as gravity drags a joist free from its remaining pockets, the black wooden beam suspending in mid–air for a second before twisting and tumbling down towards him.

Enzo is helpless; he cannot get out of its way; there is nothing he can do to avoid the beam's path. It is falling down, straight down, straight down towards him. It is coming.

"Oh, please no." He raises his arms over his head in a futile gesture of protection. He tenses. The end. The end is—

The beam misses him by a hand's breadth and it lands upright and vertical, as though a lance thrown by a funcitta down into the sea, and it lands on the end of the beam which for these past days has kept Enzo pinned in his prison.

There is good news: the beam across his legs is flicked upwards like the unweighted end of a seesaw. There is bad: Enzo's legs are its fulcrum.

Pain. Pain more intense and more concentrated than before: in his legs, in his hips; in his everywhere, there is nothing but unadulterated, inhuman, vicious, diabolical pain.

Enzo looks up at the sky and screams.

CHAPTER 22

"Prudence?" Lilla whispers. "Are you awake?"

"In this cot? With all your fidgeting? How could I not be awake?"

Curtained off with sheets in an area at the back of the warehouse, they have spent an uncomfortable night clinging to each other for warmth. About them, exhausted doctors and nurses grab a few minutes rest between shifts.

"What is it, Lilla? What's keeping you from sleep?"

"It's nothing, really."

"Hmm. Nothing doesn't do whatever something is doing to stop you from sleeping, now does it? So, come on, out with it: a problem shared is a problem halved."

"I keep thinking about the warships that arrived yesterday?"

"Yesterday," Prudence murmurs, keen not to disturb others. "Now what day was yesterday? I've been here so long, I can't even remember what day it is."

"Today is Wednesday."

"And what of it?"

"It doesn't matter what day it is, Prudence, it was the ships I was thinking about; those big Russian and British ships with all those big guns."

"Go on. What about them?"

"Well, I overheard two of the nurses talking and one said that there are so many people buried in the ruins we've no hope of digging them all out. The other one then said that this presented the doctors with something called a health hazard, because dead bodies can bring about a plague. She said all those warships have come here to destroy the city, to bury the dead beneath what's left of the city so the plague can't get out. Do you think that's true?"

Prudence scoffs, quietly. "Idle gossip. That's what that is. You mark my words, young lady."

"But is it true? Can you get the plague from dead bodies?"

"I believe it can happen. Typhoid. Cholera. Food poisoning and tummy bugs too. That's why these sailors are working so hard to bring fresh water ashore." She fixes Lilla with a calculating look. "That's not what's got you all anxious though, is it? You're more worried that if they do start an artillery barrage, we'll not get to find Enzo."

"Yes. That's exactly what I was thinking."

"In which case, there's no benefit to be had by lying here worrying about it, especially with you wriggling like a hooked fish."

On their way out, Prudence approaches Dottore Roselli to ask if he can spare them for an hour.

The good doctor appears to have aged twenty years overnight. "Yes, you've done more than your fair share," he states. "I am grateful to you, Prudence. Messina is grateful; she could not have managed without you. You and our queen. Fortunately for Messina, more naval ships are coming and each arrival brings more doctors and more medical supplies."

"Is it really all as bad as people are saying?" she asks, her brow furrowed in concern.

"Worse than we could have imagined. From what I have heard of the devastation both here and across in Calabria, there may be as many as 200,000 dead or missing. They are saying that all the pupils in the College at Reggio have been killed." He lifts his glasses up off his nose and wipes his eyes. "My nephew is there." He winces. "Or perhaps was, I don't yet know for certain; the confusion is considerable. You must go. If you have someone to find, you must do so as soon as you can. By now, anyone still trapped in the ruins is likely to be suffering from acute hypothermia."

Outside, the only blessing would seem to be that the sky has wasted itself of rain, the depleted clouds now crowding around the table of Aspromonte quibbling about which of them is responsible for their profligacy. And while they argue, more and bigger ships are arriving and detachments of Russian and British troops ferried ashore.

Stepping over canvas covered bodies and fallen masonry, Prudence pulls Lilla with her along the ruptured esplanade. A barge of redcoat Royal Marines is tying up.

"Excuse me," she calls. "Lieutenant, could I have a word?"

Mildly surprised to hear English spoken without any trace of local accent, the young officer turns. "Yes, Madam." He tips his cap as he walks towards her. "How may I be of service?"

"I'm perfectly sure you will hear what I am about to say many times over during the next few hours, Lieutenant, but I find myself in need of your assistance."

"Of course, Lieutenant Aubrey Lock, Royal Marines Light Infantry."

"Yes, Lieutenant," Prudence replies, "I can see by the colour of your jacket you're a Lobster."

"Oh, er, well, I... We've come in on HMS Minerva. Left Valetta... Malta, late last night. Couldn't have got here any sooner. Sorry."

"Yes, I know where Valetta is, thank you. I'm Prudence Robertson, pleased to meet you, and this is my companion Lilla Lunapiena; as I have already said, we need your help."

Lieutenant Lock raises his head to take in the scale of the damage to the once beautiful edifices that line the back of the esplanade. Several palls of dirty grey smoke give evidence to the fires that still rage through the city and a group of bewildered locals huddle together around a brazier, enviously eyeing the supplies the marines are unloading.

"I hope you don't mind me saying, Mrs Robertson, but I didn't in my wildest dreams imagine this level of destruction. I thought initial reports must have been exaggerated."

"Quite so, Lieutenant, though as you can see for yourself, there are some of us who are very much alive; which is exactly what I need to talk to you about."

"Yes, of course." His tone implies that whatever the size of the wheel, he will be only too happy to put his shoulder to it. "As I said, how may I be of service?"

"I need you and some of your men to accompany Signorina Lunapiena and me to a house a short distance from the Duomo. We believe there may be a man trapped, a relation of Signorina Lunapiena's who is very dear to us."

The Lieutenant smiles. "And just how far into the city is this house?"

"Not so far," she lies.

Lilla gasps, glancing up at Prudence, who in return squeezes her hand rather too hard for comfort.

"I see," the Royal Marines officer says, considering. "Slight fly in the ointment is that I have my orders and they are to bring this cargo of food, blankets and medical supplies ashore and thence to return to HMS Minerva with all the British nationals who are ready and waiting for disembarkation. A further issue is that the Russians have been delegated the sector around the basilica and we have been allocated ours, which is to the south of here. The Russians have already lost a dozen or so of their brave souls, killed while trying to free people from their houses, and I wouldn't want to go treading on their toes, so to speak."

"No, Lieutenant, I can see how that would make life uncomfortable for you. Although," Prudence breathes deep, stands as tall as she can manage and squares her shoulder, "you might like to give some thought to what it must be like to be trapped in the cellar of a collapsed house for forty–eight hours without food or water. And in the middle of winter."

The Lieutenant wilts. "Yes, I can only imagine that must be ghastly. Might I inquire as to whether this, er, relation is a—"

"A British citizen?" she interrupts. In order to curb her reaction to the coming white lie, Prudence is already squeezing Lilla's hand. "Yes."

"I see. So, is this individual registered with the British Consul?" He scratches his chin.

Prudence breathes deeper. "My dear fellow, I was a personal friend of the late Ethel Ogston, wife of the British Consul, and Mr Alfred Ogston has sustained life–threatening injuries and has been evacuated to Palermo along with his niece, now the only surviving member of his family. Whatever protocols you might want to adhere to are simply no longer relevant."

"I see," he says.

As far as Prudence is concerned, he doesn't, yet. "And if that doesn't inform you sufficiently as to the general breakdown in order, then you might like to give some thought to the Captain of the Piemonte?"

"The Piemonte? The Italian cruiser out in the bay? What about her?" he asks, intrigued.

Prudence squeezes Lilla's hand one final time. "Captain Passino of the Piemonte lives at an address adjacent to the house we need to visit. He was ashore the night of the earthquake and hasn't been seen since. If I showed you where he lives and you were fortunate enough to locate him, wouldn't that prove a considerable feather in your cap?"

The Lieutenant's detachment is watching the battle of wills with open humour. He glances down at Lilla, frowning. "Is your good friend always this insistent?"

Lilla looks up at Prudence, "What did he say?"

Prudence translates and Lilla nods, "Always. It's no use arguing with her. She's a personal friend of Queen Elena, too."

Lieutenant Lock looks back at Prudence, "What did she say?"

Prudence translates and the Lieutenant's face crumbles in surrender.

He turns to his men. "Sergeant Carson," he barks, evidently keen to be seen to reassert his authority, "get a message back to the ship with one of the other barges that we've been detained on an errand of mercy. Set two men to stand guard over these supplies and make them aware that they must not leave this mooring until we return. Not under any circumstances, is that clear? The rest of you, follow me." He turns back to Prudence, bows, smiles and extends his right hand as though requesting both women join him on the dancefloor. "Right you are then, after you Mrs Robertson, Signorina Lunapiena."

They lead the Lieutenant and his marines along the debris—strewn front, and when they turn away from the sea, up towards the theatre, they are reminded of the unfortunate man they had come across the day before; the man sitting in his underclothes and opera hat, nestling the corpse of the young girl in his lap.

"Doesn't that seem like a lifetime ago?" Prudence mutters.

"I beg your pardon, Mrs Robertson," the Lieutenant calls, as he struggles to keep up, "didn't catch what you said."

"I said, there must be a factory somewhere beneath the city making all this broken brickwork; these mountains of rubble seem to have grown taller overnight."

"You mean, you were here yesterday?"

"Yes."

"What on earth for?" he asks, his measured King's English garishly at odds with the anarchy of his surroundings.

Prudence glances up at the smoke obscured sky.

Lilla, though not knowing his language, understands his tone and rolls her eyes. Hurrying on, she leaves the novice and his retinue in her wake, and returns her attention to her climbing, clambering, scaling and scrambling. "Enzo. Oh, Enzo," she whispers, picking up her pace.

If the once beautiful Via Pozzoleo that runs up beside the Teatro is disordered and dishevelled in raiment, then the Garibaldi has shrugged off not only its garments but also its flesh, leaving the skeleton of its insides now starkly exposed. One of the houses in the Corso Cavour has been opened up as though the front wall was nothing more than a hinged door, now pulled back and discarded into the street. A naked man hangs by a coat hook, a look of surprised annoyance on his face, as if his situation is but a minor irritation. They all stand and gawp, before realising that in spite of the unusual and gruesome nature of the spectacle, it is disrespectful to stare.

"Someone should bury him," Lilla says to no one in particular. "How can he begin his journey to heaven when he is trapped in hell?"

And as they are picking their way gingerly around the carcass of the property, each one of them stunned into silence by the painful enlightenment that God can be both benevolent and yet beastly, her call is answered and the house emits a whining creak and despairing groan, and very suddenly sinks like a weary horse down into the street. A fog, like that of ground pumice, envelopes and suffocates them.

When the dust has settled, Lieutenant Lock pats himself down, checks none of his men are injured and turns to the ladies. "Is this place far, Mrs Robertson? I really don't think this is such a good idea, these streets are awfully narrow and these houses are very unstable, any one of them could come down without the slightest warning."

"No, not far, now." Grabbing hold of Lilla's arm, Prudence sets off up the Cavour. "We'll turn right in a minute and then it's only a short walk along the San Agostino to the Via dei Templari. First, I'll show you where Captain Passino lives."

When they eventually reach the house in the Agostino, the façade has collapsed and a fire rages from its basement. Atop a mound of bricks, a cross fashioned from split timbers has been wedged upright.

"Well, I suppose that tells us all we need to know," Lock says.

Again, Lilla glances at Prudence, though this time her look suggests she is now aware of and accepts why her companion felt it necessary to tell the officer a white lie in order to persuade him and his men to accompany them on their journey into the city. And as if to lend added weight to the security their presence supplies, a few awkward paces further on lies the body of the robber, Tulliu. A mangy dog standing guard, growls and then barks at them, baring bloodstained teeth, daring them to steal his prize.

Lilla pauses and stares.

Noticing her reaction, the Lieutenant asks, "Do you know this man?"

"No," she replies, thinking how best she can explain her sudden fascination without giving away the fact that she and her companion have already trodden the same street on the very same mission. "He is food for the dog."

"Sergeant Carson?"

"Yes, sir."

"Shoot the dog."

The sergeant, a tall and deep–chested man, whose impassive features betray no emotion, takes a rifle from one of his men and aims at the dog. "Very good, sir."

Lilla flinches at the shot.

Just beyond the entrance, the narrow Via dei Templari is blocked by a wall of debris seemingly as high as the houses had once been tall, so they retreat back into the Agostino and wend their way on into the Monasterio, where they locate an alley through which they hope to access the Templari.

The buildings either side of the narrow alley have shifted towards each other so that their gables touch, forming a neat triangular tunnel.

Lieutenant Lock blocks their way, holding up his hands as one would when attempting to halt a locomotive. "I'm sorry ladies, I can't let you go down there, it's too dangerous. The entire structure could come down any minute."

Prudence glances at Lilla and subtly inclines her head.

Lilla steps to her right; Prudence to her left.

The Lieutenant looks from one to the other. "Sergeant Carson?"

However, before the burly sergeant can move to restrain either of them, Lilla dodges and rushes past down the tunnel.

Once more the Lieutenant surrenders. "Does this girl know no fear?"

"Now you come to mention it," Prudence replies, a grin sweeping across her face.

"Right. Men, follow me and if you hear any of these houses as much as whisper, it's every man for himself."

The half–dozen men hesitate and more than a couple stand and look at each other, wide–eyed. "But, sir," one of them says.

"No time for the faint–hearted," Lock replies, visibly nervous. And then, louder than he intends to, he mutters. "Right, for fools rush in where angels fear to tread."

Carson stiffens to attention. "Beg pardon, sir, but where that angel has rushed, only a fool would dare follow," he says. "May I ask if we are to steal stealthily or dash boldly, sir?"

"Your guess is as good as mine, sergeant."

Carson turns to his troop. "Come on, you men. Let's be going after that angel."

They set off after Lilla, none of them knowing what they will find in the street beyond. Some run, some trot and others walk, slowly, keeping their eyes fixed on the overhanging masonry.

When they gain the other side, they are faced with the ruins of the old Templar church. The bell tower has crashed down into the street and the gospel wall has crumbled, revealing the austere nave and beyond it the altar table.

Lilla is standing, waiting.

Lieutenant Lock arrives by her side. He is panting, whether in fright or from his exertions she isn't sure.

"Which is the…" he begins to ask. But when his eyes follow Lilla's, he realises that there is not one house left intact. The trembling of the earth has brought down each and every dwelling. Walls lean menacingly, roofs suspend in defiance of gravity and furniture balances precariously on ledges, as if placed deliberately by the hand of a giant child.

"That one." Lilla points, her eyes watering.

"My word," Lock mutters. "How can anyone be expected to survive amid such devastation?" He looks at Lilla and notices her distress. "I'm sorry, signorina, I didn't mean to…" He takes her hand and ushers her towards the foothills of rising masonry. "Mind your feet. I see you've already suffered an injury to your leg. Mrs Robertson, stay close behind me. You men, give the lady a hand."

They make their way along the street until they reach what's left of the Ruggeri house. The walls have collapsed outwards into the street, building their own monumental tumulus; bricks and mortar, tiles and plaster adding to its height with each aftershock.

Once again, Lieutenant Lock warns against going closer, adding, "I can't order any of my men to go into the house. As I told you, the Russians have already lost a dozen or so men to… It would be beyond the bounds of common sense. I just cannot sanction it."

They stand and survey the ruin, the inside of which they are prevented from seeing because of the mound of debris on which Lilla had slept, her head resting on Lucrezia's still form.

148

"I realise that, Lieutenant," Lilla says, "and I would not ask you to risk your life for my fiancé. But if he is dead, I have to see for myself. I have to be certain. And that is why I have to go."

The capable, stern—faced Sergeant Carson steps forward and comes to attention. "I'll go with the girl, sir. We won't be more than a minute."

"All right, sergeant, but be ready to return immediately."

"Yes, sir."

"Anyone else care to volunteer? An extra tot of rum for whoever accompanies Sergeant Carson."

While others study their mud encrusted boots, a short, wiry individual, his nose ruby—red, shuffles his feet.

"Is that a yes, Spinetti? Your family are from near here, aren't they?"

"From Naples, sir."

"Well, near here, then."

"If you would call London near to Edinburgh, sir," Private Spinetti corrects, petulantly.

"What I mean is," the lieutenant carries on, clearly irked by his man's propensity to define near, "you speak the lingo, so be a good fellow and translate for Sergeant Carson, would you?"

The man nods and like an underfed street urchin promised a hearty meal, he hurries to Sergeant Carson's side.

"Very good."

Lilla looks up at the sergeant and the man from Naples, the light of admiration shining in her eyes. "Thank you," she says and, glancing at Prudence, adds, "You're not to worry." And as though practised in scaling a heap of jumbled bricks and masonry, Lilla turns around and begins picking her way deftly up the slope.

The two marines follow more circumspectly, checking their every step and ensuring that wherever they tread they do not risk dislodging or disturbing the debris.

Once at the top of the mound, Lilla pauses and raising her fist to her lips she bites on her knuckle to stop herself from screaming.

She had expected to find Lucrezia's body and had steeled herself. Yet, the poor girl is so startlingly pale and still, she appears to have been sculpted out of the same white marble as that of Neptune's statue. Lilla's eyes are drawn to the missing finger.

"Now, now," Sergeant Carson whispers. "Do you know this girl, Signorina Lilla? Tell her what I just asked, Spinetti."

He does so.

Lilla nods, dreamily. "Yes, she is Enzo's little sister, Lucrezia. The man we saw near the dog, he cut off her finger to steal her communion ring."

The little man, Private Spinetti, rests a comforting hand on her shoulder. "I guessed by the way you were looking at him you must have met him before. Tried to rob you, did he?"

Lilla nods again, reluctant to relate much of the episode in case the memory buckles her knees. "Yes. One of the Russians shot him. He was a bad man. The worst,"

"Every city must have its sewers."

"What was that?" Carson asks.

Spinetti translates.

"Just as well, eh?" the sergeant mutters, before adding in a tone that would embolden the most nervous of recruits. "Right, let's not tarry. No guessing how long we've got."

The three of them gaze up at what remains of the Ruggeri household, wondering which section is the most likely to fall. Most of the front wall has already collapsed, as has the roof, which has brought the floors and landings with it.

"Ask the young lady where she thinks this fiancé of hers might be?"

Spinetti does so. The creases and lines about his eyes suggest he has passed much of his life staring in the face of wind–driven saltwater and his ruddy complexion advertises his affection for rum.

"If he's anywhere," Lilla replies, warming to the man, "he'll be in the cellar. His father shut him in there before the earthquake."

Like thieves sneaking into a house, they step soft–footed across the threshold and inch their way inside. The stairs have come away from their fixings and the cellar entrance is buried beneath an avalanche of timber and masonry.

"Sergeant, you are too large for this sort of thing and the girl, well… You two stay here," Spinetti says, "I'll see if I can't find a way in."

"Steady as you go," Carson whispers.

The diminutive man picks his way towards the back of what used to be the ground floor. He pauses occasionally, looking around, assessing which of the timbers he can move without dislodging others and grasping the odd brick, piling each one carefully to the side. He struggles with a timber, grunting and groaning, and then once it is secure, he bends and crawls beneath an upright table, and disappears from their view.

Lilla looks up at Sergeant Carson, her concern reflected in his expression. Both would like to call out and encourage the brave man not to venture too deep into the house in case they cannot reach him should the building start to fall; however, the eerie silence seems to be the only brace holding up the walls and they are nervous of fracturing it with their jitters.

They listen to Spinetti scrabble about, the rasping of his boots against dusty surfaces, the scratch and scrape of brick against brick, the thud and clink of loose stones dropping into the cellar.

"I have…" he calls, softly. "If I can only… shift this… block, then I can reach…"

Lilla and Sergeant Carson hear an exasperated sigh, followed by a sharp intake of breath, as if the man is setting himself for some intense physical task. And whether the courageous Private

Spinetti nudges a supporting beam or eases out a loaded brick, they do not know, but the old house shivers and moans like a bereaved husband and what's left of the roof takes leave of its precarious moorings and plummets down towards them.

"Out, Spinetti. Get out," shouts Carson.

Lilla is not so fast to react and the wall beside them shudders and collapses, a slab of bricks and snapped wood slipping and sliding onto her already wounded leg.

Sergeant Carson grabs Lilla round her waist. Dragging her to him, freeing her leg and lifting her clean off the ground, he throws her onto his shoulder and clambers as fast as the uneven terrain permits out of the house. Huge blocks of masonry, lumps of plaster and mortar, and wooden beams as thick as a man's trunk tumble towards them.

"Mr Spinetti?" Lilla screams, reaching out.

The sergeant, though, ignores her plea. He is focusing all his concentration on staying upright, knowing that one slip, one stumble and the pair of them will end their lives entombed in the ruin.

They make the top of the hill of rubble outside and, facing the way they have come, Lilla sees Lucrezia's marbled form.

She looks away and watches the last moments of the house she once dreamt she might live in with Enzo; a home she hoped she might grow up in with Enzo and their children. Now though, as she bounces and bumps against the sergeant's shoulder, Lilla realises that hope is for fools, that dreams do not come true and that there is an end to love.

"Oh, Enzo," she sobs. "Enzo, my love."

Behind them, the walls fall, throwing up yet another veil of powdery fog which pursues them down the slope. Before they reach the bottom, they are overwhelmed and Carson kneels, drops her from his shoulder and cradling her as though she is little more than an infant, he clutches her face to his chest.

They shut tight their eyes. They cup their mouths with their hands. And they wait and wait and wonder whether they have done sufficient good in their short lives that God will see fit to spare them.

CHAPTER 23

Ashes and Dust. All is ashes and dust; the smallest specks of everything that once, when joined together, amounted to a person. Wasn't that what Enzo had told her? Hadn't he said that we were all little more than a fortunate union of little specks of dust?

Now, though, there is dust which amounts to nothing. It is all that is left of someone once treasured, and it settles on her face and sticks in the corners of her eyes.

Lilla tries to breathe and finds she cannot.

St Francis has clutched his lamb so hard against his chest that not only is Lilla unable to expand her own chest, but her right hand is also crushed flat like a stopper against her mouth.

She wriggles, not unlike a new—born lamb, and Sergeant Carson, embarrassed by his zeal, relaxes his iron grip. "Begging your pardon, miss."

She should thank him, rough though he was in his handling of her. Except, how can she thank him for saving her life when she isn't absolutely sure she wants to be alive. Wouldn't it have been kinder to leave her in the ruins of the house with Enzo? To end her life right then so that she could start the next with him? Surely, the two lovers would have been released. Two winged angels. Two free spirits. Free to soar up into heaven to love again, to be reborn together and to live again in that next world promised to them by the scriptures.

Lilla is crying, her tears dribbling down her cheeks like rainwater dribbling down a dusty window.

"Enzo!" she cries, wrestling herself from her saviour's arms.

They stand, as the last blankets of the dust begin to settle, ghostly statues in a barren landscape, and turn to look at the ruins of the once beautiful house in the Via dei Templari.

For a few seconds, in a silence of nothing, they wait, wiping the dust from bleary eyes, coughing and spluttering, unsure of how they have survived.

And then, as if by some illusion of smoke and mirrors conjured from the shuffling hands of a diabolist, they perceive a spectre standing on top of the mound they had just seconds ago scrambled down.

A surge of hope rises within her and Lilla toys with the ring in her pocket. She closes her mind to possibility and then very quickly opens it again, the battle between that which her heart wants so desperately to see and the image of that which she truly sees, swaying in favour of her desire.

"Enzo," she whispers, softly. "Is it you?"

However, the sway in momentum does not last and, like a negotiated truce during which two warring factions are permitted time to comprehend the ridiculous futility of their differences, the fog of battle clears and the truth becomes more real. This pale spectre who has walked through the maelstrom of the collapsing house cannot be Enzo, for he is both too short and too thin.

"Spinetti," Carson says, a mixture of relief and affection conspicuous in his tone. The affection, though, is short–lived. "Don't just stand there, man. Get back in line this instant."

The little man treads carefully down from his elevated position, patting his uniform and shaking the dust from his hair.

Lilla, like her hopes, crumples to the ground and raises her hands to her face.

Spinetti ignores the orders of his sergeant and makes his way over to her. He stands, patiently waiting for her to set aside her distress and when she does not, he bends and places a paternal hand on her shoulder. "I am sorry, I could not help them. The walls, they... I did not have time. I'm sorry."

Slowly, she looks up. "Them? You said them. Who do you mean? What did you see?"

"In the cellar..." Spinetti replies, his eyes downcast, although not towards her. "There was a young man. I'm sorry. There was nothing more I could do."

Lilla stifles a howl of sorrow.

"You must not worry," Spinetti consoles. "Now, he is with God. He is at peace; in a better place."

"Did you see his face?"

The diminutive marine looks away towards the rest of his group, either pretending not to have heard her question or imploring them to tell him how he should answer.

"Please, Mr Spinetti, did you see his face?"

Tears leak through the dust caked in the corners of his eyes as he crouches down so that she will be able to read his expression and will therefore not mistake or misinterpret what he is about to say.

"Yes, a young man. I could only see his shoulders. He had dark hair and he was wearing the uniform of a sailor. Please, I beg of you, Signorina, spare the eyes of a man who knows too well when another man is dead, do not ask me for further description."

For a minute or perhaps two, they stay holding each other, their mud–streaked cheeks touching, their tears meeting and mixing; one bereaved, the other bewildered, both of them lost and alone and yet united in their misery.

Lilla grows aware that they are being watched by Prudence, the officer and his men. "Thank you, Mr Spinetti," she murmurs, "I thought there might have been a chance... I thought I knew he was... I suppose I didn't want to give up on him. I couldn't let myself. I'm sorry I made you risk everything for him and I'm sorry I made you see those things. I will always be grateful to you that you..."

Spinetti hugs her one last time and, getting to his feet, he reaches down and encourages her to do the same. "Come, Signorina Lilla, we must leave now; we are not safe here. Say goodbye to your Enzo. Say goodbye and know that at least you have had the chance. So many have not been afforded even this much."

When Lilla tries to stand up, she finds her legs, particularly her right one, will not support her. She looks down and glares at it, angered by its refusal to obey her command. The bandage that Prudence had two days before tied so neatly and tidily around her calf, is now a more vivid red and splinters poke out from it like the jagged spines of an agave.

"Is Lilla all right?" Prudence calls.

"That doesn't look so pretty, now does it?" Spinetti says, a gentle sympathy to his hushed tone. "Come on, I'll carry you." He reaches down for a second time and pulls her up and slides her piggyback onto his shoulders. "Hold on round my neck and I'll support you." Then, turning to face the group now gathering around them, he says, "She's hurt her leg."

"My fault," Sergeant Carson volunteers. "I had to pull her up quick otherwise we might not have made it out of the house. How you made it out is a miracle, Private Spinetti."

"Wouldn't want to miss out on that extra tot of rum, now would I, sergeant." He grins, cheekily. "We'd better get her back to the aid station, her leg's not good. Mrs Robertson, would you care to have a look?"

Prudence bends, examines Lilla's leg and quickly straightens. "Oh, you poor thing," she mutters, "that'll need some attention."

"Sorry, Ma'am," Sergeant Carson offers, "I–"

"Not your fault, Sergeant Carson, it's mine. I knew I shouldn't have let her go up there in the first place."

As they pick their way across the Via Cardines, they notice that the Santissima Annunziata dei Catalani has fared better than the other churches, a sight which gladdens and encourages them.

"Mr Spinetti?" Lilla asks, wincing and gripping him tightly around his neck.

"Yes, Lilla."

"Why did you leave Naples and go to England." Her head bounces against his shoulder and her leg pains her as they negotiate a zigzag path up the rubble–strewn street.

He tries to shrug, then remembers he cannot do so with his arms supporting his burden. "I don't know; why does anyone leave the place of their birth? Because they believe their lives will be better lived in another place, that's why."

"But why England?"

"Why England? Because my family had been making ice cream in Naples for many generations and the great Queen Victoria of Britain wanted people to do the same for her in England."

"I have met our queen, Queen Elena," Lilla mumbles, dreamily. "She is a fine queen. Is this Queen Victoria like her?"

"Not anymore. She passed on a few years ago. There was such a funeral, so grand."

"Did she ever visit Naples?"

"Not to my knowledge."

"Then how did your family meet her?"

"My mother told me our family made ice cream for Queen Carolina of Naples, one of whose friends was the wife of a British Envoy. This lady had a great liking for ice cream and she lived at the beautiful Palazzo Sessa, where she met and fell in love with an English Admiral. When she returned to England to give birth to his daughter, she told people about our ice cream and our family became so famous that some years later Queen Victoria offered my parents a place to live near one of her palaces so they could make ice cream for her. That is how we came to move to England."

"What is it like to move to another country?" Lilla asks.

Spinetti sighs, a weary, perhaps wistful sigh, which suggests deep down he would rather things were other than they were. "Oh, it's not so bad. It depends on what you have to leave behind. If you have friends, it is naturally very hard."

"Did you have friends?"

"Yes, some."

"Was one of them a special friend?"

He sighs again and shrugs, though this time he does so attempting to shift her further up his shoulders. "At the time, I thought so. But I was young, eh, and every young man likes to think that the first girl he falls in love with will be the last."

"How old were you?"

"Seventeen. Perhaps not old enough to know what was best for me."

Lilla raises her head, leans forward and tries to look him in the face. "I am nearly sixteen," she states, as though his musing has somehow offended her.

"Well, young lady, at sixteen your life is just beginning, so there can be no better time for you to move to England."

Lilla tenses, sticking her legs out straight, like the buffers on a steam engine. Her reaction is ill–judged and a bolt of pain shoots up her right. She slumps back down against his back. "She told you."

"No, she didn't. I overheard the lieutenant talking. Mrs Robertson told him that your family were killed by the enormous wave and I understand from what I saw in the house that there is no longer much that binds you to this wreck of a city." Private Spinetti looks down at the blood–soaked bandages now hanging in tatters from her right leg, and quickens his pace. "Lilla," he whispers, "in my forty years, I have learnt a great deal about women and I have learnt to recognize love when I see it."

"Oh, yes," she scoffs, "a girl in every port. That is why men like to be sailors, I have watched them by the harbour."

Spinetti gently squeezes her thighs against his ribs. "That is unkind, Lilla, and not the kind of love I was talking about. No, what I meant was Mrs Robertson looks at you the same way my mother used to look at me in the last days of my leave. It is the look of a love that not even a thousand words can describe and it tells me she does not want to let you go. This was why you asked me what it is like to move to another country, wasn't it, eh?" Spinetti squares his shoulders and bends his back. "Think of it this way, Lilla, I may be able to carry you to the aid station, but I can carry you no further. And when your leg is recovered and you leave the aid station, do you want to be taking your first steps all on your own or would you rather have another's love to help you?"

Now, even though the buildings near the station end of the Via Primo Settembre do not seem to have suffered as badly as those around the Piazza Duomo, their route is littered with still more canvas—covered human debris.

At the aid station, the queue of gaunt, unhappy faces has lengthened and true to her nature, Prudence walks boldly and directly into the tent, where she wastes no time in informing Dottore Roselli that Lilla's leg requires both cleaning and suturing.

Spinetti lays Lilla gently on a cot. He kisses her on her forehead, smiles briefly and makes to leave.

However, before he can walk away, she calls to him, "Mr Spinetti?"

He turns back to her. "Yes, Lilla?"

Her hair the texture of pale clay, Lilla's eyes water and her lips tremble. "Thank you for risking your life to find Enzo. I will never forget your courage and your kindness. And would you," she bites her lip in an effort to rein in her emotion, "thank Sergeant Carson for me; he risked his life to save mine."

The little man had borne her seemingly without effort, and without the slightest complaint, all the way from the Via dei Templari, and now, behind the bulb of his ruby–red nose, his eyes betray his affection for her. "Remember what I said, Lilla. One must embrace love when it is offered so readily."

Spinetti melts back into the sea of people crowding the station.

"Now then," Prudence says, looming over her, "let's get this leg of yours sorted out, shall we?" She frowns as, with a pair of long tweezers in one hand and a swab in the other, she examines the splinters and shards of brick poking out from the bandage. "I can't put it any other way, Lilla, this is going to hurt; you'll have to be brave. Try not to cry out. Try to set an example to the others hereabout."

Lilla nods, propping herself up on her elbows. "What were you talking to Dottore Roselli about?"

"Oh, nothing. He just wanted a quick chat."

Instead of satisfying her curiosity, Prudence's evasion pricks it. "No, please tell me. Didn't you say it was important for us to be honest with each other? I saw you talking, he kept looking over at me. What did he want?"

Prudence tut–tuts. "Now then, young lady, the conversations that go on between doctors and their nurses are confidential, so I don't have to repeat what he said. But, if you can't control that busy mind of yours and you won't lie back and rest, Dottore Roselli said he is running low on a certain type of serum and he wants me to go down to one of the other aid stations, the one in the Villa Mazzini, to see if they can spare any."

"What's a serum?" she asks, not yet wholly satisfied with her explanation.

"It's a liquid made from the blood of horses and, if you must know, it's called Anti–Tetanic Serum. It's a modern medicine; not been around for long. Dottore Roselli says you should have an injection of it to stop you from developing the bacteria that cause Tetanus."

"What happens when you get Tetanus?"

"My, aren't we the one for questions. Well," Prudence pauses in drawing a splinter, "one symptom is that you get muscle spasms, most commonly in your jaw. Lockjaw, they call it, a little dose of which wouldn't necessarily be a bad thing for you at this moment. Now lie back and think nice thoughts while I pull this wretched sliver of wood out of your leg; enough with the talking."

Chapter 24

Whispers. All Enzo can hear are whispers. And beyond the soft yet sharp, breezy yet harnessed tones he can hear, he can see only the same patch of what his eyes tell him is a khaki–coloured square of canvas. As far as feeling goes, he can, if anything at all, only feel the strangest rigidity in his limbs. No, feel is too categorical, too definitive; perhaps detect or vaguely sense are more accurate descriptions.

"How is he doctor?" a woman whispers, concern very plain in her tone.

Enzo attempts to move his head so that he can see who it is that is talking; however, the orders his mind wants to despatch to his muscles seem to be stuck fast in the very centre of his brain.

The doctor sighs, the demoralised exhalation of a man who labours at a task he believes futile. "His injuries are severe, as is his hypothermia. You can see by the blankets and the intravenous solution that we are trying to warm him, though we will not know how effective these measures are for some time. His temperature is dangerously low."

Dangerously low. The words echo through his head the way a priest's eulogy echoes through the hollows of a church. He tries to make sense of the words and even though their meaning is perfectly clear, he is confused by the doctor's prognosis. Enzo does not feel cold: his teeth are not chattering, he is not shivering, and yet he has not the wherewithal to summon the correct language or move his mouth to articulate his objection.

"What state was he in when they found him?"

"The Russians who brought him in said he was only partially conscious. They said he persisted in trying to crawl into a small cupboard that lay nearby, that he kept trying to throw off his clothes and that he was delirious to the point of hallucination." The doctor pauses and sighs once more. "This we call hide–and– die syndrome; and the throwing off of clothes, this is paradoxical undressing; these are normal manifestations of severe hypothermia. The hallucinations? For someone who has been trapped in such cold for so long, they are also to be expected."

To be expected. Of course, his incarceration, his treatment at the hands of the criminal, his isolation! At times he had to let go of his mind like a man untying the knot tethering a kite. How could he do otherwise when his mind was all that appeared to function?

"He must be malnourished," the woman says. "Malnourished and exhausted. He can't have eaten or taken on fluids for nearly three days."

"Inanition, you mean? Yes, to a degree. But only to a degree. When we examined him, there appeared to be scraps of salami in his mouth and his breath smelt very heavily of alcohol. The food may have sustained him, but the alcohol has only exacerbated his condition."

Exacerbated his condition. The Malvasia? How can the wine have done any harm? Without it, he would surely have died of thirst and, in all probability, boredom and frustration.

"Doctor, you said his injuries are severe. What exactly are his injuries and how severe are they?"

"They are similar to most of the injuries we are treating: classic fractures of the vertebral column, the pelvis and limbs, many of them compound; nerve compressions that cause paresis, by which I mean either partial or permanent paralysis; and pressure sores and cellulitis which inevitably lead to gangrene. In this young man's case, some part of the structure of a house fell across his legs, immobilising him for a sustained period. And, because of his resulting hypothermia, he seems to have lost the ability to communicate. So as yet, we have been unable to ascertain both the extent and the seriousness of his injuries; this inability to speak is in itself not unusual, what with his body temperature being so drastically reduced." The doctor sighs again, this sigh even longer and even more resigned than the last. "I was told that when they found him, he was crawling, using only his arms. Perhaps this is why they are in such a terrible way; it would provide a logical explanation for why they have suffered so many contusions and lacerations. But, as yet, we been unable to ascertain whether his greater paralysis is caused by nerve compression or some more substantial injury to his lumbar vertebra or pelvic bones. Until he can communicate otherwise, we can only assume they have suffered some critical damage."

Critical damage. How can they be so damning in their diagnosis? Using only his arms, hadn't he climbed out of the cellar past his brother's lifeless form? Oh, poor Vittorio, still wearing the same uniform their mother had insisted they wear to the theatre. Hadn't he had to crawl past the lifeless form of his little sister? Oh, poor Lucrezia, her hand mutilated by that craven individual. Hadn't he crawled through the rubble like a lizard? And now, after all his courage, his effort and simply because his legs refuse to obey his instructions, they can only assume he has suffered some critical damage.

The woman falls quiet for a while, no doubt shocked by the catalogue of the patient's injuries. "What about Tetanus? Have you given him an injection of Anti–Tetanic Serum?"

"No, we have run out. I am told there are a number of American warships on their way here; we are hoping they will bring us a supply of the serum. If he develops the symptoms, or perhaps I should say if he lives long enough to develop the symptoms, we will have anywhere between one and four days to begin treatment; by that time, we hope to have the anti–toxin available. That he should have survived so far is as much down to his physical strength as it is to what God has planned for him."

What God has planned for me. So many plans! They'd had so many plans. What use are they now?

"Leaving God aside for a moment, doctor, what is your prognosis?"

"In the short term, he is stable. But his temperature is thirty percent below what it should be and if that decreases further and his blood pressure drops, he will fall into a coma. As to whether he will walk again? I'm afraid we will not know that for some time."

For some time. But how long is some time?

"Do you know where he was found?" The woman has dispensed with her whispering; her voice is now clearer, stronger, more pressing.

"No, Mrs Robertson, sorry. As you can see, there are too many of them for us to bother with where they have come from. They just keep coming."

"Do you know his name, doctor?"

"No. No, we don't. All I can tell you is that in his delirium he kept repeating the name Lilla. That was all he said, over and over again, Lilla."

CHAPTER 25

All of a sudden, she wakes up.

At first, Lilla isn't properly certain what it is that has rescued her from her nightmare; a nightmare in which she found herself standing on the edge of a tall parapet, watching Enzo fall away from her, an expression of horror and of finality screaming from his eyes as he is consumed by a sea of swirling smoke.

Then, just as suddenly as she wakes, she realises that what has woken her is the excruciating pain in her right leg. The pain, though, seems peculiarly ambiguous in its nature; for it is at once both harsh and yet merciful. Harsh, because the sheer terror of the nightmare has caused her to squirm in her sleep and rub her injured leg against the frame of the cot. And merciful, because the intense pain has woken her, rescuing her from the ghastly dream.

A child lying in a cot nearby whimpers, reminding Lilla that she is not the only one to be suffering.

Something is poking against her thigh, adding to her discomfort: a stone or a little lump of brick perhaps. She feels for it.

"Oh, Enzo!"

To distract from the pain, she draws from her pocket the signet ring.

Lilla toys with it, slipping the ring first on one finger and then on the next until she comes to realise that whichever she tries, the ring will not stay firmly in place because her fingers are too slender. She studies it, turning the ring over and over, exploring its firm texture, caressing and fondling it, pressing it in her palm, appreciating the broad circularity of its shank and enjoying the solidity of its weight.

"Your keepsake is heavy, like my heart," she whispers. "It is all I have left of you, Enzo. It is all I have to show for our love and I will carry it with me always."

The ring is fashioned in silver, plain to the point of austere in appearance and not much larger than her thumbnail. The shank is worn smooth and rounded, and engraved in the flat, shield–shaped head is a single cross—formée, a Christian cross similar to the Maltese Cross, in as much as the cross is narrow at the centre with the arms flared out towards the perimeter.

The hurricane lamps hanging from the roof of the tent lend her only a dim light, so when Lilla holds the face up, only the indent of the engraving and the scratches on the surface catch her eye. The ring is evidently no decorative jewel, no ornament or trinket; rather it is a statement of belonging, a mark of nobility or heritage and quite possibly a seal with which to autograph a wax–bound letter.

One hot summer's afternoon as she and Enzo had sat shaded and cooled beneath the boughs of the vast fig tree in the Mazzini, he'd told her the story of how his mother came by the ring and why she had given it to him.

"To follow your heart through happy and sad," she mumbles. "Through happy and sad."

"Are you talking to yourself, young lady?"

"Yes, Prudence, I am. There is no one else to talk to, is there?"

"No, I suppose not. But, as we say, talking to yourself is the first sign of madness."

"Would it surprise you if I was going mad?" Lilla scoffs. "Isn't the madness of this place catching, like a disease?"

"Oh dear, what's got you all riled up then?"

"Nothing. You surprised me, that's all? Where have you been, Prudence? How long have I been asleep?"

"I've been down to the aid station at the Mazzini. If you recall Dottore Roselli wanted me to scrounge some of that Anti–Tetanus serum."

"And did you?"

The older woman looks her young charge very directly in her eyes, appraising her, examining her in much the same way as Lilla had not a few minutes ago examined the signet ring. "No, as a matter of fact I didn't; they've run out same as here. As far as how long you've been asleep goes: I suppose I've been gone three hours, the streets are still not easy. How is your leg?"

"Sore. It hurts when I move it and the girl over there," she nods towards the next cot, "keeps moaning. It's impossible to sleep."

"My, we are in a state, aren't we? Well, young lady, you'd better take that pot of yours off the stove before it boils over; it won't do you any good to get all het up about life. And for your information," Prudence leans closer, whispering, "that girl is a sight further under the weather than you are. Your leg might stop you from walking for a bit, but the only way that young girl is ever going to join in at passeggio is if some kind soul pushes her in a wheelchair."

Prudence fusses over Lilla's leg for a while, inspecting the bandages which extend from her knee all the way down and around her foot. When she is satisfied the wounds are no longer bleeding, she stands back and pats Lilla affectionately on her shoulder. "Come on now, buck up. You might have what we call the morbs, but they won't do you any good."

"What are the morbs?"

"Morbs? Well, you get the morbs when you can't see your way through, when you get all melancholy. Morbid, I suppose. Now then, I have some news and you have a visitor, which would you like first?"

Lying as she is on the cot, Lilla's eyes water. "Do you have a piece of cloth or something, Prudence?"

Prudence pulls a handkerchief from her cuff.

And whether it is the pain in her leg, the misery of her bereavement or simply the accumulation of her tiredness that breaches the dam, Lilla dissolves into a flood of tears. "I'm sorry, Prudence, I didn't mean to complain, it's just that… I won't complain again, not ever again, I promise. I know I'm lucky and I know I should be grateful, it's just that…"

"I know." Prudence soothes, bending towards her, taking Lilla in her arms and hugging her gently. "It's all been something of a trial, hasn't it? It'll soon be over. Why don't I give you the good news, eh, then you can see your visitor?"

Lilla sniffs and wipes away her tears. "Can there really be any good news? I hope so; it seems as though the last few days have brought us nothing but bad news. Please, Prudence, tell me what we can hope for?"

"Well, my love, the good news is that I've met up with Mr Gordon and you'll be pleased to hear he is alive and well, and that he has offered to arrange us passage to Naples. I've also had word from the Duca di Lantra that the British Ambassador has given me leave to take you to England. All being well, we are to depart on the first available boat tomorrow morning and when we get to Naples, if your leg is mending as it should and you are fit enough to travel on, we'll take a passenger ship for England. There, that's the best bit of good news we've had in a while, isn't it?"

"Yes, Prudence. That is good news. I can't wait to be gone from this sorry place. Now I've made up my mind to leave with you, it's as though Messina has become some terrible place I never want to see again. Does that make sense? It doesn't to me, I used to love the city."

"It's perfectly natural, dear. I remember experiencing the identical sentiment when I left England to go to Rome. Suddenly, I couldn't think of one good reason why I wanted to be in England a minute longer. Strange thing, one's mind; it plays tricks. But don't you worry about the city: every time nature knocks it down, nature sees that it is rebuilt again. Life, as I've learned, is one continuous circle of seasons. You know, for every winter there will come a spring and then summer."

The sunlight of a smile returns to Lilla's eyes. "Oh, you always manage to find some good even in the worst of situations. I hope one day I'll do the same."

"You will, my angel. As sure as God makes little apples, you will."

Lilla giggles, nervously. "You know, Prudence, I've never met anyone who puts words in such a grand way. Is that how everyone speaks in England?"

"No," she winks, "only me. Others speaks a version of the same, though not so correctly."

"Can I see my visitor now? And please, Prudence, don't be too far away."

"I won't. Don't worry, I'll be on hand. Now, lie back while I go and get him."

However, Lilla doesn't lie back. She rests up on her elbows and looks over at the child in the cot adjacent to hers.

The girl, probably five or six years younger, is dark-haired and her complexion dark like Lilla's.

Perhaps she is from the Borgo del Ringo; Lilla doesn't recognise her though.

Her nose is snotty from her snivelling and crying, and she stares at the ceiling as if imploring it to fall and envelope her. From her chest down, she is swathed in blood-soaked bandages and pieces of ripped clothing. Her chest rises and falls in rhythm and occasionally, her arms twitch with involuntary movements.

She senses that she is being watched and though she inclines her head towards Lilla, it is painfully obvious from the way she has to look hard by the corners of her eyes, that she cannot move her head freely.

"It's all right," Lilla says, trying her best to inject her tone with some authority. "It'll be all right, you'll see."

"Lilla?"

It is Pipo.

She lies back and turns her face towards him. "That girl; she's frightened."

"It is not a crime to be afraid," he begins, "even to be afraid of dying. We are all afraid at some time or other and we are all afraid of different things." A mournful soul, his eyes betray his greater sadness.

"How did you find me, zio Pipo?"

He looks down at the ground immediately in front of his feet: it is his signature. "I have been looking for you and when I came, I saw Mrs Robertson." He reaches out and lays his hands on her arm. His palms are hard and rough, as one would expect from a man whose days are spent hauling line and dragging nets, and yet they are gentle and soothing, like those of a father coddling his new–born.

"Zio Pipo…" Lilla begins, but then loses her way. Or maybe it is the words that get lost somewhere in her head, even if, given her emotional fragility, she knew what they were going to be.

She makes to speak, but Pipo raises his hand, palm outwards, towards her. "I know," he says, "I know. The English woman wants you to go away with her; she has told me and asked for my blessing." He quiets for a few seconds that seem to last for hours. The fisherman is thinking, a methodical process that she has known take days if not weeks. "I have given her my blessing and, because your father cannot be here, I have given her his, too. But Lilla, you must tell me if this is what you want."

"Yes, it is. I think so, yes."

Lowering his hand, Pipo inclines his head to present her with his ear, raises his eyebrow and juts out his chin in expectation, waiting for her to speak.

"Are you saying my father would want me to go? Are you telling me he would want me to take what I am offered? After all, apart from you and Concettina, I have no reason to stay."

"We must all hope for a better future, Lilla, and this woman offers you that hope. Do you remember what your father used to say?"

"About hope? Yes, zio Pipo: he used to say that without hope a person drowns."

"And this boy, Enzo Ruggeri, he offered you a similar hope."

"You knew?" she says, as much an exclamation of surprise as a question.

"Yes, we knew, both your father and me. We discussed most things. Being out on the water for such long periods leads to such conversations: it presents one with time to think, to consider, and I think he wanted to know what I thought as much as he wanted to know his own mind."

Lilla smiles, remembering. "He was up when I left and he caught me as I was leaving. We talked. He wanted me to go."

"Not so," Pipo disagrees. "He knew in his heart that he could not keep you with him for all time and he knew it would be wrong to prevent you from going."

"Unlike Enzo's parents," she snaps, "who locked him in the cellar, sealing him in his grave."

To draw her from her maudlin, Pipo says, "I did not know you had talked to your father that morning."

"Yes, zio Pipo, we talked." She looks up at him, her eyes wide, questioning and then softening as she realises that he needs to know just as much as she needs to remember. "He told me I would break my mother's heart if I left."

"And how did you reply?"

"I told him I would break mine if I didn't. I told him I must go." Lilla stares into her memory, reliving both the darkness and the light of it. "And he said, "Yes, my little angel, so go you must." That was the last thing he said to me."

Pipo smiles, a sad, reluctant, resigned smile, yet a smile not without its hope or promise. "Then go you must, Lilla, and you must go safe in the knowledge that should you ever return, Messina will be here, we will be here."

Chapter 26

"Good morning, Lilla. How did you sleep?"

She rubs her eyes and yawns. "Not very well. Sorry, I didn't mean to... What I meant was, I slept all right." She stares at the empty cot across the way. "Where has the girl gone?"

"They've taken her to the sick bay in one of the Italian Battleships that came in this morning: the Marco Polo or the Napoli, I'm not sure which one. It's probably where you would be going if it wasn't for the fact that you're coming with me." Prudence studies Lilla's face. She frowns. "Your leg? Painful is it?"

"No, it's fine. Really."

Her answer does not fool the English woman. "Now you listen to me, young lady, it's all very well you wanting to tough it out and not complain, but I can see the pain in your eyes. So, when I ask you if your leg hurts, please do me the kindness of replying honestly. I'll ask one more time? Is your leg painful? Come on, pipe up."

Lilla looks down at her bandaged leg as though it is an unwanted bequest she has only recently inherited. "I'm afraid I was dreaming and must have banged it. It's like a thousand bee stings all in one place and I don't know what my foot is doing, I can't feel my toes. But after seeing that girl," she nods towards the empty cot, "I don't know if it's right for me to complain, and that's part of the problem, because I don't know what hurts the most my leg or thinking about leaving, and especially leaving Enzo all alone in the cold cellar and thinking someone who didn't even know him might just bury him without knowing he's there, I, I…" Her monologue increases in pace and pitch; a runaway tram destined to crash when it runs out of rail, "I don't know if it's right for me to leave him like this, Enzo and my parents, shouldn't I be there to see them into their graves, surely they cannot have expected to leave for the next world without someone being there to say goodbye, I—"

"Steady on girl. Slow down for a minute." Prudence raises her hand to Lilla's forehead. "You're running a temperature," she ponders for a moment, "which probably means your leg is infected. I'll go and ask for our good Dottore, see if he's still here. Lie back for a while, there's a good girl, and I'll be back in a jiffy."

Lilla does as she is told and she tries to be patient, like all the other patients; a model patient so that she might please Prudence in the same way she used to want to please her mother: she would have done anything and everything her mother ever asked and now she will never again have the chance to please her mother, because she—

"So, what is up with our little angel of the full moon today?" The doctor asks, resting his hand on her forehead in the same manner Prudence had only a minute or so before. "A fever, eh? Well, let's have a look at your leg." His kindly eyes seem to have recovered something of their inner warmth and wisdom; they seem restored.

Carefully, as though the bandage is holding together some fragile pottery, the doctor begins to peel it back.

Lilla winces.

"Oh, you should see how things have changed out there Lilla," Prudence says. "It's as though half the world has turned out to lend assistance. Why, it's busier than Piccadilly on a Friday

176

afternoon. You should see the Strait: all the coming and going. General Mazza has arrived to take charge; he's declared martial law and says that by the end of the day he'll have four thousand soldiers in the city."

As Dottore Roselli teases the bandages away from Lilla's calf, he too winces.

Prudence lays her arm on Lilla's shoulder and tries to maintain eye contact with her. "HMS Minerva's gone over to Reggio. HMS Exmouth has arrived with thirty thousand blankets and HMS Duncan, that's another battleship, has put in: rumour has it she's carrying 50 tons of corned beef and half as much flour and coffee. And the best part of it? The Red Cross have arrived to take over the aid station here in the Piazza Cairoli, and the Princess of Teano and the Princess d' Antuni del Drago have chartered a ship in La Spezia, and with them they will bring more doctors and nurses."

"Who is the Princess of Teano?" Lilla asks.

"Well, the Princess was born in England and not only is she a princess, she is also a Duchess, of Sermoneta." Prudence smiles in her recollection. "She is a very beautiful woman, always the height of fashion, quite the toast of society in Rome; believe you me, any social engagement without her presence would simply not be worth attending."

Lilla winces and raises her head, trying to see what the doctor is up to.

Prudence swiftly moves into her line of sight to distract her. "A great shame, though. Her son, Onorato, was born with considerable infirmities, poor fellow. And the Princess d'Antuni del Drago? Well, the good lady claims to have lost her child to a ghost. A strange cove she may be, but she is a formidable woman and I'm sure her presence will be much appreciated."

They both hear the Dottore exhale as he removes the last of the bandage. "There is one part of the leg that has turned septic and there is one small area of necrotised flesh. I will have to excise this, clean it and dress it…" And with a practiced sweep of his hand, he removes his round glasses from his angular nose and fixes his patient with a steely glare. "This may be a little uncomfortable, Lilla. I'm afraid I don't have any suitable anaesthetic with which to dull your pain."

"I have a phial of chloral hydrate," Prudence offers. "I brought it with me from the house at Isola Bella."

Chewing one arm of his glasses, the doctor considers. "Alright, but just a few drops in a glass of water. I don't want our little angel of the full moon unconscious; only her reaction will alert me to when I am in danger of removing any flesh that is healthy."

Prudence steps back and begins to rummage in her purse. "Is there anything we can do to stop the infection recurring?"

Dottore Roselli ignores her question as he searches Lilla's face for the slightest symptom of septic shock. "How do you feel, Lilla?"

She wilts beneath his examination before summoning what is left of her depleted reserves: "I'm fine. Really, I'm fine. I'm just a little tired."

"Not too confused."

"No, I understand what you're saying."

He lifts her hand and feels at her wrist, checking her pulse. "Do you feel dizzy? Can you sit up, if I ask?"

"Yes."

She makes to, but before she can do so, with his free hand the doctor eases her back down.

When he is satisfied her pulse is not racing, he says, "Good. Good girl. I will be as gentle as I can be in this ridiculous light." He pauses, turning to address Prudence. "And afterwards, the best you can do for Lilla is to take her away from this city. Get her out of here. In this crude apology for a hospital, infection breathes the same air as the patients. Now, I will go and sterilize the necessary surgical instruments and come back as soon as they are ready. Be strong for a while longer, Lilla."

With the promise of further pain, she is again moved to tears. However, gradually learning from her new tutor the subtle difference between being in one instant stoic in the face of adversity and in the next honest regarding her physical state, Lilla manages, somehow, not to fold.

"When can we leave, Prudence? Didn't Dottore Roselli suggest it would be better for both of us if we did?"

"Yes, poppet, that's exactly what he said. There are still more injured coming in and he is very pressed, but more and more doctors and nurses are arriving. I hear Dr Douglas is coming from Rome with three nurses, the British Fleet in Malta are sending more and your government is mobilising all the medical forces it has at its disposal. Very soon, we'll only be in the way."

"When are we leaving then?"

Prudence beams. "Tomorrow. New Year's Day. A new year and a new beginning for the pair of us."

"How can you be so sure?"

"Because of what Mr Gordon told me. He said he was indebted to you for taking up so much of his time when he met you outside the Trinacria; said if you hadn't kept him talking, he'd have been in the telegraph office when the roof came down."

Lilla winces, though this time not from the pain generated by her leg, more from the mental anguish generated by the untimely reference to people being buried beneath fallen roofs.

"Sorry, Lilla, that wasn't very tactful of me, now was it?"

Lilla dredges up a wan smile. "That's all right, Prudence. Go on, what else did Mr Gordon have to say?"

Her apology accepted, she carries right on: "Mr Gordon told me that there's a big German liner on its way. Oh, what is she called? Ah, the Bremen, that's it, the Bremen; on her way back from Australia. Came through the Suez Canal, would you believe. They say she'll be stopping to pick up here in Messina tomorrow and then going on to Naples. Mr Gordon tells me, he knows the people at the North German Lloyds line and he's going to try to get a message to them, asking if he can reserve us passage. Although that," she says, as a cloud passes over her thoughts, "depends on how your leg fares."

Dottore Roselli reappears, in his right hand a glass jar containing some clear fluid in which jangle a pair of long scissors and a scalpel, in his left a cup of water. "Would you...?" He inclines his head towards a small occasional table standing by the adjacent cot.

Prudence moves the table closer.

"Thank you. Now, be kind enough to pass me the phial of chloral hydrate, fetch me some carbolic acid and a swab, and, while you are at the dispensary, some more surgical spirit and some clean bandages."

Prudence Robertson nods obediently and leaves.

"Now, my little angel of the full moon," he says, as he snaps the end off the glass phial, holds it up to the light and administers three drops into the cup of water, "I apologise for not having fruit juice or a little wine to improve the taste, so hold your nose, this will make you feel a little sleepy. Don't be alarmed, that is exactly what it should do and what I want it to do. But please, try not to get too sleepy, I need you to stay awake to tell me when I am hurting you. Do you understand?"

Lilla nods, forewarned and forearmed, if quite naturally petrified.

Chapter 27

A stretcher. Lilla has never imagined herself being carried on a stretcher. Surely, this frame of wood, onto which a canvas sail is usually nailed, is used solely for the removal of the deceased from the house in which they have died; the same house in which they were very probably born. In consequence, to be carried alive on a stretcher is a pleasing if slightly unsettling experience.

Her head bounces with each step her out–of–step bearers take, disturbing the residue of nausea that had woken her several times during the night.

Prudence walks beside her, watching her feet lest she trip in one of the wide fissures that follow the tramlines down the harbourfront. "Are you feeling all right, Lilla?"

"No. I feel sick. I–" She leans over the side of the stretcher and vomits.

Her stretcher–bearers, two grey–jacketed Bersagliere, their wide–brimmed vaira hats decorated with capercaillie feathers, pause until she has finished.

"Better, now?" one of them asks, wrinkling his nose.

"No, not much," she replies, wiping her mouth. "I feel as though my head has bounced all the way down the steps of the Chiesa San Gregorio."

"Don't worry, my dear," Prudence says, glaring at the soldier. "That's just the effects of the chloral hydrate; it'll wear off soon enough."

"Not soon enough for me; I need a toilet. Where are we going? Is it far?"

"No, these kind gentlemen are taking us to a tender which will get us out to the ship we are taking to Naples. It's not far now and Mr Gordon will meet us there."

"I've never been on a grand boat before," Lilla mentions, as much to herself as to her attendants. "Come to think of it, I've never so much as been across the Strait. I think the furthest I've ever been anywhere is Ganzirri and that was only to see relations of Rosario and Gaetano." She claps her hands to her face. "Oh, I can't believe it: this is the first time I have thought of them since the morning of the…"

The lead Bersagliere falters in his stride. "They say there are a thousand or more dead in Ganzirri. They say the wave washed away the whole village."

Lilla glances up at the stretcher bearer, firing him a look of unadulterated hatred before realising that it is not the man's fault that he does not know how one should impart bad news; if, that is, there is a good way. "Will the sea be rough today?" she asks, looking away from him.

"Well," Prudence considers, studying the overcast sky, "There's a few line squalls coming through and there's a cold wind from the north, but we shouldn't be troubled: a ship as large as the Bremen will make light work of it, don't you worry."

"How long will the journey take?"

"About twelve hours, so Mr Gordon said. If we get away by dusk, we should get in at dawn. And a beautiful sight it will be, too. Vesuvius will be snow—capped, the—"

"What's Vesuvius?"

"A volcano."

"Like Etna?"

"Yes, like Etna," Prudence replies, a worn edge dividing her patience.

"Enzo said there is a monster trapped under Etna; is there another one trapped under Vesuvius?"

"She likes to ask questions, eh?" one of the Bersagliere quips.

Prudence ignores him. "Not like Typhon is under Etna, no."

"Are there volcanoes and earthquakes in England?"

"Oh, I see where you're going with this, Lilla. Yes, we have volcanoes in England and, thankfully, they're all sleeping; we don't disturb them and they don't disturb us. That's the way it's been for a good while and I see no reason for it to change. As for earthquakes, I do believe we had one a few years ago: The Great Colchester Earthquake, if I remember right. A few tiles fell from a roof; a few garden statues came to life. You're not to worry, my girl, we'll encounter nothing that measures against what's gone on here."

All along the seafront, soldiers and sailors are putting their backs into clearing the rubble and shoring up facades with beams and sawn timbers they have requisitioned from inside the hollowed–out houses. Hundreds of wooden barrels of fresh water line the road in rows three–to–four deep and a man wearing an apron busies himself butchering a carcass of beef. Further along the quay, the road has slipped and submerged, and a lamppost pokes up from the water, bent at an angle.

Lilla does not need to see the harbour to know that it is a hive of activity; lying, looking up at the quarrelsome clouds, all she can hear is the constant thrum of engines punctuated by the mournful bawl of ship's horns.

Her stretcher–bearers halt and lay her down.

Lilla looks up: "Mr Gordon!"

"Yes, one and the same. Can this be the same young Lilla Lunapiena I met outside the Hotel Trinacria in the minutes before such calamity broke upon this once beautiful city? The same young lady who granted me one of the best scaniatu I have ever had the pleasure of sampling? Good thing you did, too. That scaniatu was the last morsel that passed my lips for many hours."

"I'm sorry, Mr Gordon, I don't have any more scaniatu. I'm very pleased to see you have no injuries. You went off to the telegraph office at the station."

"I did, correct. And had it not been for our conversation delaying my arrival, there's a good chance I might not be here in person to meet you now."

Not yet educated in the niceties of verbal exchange, Lilla cuts right to the chase: "Have you managed to get us on board the ship Prudence told me about? Was it easy? I should think there are lots of people who can't wait to get away from here."

In contrast to most others milling about the front, and certainly in contrast to Lilla and Prudence, Nathaniel Gordon has somehow managed to maintain his sartorial refinement. He hitches up his trousers and squats, miner–like, so that he no longer has to look down at her. "Yes, young Lilla of the full moon, difficult though it has been, I have. And not only that, because of the injury to your leg, a nice couple have agreed to move quarters and let you and Prudence have their cabin; a cabin with a sea view, no less.

"Oh, Mr Gordon, you are a clever man. How can we ever repay you?"

"Why, Lilla, it is I who will forever be in your debt. Consider this a part payment." He stands, slowly, his limbs audibly objecting. "Prudence, I had thought that I might travel back with you to Naples, what with most of Messina having been brought to ground. However, my office thinks it imperative that I stay, there being no end of claims to process as a result of this catastrophe," a word he pronounces in French, "and I have managed to locate some lodging at Le Phenix, a boarding house down the way, one of the very few that remains intact. So, I'm afraid I won't be accompanying you and trust you will be able to make arrangements for the rest of your journey to Britain when you arrive in Naples?"

Prudence scoffs, though not impolitely, "I should think, Nathaniel, that after what has befallen us these past few days, very little will be beyond our combined abilities." She grins down at her new companion. "Isn't that so, Lilla?"

A blue–uniformed sailor strides purposefully through the crowds towards them, his cap banded by a black tally ribbon with gold lettering spaced either side of a white flag with blue anchor and crossed key. "Herr Gordon," he bows. "I am Second Officer Speckmann. Kapitän Nierich sends to you his compliments and respectfully requests that we bring your passengers to the ship as soon as possible."

"Thank you, Second Officer Speckmann. And please extend to the Kapitän my grateful thanks for agreeing to accommodate these good people. As you have no doubt noticed this young lady is unable to walk, so if you would be kind enough to…"

"Yes, of course. At once." He nods to the two crewmen who now stand at attention beside him.

His pained expression a mixture of relief tinged with regret, Nathaniel Gordon turns to the two women. "Prudence, these men will load Lilla into the launch and convey you both out to the SS Bremen." He looks down at Lilla as the crewmen carefully lift her makeshift stretcher. "Young lady, as I said I am much in your debt. If ever I can be of service, Prudence will know how to contact me. Good luck, Godspeed and I hope one day we will meet again."

CHAPTER 28

The journey to consciousness is slow and troubling and begins with him staring wide–eyed into a formless void filled with blue–grey water that promises eternal peace and contentment.

He is floating, neither descending nor ascending, simply watching and waiting for something to happen. Is he to be drawn down beyond reach, his self, both mental and physical, to be consigned to a watery grave? Or should he fight, fight to be conscious once more, fight to live and not to slip away?

And as he floats, he perceives a voice calling him, calling his name, encouraging him up to a surface that is encompassed by sky and land, one that has form and substance.

But who is calling his name?

The voice belongs not to Lilla; for whoever it is that is calling him is a man, his tone gruff and imperative, a world away from Lilla's cool and lively variation.

Enzo stares up at the same square of khaki canvas he remembers staring at as he slipped so gently into his coma. The canvas ripples, like a windblown curtain.

Movement.

He is awake. He realises he must be.

He tries to turn his head and... he succeeds.

"Enzo, can you hear me? Can you see me? It is me, Pipo."

He blinks, slowly, urging his eyes to focus. This man; this face. His expression is sad, like that of a man who follows the casket of a friend.

"Pipo, what are you doing here?"

"Looking for... a relation. I asked the doctors if someone new had been brought in and they thought, because you have not spoken and therefore could not identify yourself, that you might be him." Pipo looks down away from the cot, his expression forlorn and filled with guilt. "Please don't think I am not pleased to find you, Enzo; I am pleased to find anyone alive and to find someone one knows is a blessing."

"Yes, Pipo, thank you, you are right: I am alive even if I don't feel so." He struggles to raise his shoulders off the cot.

"You must rest. The doctors tell me that for many hours your life has been in the balance. They tell me you were so cold that your skin was like stone to touch. How do you feel?"

"Tired, Pipo. Like everyone, tired. Tell me, what is it like outside? How long have I been here? Have you—"

"Outside? Beyond this tent? I'm not sure I know how to describe such devastation. All I know is that for the time being Messina is lost. Her eyes no longer see; they have turned dull, like those of the swordfish when she knows there is no longer any reason for hope. As to how long have you been here: the doctors say you were brought in yesterday. A party of Russian sailors found you crawling along the street. They say your legs do not work, is that so?"

Enzo grunts as he tries and fails to ease himself up onto his elbows. "To order one's body to respond when there is no sensation is like ordering a corpse to rise up and walk. As you can see, Pipo, they..."

The old fisherman places his comforting hand on the young man's shoulder. "No matter. Rest. Keep still. Perhaps when you are warm again, life will return to them."

187

"Pipo?"

"Yes, Enzo."

"You say you are looking for a relation; have you been to other aid stations? Is there no one who knows who is missing?"

Arching his eyebrows and splaying his hands, he shrugs. "No one knows who is missing and no one knows who has survived. There is no council to make a reckoning, for nearly all the officials died in the earthquake or were killed by the great wave. There are thousands missing. Not hundreds, thousands."

"And Concettina?"

"She is safe." He crosses himself. "We were fortunate. Others were not so."

Enzo chews his lip, his eyes water and much to his shame he finds he is incapable of raising his hand to his face to conceal the evidence of his anguish. "Pipo, do you have any news of Lilla? I left her in the harbour. I..."

The old man's face crumples and creases, and then breaks into a smile that borders, but only borders, on ecstatic. "Yes, Enzo, Lilla is alive. She is injured, like many, but only her leg, which I am pleased to say will heal."

"Oh Pipo. Oh..." He tries to raise his hands to his face again and it is as though the relief of knowing Lilla survives empowers his arms. "Oh, Pipo. Thank God. Thank the Madonna: I thought she had abandoned us. I thought we had all been forgotten." Tears flow, cutting a path like a river through the dust and dirt caked on his cheeks, and he sobs openly, unconcerned that those who may be less fortunate have no alternative other than to bear witness to his joy. When he manages to regain his composure, he asks, "What of the Lunapiena family? Did they survive?"

This last of his questions causes Pipo to replace his smile with an expression of such profound and unbearable heartbreak, that Enzo realises no spoken answer is necessary.

"All of them?"

Pipo nods.

"I am so sorry," Enzo whispers. "So very sorry. I know how much you loved them; how much they meant to you."

"Yes," he mutters, looking down once more and fingering nervously his cap. "I am a hollow man. If it was not for my family, I would find little reason to continue."

"But we must, Pipo. We must continue. Out of bad always comes some good. What we must do now is find the good, this will provide us with every reason to continue." Enzo studies the fisherman: the bags beneath his eyes in which he carries his sadness, the lines about his eyes in which he carries his wisdom, the light within his eyes in which he carries his memories. That light even now as he avoids Enzo's look, is dimming with every breath. Some other misery, not yet spoken of, bothers him.

"What is it, Pipo? What is bothering you?"

Pipo dithers. He toys with his cap. He feeds the rim through his fingers; he thins his lips, his moustache swallowing his mouth, his eyes darting left and right, avoiding even the slightest prospect that they might engage with those of the young man lying on the cot.

A shiver dances through Enzo's limbs, causing his legs to twitch uncontrollably.

The fisherman notices. He smiles, albeit that his smile would achieve only a middling position in a race of smiles. "Look! Your legs! They move! Your muscles are beginning to work again. The doctor told me there was a good chance your paralysis would be temporary. That is more good news."

"Yes, Pipo, that is more good news."

However, the elation of realising that Enzo may not have lost the complete use of his legs is short–lived and there develops an atmosphere similar to that of a sudden lowering of air pressure before a storm.

The old fisherman turns away, as if to hide embarrassment.

"Pipo," Enzo says, his voice dark and intimidating, "there is more bad news, isn't there?"

The silence between them extends, only to be interrupted now and again by the squeals of an infant and the groans of the aged.

"Pipo," he repeats more insistently, "I have lost my family and my home, yet I have been spared. If you have more bad news, and I cannot imagine how there could possibly exist any worse news, please tell me now." He waits, anticipating, his expression dour and anxious. "Now, Pipo, tell me now or the fear of not knowing will surely kill me."

Still facing away, Pipo Sorbello, sways from one foot to the other and dips his head from side to side as if debating with himself.

Finally, he decides. "There is a woman with Lilla, an English woman. Her name is Mrs Robertson—"

Robertson. Robertson. "Wait," Enzo interrupts, frowning in concentration, "I know this name. I heard the doctor speak to a woman by this name when all I could do was hear. When I could not so much as turn my head to look at them, I heard the doctor discuss my state with her." His frown deepens, like the sea floor to the north of the Strait. "This Mrs Robertson, she knows Lilla? How does she know her, I've never heard Lilla speak of her?"

Pipo glances and quickly returns his gaze to the floor. "She is from Taormina. She has been working in the aid station in the Piazza Cairoli. It was where Lilla was taken after she was injured while she was out looking for you."

"She came to look for me?"

"Yes, with this Mrs Robertson and some British Marines. They went to your house in the Via dei Templari; the house collapsed and Lilla was injured."

"But I was at the house. I was trapped in the cellar."

"You must have freed yourself and left. When I asked the doctor about you, he told me you were found crawling through a street in the north of the city. He told me your legs would not work and that you were dying of cold." Pipo glances again, this time a look of guilt suggesting the doctor had broken his oath in revealing so much about his patient.

Enzo studies his bandaged hands. "I don't remember crawling? All I remember is trying to free myself from the cellar. I remember I was trapped for hours, perhaps days, and then the ground shook and the beam pinning my legs moved and I was able to climb up. I don't remember crawling, though. All I remember is a desperate need to find Lilla. That is what kept me going; the thought of finding Lilla." He quiets for a moment, contemplating his luck, in equal measure both good and bad. "So, I found a way out, that was why I was not there when she came." He quiets again, his expression suggesting he is coming to terms with the extraordinary twists and turns of fate. "What a terrible irony, eh? Trapped all that time and free just when it would have been better not to be."

"Yes, terrible. Terrible because Lilla believes the ruins of your house are your grave, Enzo. She believes you are dead and, what with her family the same," he crosses himself and hangs his head in respect for a second, "Lilla also believes that there is nothing left to keep her here. And that, Enzo, is why she is leaving Messina today, with this Mrs Robertson, to go to live in England."

CHAPTER 29

Their transfer out to the liner seems to take a long time and when they arrive, Lilla gazes up in awe at the steep sides of the ship, wondering how on earth they will manage to get her stretcher up on deck. They tie her into a canvas boatswain's chair and haul her up in a series of slow and irregular ascents.

An armada of skiffs crammed with survivors mill around the SS Bremen and occasionally a lone voice calls out a plaintive appeal in the hope of being granted permission to board. The grand ship is, though, already packed with gaily–dressed passengers who line the rails pointing, gasping in horror and weeping in sorrow for the ravaged city.

As Lilla is hoisted skywards, the devastation along the front and high up at the back of the city becomes all the more apparent.

"Oh, Messina," she whispers, "how will you ever recover?"

Waiting at the rail is Kapitän Nierich, a warm, ruddy–faced man in his late fifties, his bright eyes beaming over a generous handlebar moustache. "You must be Signorina Lunapiena, the young lady Mr Gordon has spoken so highly of." His Italian is clipped and Germanic. "We have arranged a cabin for you," he ushers an officer forward. "This is Assistant Purser Lehmann; he will escort you."

Lehmann bows and clicks his fingers, at which two crewmen come forward, untie Lilla from her confines and deftly lift then lower her onto another stretcher.

"Kapitän Nierich?" Lilla asks, careful to address him correctly, as Prudence has suggested she should.

"Yes, Signorina."

"What about all those other people? Can you not find room for them, too? After all, you have a very large boat."

He paws at his moustache, considering. "Quite naturally, I would like to accommodate all of them. However, we have already taken on board six hundred, our steerage is now overflowing and some of your fellow travellers will have to sleep on deck this night. I am sorry, but we simply don't have the capacity to take any more." He turns to the rail. "Ah, Mrs Robertson, so good of you to join us. You are our last addition."

Prudence, not having enjoyed her trip in the boatswain's chair, pats down her skirt. "Thank you, Kapitän. Though I'm used to the more conventional access to a ship of this grandeur, I am grateful to you for accommodating us at such short notice."

"I assure you, Mrs Robertson, the pleasure is all ours." Kapitän Nierich bows.

The grand staircase, the reception rooms, the lounges, smoking and dining rooms are a wonder to behold, and as Lilla is carried to their quarters, she can only stare wide—eyed at the sheer opulence of her new surroundings.

"This cabin is larger than my house," she says, a reference that instantly brings to her mind the family she once had and the home she is leaving behind.

"Now, now, Lilla. There's nothing to be gained by you getting all upset about what you can't have," Prudence chides. "We must appreciate what we have while we have the pleasure of it. Mr Lehmann says a nice couple have given us their berth and their charity does not deserve to go unappreciated."

"Yes, I know that," she mutters, as one of the crewmen picks her up and lays her on the bed.

Prudence glares at her.

"Thank you," Lilla says, fuming silently for a minute before continuing. "But I am allowed to miss my family, to miss my home and to miss Enzo, aren't I? I wouldn't be human if I didn't feel sad and I..." She begins to cry and soon enough to sob.

"Yes, my girl," Prudence soothes, sitting beside her on the bed, "of course you are. What you have endured these past few days would be enough to make anyone cry." She reaches around her young companion, lifts her by her shoulders and cradles her head. "You've been a very brave girl; braver than anyone can know. You cry, Lilla. Cry for your city. Cry for your loved ones and the love you have lost. Cry now and for as long as you want. Leave your tears behind you so that tomorrow you can start anew."

And they stay sitting together, the older lady with her younger charge, while Lilla's tears wash away the tragedies of recent days.

Beneath them, the decks begin to shudder and tremble and they feel the SS Bremen sway and turn towards open water.

Like only four others, their palatial cabin is situated on the bridge deck, and when Lilla's sobbing has subsided, Prudence leaves her to open the doors onto their very own private promenade.

"Come on now, enough tears for the moment. There's a chaise longue outside. I'll take some of these pillows and wrap you up; it's still awfully cold outside."

Once warm and comfortable, they sit in silence and watch the enormous ship thread its way between the myriad smaller boats coming and going across the Strait.

"There," Prudence says, pointing, "the British warships are tending to the Calabrian coast now. Mr Gordon told me they've sent a party of doctors and marines to set up a hospital at Villa San Giovanni. And that great warship is HMS Exmouth, she'll be delivering supplies and men to Catona and Scylla." She pauses, briefly, and looks down at Lilla. "Mr Gordon said all the world has come to rescue Messina."

The heights of Aspromonte are shrouded in an evening mist made darker by the smoke from many fires.

"The hills look exhausted," Lilla murmurs. "They look grey and weary, like an old man who is tired of walking."

"They do, my young girl," Prudence replies, gazing out from the protection of their nest high up in the ship. "They look as though they've been beaten to within an inch of their life, as though they need fresh air and sunshine to breathe new life into them."

"I know how they feel," Lilla says, yawning. "I don't think I've ever felt so tired."

"Right then," her nurse decides. "For you Signorina Lilla Lunapiena, a proper wash is next and some clean night clothes; you look grubbier than some street urchins I've had the displeasure to step over. And after that, a good night's sleep in those newly pressed sheets. It's time for you to be treated to some of the finer things life has to offer."

Lilla tries her best to muster a smile, but her fatigue, forced upon her by not only by the physical challenges of the last few days, but also by the sadness, the sorrow and the misery, get the better of her.

"Prudence?" she mumbles, looking up.

"Yes, dear."

"I don't know how I'm ever going to thank you for looking after me."

"Oh, don't worry, there'll be plenty of time for that later. If you can remember where you've come from, you'll always be humble. If you don't forget that, you'll have thanked me enough."

"Prudence?"

"Yes, Lilla."

"We did as much as we could to save Enzo, didn't we? We couldn't have done anymore. I mean, could we? Do you think there was anything more we could have done?"

"No, Lilla," she whispers, kissing her on top of her darkly—matted mop of curls. "You did, we did, everything we could possibly have done. No one could have done more to find Enzo than you."

"Prudence?"

"Yes, dear?"

"Would you mind if I slept here for a few minutes, I..." And as the Calabrian coast dissolves into dusk, Lilla yawns, her eyes fall shut and her question is lost to the ever—changing tides of the Strait.

CHAPTER 30

"You cannot move," the doctor states, his face a mask of concern. "You must not move. It is very likely that you have internal injuries and if you bleed, you will die."

With considerable effort, Enzo hauls himself up and onto his side. "I understand. I understand that you have already saved me once, and for that I am as grateful as any you have saved during the last few days."

"No," the doctor replies, summoning a weary authority to his tone, "clearly you don't. What I am saying is, I cannot permit it, I won't permit it."

Enzo, reaching out and grabbing him by the lapel of his once–white coat, draws his face close to the doctor's so that the man cannot escape either the heat or the force of his glare. "Listen to me, doctor. Please understand, I said I am grateful and more than that I cannot say." His knuckles white, his face wracked from the pain caused by his moving, a sheen of sweat breaks at his brow. "And if my legs would support me, I would ask them to walk me out of here even if I had but one cup of blood left in my body. So, you can either help me and reduce the risk of me injuring myself further, or I will crawl out of here in the same manner I crawled out of the cellar of my father's house." The pitch of his voice rises in frustration. "Now, help me or stand out of my way."

When the doctor neither moves back nor forward, but merely stands staring directly back at him, daring him to move, Enzo hauls against the doctor's lapel, and, overbalancing, he topples out of the cot and lands flat on his face.

A nurse rushes to help him, but the doctor waves her back.

Pipo kneels beside him. "For the sake of your mother's memory, listen to the doctor. You have come so far. You have lived where others have not; is that not charity enough for any man?"

Enzo again hauls himself up on his elbows and, through the forest of legs planted by those gathering to watch, he begins to crawl awkwardly towards the entrance of the tent.

"What is the name of the boat, Pipo?" he asks, gasping for breath and then spitting dirt from his mouth.

"Please, Enzo, stop." he replies. "This is too hurtful to watch."

"What boat?" Enzo asks again, his gaze focussed on the trampled ground immediately before him. "What boat? he yells, all of the frustration, the hurt and the wrong he has suffered let loose in his tone.

"A German boat, the Bremen."

"Are you certain, Pipo? How do you know for sure?"

"They told me at the aid station in the Piazza Cairoli. Lilla was not there; she had already left."

"When does the boat leave?"

"Before dusk," he answers, softly.

"How long do we have?"

And when no answer comes, a second shiver afflicts his limbs and his legs quiver and twitch.

"How long do we have," he screams. "Answer me! How long?"

"Not long enough at the speed you are crawling."

Before Enzo, a path opens through the forest of trees and he can see a dull light emanating from between the flaps of the tent. He stops, turns and looks up.

The doctor stands above him, looking down. "You men there," he orders, shaking his head in resignation, "pick him up, gently. Mr Sorbello, you should find a handcart outside; please, bring it back when you've finished with it." He pauses, evidently reconsidering some part of his offer. "In fact, bring him back, too, if he's still alive."

"Thank you, doctor," Enzo says.

"Don't thank me, young man." His expression is harsh beyond unforgiving. "If you are hellbent on dying, better you do it outside where you will not distress those others in here who are equally hellbent on living."

The cart is rudimentary at best; one with long handles, small wooden wheels and a modest platform. Understanding what needs to be done, men loitering by the entrance lend a hand and soon enough Enzo is wrapped in blankets and propped up on board; a swordfish on its way to market.

He looks up at the sky. How long before dusk, he cannot work out. The clouds obscure his view of the sun and light rain falls, causing him to blink repeatedly. All he is sure of is that if the sun is not already sinking behind the mountains, it won't be long before it does as across the Strait the Calabrian coast darkens with every minute that passes.

Fortunately, the Via Boccetta is wider than most other streets and the harbourfront only a few minutes' walk.

Along the route, soldiers and sailors of every regiment and ship and, judging by the different colours and styles of uniform, every nationality are clearing rubble and shoring up buildings. So many, that Pipo has to call to many of them to stand aside lest he run them down.

When they reach the front, the sight that greets Enzo's eyes is beyond his comprehension. "I would not believe it, if I was not seeing it," he says.

An alternative city of tents and awnings has grown up along the marina, and the bedraggled inhabitants stand and sit outside, each staring with the unfocused gaze of normal folk who have had to face abnormal challenges. The well–dressed beside the poorly, the peasant beside the bookkeeper and the old beside the infant: they all share a common bewilderment. And beyond them out in the waters: "There must be more ships in the Strait than houses left standing in the city," Enzo remarks.

"Yes," Pipo shouts over his shoulder. "Our navy and everyone else's. I hear the Americans are sending help, too." The cart jolts over a discarded brick and his passenger is jerked up into the air. "Sorry," he says.

"No matter, my friend. Hurry now. Don't mind me, be as quick as you can. Do you know what this ship, the Bremen, looks like?"

"No. All I was told is that she is an ocean–going liner, so she'll be big." Pipo pauses in front of a boarding house, Le Phenix, intrigued that the building seems to have come through the terrors of the earthquake unscathed. He turns the cart to face the harbour so that Enzo has a better view.

In spite of the wretched pain in his hips, Enzo pulls himself upright and strains his eyes. "There are so many," he mutters. "So many. How can we possibly know which one is the Bremen?"

Unseen behind them, a man steps out of the front door. He wears a heavy woollen overcoat with a velvet collar and a round hat with a curled brim. His way blocked by the cart; he steps carefully round the side.

"Excuse me?" Enzo asks.

"Sorry? I beg your pardon," he replies, in perfect if stilted Italian. And taking in the curiously propped–up posture and the bandaged hands of the young man addressing him, he says, "Yes, of course. What can I do for you?"

"You are English?"

"Yes, my name is Gordon."

"Do you know much about ships, Mr Gordon?" Enzo asks, tentatively.

The man hesitates then smiles. "We British are an island race, much like you Sicilians. So yes, I know a little."

"Would you know the Bremen?"

"Mm, as a matter of fact I do. About five hundred and fifty feet long, hull dark, superstructure light and two white funnels." The man looks out across the Strait. He points. "There. See that one, over there, to the left of the battleship; that's her."

And at the very moment he points the SS Bremen out to Enzo, the ocean–going liner blows two long mournful blasts of her horn, a plume of white water bursts up from her bow and the water boils furiously at her stern.

Enzo slumps back down onto the board, his eyes dull, his face as much a picture of desolation as the scenes along the waterfront. "Not now," he whispers. "Please God, not now."

Mr Gordon is watching him. "I say, young man, you've gone awfully pale. Are you sure you're all right?"

Pipo leans against the side of the handcart, looks down and sighs. "No," he says, a philosophical lethargy to his tone, "he is not all right. For the moment, he is broken. But, sir, please don't underestimate this young man; he is stronger than even he knows. He will survive, we will survive and for as long as the Madonna chooses to watch over us, so too will Messina."

BOOK 2

MIRA

1943

Chapter I

When first the soldiers had come, the day after her twenty–fifth birthday in the June of three years before, they had grinned and laughed and treated her like an older sister. They had promised to take her to lands they said she could only dream of and they had tried to infect her with their enthusiasm for a war they said they could not lose. After all, they had proclaimed: God, Mussolini and Right were on their side.

Mira, on the other hand, had understood the one simple and undeniable truth they had all too readily ignored, which was that hard on the heels of war comes death. Mira knew it and knew it well, for war had already made her a widow.

Of late, and since the First Army has been defeated in North Africa, Mira has noticed a certain sourness lurking behind their boyish charms: their grins have faded to pouts of wistful longing and they no longer look upon her as a sister; for when they look at her now, their eyes resemble those of a dog that knows it must not pass on scraps of food lest it is never offered them again.

The walk from Ganzirri up to Torre Faro takes her the better part of an hour and Mira walks because, these days, no one stops to give her a lift. No one stops because owing to the rationing and the conscription, there is no longer anyone to stop.

Still, the walk does her no harm, the hours after first light are cool and the view across the sparkling blue waters of the Strait to the green hills of Calabria a balm to her soul. This morning is one such morning and Mira knows she should be feeling light and carefree; but she isn't, for because of the rationing and the ridiculous price of black—market coffee and flour and sugar, she will soon have no alternative other than to close her café in the Piazza Chiesa.

The rasping noise of what sounds like several motorbike engines distracts her from her maudlin. Mira looks back down the road. Nothing, no motorcycles, no traffic. She turns and looks south along the coast towards Messina.

The breeze blows her long dark hair about her face and she sweeps it back with her hand.

There! Coming up the Strait. An aeroplane. A single engine; long, slender, curved wings. Fast, very fast. And low, very low.

No one is shooting at the plane, so she not unnaturally assumes it must be either Italian or German; and Mira is about to look away when she notices its strange grey—blue colour, like that of bream in sunlight.

The pilot spots her and dips his wing. He waves a single, cheerful salute, and he is so close that Mira can see the whiteness of his teeth and the cavalier twinkle in his eyes.

She lifts her hand from her face. She laughs. She waves. And with a deep booming roar, the vibrations of which stir the pit of her stomach, the war machine levels and streaks, almost skimming the waves, through the neck of the Strait and out into the open waters of the Tyrrhenian Sea.

Mira is transfixed by the machine's grace and elegance. "Oh, if only war could be so... so beautiful."

The grey—blue colour she has not seen on other planes, yet the blue roundel with a red centre painted just behind the bubble of the cockpit she has.

"Not Italian. Not German," she says to herself. "Ah, British!"

The silence the aeroplane leaves behind is deafening, and in a rare moment of self–consciousness, her cheeks blushing the shade of sun–ripened tomatoes, Mira turns from the Strait to check that no one has been watching her.

"Waving to the enemy, Mira," she whispers, grinning. "Whatever next?"

She kicks the dust from her feet and walks on.

"Aeroplanes, ships, tanks, guns, bullets and bombs: is there nothing more to men than metal?"

Since the second–to–last day of January, the burden of that metal has weighed heavily on her shoulders. After all, why wouldn't it? One lives surrounded by metal; one plans the day according to metal; and one's loved ones die because of it.

She remembers the day at the end of January, one that had started cold and remained quiet until half–past midday when nine of the American four–engined bombers had appeared over Messina. Like lots of thin matchsticks, their bombs had tumbled and burst in the streets and the harbour, and in a matter of seconds, once grand palazzos had been disfigured, buildings had been disembowelled and citizens had fled in terror. Worse, though, was to come; for the next day, the Sunday, the men had been going across the city to the Campo di Gazzi to watch Messina play Catania, without doubt the most important derby of the football calendar, but... the game had been cancelled. Okay, so a little inconvenience was to be expected, but cancelling that particular game of football?

Through the end of May and June the air raids had become heavier and more persistent, the papers reporting that the bombing had become so violent it was impossible to count the dead among the mounds of ash. And now, in the heat of a Sicilian July, people were beginning to wonder if the destruction would ever cease.

"Oh Messina," Mira shouts to the Strait, "have you not suffered enough?"

Chapter 2

Mira's father sits on the wooden stool, weaving his long, hooked needle and thread in and out of the net spread across his knees. He is muttering to himself about his poor hearing and his failing eyesight, excuses he all too often employs to ignore his wife and daughter. He sighs, shakes his head and sets his net aside, stretching out his thread and getting to his feet in a series of awkward mechanical movements, as though his bones are iron and his limbs drawn together by a series of inefficient pulleys. "What are you doing back at this time of day, Mira?" he asks. "Is the café closed?"

She sighs, petulantly. "What other possible reason could there be for my being home at ten o'clock in the morning, papà."

Her mother appears at the door. "Please, Mira. Please take that tone out of your voice when you speak to your father. You may think you are a grown woman, but that does not give you the right to be rude." Francesca winks playfully at her husband, knowing full well Mira is watching her. "So," she says, turning to address her daughter directly, "why are you here? Run out of soldiers to serve?"

"No, mama, we have run out of coffee. In fact, we have run out of nearly everything, including sugar, which means I can make neither granita nor brioche." She sits herself rather clumsily on the stool beside her father and runs her fingers through the curls of her long black hair. "So, yes, papà, I have closed the café."

"And after Monday's bombing, now we have no newspapers," Enzo adds, rubbing at his moustache and stepping inside to sit down at the kitchen table. His face carries a resigned, weathered aspect; an aspect that only increases in its resignation when he notices his wife and daughter follow him.

Inside the small front room which serves as kitchen, living room and scullery, her mother busies herself preserving the day's catch. Tomatoes boil noisily in a pot and above the stove hangs a small, framed photograph of the adamantine, the handsome, the vainglorious Benito Mussolini.

"The papers, who needs papers?" Francesca scoffs, glancing at the photo. "I cannot believe the news is all so bad. Why don't they give us a little good news from time to time?"

"Mira," her father asks, "apart from the printing house, what other news of the bombing?"

"Yesterday, Tenente de la Grascia told me that there were sixty aeroplanes in the raid. He says three German planes were shot down and that the destruction of the central railway terminal and the yards is almost total. Also, he said that many of the warehouses by the harbour were destroyed, some of which are still burning," Mira sighs again, this time in sadness, "and he said some bombs fell on the quay, damaging the statue of our Madonna."

"And what was your tenente's verdict, eh?" he chuckles. "Tell us, please. We wait with bated breath to hear what more your tenente has to say. Did he not declare at church on Sunday that there would be no more air raids on the city? Did your tenente not say that from now on the Americans and the British would bomb only the airfields to the south, so that the might of the Luftwaffe and the Regia Aeronautica would be denied the airfields from which they will disrupt the landings he says will soon take place?"

Francesca winces as Mira fixes her father with a fractious stare; fires far more incendiary than any bombing could deliver blazing fiercely in the darkness of her eyes.

"Papà, you have no cause to sneer at Tenente de la Grascia. May I remind you how generous he has been."

When her father doesn't react to her dig regarding the Tenete's gifts of soap, Mira fumes and when the volume of her fumes exceeds the pressured confines of the front room, her temper flares: "Oh, yes, papà, we all know how very generous you are with your labours that you donate much of your catch to him. Oh, how very grand it is that you put yourself to so much trouble for your neighbour!"

In an effort to pour sand on her incandescence, Enzo says, in a low, serious tone: "May I remind you, Mira, that not two weeks ago a lampara in Mortelle was shot by a nervous sentry; a lampara they suspected of sending signals to the enemy, while all the time he was using his light solely to attract the squid he needed to feed his family? And shot by an Italian sentry at that."

"No," she replies, startling him, "you may not remind us because you have no need to. If you think mama and I sleep soundly wondering whether or not you are going to return from your early morning fishing trips, then you are very sadly mistaken. Why, even on the morning after the last air raid you could not keep yourself from going out in your boat." Mira's tone becomes angrier and yet at the same time more imploring. "And what happens? After the night raid, early the very next morning comes the day raid on Villa San Giovanni: ships left on fire, a ferry sunk and two explosions so large they nearly obliterated the town. And all this while you sit out there on the water, casting your net and watching like a wide–eyed child. Is that the kind of behaviour one expects of a responsible husband and father?"

He rubs his moustache in thought. "Mm, you want to eat: I need to fish. The world does not stop turning simply because some general has a grudge against Villa San Giovanni. Nothing much good comes from there, anyway."

Francesca shakes her head and raises her eyes to the ceiling in prayer.

That Mira cannot rile her father annoys her even more and she throws up her hands in dismay. "And please, papà, and you mama, please try to desist from calling him your tenente. He is as much your lieutenant as he is mine. Besides, do you really think he likes to be here? Do you really think he wants to be here?"

Enzo snorts, dismissively. "You are right in what you say, Mira. I should be more sympathetic towards him. However, he is not my neighbour; he comes from Bologna." He pouts. "Answer me this, young lady, why do I bother to feed a man from Bologna when all he does is fire his cannon and scare the fish?"

"Why?" Her tone rises. "Why? Have you forgotten that the evening before the first air raid you told me that the man who has to suffer war deserves our pity? And did you not say the same of my husband when he died?"

"Enzo Ruggeri!" her mother chips in. "It is beneath you to mock men who serve their country so faithfully. May I remind you how few of our soldiers returned from Russia."

"They say this lieutenant returned under a cloud," he mutters. "They say he was demoted for some breach of discipline."

Mira groans in exasperation. "They, papà? And just who is they?"

"Perhaps," Enzo continues, thinking aloud, "that is why he still wears the uniform: to legitimize his ill–discipline."

"No, papà, you don't know him like I do. Aldo does not hate anyone. The worst his preferences permit is for him to dislike people from Modena which, he tells me, is no further than a few hour's walk from his home. And even then, he laughs when he tells me this. No, papà, if you took the time to get to know him, you would understand that first, he is a gentleman and second, he is intelligent

211

and has no more love for war than you. You know, Aldo was a student at the Università di Bologna before he volunteered for service."

"Aldo? Oh, Aldo is it now?" Enzo replies, his tone openly dismissive. "Well, perhaps when he leaves, he will take you back to that city of his and set you up in a fine house; that is, if there will be any houses left standing by the time this war is finished. Tell me, Mira, should I expect a visit from him soon? It had better be soon if this invasion he insists on talking about happens."

They sit and stare each other down across the wooden table until the second, inevitable conflagration of Mira's ever—combustible frustration occurs. She kicks her chair back as she stands up from the table, balls her hands into fists and...

There is a knock at the door.

Francesca crosses herself and glances at the ceiling; her prayers are answered.

Father and daughter continue to stare at each other, each one waiting for the other to move towards the door.

Neither of them does so.

There comes a second rat—tat—tat—tat, followed by a polite, manly cough, suggesting the caller may have been standing outside, waiting for their argument to run its course.

Whoever it is that has come calling can wait, as for the moment neither father nor daughter are for moving and, as is always the case following one of their petty squabbles, it is Francesca who takes it upon herself to defuse the situation. She steps over to the door and pulls it back.

With the stark sunlight behind him, the shadow of the caller is cast onto the stone floor of the room, suggesting he is a man of ordinary height and build, and yet, judging by Francesca's studied almost reverential silence, no ordinary man. He wears the uniform of a soldier and, not merely a soldier, an officer, as his cap is peaked, rather than the bustina side cap worn by his men, and his calzoni curved breeches perfectly pressed.

"Signora Ruggeri," he says, bowing, "my name is Tenente Radaldo de la Grascia. Please be so kind as to forgive my intrusion," his voice is warm and lilting, a tenor's tone, smooth and confident, "but would it be possible to…"

"Yes, of course, Tenente. You would like to speak to Mira. Please, please come in."

De la Grascia steps in and turns to survey the small, rather untidy, front room, by which time both Mira and her father have hurriedly laid aside their differences and stood to receive the visitor.

"Ah," de la Grascia begins, "you must be Mira's father, Signor Ruggeri. My compliments, sir, Mira has told me much about you and, if I may say, it is an honour to meet you." He takes a stride towards Enzo and offers his hand.

Mira's father, spellbound by such a formal introduction, immediately spills whatever wind he may have been filling his sails with in order to appear intimidating in the face of a man about whom he has so recently been less than complimentary, and wipes his hands on his shirt, taking de la Grascia's hand and pumping it enthusiastically.

The lieutenant waits patiently for Enzo's enthusiasm to wear itself out. "May I say, Signor Ruggeri, how grateful I am, or perhaps I should say how grateful I and my fellow officers are, for the continued gifts of your catch?"

"Yes. Yes, of course, Tenente," Enzo blusters. "Although it is I who should be thanking you for your continued gifts of… err, well, gifts. Please, sit down." He glares at Mira as if she should have warned him of the lieutenant's impending visit.

In return, she shrugs her shoulders and glares back.

Mira offers de la Grascia the chair on which she had been sitting, wiping it with the hem of her skirt as she does so. "The soap," she says. "He means the soap, for which we are all very grateful and no doubt the better for. Please."

The lieutenant sits and smiles. "It is nothing. A gesture."

Francesca shuffles her hands, nervously. "Would you like a cup of…"

"Mama," Mira interrupts, "how would it be possible for us to offer a cup of coffee when I have had to close the café because I have run out?"

"A drink, perhaps?" Enzo grasps a dusty bottle of Amaro from the sideboard. "Mira, a glass for the Tenente."

De la Grascia removes his peaked cap, sets it carefully on the table and holds up both hands in surrender. "Thank you, but you are too kind and time will not permit me."

"Oh, yes," Enzo agrees, frowning at his own incompetence, "it is too early for Amaro."

"No, Signor Ruggeri, please permit me to disagree: it is never too early for good Amaro; however, sadly I cannot stay to enjoy your hospitality. No, I have come to call on you for a number of reasons. The first is that I notice the café is closed and as much as I mourn the loss of your welcome —"

Enzo raises an eyebrow and shoots his daughter a consternated look.

"— I was concerned that perhaps you were not well, Signora Alberti, and thought that if that was so, I could ask my medical orderly to provide you with whatever remedy you might be in need of."

"Thank you, Tenente," Mira replies, embarrassed by both his acute manners and his protracted inquiry. "Your concern is appreciated. As you can see, though, I am quite well. The café is closed for the simple reason that we have no sugar, no coffee and no flour."

"Ah, good."

"Good?" Mira repeats, baffled. "How can it be good to run out of the very ingredients I need to serve my customers?"

"Because, Signora, that means that from now on you will have to rely on us, more particularly me in person, to supply you with whatever it is you need. In this way, I can repay you for all the kindnesses that you have shown me over these past weeks."

Enzo frowns. Francesca smiles.

Mira, perhaps against her better instincts judging by the way she doesn't leap at his offer, says, "Thank you, Tenente de la Grascia, whatever you can spare we will naturally be very grateful for."

He holds up his hands in surrender. "Please don't think me too generous. I have an ulterior motive, which is that if my senior officers are not supplied with a regular diet of coffee, granita and brioche, they will only become even less human and will therefore cause me trouble; trouble I can live without. So, I will be grateful for your cooperation and it goes without saying that nobody other than the three of us needs to know from where your good fortune stems."

"But will we not be able to get supplies from Villa San Giovanni or Reggio?" Enzo queries.

"No, from today the only supplies sent across the Strait will come in the form of German tanks."

"So, you will be our only source of food?" Enzo asks, perplexed. "How are we going to repay you?"

"Signor Ruggeri, you have been a ready source for the best fresh food in our mess and without your contribution, our palates would have died of boredom weeks ago. And," he holds up his hand to stave off Mira's father's objection, "I am aware fishing is equally as dangerous an occupation as soldiering, particularly at the moment, so I will be making certain that all our sentries know that you are to be allowed free access to the beach and to the waters, though it may suit us both if you confine your fishing to the waters close inshore."

Mira fidgets as she restrains herself from reaching out and hugging the lieutenant.

Her mother, though, is not so controlled of her emotions. Francesca steps over and, being the same height standing as he is sitting, grasps de la Grascia to her ample bosom.

Enzo blanches and drags her back.

Such a flagrant display of gratitude, the lieutenant had not in his wildest imaginings accounted for and he coughs with embarrassment before adding, "I should also advise you that from now on some foods will become scarce."

"Thank you, Tenente, you are..." Francesca starts forwards again, causing Enzo to sway in her direction like a chestnut tree in a gale, "...too, too kind. We had anticipated shortages and the Madonna knows we have been living with rationing for far too long. In consequence, Mira and I," she glows at her daughter, "we have been corning fish, preserving tomatoes and figs and lemons, and drying pasta and storing up our olive oil. We—"

"Yes, Francesca," Enzo interrupts, patting her patronisingly on her shoulder as though she is a grandmother too easily confused by her grandchildren, "as I'm sure the Tenente knows only too well, hoarding is against the law and we are simply looking after the daily provisions others have no means to."

"Really, father," Mira chides, "you have no reason to fret, Tenente de la Grascia is neither Carabinieri nor fool. It is as much beyond his regulations to provide us with soap as it is mother to hoard food."

Enzo glowers once more, although again more probably at his repeated incompetence.

Radaldo de la Grascia, keen not to become embroiled in a struggle for family power, gets to his feet, picking his cap up as he does so. "In fact, if I was to be completely truthful, Signor Ruggeri, I believe that within two years most food, particularly rice and potatoes, will increase in price by over 1,000 per cent, and bread and milk by as much as 500 per cent; so, you are wise to act accordingly."

Mira, Francesca and Enzo stare at each other, wide-eyed in amazement tinged with fear.

"Oh, this cannot be," Enzo says. "Why, if food costs as much as you predict, there will be no one to eat it because there will be no one who can possibly afford to buy it."

The Tenente's face stiffens at the indignity of Mira's father questioning his knowledge. "Very well, then."

"Tell me, Tenente," Enzo straightens his back, assuming his rightful superiority as master of his house and therefore chief arbiter, "how can you be so certain of these... How is it that you have acquired such mathematical precision in your predictions?"

"Signor Ruggeri, I–"

"Ah, of course, Mira told us that before you enlisted in the army you used to be a student at the Università di Bologna. What subject did you study? Prophecy, by any chance?"

"Father!" Mira shrieks.

"No, sir. I studied sociology."

Enzo scoffs, much as he would have done if the Tenente had answered that he was studying the mysteries of female behaviour. "Well, on Sunday you told us it was unlikely that there would be more air raids for the foreseeable future and yet we suffered one the very next day. Did you not tell us that there would be no more air raids until after the invasion which, if I recall correctly, you said would happen in the next few weeks? Is that not what you said?"

"Yes, Signor Ruggeri, that is exactly what I told you and I have to admit I was incorrect; a miscalculation for which I apologise."

"Incorrect? A miscalculation?" Enzo repeats, a broad self-congratulation unattractively clear in his tone.

"Yes, sir. But only a minor miscalculation."

"How so, Tenente de la Grascia? How minor?"

"Well, Signor Ruggeri..." Though he addresses her father, he is looking at Mira as he speaks, his expression now far more serious. "You may like to recalculate the extent of my shortcomings when I tell you that during the night British paratroopers landed at Ponte Grande and as we speak the Americans are coming ashore at Gela."

CHAPTER 3

Francesca stirs. "What is that noise, Enzo? I feel as if I have only just got back to sleep after all that commotion out in the Strait."

"Someone is knocking at the door," he mumbles. "Go back to sleep, I will go and see."

"Don't they know it is the middle of the night?"

Throwing on his shirt and trousers, Enzo, yawning and rubbing his eyes, makes his way into the front room. However, he hasn't made it to the door when the knocking is repeated, this time even more urgently than before. "All right, all right, I'm coming."

Sliding back the bolt, he lifts up the latch and pulls back the door.

Two black figures. Or more accurately, perhaps only one and a half, as the second of the two is bent low and only standing because he is supported by the other. Though dawn is still an hour or so distant and the moon obscured by cloud, the figures seem somehow darker even than the night.

"What do you want?" Enzo snaps, irritably.

"Your help, sir," the more upright of the two answers. "I need your help. Please, this man is hurt and I have not the strength to carry him any further."

"Hurt? What kind of hurt? You look more like drunks to me."

"Please, sir, I will explain." The man's tone is gruff, yet his desperation is evident in the rasp of his voice and the manner in which he gasps for air. "Please let us come in for a moment? I beg of you." He leans in through the door so that it is impossible to close it without forcing him out.

"Wait a minute," Enzo grumbles. "I will light a lamp."

"No, please. Don't make light until you have drawn the blinds. I will explain. Black out the windows, please."

"First you ask for sanctuary and then you ask for anonymity; you want much for a man who wanders around in the middle of the night." Enzo stands back to let them pass into the front room. "Who are you? Where are you from?"

"My name is Sottocapo Falanga."

"A leading seaman, eh, what sort of an excuse is that? Oh, never mind, you might as well come in. But no funny business, eh. It is late and what with the bombing on Villa San Giovanni, the cannons behind Sant Agata blasting away and that business with the explosions out in the Strait, none of us have managed any sleep."

As the man who has introduced himself as Falanga staggers across the threshold, he loses his grip and his companion slides to the floor.

Enzo bends and tries to take hold of the second man, but manages only to get him halfway to his feet when his hands also slip from the fellow's arms. "What is this he is covered in, grease?"

"No, sir," Falanga gasps, "it is oil, fuel oil. Please, get him to a chair but take care not to touch his face, his arms or his legs, they are burnt. Quickly, now, I promise I will explain."

"Burnt? How? What do you mean burnt?"

"Papà, what is going on?" Mira asks, from the doorway to her room.

"Light a candle and draw the blinds, Mira. It would appear this man is hurt. Falanga, help me get him to the chair by the table."

Between them, they manhandle the slippery form up off the floor and with some help from another chair wedged under his arm, they manage to get him to slouch at the table.

"Papà!" Mira exclaims, failing to stifle her horror.

Black from head to toe, the man appears to have been bathed in a thick, shiny paint, so much so that it is impossible to tell the colour of his skin. His shirt, if at some time he had been wearing a complete shirt, is ragged and soiled like that of a beggar, and his shorts are stuck fast to his legs.

She holds the candle closer to him. "Oh, look at his face, papà. Poor fellow. The skin at his eyes, it is raw."

"Mira, wake your mother and ask her to heat some water and bring cloth, salt and what sugar we have left. Olive oil, too. Tell her she must make a paste: we must remove as much of this oil as we can." Enzo lights a hurricane lamp and hangs it from the ceiling. "And you, Signor Falanga, take this cloth and clean yourself as best you can. Are you hurt? Do you have wounds that need attending to or can we see to this man first?"

"No, I am fine compared to this man," he replies, even if he doesn't look like a man who is fine, as he too is painted in a similar dark film of oil. "My head rings like a bell, my mouth is dry like a desert and I am exhausted from swimming for so long, but please, see to this man first. If not for him, I doubt that I would be here to talk to you."

"Then sit, over there, wipe yourself down and tell me why you have been out swimming in the Strait in the middle of the night."

Mira returns with Francesca.

On seeing the figure slumped at the table, she says, "Oh, the poor man." However, she does not pause to ask who he is or where he has come from, she merely begins to pour a bowl of water, gather some strips of cloth, jars of dried salt and sugar and one of the bars of soap the Tenente has given them. She places the bowl on the table and stands stupefied, as she contemplates where she should start cleaning a man who is so completely coated in oil.

"Take his shirt off," her father barks, in an effort to distract her from her stupor. "Clean what you can." He sighs. "And be careful not to get the salt near his face. What we do with his burns, I've no idea. Perhaps we should take him to the military hospital in Messina."

"No," Falanga states, with more than a hint of fear in his tone, "I don't think that would be best. Signor..."

"Ruggeri. Enzo."

"Is there not a doctor nearby who can attend to him?"

"Yes, possibly." The fisherman is intrigued. "Though he would certainly benefit from the care they can provide. They will have the necessary detergents and disinfectants, and as for his face... So, I ask again, please tell me what you are doing here and why you don't think it would be best to get your companion to hospital."

"Here? What am I doing here? Why, I am surviving, nothing more. On the one hand I have the misfortune to be one of the crew from the submarine that has just been destroyed. And on the other, I believe I have the good fortune to be the only survivor. You must have heard the noise."

Enzo nods. "We heard it and saw it: the artillery barrage, the great explosions, the flames. If the air raid on Villa San Giovanni was not enough to keep us from our sleep, your pyrotechnics removed all hope." He studies his guest for a moment. "And this poor wretch? You bring him here, instead of raising the alarm. You seem to me to be reluctant to get him to a hospital. Why is that?"

Falanga pauses in his ablutions and fixes his host with a look that suggests he is unsure of the reception his reply is about to provoke. "Because, Signor Ruggeri, this man is English and I fear the Germans will not treat him well."

"English?"

"Yes, English. He is from the boat that destroyed us."

222

Mira stops and stares at him, her expression quizzical, as though she believes Sottocapo Falanga has swallowed too much seawater than is good for his senses.

"From the boat that destroyed you," Enzo notes, his eyebrows raised, his lips bridled with curiosity. "You mean to tell me this man destroyed your submarine and killed your compatriots, and yet you have saved him from the very same death he wished upon you?"

"Yes, Signor Ruggeri, you are correct. Strange isn't it? In sinking our submarine, he tried to kill me; of that there is no doubt. And yet, by throwing me the lifebelt from his boat, he saved my life and in doing so provided me with the chance of saving his. Of course, he could not have known his boat, too, would be destroyed and that he was going to end up in the water with me; that was simply the result of good gunnery and bad timing. As I said, it is a strange war, eh? I do not expect you to understand. Pah! How could you?" He scoffs, though not so disrespectfully that his host might take offence and confuse his irony as anything other than his contempt for war. "I for one certainly do not understand this war and I can only hope you are not the fascists so many of my crew professed to be." He waits and watches, and adds, "Please, sir, I beg of you, please tell me you're not like those others."

"No, sottocapo, you should not concern yourself. I…" He glances at Mira and Francesca, "We are not like those others. We are neither fascist nor communist; we are fisherman and therefore our politics are governed by elements beyond our control, much like your orders are given to you by your officers." Enzo attempts something that approaches, but falls short of, a reassuring smile.

"Really, father!" Mira grumbles, returning to her task. "This poor man is not interested to know your politics; he merely wants to know if he can trust you not to hand the man who saved his life over to the Germans."

Enzo glowers at his daughter and snaps, "Yes, I am perfectly aware of what he wants to know. What *I* want to know is whether or not I can trust him." His tone softens to something more conciliatory. "The sottocapo would seem to me to be a very fortunate man. For one thing, he is the sole survivor from his submarine; one, just one, of probably more than fifty men who have perished. For another, he was saved from almost certain drowning by the compassion of a man who had not moments before been trying to kill him. And finally, and perhaps more miraculously, he has been lucky enough to catch the tide at such a time that it has swept him in towards the shore, when in another ten or so minutes it would have swept him out to his death. All that, and he has brought with him a man who he would like us to believe is our enemy." He sits back in his chair and briefly crosses his thick forearms. "If I was a suspicious man, I would wonder if perhaps Sottocapo Falanga you were trying to trap us; to find out if we sympathised with the Americans and the British."

A silence of profound contemplation hangs in the air, broken only by the dripping of water into the bowl, as the two men gaze at each other; one perplexed that his integrity should be doubted, the other unprepared to relent in his suspicions.

The third man stirs, lifts his head and mutters a groan of pain.

"Fools," Mira says. "Both of you fools. Can you not see when a man is dying before your very eyes?"

Once more, Enzo glowers at his daughter.

"Signor Ruggeri," the sottocapo begins, "do you seriously believe I would injure this man so gravely simply to question your loyalty to a war which none of us wanted and which is already beyond lost?"

The third man groans again, this time in an attempt to make himself heard.

"He is trying to speak and whatever he is trying to say sounds distinctly Italian," Francesca says.

"Ha!" Enzo points, accusingly, at Sottocapo Falanga, "There you are. You don't know who he is. He is not even English."

"I am English," the man murmurs softly in Italian. In itself, his use of Italian is unsurprising; however, what is astonishing is that he speaks it in near perfect local dialect. "I am as English as you are Sicilian," he says, "and I speak your language the way you speak it." He raises his hands and begins so very tentatively to feel the skin around his face, wincing every time he touches a raw part of flesh. "My name is Nicholas Lock. I am an officer in the British Navy. Now, please, will you stop arguing and will one of you kindly tell me where in God's name I am?"

CHAPTER 4

While Enzo and Falanga stare in wonderment, Mira is the first to react. She kneels down beside the table and placing her hand underneath the man's chin, she tenderly lifts his face.

"You are in Ganzirri," she replies, examining his blackened eyes, "it is a small fishing village just to the north of Messina. My name is Mira and my father's name is Enzo."

"How did I get here?"

"There is a man, here. Sottocapo Falanga. He brought you ashore, to our house."

Nicholas Lock sits more upright and starts to feel at his face. "What has happened to my eyes? I cannot seem to open them."

Mira frowns, not so much at the raw flesh about his cheeks and forehead as at the fact that his eyes, though still coated with a film of oil, are only partially open. His eyelids, she notices, are badly burned, their soft tissue disturbingly charred in appearance. Taking his hands in hers, she lowers them away from his face and presses them gently into his lap. "You have suffered burns, Signor Lock. For the moment, you cannot see and you will need time to recover. Try not to alarm yourself."

He struggles to lift his hands again and she holds them down, this time more firmly.

Mira purses her lips in disapproval and glances first at her father and then at Sottocapo Falanga.

They, too, grimace in discomfort as they realise the extent of the injuries.

Turning back to her patient, she says, "It is better that you do not touch your face. Your hands are not clean and it will be better not to risk infection. Please, try to be calm and let us take care of you. We will need to remove as much oil as we can and then we will find a place for you to lie down."

What passes for a smile creases his lips, his teeth glowing bright white against his charred features. "Thank you, M…"

"Mira," she says.

"Thank you, Mira. I would like to; I feel awfully tired and my head feels as though it is still aflame. Do you have anything I can take for the pain; it is quite intense."

"Signor Lock?" Enzo asks.

"Yes."

"I am Mira's father, Enzo. I must ask you a question, though I understand it will be difficult for you to answer, so please take your time to think before you reply."

"Yes, Enzo."

"Sottocapo Falanga has brought you to our house. You are safe here, but I cannot guarantee that you will be completely safe from capture. With your injuries as they are, would you prefer us to hand you over to the military so that you can benefit from better treatment at one of their hospitals?"

For a few seconds, all the response they receive is his laboured breathing as Nicholas Lock struggles once more to raise his hands from his lap. Again, Mira presses them back down. When he understands that she will not let him scratch the irritation prompted by the burns, he asks, "I should imagine their hospitals will be too busy treating their own men to be concerned with attending to a prisoner of war. Do you have a doctor who can help me? One that you can trust."

"We do," Enzo replies, "he is an old friend. You need not concern yourself; as I have said, you will be safe here."

"And you…" Nicholas winces as pain wracks his body. "And you, will you be safe? Having me here will only lead to trouble for you and your family. Perhaps very bad trouble. Can you promise me you will be safe?"

Mira looks across at her father, widening her eyes in amazement that a man so brutally injured should find the strength to voice concern for others.

"Safe?" Enzo says, as though he is recalling a distant and pleasant memory. "No one is safe, Signor Lock. Not in Ganzirri, not in Messina and judging by the bombs that fell yesterday and last night, especially not across the water in Villa San Giovanni. What I will promise you is that you will be safe with us. Sottocapo Falanga will not betray your presence," he glances at the submariner, then at Francesca, "and neither will we. As I have already explained to the sottocapo, we have no love for troublemakers, be they fascists or communists."

The spasm of pain twists the Englishman once more and a curious rictus grin infects his face. "In that case," he mutters, "I don't have the energy to argue. In fact, if you will permit me, I think I'm going to pass out."

Mira, confused not only by his courtesy in asking her permission, but also by wondering exactly how she is supposed to stop him, hesitates. Enzo, Sottocapo Falanga and Francesca are helpless to prevent him from falling as, even in the modest confines of the front room, they are too far away to reach him in time. So, they all watch as he leans, at first haltingly, like a sailboat listing in a blustery gale, and second inevitably, falling faster and faster as gravity draws him down.

Enzo stands up, slowly, and straightens his back. "Mira, go to Dottore Roselli; tell him of this man's condition and ask him to come with whatever medicines and dressings he has left. Tell him that though his old bones may object to being disturbed at this hour, if he does not come right away, he will no longer be the beneficiary of fresh fish on Fridays. And do not go by the road, there are too many patrols: take one of the boats and row across the lagoon."

He studies the prone figure for a moment and scratches his head in thought. When he has reached a conclusion, he looks at his wife. "Francesca, if you have clean sheets, make up Mira's bed. Sottocapo Falanga and I will clean this man, and as soon as we have finished, we will bring him."

"You are going to keep him here?" she asks, incredulous. "An enemy?" She glances at the photo above the stove.

Her husband glares at her. "He is not our enemy, Francesca; he has come to us from the sea. And you know very well, I cannot ask our neighbours to put themselves at risk if I am not prepared to do the same. Go on, woman, hurry now."

Francesca scuttles from the room.

Mira pauses by the door, her eyes shining warm in the light of the hurricane lamp. "Thank you, papà."

Enzo smiles, perhaps a shade resignedly. "Thank me by being careful, eh, my daughter? And think of some excuse in case you are challenged. Now go. Make your feet soft so no one will hear you."

She lifts the latch on the door and is gone, leaving her father and Falanga to begin their cleaning.

Enzo takes a strip of cloth, the bowl of water, the olive oil and the paste off the table and kneels beside the Englishman. With Falanga's help, they role the unconscious figure over onto his back. "Now, let's remove the rest of his shirt and his shoes. Pass me that fillet knife," he nods in the direction of a sideboard, "and we'll cut off his shorts. You know how to polish wood, Sottocapo Falanga?"

He nods, a little uncertainly.

When the recumbent figure is naked, Enzo takes a strip of cloth and folds it into a round pad. "Like this, eh? Then, take some of the salt and sugar paste onto the cloth and dip it into the olive oil." He does so and holds his cloth up so that the other man will see how much or how little paste he has put on the cloth. "Use only a little; we don't have much. Then, wipe as much of the fuel oil off the skin as the cloth will clear, allowing the cloth to absorb it." He paws at Nicholas Lock's right forearm. "Remember, the paste is abrasive and we do not want to break the skin, so do not press too hard. When your cloth is dark," again he holds it up, and whereas before there was a fresh white ball of cloth, now there is a gluey black mess, "leave it and use a fresh piece."

For the better part of an hour, they work, alternately dipping, wiping and discarding pieces of cloth; the silence disturbed only by the occasional mumbling of the invalid whenever they clean too close to his wounds.

When the silence of their concentration weighs too heavily on him, Enzo asks, "Your submarine? Was it completely destroyed?"

"For certain, Signor Ruggeri. We have come from Taranto and our journey was made all the longer by having to avoid so many British warships. When we surfaced, the hatch was opened and all that foul air of bodies confined for too long in too little space escaped and was replaced by fresh air. This air is like a drug and it causes me to dream of the Mistral, the cool wind that blows from the north. I was standing at the bottom of the conning tower, thinking of the wind when all of a sudden there was a mighty explosion and I found myself outside the submarine, swimming through the oily, fiery water."

"You were indeed very fortunate, eh?"

"As God is my witness, Signor Ruggeri." Sottocapo Falanga crosses himself and kisses his knuckle. "I've heard the bombing here has been terrible and last night, we could not pass through the Strait until it had finished."

"It has been bad, that is true," Enzo says. "Before dawn on Wednesday, they bombed Messina: the ferry slipways, the train yards, the oil depot. I tell you, my mother would have been able to smell the burning oil in heaven so high was the pall of smoke. Later, during the morning, they returned with over 200 aeroplanes to complete the job, and yesterday, as you know, Villa San Giovanni and Reggio di Calabria received the same punishment. I suppose it is because of all those tanks and troops the Germans are sending across from the mainland. Do you know how the invasion is going?"

Falanga shrugs, briefly, before bending back to his cleaning. "No, they don't tell us much; they don't want us to think the defence of Sicily is a lost cause."

"Is it?"

"You had better ask Generale Guzzoni. He knows better than me."

"Where are you from, sottocapo?"

"Me?" He sighs, a long and constant outgoing breath of despair. "From everywhere and nowhere. I was born in Puglia and raised in Naples, before going wherever there was the promise of employment. One day, there wasn't, so the Fascists found work for my idle hands in the navy."

"Driftwood, eh?"

Falanga smiles. "Yes, driftwood. Plain and simple driftwood."

Enzo holds the Englishman's arm and rests his hand against his own thigh. He dabs his ball of cloth in the bowl of paste, wipes at the back of the blackened left hand and inspects the congealed residue of what he has removed. When he is happy the hand is sufficiently clean, he moves on to the fingers and notices Lock's signet ring. He wipes it and studies the simple engraving on the face, his thoughts for a moment distracted from his task.

"I have been thinking, sottocapo," he says, leaning back to rest. "I think it would be best for you to leave now. You must go and report to whoever it is right for you to report to before they come searching for you."

Without looking up, Falanga replies, "There is no one to search for me, Signor Ruggeri. As far as they are concerned, I have drowned with the rest of the crew. You see, as I neared the shore I believe I heard the motors of a Motoscafo Armato Silurante, one of our fast boats. They were probably searching for survivors."

"Did you not try to attract their attention?"

"No," Falanga sighs. "By that time, I was as near the shore as I was to them and in the dark, they did not see me." Now, he too sits back on his heels. "And besides, I decided that if I was rescued, I would only find myself sent back to another of those tin coffins and to survive one sinking is a blessing, to risk the same again would only serve to tempt fate beyond all reason. No, Signor Ruggeri, I would rather take my chances hiding out in the hills and from what I have heard, the Germans will only be able to hold Sicily for another month at best. Generale Guzzoni is telling everyone that he will never give up; that he will fight to the last man." He scoffs. "In my experience, when a general makes bold proclamations of this nature, it usually means he is about to run away, and believe me, I have no intention of being his last man. Do you know anyone who will help me?"

Enzo thinks for a while. "Yes, I believe I do. When Dottore Roselli comes and if there is enough time before first light, I will take you to the house of a friend."

They bend forward and set to finish their cleaning.

"Signor Ruggeri?"

"Yes."

"Do you think I am a coward?"

Again, Enzo considers. "Sottocapo Falanga, it does not matter what I think." He pauses and sighs. "But I will say this, a coward uses his head where a fool loses his life and if I had not run from many storms, by now I would be sleeping with the fish and my family would have starved."

"Then perhaps you should stop calling me sottocapo and call me Filippo."

"As you wish, Filippo. Come, we have nearly finished. Let's get him into the next room and into the bed."

The front door opens and Mira enters, followed slowly by an elderly gentleman who is bent almost double, his hair wispy white, his shoulders small and round.

"Hurry up and close the door," Enzo barks. "Ah, Dottore Roselli. Good of you to come. Mira, were you seen?"

The doctor grumbles, "Do you seriously believe I am young enough to be playing at fugitives? Of course we were seen. A German patrol stopped us as we were crossing the main road."

Mira grins. "Not to worry, papà. The Dottore told them we were on our way to deliver a newborn and he told them they had no right to prevent him attending a mother to be, especially when any one of them might be the father."

"Now," Dottore Roselli begins, "what is so urgent that you threaten to deny me my fish?" Bent as he is, he cannot miss the figure lying on the floor. "Oh, I see."

Enzo grabs at a strip of cloth and lays it across Nicholas Lock's groin.

"Papà," Mira groans, "Modesty is all very well, but you forget I—"

"Yes. Come, Filippo," Enzo says, ignoring her, "let's get him into the bedroom where the Dottore can examine him in peace."

They heave the Englishman up from the floor.

He comes to and struggles, his sinews tightening, his anxiety rising, his hands gripping tightly the arms of his porters.

Mira bends to his ear and whispers, "Signor Lock, my father is only trying to help you to the bedroom," she hesitates, "to my bedroom. Be a good boy and try to relax. Soon, you will sleep."

And as a baby calms at a mother's cooing, so he loosens his grip and falls tranquil.

Enzo glances, then frowns at his daughter as much to say that he disapproves of the power she has so quickly assumed over a stranger, albeit an injured, barely conscious stranger.

Mira smiles and returns his look with one leaving him in no doubt that however long he should live, he will never understand the subtle influences of her gender. "Now, papà, be careful with him," she adds, rubbing salt into the wounds of his ignorance.

"Enough, the two of you!" Dottore Roselli grumbles, raising his hands above his head in appeal. "I don't know; keep an old man from his sleep while you busy yourselves scoring points off each other. Francesca, you had better assist me; these two cannot keep from their ridiculous competitions."

CHAPTER 5

Mira, Filippo Falanga and Enzo sit in silent expectation, the patient's nearest if not dearest awaiting the outcome of his operation.

When Francesca returns, Enzo looks up. "How is he?"

"The good doctor says he has seen worse; that is good. But he also said the last person he saw in such a pitiful state was you, the day he met you, all of thirty–five years ago, and that is bad."

Enzo sniffs, hunching his shoulders and splaying his hands. "That is just like the good Dottore, eh? Always the good news corrupted with a spoonful of bad. How long will he be with his examination?"

"Do you have somewhere to be?" his wife asks.

"No, I have nowhere particular to be. What with all that noise during the night I should think any sensible fish is covering his ears at the bottom of the Strait. However, this gentleman," he nods at Filippo Falanga, "has to have a place to stay. It is a question of whether I take him or Mira takes him."

Francesca carries a bowl, once white but now pink, piled with scraps of cloth, most varying shades of crimson, others vividly scarlet. "Then, husband of mine, you must take Signor Falanga. Dottore Roselli would like to speak with Mira before she opens the café; there are medicines he does not have which he believes Mira may be able to procure for him."

"Yes, I thought as much," Enzo says. "Come sottocapo, sorry, Filippo, you look clean enough and what with the curfew, we are not likely to have to shake hands with anyone."

"What about the patrols?" Falanga asks, his unease evident in the perpetual quivering of his legs.

"Don't concern yourself. They change over at about this time; we will not be troubled. Let's go."

"Papà?"

"Yes, Mira?"

"Please be careful, you know what we say."

"Ah, yes: the appreciation of a good deed is to be measured in bruises." He pauses by the door. "If Dottore Roselli has what I believe he has in store for you, I suggest you do the same." He looks hard at her, then ushers his charge out of the door and they are gone.

"Francesca," Dottore Roselli calls from the bedroom, "where are you with those clean cloths? And if you have it, bring me some ground turmeric, this gash on his shin refuses to stop bleeding."

By the time the good Dottore has completed his examination and treatment, and cleaned his hands and clothes sufficiently to make himself respectable, light is tiptoeing stealthily over the peaks beyond the water.

"Please, Dottore Roselli, sit at the table, Mira will make us coffee."

"Real coffee?" he asks in surprise, lowering his creaking bones onto the chair.

"Yes," Mira replies.

"Not that terrible chicory stuff the Germans drink?" He removes his round spectacles and runs his hand across either side of his wrinkled face, as though he is encountering great difficulty imagining what his ears are hearing.

236

"No, Dottore, real coffee."

"Please, Mira, Francesca, if you have need of my services at any time of day or night, please feel free to call. Why, I might even put you on my round of daily visits."

"We don't have that much, Dottore," Mira replies, "and the black market price is beyond our pocket."

"Then, where do you get it from?"

Mira glances at her mother.

"I think you can trust Dottore Roselli to be discreet," Francesca says, as she leaves the room.

"From the Italian Tenente at the battery at Capo Peloro."

"Ah, yes, Tenente de la Grascia," Dottore Roselli exclaims, grinning, his eyes suddenly lively and bright with mischief. "I was hoping you would say that. You should know, Mira, that the gossips in the village are consumed by their speculations as to exactly how you manage to keep your café open." He pauses, thinking for a moment before adding, "However, you need to consider how long you should keep the place going: there are those with green eyes who, when this war is over, may permit their jealousies to resent your..."

"My fraternising with the enemy? And just who do these gossips believe is the enemy, eh?" Mira asks. And before he can object to her broader description of her behaviour, she goes on to say, "Don't worry, Dottore, I have long since learned to serve the Germans the fake coffee. Surely, the rest of the village has noticed my café is only frequented by Italian officers; those who have more discerning palates. But you said you were hoping I would say that it is through an Italian officer I come by coffee, why?"

Dottore Roselli replaces his glasses and studies her without judgement. "Because, Mira, I need you to procure some medicines from the Tenente; that is, if you think he can be trusted not to ask who or what they are required for."

The doctor's proposal and subsequent query hang in the silence.

"How bad are the Englishman's wounds?" she asks.

"Well, he has, as no doubt you have already seen, serious burns to his arms and legs and his face. These burns have already dehydrated him to a point where he desperately needs fluid. An oral solution you can make up with some lemon juice and salt; only a very weak solution, mind, and only in small quantities. Here," he hands her a section of thin rubber tube, "take this, it is a tourniquet tube; it will be easier for him to drink through this. As far as treating this man is concerned, I want you to find some aloe leaves; the gel inside can be applied directly onto his burns and then covered with a loose bandage. May I assume you know the difference between the aloe and the agave?"

"Yes, of course."

"Good, because the agave is not at all suitable. And if you have garlic, mash a clove and mix it with a little water to form a paste; you can use it to clean his wounds, if they begin to weep."

The doctor leans forward, rests his elbows on the table and steeples his fingers. He waits, studying Mira more closely, waiting while he makes sure she is concentrating. "What you need to get hold of for me, what is no longer available to me, are drugs and gauze bandages. The army doctors may have the drugs, oral or intravenous, it doesn't matter which. And, a sulfa drug would be better than penicillin; they are more effective against the bacteria which causes infection. But, Mira, please don't refuse the penicillin if it is the only one of the two available; our patient will in all probability contract some infections and the drugs will be necessary for him to overcome them. Gauze bandages: you will need to dress the wounds and, while I think of it, you will need to keep his eyes covered and moist with the aloe for it is his sight that is the greatest concern."

"Will the people I ask for these drugs not work out that they are required for something more than the infection one gets from treading on the spine of a sea–urchin?" Mira asks.

The aroma of freshly–percolated coffee infuses the air, swiftly followed by Francesca placing on the table three tiny cups only partway filled with steaming black liquid.

Dottore Roselli chuckles, a long, slow rasping chuckle filled with a hapless irony. "If they don't suspect it when you ask for these drugs, they will surely know it when you ask them for morphine; and without it, I would be surprised if your Englishman lives through the pain he is soon to endure."

Chapter 6

"Halt and identify yourself," the sentry shouts.

Mira ignores him and without faltering in her stride walks on confidently until she reaches the boom barrier.

"I said, halt and identify yourself." The sentry, his scrawny frame resembling a coat–hanger overladen with a jumble of drab, tatty clothes, thrusts his rifle menacingly at her.

"Good morning, Comune Simone. As you can see, I have to stop unless you raise the bar. And as for identifying myself? From your many visits to my café you know perfectly well who I am."

"Of course, I do, Signorina Ruggeri. But—"

"Comune Simone, perhaps it is you who needs help with your powers of identification, for whilst I appreciate your compliment, your eyes cannot deceive you to the extent that you believe me young enough to be addressed as Signorina."

"Yes, of course, Signora Ruggeri, it was only that—"

"And I am sure you must also know that my husband was once, as you are now, a soldier of the Italian army, so Signora Alberti will do, thank you."

"Yes, of course, Signora Alberti. I apologise for my initial rudeness, but Il Duce has warned us to be wary of people belonging to something called a Fifth Column and it is therefore our duty to be vigilant."

"A Fifth Column? Whatever is that?"

"I do not know, Signora Alberti."

"Then how are you supposed to identify them?"

"I don't know that, either."

"Ah well, if Il Duce has warned you to be so, Comune Simone, then I suppose you should be... vigilant." Her dominance over the old private established, Mira surveys the battery beyond the coils of shiny barbed wire.

Poking up from the dunes of the promontory which define the Sicilian neck of the Strait, long and slender gun barrels point skywards from behind neat rows of sandbags. And from the stout stone ramparts of the substantial if quaint Roman fort, heavier howitzers nudge their snub–noses up, like hog's snouts sniffing for swill.

Yet for all its lethal potential, the Capo Peloro battery is a picture of relaxation and calm, as most of the men, some semi–naked, lounge cross–legged, chatting and smoking and laughing as they deal playing cards. From the few olive trees hang their once light–grey uniforms and littered here and there lie their Nicholas helmets, relics of the First Great War. They seem casually content and carefree, as though they have woken from their slumbers to find themselves quartered in a retirement home for gunners.

"I must compliment you on your artillery, Comune Simone. You certainly boast an impressive array of canoni." Mira's eyes sparkle with mischief.

The grey–haired, grizzle–faced soldier stiffens to attention, the way he might when addressed by an officer. "Yes, Signora, Il Duce has provided us with the best howitzers and the best available anti–aircraft guns: three complete batteries, eighteen in all. Nothing will pass through the Strait unless we permit it," he adds, proudly.

"And were your guns the ones making all that terrible noise during the night?"

Her question confuses him and he shifts his weight from one foot to the other, as though he has forgotten to put on his regulation boots and the sand is sizzling his soles. Eventually realising that she is being facetious, he straightens. "The enemies of fascism must be made to pay the price of their aggression, Signora."

"Yes, Comune Simone, they must, mustn't they." Mira is careful not to overplay her humouring him to the extent that he recognises it. "Now, perhaps you would be kind enough to ask Tenente de la Grascia if he can spare me a minute of his time?"

He looks about, nervously. "Yes, of course I would, Signora. The only problem is that usually there would be two of us out here, manning the barrier, but because of the men who have been sent south to Ponte Grande, we are short of staff and I cannot leave my post to go and alert him to your presence."

A small handful of seemingly adolescent soldiers lark about not too far from the sentry post; they notice Mira and mosey over towards the barbed wire, curious like cattle. However, the majority of the men are of later middle–age, owing to the fact that so many of their sons have already surrendered their lives in the sands of North Africa or the snowy wastes of the Eastern Front, and nowadays there is no one else left to protect their homeland. One of the younger conscripts wolf–whistles, another shouts an invitation and a few simply stand and stare as though they have not yet enjoyed the company of a woman.

Mira smiles and waves to them. "No matter, Comune Simone, I am sure Tenente de la Grascia will want to know why his men have ceased maintaining their cannons, if indeed that is what they were supposed to be doing. I'll wait."

Apart from the stone fort and the rudimentary sentry post, the Capo Peloro battery boasts an austerity completely at odds with its relaxed atmosphere.

"Officer to the gate," shouts Comune Simone, in a stern, authoritarian tone.

A door in the wall is pulled inwards and the Tenente appears. He pauses, seats his cap at an angle a degree or two off–centre and strides with a businesslike gait towards them.

"Tenente," Comune Simone announces, coming to attention, "a visitor is asking for you."

If the other artillerymen appear by their casual attire to be on holiday, Tenente de la Grascia seems more likely to have come from a forum of tailors. "Thank you, Comune Simone." He salutes and the sentry, returning the salute, stands at ease.

Turning to Mira, he smiles, inclines his head and raises an eyebrow. "Ah, Signora Alberti, how is it that on such a beautiful summer's morning the Capo Peloro battery is graced with your very agreeable presence?" Not content with his theatrics, he now raises the eyebrow again and inclines his head gently towards Comune Simone in such a way that the sentry cannot see his half–serious expression.

Mira catches on, her lips curling in amusement. Stepping to one side so the sentry can both see her and hear her reply, she adopts a less agreeable attitude. "Tenente de la Grascia, I am sorry, but I have come here to register a complaint regarding the behaviour of some of your men."

"A complaint?" The Tenente turns, bridling his mouth and frowning in concern at the sentry, as if to convey that this issue is most unfortunate and that, probably, he is about to have to eat a plate of unpalatably humble pie. He nods towards the boom separating him from Mira and the sentry hurries over to raise it.

"Thank you, Comune Simone." He lowers his voice. "I believe matters of this nature are best dealt with informally, so perhaps Signora Alberti and I will walk and discuss whatever transgression my men, or those from another unit, have committed. If," he turns back to Mira and bows, "that is acceptable to Signora Alberti?"

"Yes, Tenente, I suppose it would be better for the men involved if we kept this unofficial." Mira, though, struggles to keep a straight face, so she turns about and, swinging her feet ponderously, strolls off down the dusty lane.

De la Grascia catches her up and falls in step beside her.

The day is fine, if a little warm for a man in full uniform, and the village peaceful. High above them, an aircraft drones a mournful dirge and rock sparrows flit among the cypress trees, perching only to watch the couple who, on another day in another life, might be no more remarkable than two lovers engaging in an early morning tryst.

"Please excuse the charade, Mira," he says.

"No matter, Aldo."

He beams in acceptance of her familiarity. "Perhaps I should explain. Please, let me, I should like to. It might help you to understand that whilst command is a burden I shoulder out of choice, the politics of giving orders are sometimes complicated."

"Yes, please, I should like to understand why we have to put on an act in front of your men."

"My man: not so much my men. I will explain. Comune Simone," he begins, very obviously taking his time to choose his words carefully, "is unlike most of the other men and I try for his own good to keep him separate from them. You see, Mira, most of the men under my command are from Sicily, some even living nearby, and Simone, unfortunately, is the fly in their ointment. He claims to be a Sansepolcrista, an old and ardent fascist from when the movement was first formed in the Piazza San Sepolcro in Milan more than twenty years ago.

"As a result, I have no doubt that when the time comes for each of us to choose his road forward, Comune Simone will not only give up his life for his cause, but that he will also willingly help others do the same. For this reason, he cannot be trusted and for this reason, I have to keep him… quarantined, if you like, both for his sake and ours."

"And when is that time coming, Aldo?"

"Soon, I think: a month, perhaps sooner. Augusta is now in British hands and the Germans are saying Admiral Leonardi surrendered the port too easily: they are saying that some of our officers deserted their men and that the 206th Coastal Division surrendered without a fight. Right now, the Americans are close to Agrigento and their General Patton will be in Palermo within a few days. The Germans, they are far more stubborn than our troops, they will not give up without a real fight. Mark my words, Mira, all these troops they are bringing over, pah! They will soon enough be sending them back. Who wants Sicily apart from you Siciliani, eh?"

"And you, Aldo," she says, halting and turning, looking deep into his eyes, inquiringly, sympathetically, and yet vaguely insulted by his casual indifference to her homeland, "what will you do when the time comes? Will you fight to the last? Do you believe in the cause with the same selfless regard as that of your narrow-eyed Sansepolcrista?"

Tenente de la Grascia returns her look with one equally inquiring and yet profoundly resigned, as much as to say he is unsure of how else he should or can act. "Mira, though we would all like to believe otherwise, our lives are never simple. I am only one of many who on hearing the seductive tunes played by Mussolini's band all too readily jumped aboard his wagon. He promised us glory and has delivered us nothing but misery. I sometimes wonder if I am naïve."

"You don't strike me as naïve, Aldo." Mira lays her hand on his arm and squeezes it gently, fondly. "And I believe there is more to you than merely your desire to atone for the sins of your youth. No, there is something else that bothers you, isn't there? Something far more important, something more fundamental that has upset your belief in the cause, as you put it."

He stands back from her, allowing her hand to fall from his arm. "Yes, Mira, there is and it is this: I cannot forgive myself for the ills ordinary fools like me have bestowed upon this fine

245

country. When Mussolini passed the Leggi Razziali, the racial laws that disfavour our Jewish citizens, I should have seen through the propaganda. In a way, I did, for it was at that time that I began to doubt my allegiance and I began to question the sacrifices ordinary people were making in the name of our country." At this, de la Grascia pauses, no doubt remembering. "And even now," he sighs, "while the Germans are sending their troops to fight here, across the Strait, our troops in Savoy and Provence are being ordered to arrest Jews and send them east in cattle trucks. I have heard they are being deported to work camps, or perhaps even worse, death camps. Tell me, how is it possible for intelligent men to behave in this manner?"

Mira tries and fails to suppress her look of horror. "I can't believe anyone would do such a thing, Aldo. Surely, that is just idle gossip thought up by those who want us to hate the Germans."

"I hope it is. Or rather, perhaps I wish it to be so. It is difficult to tell the propaganda from the truth these days; it has been so for far too long. All I do know is, what is important to me now is the welfare of my men. That is all I have left."

The sombre couple stroll on down the line of barbed wire until they have reached the sandy beach at the eastern end of the promontory. Before them, across the rippling waters of the Strait, stand the verdant heights of Aspromonte, a sprawl of white clouds cloaking its many peaks. To their left, shimmering in the heat haze, stands the monolith of Scylla buttressing out into the Tyrrhenian, the grey battlements of Ruffo Castle stark against the terracotta roofs of the little houses below. And to their right, lie the villages of Cannitello and Pezzo, and beyond them Villa San Giovanni, from which a dozen or more ominous palls of dark smoke rise and then disperse in the breeze.

"Oh, this view," Mira whispers. "Sometimes when I look out across the Strait, I find it hard to believe people can hate so much that they would kill one another."

As a warship carves a white bow wave through the azure sea of their tranquillity, they linger and watch and wish life was other than it is.

She takes his forearm and leaning her head down against his shoulder asks, "Aldo?"

"Yes, my beautiful Mira. What can a simple man from Bologna do for the woman he would very much like to love?"

"Oh, Aldo," she moans, "how can you think of love at a time like this."

"Oh, Mira, how can you not?"

CHAPTER 7

"How do you know how much to give him?" her father asks.

"I am assuming," Mira replies, as she holds the small glass phial up to the light, "that each of these six bottles is to be used one at a time; the larger first and the smaller after."

"Assuming?" he repeats, more than a little concerned. "If you have to assume, shouldn't we ask Dottore Roselli to assume? At least he assumes with authority."

"Thank you, mama," Mira says, as Francesca finds a place for a bowl of steaming water on the table beside her.

The green canvas kit bag on the floor shows on the flap a white circle enclosing a red cross, and beige wax–paper packs labelled green and marked R ESERCITO ITALIANO are piled on the table. Bandage dressings, triangular bandages and eye dressings lie jumbled beside a leather roll of surgical tools, inside of which fine suture scissors, needle hooks and tweezers nestle in individual sleeves. Safety pins, eye solution, tins of foot powder, iodine swabs and a tube of sulfadiazine ointment for burns add to the clutter. And as if the last was more than Mira could have hoped for, Tenente de la Grascia's crowning glory comes in the form of two tins, both not much bigger than cigarette packets and both, Mira notes, marked in German. When she opens them, she finds that the larger of the two contains a selection of bevelled glass tubes with interchangeable hypodermic needles, and the smaller contains six ampoules of morphine, one of which she is examining in the light from the window.

"We need to ensure all this medical equipment is sterile," Mira says to her mother.

"Sterilise? All this?" Enzo says.

"Yes, papà. Do you drink from a dirty cup?" She raises her eyebrows at him. "Before I can give him the morphine, we must make sure the syringes are clean. I don't want to inject him with something harmful; he is weak enough as it is."

"But we don't have the means," he argues.

"Yes, papà, we do. These syringes look as though they have been used before and they cannot be used until they are sterile. Mama, the old cast—iron pressure cooker, please, make sure it is clean, pour in a few cups of water and set it on the stove. Place the colander inside and a metal dish on top, this way we can sterilise the syringes. The needles I can sterilise with a flame."

"Are you certain this will be enough?" Enzo asks, once Francesca has left.

"You forget, papà, when Carlo was brought back from Africa, I stayed with him in the Margherita hospital for the last four weeks. I fed him when he was conscious and I tended to him when he was not. In four weeks, with little else to do other than sit around and cry and wait for him to die, I learnt a great deal from the doctors and nurses."

"Obviously not enough to save that fool of a husband, eh?"

Mira rounds on her father and spits venom, "Papà, I know too well that Carlo was not your flavour of man, but that is not the kind of remark I expect from you. You! A man of such compassion that you allow a complete stranger into our house. A complete stranger, not only a man who may die of his wounds, but also a man who, if he is found by the Germans, will no doubt be responsible for all of us being stood against a wall and shot."

Enzo withers beneath her tirade. "Yes," he mumbles, "I am sorry, I–"

The patient stirs, his arms and legs twitch. "Where am I?" he asks in English, raising his hands to the bandages covering his eyes.

Mira leans over him and taking hold of his hands, pulls them away and places them down either side of his torso. "Ssh, rest, Signor Lock. Calm yourself. Try not to talk too much. I know you can understand Sicilian, so if you need to talk, try to speak our language." She waits, looking for some small acknowledgement that he has understood. When there is none, she carries on, "Now, as to where you are: you don't remember?"

"No, not much, I..." he replies, this time in Sicilian. "I think I must have been dreaming." He struggles against the bed, first trying to lift his shoulders, then his legs. "Where am I? How did I get here?"

Mira ignores his questions and asks in a tone pitched perfect in calm and reassurance, "And what have you been dreaming?"

Her father looks at his daughter as though he is sure she has lost her mind.

"Dreaming? Oh, I was dreaming of when I was a boy. I was sailing on a lake. It was night and the breeze was so warm and the stars were shining so brightly." In falling some way back into his dream, he ceases his struggle and very gradually his limbs fall limp.

"That was a good dream," Mira murmurs, shooting her father a look that tells him he is ridiculous for having thought she may have lost her mind.

"Yes, it was until something terrible rose out of the water. Whatever it was brought a loud noise and a white light and... Am I awake now or am I still dreaming?"

"No, Signor Lock, you are awake; for if you are dreaming, then so are we. I think what you were dreaming of was how you came to be here."

He grimaces and tries again to raise his hands.

Once more, Mira presses them back down. "You were on an English boat; you had a battle with a submarine; your boat and the submarine blew up. Fortunately for you, you were rescued from the water by one of the Italian sailors from the submarine. He brought you here, to our village of Ganzirri on the shore of the Strait, to our house. This is where you are and that is how you come to be here."

"Yes, now I remember, you are Mira. Did anyone else get ashore, Mira?"

"As far as we know, no. But that does not mean to say there are no other survivors. Sottocapo Falanga, who brought you here, said that a Motoscafo was nearby; it is possible they may have rescued others."

Francesca comes back in and Mira hands her a needle and a syringe tube. "For fifteen minutes, please, mama; then let them dry and bring them back."

Turning back to her patient, she says, "Now, I want you to drink some of this fluid, it is to stop you from becoming too dehydrated. We have no intravenous fluid, so you will need to drink as much as you can. Do not concern yourself with the bedclothes; they are the least of our concern."

He draws on the tube, gags, coughs and splutters, and eventually manages to swallow. "Thank you," he whispers and lies silently for a few seconds. Then he moves his head slowly from side to side, wrestling with some thought that bothers him. "I don't understand, why haven't you given me up?"

Mira glances at her father, her look designed to prompt him to respond.

"Because you are wounded," Enzo replies, "and because you have come to us from the sea."

"But I am British. I am your enemy."

"Signor Lock, no man who comes to us from the sea is our enemy unless he means us harm. We are fishermen and our duty is

251

to those of the sea; that far outweighs our duty to whatever flag he bears. Besides that, we know what it means to..."

Nicholas Lock lifts his head from his pillow and, though he cannot even see the tears forming at the corners of Enzo's eyes, he perceives the anxiety in his voice. "What it means to... what?"

"To be desperate to survive, Signor Lock." Enzo blinks and clears his throat. "Now, I leave you in my daughter's capable hands. We will talk later, when you have more strength. For the moment, rest. As I said before, you are safe now, so rest."

"Thank you, Enzo. That is your name, isn't it, Enzo? I feel sure it is; you must have told me."

"Yes, Signor Nicholas, my name is Enzo, Enzo Ruggeri. We will talk later."

Before he leaves the room, her father squeezes his daughter's arm affectionately; his expression tinged with melancholy, if not exactly apology.

Mira smiles, wanting him to know that she does not hold his unnecessary and ill–judged remarks against him.

So, her father did not approve of her husband. So what? And why does that matter since her husband is no longer around to upset his father–in–law? She offers the tube up to her patient's mouth. "Come drink, a little at a time. Not too much, just a little."

When he wearies from lifting his head, Nicholas rests back down, but after a few minutes, he tenses and shudders as if in pain. "Mira?"

"Yes, Signor Lock."

"Mira, I think I am lying naked in your bed, is that right?"

"Yes."

"In that case, you had better call me by my given name. I think you must already know me better than most others I have met. Please call me Nicholas."

"Of course, Nicholas."

His body is once more and very suddenly wracked by a spasm of pain. "Mira, am I blind? Is that why I cannot see?"

"No, Nicholas. You cannot see because the skin around your eyes is burned and Dottore Roselli wants to keep them covered for the moment."

"Well, I'm grateful to Dottore Roselli for his time. Is he here?"

"No, not now. He will come by later."

"I'm so sorry to put you out, Mira."

"No matter, Nicholas. How do you feel, right now, I mean how do your burns feel?"

"They sting a good deal and my face is on fire, yet I am cold. How can that be?"

"It is because of your burns. You are cold because your body has surrendered much of its heat. When I have given you some morphine and dressed your burns with fresh aloe, I will cover you with a blanket and you will be warm again."

"Morphine?" he murmurs, his voice tiring. "Where did you get morphine from?"

Francesca returns, and with the aid of a towel, she carries a hot metal plate, on which a glass syringe tube, a plunger and needle lie. She sets the dish down on the table, frowns in sympathy and leaves.

"From a friend, Nicholas. From a friend. Now, I am going to give you an injection which will help you dream some more. Try to dream nice dreams." She picks up the syringe tube, screws the needle on top and lays it back on the dish in such a way that the needle rests free of contact. Next, she breaks the bulbous nipple off the top of a larger ampoule and picking up the syringe, draws some of the clear liquid into the glass tube. "Rest now, Nicholas. Banish dark thoughts and free your mind to wander." Holding the syringe up to the light, Mira presses the plunger and notes the fine jet of morphine which squirts silvery from the needle. "Nicholas, walk in the afternoon sun on the slopes of Aspromonte. Look down across the Strait at our beautiful village. Feel safe and well; I will sit by you to make sure you do not stray too far."

Chapter 8

"What time is it?" Nicholas asks, unsure as to whether he is either awake or dreaming or whether, if he is awake, anyone is nearby to hear him.

"Please?" Mira replies, in a voice soggy with sleep.

"I'm sorry; forgot where I was and spoke in English. What time is it?" he asks again, though this time in Sicilian.

"I don't know. Perhaps a half hour before dawn."

"Was there an air raid during the night? I don't know if I heard one; I think I did."

"Yes. Reggio and San Giovanni again. Now, though, it is too close to first light. Your air force is nothing if not predictable. Breakfast and dinner: in between, but never during. How do you feel?"

"Oh, not too bad." He hesitates. "Mira, you are sleeping on the floor? Because of me?" The air in the room is sultry, an oppressive saturated cloak that clings to his skin. A bead of sweat dribbles from his neck.

"There is only one bed in my room," she states. "Or should I say, there is only space for one bed." Mira chuckles, "We are fortunate. There are four rooms in my parent's house: one for my parents to sleep, one for me, a washroom of sorts and the room in which we cook and live. Most people only have two rooms: one for cooking and living, and one for everything else. Even though we have only the water papà collects from the village pump, he wanted a private room for washing, so he built one. A necessity, he calls it. A luxury, my mother called it until she got used to using it. Ha! That didn't take long now, eh?"

"I'm sorry you have to sleep on the floor on my account."

Her hand is at his chin and he senses the rubber tube against his lips. He sucks and draws in the sweet, citrus–flavoured water.

Mira withdraws the tube and waits for him to swallow, before offering the tube up once more. "Don't concern yourself, Nicholas. I am quite used to it. Until… Well, until recently, I shared this bed with my… my sister and before that with my brother, too. Nowadays, I get to sleep on the floor more often than I would like, because when Maria comes to stay, she sometimes wriggles in her sleep and then I am more comfortable on the floor."

"Maria?"

"The grand–daughter of a friend of papà's. Maria and Beppe: they are like my brother and sister, though Beppe no longer comes to stay."

"What about your brother and sister? Where are they now?"

He feels her shift, perhaps uneasily, on the bed. "I don't mean to pry, Mira, I–"

"You are not prying, Nicholas," she soothes. "You cannot see, so it is only natural that you are inquisitive. The dark makes us question, don't you think? It is what I do when I don't sleep: I question." Mira sighs. "Knowledge is, or so my father has always maintained, enlightening and without light we would all be living in the dark. That is why he taught us to read and to think for ourselves. That is why we have not heard from my brother for many months; he is either dead, in a hospital or in a prison camp in Tunis."

"I'm sorry, Mira."

"Don't be; it is not your fault. My brother joined the army for probably the same reasons you joined the navy: because you had no choice, because it was your duty and because you wanted to."

"And your sister?"

"My sister is younger, she is married to another of our fishermen, they have only been together three years and already have three children. They live in Mortelle, not far away on the north coast. But we are different, my sister and me; she does not like to think for herself; she does not question everything the way I do."

Detecting a note of regret and longing in her wish, he searches for some comfort he might supply this woman he cannot see and yet who sleeps beside him on the stone—hard floor. "There's nothing wrong in wanting to know why life is the way it is," he says.

"No, Nicholas, you are so very right. If we do not ask, how can we make things better? The only trouble is that I sometimes think my father wishes he had not taught me to question so much; for if he had not, perhaps we wouldn't fight each other so."

"You fight? Each other? Why?"

Mira chuckles or rather, perhaps because the darkness affords her some licence, she snorts a little indelicately, as though she has led him like an ass round the very same perfect circle she leads herself every night. "That is exactly the question, isn't it, Nicholas. Why do I fight with my father, especially when he is the man who I respect and place above all others? And why do men fight, when they can more easily sit in my café, sip coffee and argue until the hunters return with the swordfish? They would certainly achieve just as much that way as they do by running around killing each other, and at least they would have the hope of some fish as a reward for their patience and respect."

In trying to dispel the numbness in his legs, Nicholas tenses his buttocks and eases his weight from one side to the other.

He feels the coolness of her hands at his waist.

"I must change your sheets. If you can sit up for a moment, that would help me."

He does so, too quickly. Pain flashes through his arms and across his chest, and he moans.

"Slowly, Nicholas. Slowly." She wraps her arm round his shoulders and holds him upright as she slips the sheet away from beneath his raised torso. "You need to be careful, or you will only make more work for Dottore Roselli when he comes this morning."

"Sorry, I—"

"And you will have to learn to stop saying sorry," she interrupts in a calm, matter-of-fact tone. "Clearly, you are a man of some independence and therefore not used to being cared for. Tell me, did your mother make you do your own washing like my mother makes me do mine?"

"Probably. But then, I have no idea how old you are. I have no idea if you are old enough or too old to do your own washing." He eases himself back down and hurries on with his talking. "I would guess from your voice that you are young, but no longer a child." He makes to smile and then stops when the taut skin of his cheeks stretches and stings.

"Yes, that serves you right for trying to be impolite, Nicholas. A woman's age is not relevant to how others should see her. Her years are only of concern to her."

As though to make up for his lapse of manners, he says, "If it makes you feel any better, I am twenty-seven."

"Then I am older than you. Please, lift up your hips so that I can remove the sheet."

"Sorry, Mira, I—"

"Enough, Nicholas. Enough," she whispers, firmly.

"It's a strange feeling," he says. "With my face as it is, I've no idea whether I'm blushing."

"Blushing? Why would you blush?"

"Because, Mira, the last person to change my bedclothes at night was my mother and the last person to see me naked was my mother. I'm almost relieved I can't see you; that would only make the situation far more difficult to live down."

Ignoring his anxiety and his embarrassment, she asks, "Nicholas, please lift up your hips once more."

He does so, and when he relaxes the new sheet is cool and dry.

"And now your shoulders, slowly, eh." Mira struggles a little against his weight. "Good. There. Now perhaps you will be quiet. I can't make up my mind whether you talk more when you are sleeping than you do when you are awake. You are puddaciari. Anyone would think you were from Lipari."

"Puddaciari? What's that?"

"It means talkative. Too talkative for your own good. In Lipari they have little else to occupy their time other than talk."

"Mira, what language was I speaking in my dreams?"

"English, mostly. A little Sicilian now and then. Sometimes a mixture."

"What was I saying?"

"Much that I did not understand. You called out for someone. A man, I think. Harry, it sounded like. Then a number. It sounded like four. You wanted this man or men."

She sits on his bed and wipes his fevered brow with a damp cloth; the silence of the night broken only by the clicking and whirring of the rotors of his mind turning, as he tries to decipher the code to whatever it is that she thinks she has heard.

"Oh, yes, of course," he says, pleased with himself, "the Harry Four."

"What are they, the Harry... Four? Are they people?"

"No," he chuckles, "they are flags. Signal flags in fact. They inform other boats our engines have stopped. It was part of my dream. From the boat I came down on. Whenever we changed

259

over fuel tanks, the engines used to cut out." He pauses, thinking. "Curiously appropriate when you consider the state I'm in. You know, all at sea, blind as a bat and for the moment dependent on you."

Though he cannot see her, Nicholas is sure she is smiling. He can sense her smile in the same way he senses the rubber tube when she lifts it to his lips. Somehow, it is there and he knows it is so. "What else did I say?"

"You spoke of your mother. You spoke of her the way I speak of my father."

"And?"

"And nothing. We will speak of it later, when what you say is not decided by the morphine."

"Yes, Mira, let's talk later. I'm awfully cold and tired." He lifts his hands.

Gently, she presses them back down, just as she has so many times already. "Here, I will give you one of my blankets. Now, go to sleep, Nicholas. You save your strength for Dottore Roselli and I will save mine for the café... That's if some kind soul has left me some coffee to serve my customers."

Chapter 9

Young Maria is sitting on the low wall opposite the church in the Piazza Chiesa, kicking her feet. "Ciao, Mira," she calls, smiling, waving and brandishing a paper bag.

"Ciao, Maria." Mira waves back and quickens her step just enough to let the girl know that she is really, very pleased to see her. The light innocence of her youthful enthusiasm buoys Mira's spirits and quietly she thanks God that hope has not yet been stamped flat beneath the boots of war.

"Your secret benefactor has left you a gift," Maria giggles. "The contents are getting smaller though."

Mira takes the bag, glances inside and frowns. "So they are. No real coffee, and only a little corn flour and sugar. Well," she sighs, "today we'll just have to be magicians, eh? Come on, at least we have some oranges for juice, let's open up." She grasps the girl's hand and leads her across the square towards her café.

As they walk, Maria studies her bare feet and frowns in imitation of the woman who, to all intents and purposes, is the older sister she doesn't have. Of course she would like to, but some things are never as one would like, are they? She raises her face and glances up, pulling on Mira's hand as if her arm is a bell-pull and Maria an impatient duchess summoning a servant. "Does that mean the Tenente will come this morning? I mean, whenever he

261

leaves you a packet in the morning, he always shows up later, isn't that right?"

"That is right, my darling; that does seem to be his way." Mira stops, nods her head briefly in the direction of the church and pauses to gaze across the Strait. The waters are in shadow.

"Will it rain?" Maria asks, guessing that must be why Mira has paused.

Normally, she would take five minutes, step inside the already open doors of the Chiesa Parrocchiale Madonna della Lettera and kneel to say a few prayers for her brother. Today, though, is Saturday, she will have time for prayers tomorrow and she cannot help but think of the waters and how they can appear so calm one moment and yet so restless the next. "No, no rain today. Tears maybe, but no rain."

In the front door to the café is jammed a leaflet.

Mira pulls it free and examines it.

"What does it say?" Maria asks.

"It says that we can choose either to die for Mussolini and Hitler, or live for Italy and for civilisation."

"What does that mean?"

At first, Mira doesn't answer, she simply scrunches the leaflet into a ball, takes a long iron key from her pocket and unlocks the door. As she stands back to let Maria walk in front of her, though, she reconsiders her silence. "It means, we don't have a choice. It means we must cherish the life we have been given."

Later, the sun breaks through the cloud and the day casts off its grey cloak.

To the corn flour she takes from the bag, Mira adds some of the wheat flour, sugar and raisins she has left. She lights the oven and bakes some small cakes which, she hopes, will excuse the absence of brioche.

Her first customers, though, turn out not to be as she and Maria have been hoping.

An open German staff car sweeps into the square and close on its heels follows a truck, in the back of which sit a dozen soldiers who, even in the face of the day's heat, wear their coal–scuttle helmets and tunic buttons fastened.

The car stops by the low wall that Maria had been sitting on while she'd waited for Mira to appear. The driver leaps out and trots around the front to open the door for the officer who, before getting out, waits for a moment while he pats the dust from his uniform. The driver stands patiently at attention.

When the officer does eventually get out, he is pursued by the two officers seated in the back. The senior of the three struts up and down, surveying first the Strait, the far shore and the water's edge immediately below the wall, and second the campanile of the church and the breadth and length and solidity of the stone surface of the piazza. Once he has satisfied himself with whatever he'd needed to see, he strolls across the square towards the church and pauses briefly, hands on hips, to inspect the statues looking down from their pedestals. Then he walks over to the café, removes his cap and sits down at the only table. His officers follow and the troops alight from the lorry to mill about, talking amongst themselves.

New customers in unusual uniforms prick Maria's curiosity and before Mira can hold her back, she rushes out to serve them.

Mira, her blood running cool, watches as the senior officer leans across the table to pinch Maria's cheek and ruffle her hair. The officers smile and laugh as the young waitress shakes her head and looks pleadingly towards Mira.

She grabs a tray and joins Maria, who quickly hides behind her.

One of the junior officers asks for früstück, which she takes to mean the menu.

Slowly and concisely Mira recites the options.

The junior officer frowns, hunches his shoulders and then laughs. "Only coffee, orange juice and cake?" he says in some language approaching Italian.

"Yes," she replies, "coffee, orange juice and cake." Though if the officer only knows what she is thinking, he will probably shoot her out of hand.

He glances at the others, who nod back. "Please, bring it," he says.

Maria looks up, bemused.

Mira smiles in gratitude, and although she recognises only the positive if reluctant tone of his acceptance, she knows full well he won't understand her response. "As if I would have anything else on offer in this stupid, bloody war of yours." Turning back into the café, she drags Maria with her.

"What did that man say?" Maria asks, as Mira places the kettle on the stove and adds a dribble of the fake coffee concentrate.

"He said he would like the heaviest of the cakes we baked this morning. So be a good girl and see what you can find."

"The heaviest?" Maria asks. "Why?"

"Because he has the hardest of heads, so he would like the hardest of cakes. Now be a good girl and select only the cakes you would usually throw to the fish, eh?" She winks.

Maria's eyes light up like altar candles and she clamps her hand over her mouth to suppress her giggles.

While the officers sweat in the sun, wince at the acidity of the orange juice, stare unconvinced into their cups and gnaw at the rock–hard cakes, the soldiers relax in the shade of the church wall and sip from their water bottles.

In the café, the two girls, or rather the young Maria and the adult Mira, are remembering the joy of a child who gets away with playing a trick on a disliked uncle and they do their best to keep from bursting into fits of hysterical laughter.

However, their amusement is short–lived as a few minutes later an old Alfa Romeo flatbed truck careers inelegantly into the piazza from the northern end and grinds to a halt in front of the café. As it does so, the four men standing in the rear are launched against the back of the cab, in which is seated Lieutenant de la Grascia. Comune Simone, at the wheel, notices the German officers seated at the table and he jumps smartly out, runs around the side of the truck, hauls open the door and stands to attention, his spine as vertical as the façade of the church. The four men in the back cease checking that they are undamaged and on noticing Simone's performance, they look at each other and snigger.

The Lieutenant steps down from his perch, adjusts his jacket so that it sits more squarely on his shoulders and bows in respect to the German officers who appear to be seated at what would, under more normal circumstances, be his table.

Comune Simone slams the door, runs back to the driver's side and, climbing back into the cab, starts the engine, grinds the gears and reverses the truck so that it no longer blocks the view of the Strait.

The junior officer stands and salutes. "Heil Hitler!"

"Yes, of course," de la Grascia responds. He hesitates just long enough to let the man know he is considering whether or not he should salute, before slowly extending his right arm and raising his palm in a more casual version of his own Roman acknowledgement.

As this is all happening and in order to save the Lieutenant's face, Mira rushes out with a second table and places it as quickly and quietly as she knows how to the left of the door to the café. Maria, by comparison, struggles out clumsily and noisily with two chairs.

"Good morning, Signora Alberti." De la Grascia grins to let her know she must not mistake the formal nature of his greeting for anything other than what it is, namely a display of good manners in front of other officers and his men.

"Good morning, Tenente."

"If you are not too busy, may we..."

With a theatrical wave of her hand, Mira offers him the newly positioned table. "Please, whichever table you like."

He turns and nods to his men.

Seemingly with one bound, they leap out of the back of the truck and join him at the table, whereupon they proceed to chatter and gesticulate as though they are discussing the merits of their favourite opera.

The German officers are clearly irked that they now have to share the café with non–commissioned officers and other ranks, and they sniff, look skyward and shun the cakes that moments before they had been trying so hard to eat.

Comune Simone strides over and, because there is no seat for him, he stands behind his Tenente, an attentive butler.

Maria appears, holding unsteadily in her slender arms a tray on which stands a pot of coffee, some cups and a plate of softer cakes.

"Thank you..." de la Grascia begins.

"Maria," she replies, grinning mischievously, plonking the tray on the table.

The Tenente catches the pot before it falls over. "Thank you, Maria." He pours the coffee and pushes the cakes towards his companions, who help themselves and munch away with gusto, if not comparative ease.

The young girl waits to see their reaction to the fake coffee.

One of the men shrinks at the taste and looks over at his Tenente who, in turn, smiles and takes a generous sip from his cup.

De la Grascia winks, grins and nods in the direction of the standing Comune.

His sergeant catches on, passes back a cup and a cake, drains his own cup and sighs in appreciation.

The German officers grumble amongst themselves.

Comune Simone sips, grimaces, tries a cake, chews, blanches, swallows and fingers at a loose tooth.

Mira glides to their table. "How is your coffee? Are my cakes to your liking, Tenente de la Grascia?"

He smiles, playing along. "Thank you, Signora Alberti, my coffee is delicious and your cakes the perfect accompaniment."

One of the Germans purses his lips and makes an all too obviously sour remark to his fellow officers. They nod their approval and, ignoring what remains uneaten of their breakfast, rise as one and make to leave.

As they do, the three men suddenly halt, come to attention, turnabout, click their heels and salute, their arms straight up and angled, perfect in both timing and elevation. "Heil Hitler!"

Tenente de la Grascia returns his cup to the table, hauls himself slowly upright and salutes in return, though without any particular enthusiasm.

The senior officer swears and though his words are unintelligible to the Italian artillerymen still seated, the message is unmistakable, so as one they stand, ready to respond to the insult.

The Panzergrenadiers watching, cut short their conversations and one by one they turn to take an interest.

Tenente de la Grascia waves his companions back down and smiles, immediately disarming the officers as though by magic he has relieved them of their weapons.

He speaks to them in their native language, his manner easy, his words as soft and sympathetic as his basic knowledge of the German language will permit him. Whatever it is that he says is clearly meant to mollify them and it does so until his final sentence, the tone of which grows harsh and unforgiving.

The two junior officers wither beneath his assault, their faces reddening with the increasing blood pressure their apoplexy provokes.

Mira witnesses the charade play out, admiring de la Grascia for the manner in which he stands up to the German officers and at the same time being uncomfortably aware of the malice transmitted in the expressions of the soldiers, who toy nervously with their rifles. When she looks back at the artillerymen still sitting, as de la Grascia has ordered them, Mira notices the look on Comune Simone's face. It is one of surprised horror, as though he can neither comprehend nor countenance why his officer has been so disrespectful to the Germans.

Under de la Grascia's glare, the two younger German officers are unsure of how to react and they stand and wait for a lead from their senior, who stares back, his expression stark, cold and resolute.

When the Tenente has finished, the senior officer replies, and though his tone holds no threat, whatever it is he says to de la Grascia, it is plainly obvious that his words hold a world of unwanted promises.

The German captain turns and speaks to one of his lieutenants, who returns to the table and places a couple of bank notes beneath a cup.

"Thank you, gentlemen. Have a good day," De la Grascia says, this time in Italian.

They don't respond to his good wishes; they simply turn away and begin strolling back to their car. One of the lieutenants barks at the men and they begin climbing back into the truck.

As they drive away, the captain refuses to look at de la Grascia; he merely instructs his driver to turn around and leave in the same direction from which they'd arrived.

The car and truck disappear, and it is as though a great balloon of tension has burst and pursued them noisily out of the piazza.

The men at the table guffaw, snort and slap each other on the back. "Bravo, Tenente. Bravo," one shouts.

De la Grascia, unlike his men, is not so amused. He doesn't reclaim his seat and neither does he join them in their irreverent rejoicing; he simply stands, rooted to the paving, and stares spellbound after the departed Germans.

Mira decides to break his spell. She strides to the now empty table and loads her tray with the dirty cups and plates. Picking up the bank notes, she counts them and whistles in surprise. "Whatever did you say to that officer?"

Hauled from the reverie of his thoughts, he comes to and smiles at her. "I merely reminded him of the fact that to leave a café without settling the bill is, even in times of war, a crime, and one which I would have no alternative but to report to his commanders."

"Was that all?" Mira stands, resting her tray against her hip. "It sounded much worse to me."

"Oh, it is difficult to be other than formal in German: the language lacks any latitude."

"And what was his reply? He didn't like seem to take to you too kindly."

De la Grascia smiles, a wan, pitying smile. "Oh, the poor fellow said your coffee was so bad that he couldn't understand why anyone would risk their life defending people who served such appalling coffee. So, I was forced to inform him that while he is a guest in our country, he should respect the people who work in our cafes even if their coffee is unpalatable. And furthermore, I informed him that your coffee is German and that if he had to complain, he was digging a rather large hole for himself. Perhaps that was the part that upset him."

Mira moves closer to him, so that his men will not overhear. "Where did you learn German, Aldo?"

At her use of his Christian name, he glances at his men and glowers playfully at her. "Oh, in Russia." He pauses, studying her quizzical expression. "Yes, I know. That is yet another facet of this ridiculous war, that one should journey all the way to Russia to learn German."

The captain turns to his men. "Come, it is time to go. That is more than enough excitement for one morning." He fumbles in his pocket.

Mira places her hand over his; an act that she is aware Comune Simone takes notice of. "I cannot ask you to pay for something you have supplied."

With his free hand, De la Grascia gently removes hers and drawing a couple of notes from his pocket, places them on the table.

Glancing towards Simone and the other artillerymen, he whispers, "That is for us to know and, even if they believe it is so, they must not see it." His look is now solemn and as he speaks, he very gently squeezes her hand. "Mira, you must be aware by now that I hold you close to my heart... No don't look so uncomfortable; I tell you this so that you will take what I am about to tell you seriously. Please, my dear one, when we have left, close the café and go home. I will explain when I see you at mass. Please, now, do as I ask."

Chapter 10

"So, your angel of mercy stayed at home today, eh?" Enzo quips, when Mira walks in.

"No, papà, he came. And he provided for me." She places the bag of provisions that de la Grascia had left for her on the table. "Yet the coffee is so bad that it provoked an argument between Aldo and a German officer."

"So why have you closed the café?"

"Because Aldo suggested I should. And before you criticise me for closing the café on his advice, I will say only that it was not particularly what he said, so much as how he said it. There was something in the way he told me that suggested it would be best not to ignore his advice."

"Aldo, eh?"

"Yes, Aldo." She moves over to stand behind where he sits in his chair and bending down, she drapes her arms affectionately around his shoulders and kisses the back of his neck. "Please don't doubt him, papà. For me, please don't."

Enzo softens to her touch. "All right, my daughter, I will try. But what I don't understand is why the generals have placed a man of supposed character and intelligence in command of a bunch of misfits. Surely, if he is a respected officer, he should be in command of frontline troops, not tucked out of the way up at Capo Peloro."

"Of course, papà, and I cannot answer your question. Why don't you ask him at mass tomorrow?"

"And how can you be so certain he will be there?"

"Because he told me he would be there. And because he also said that there would be no bombing tonight or tomorrow. For one thing, there is a full moon and for another, Aldo said the British and Americans are now bombing the airfields, and once they have flattened them and no more German or Italian planes can fly out from them, then there will be nothing to stop the British and Americans from taking the whole island."

"He sounds like he wants them to succeed."

Mira sighs and stands up, away from him. "Have you learned nothing of him, papà?" she says. "Can you not see that he is a man of honour and that he will fight until the King orders him to stop?" Exasperated, she balls her fists and plays at striking his head. "Now, how is our patient?"

"Dottore Roselli is with him and, judging by the silence, he is not happy. You'd best go and help."

In her room, the old doctor is stooped beside the bed examining Nicholas's face. He stands upright and glances at Mira.

Mira looks and gasps.

"I don't like the sound of that," Nicholas mutters. He lies prone and naked but for the blanket arranged to preserve his modesty.

"No, and you should not. Young man," the doctor begins, exhaling loudly and then drumming his fingers against his lips for a few seconds while he considers the best way to proceed. "Young man, some of the flesh, here, has necrotised." He indicates areas at the corners of both eyes, where the skin has turned an ugly shade of white. "You see this, Mira."

"That sounds even worse," Nicholas says. "Perhaps you would be good enough to tell me what you see. I realise there's not much I can do to help, but I'd rather know than lie here and wonder."

Dottore Roselli looks at Mira, evidently waiting for her consent.

She nods, thinning her lips in concern.

"Yes, that's fair," the doctor says. "I'll tell you what I see and therefore what I know to be the case. Your legs are in better shape; the bad cut on your right thigh is weeping and obviously has some infection. I don't think this is too bad and Mira can attend to it by cleaning and applying new dressings. The burn on your left thigh is responding well to the aloe; it is clean and moist, and shows no sign of infection." He pauses for a moment, no doubt thinking not only of whether, or how, he should explain to a man the extent of his injuries, but also the manner in which he should couch a prognosis that will be sure to result in pain.

Nicholas is quick to realise. "I've always believed, doctor, that bad news is best delivered quickly."

The doctor removes his glasses and breathing on each round lens, polishes them with the end of his shirt. He bends down to examine again, taking his time, first bridling his mouth in disapproval, then inclining his head from side to side as he weighs up the pros and cons of what he has decided.

"There is what we call an eschar." He points for Mira's benefit. "Three, in fact; one at each corner of your eyes and the third at the bridge of your nose. The skin at your forehead and cheeks is also wet with infection." He pauses again, then comes to some form of conclusion. "We could persist with the aloe and wait for the eschar to dry and separate naturally. However, if the infection takes hold, you risk losing both your sight and your good looks, and what is of more concern to me, your life."

"I wouldn't want you to think me vain, Dottore Roselli," Nicholas interrupts, "but I wouldn't want to end up any uglier than I am now. So, what's the answer?"

"Well, I . . ." His throat dries, his voice falters.

"Are you all right, Dottore? Do you need some water?"

"No, thank you, Mira. The Madonna has tested me with a difficult morning. Please, a moment."

While waiting for him to gather himself, Mira grasps the nettle. "What Dottore Roselli is proposing is that he removes the dead tissue."

"Debride is the correct medical term," Roselli notes. "It may sound somewhat less threatening."

In the face of such promised discomfort, Nicholas chuckles. "If you don't mind my saying, debride sounds like something awkward that happens when a groom fails to turn up at the altar."

"This is no laughing matter young man."

"Sorry, Dottore. Sorry, Mira. Laughing in the face of pain: it's a stupid habit my mother tells me I inherited from my father."

"No," she argues, "it is not only your father who laughs at such times; my father is the same." Her hostility to his nonchalance dissipates. "It is no more than how men behave when they are anxious. Why should you be any different?"

Perhaps a little frustrated that the discussion has taken a conversational turn, Dottore Roselli coughs before continuing. "As I was saying, I will have to debride the tissue, which I can surmise will be painful. Extremely painful, both during and after. And the surgery carries with it the risk of further infection and a similar prognosis to that of doing nothing and waiting. This," he shoots Mira an apologetic look, "is a far from sterile environment; though I cannot imagine, what with the high number of casualties arriving in Messina from the fighting in the south, that you would be any safer from infection in the hospital. Young man, whatever I do next, it must be with your blessing."

"Nicholas?"

He turns his head, as though he can see her. "Yes, Mira."

"How is your pain, now?"

"Honestly?"

"Yes," she moans, "of course honestly."

"Well, if you can stand me talking in my sleep, you could give me another shot of morphine: that might be a help both to me and the good doctor."

CHAPTER 11

"Please, God," Mira prays, "keep my brother safe and bring him back to us. If not for my sake, then for mama and papà. Please God, do this for me and I will be your servant for evermore."

"Remember your servant..." the priest says, in a tone so forlorn it causes some to glance up to see who is missing "... young Gennaro Ganci, whom you have called from this world to yourself."

As the boy is named, the congregation of the Chiesa San Nicholas di Bari issue a deep and mournful moan, a sound not unlike that of the sea when it retreats from the shore.

"So that is why Dottore Roselli had seemed out of sorts," Mira whispers to herself. "Gennaro Ganci."

Four days before, the eleven–year–old had insisted on going to Messina to ask for news of Rimiggiu, his older brother, one of many who were yet to return from North Africa. And not wishing to let the boy go alone, his uncle, the last surviving adult male of the Ganci family, had accompanied him and they had walked the ten kilometres into the city in bright sunshine and a freshening breeze. However, when they got to the city the sky had turned black with American aeroplanes, their bombs had fallen, a piece of shrapnel had pierced the boy's head and the uncle had carried him the ten kilometres home. Dottore

Roselli, a close friend of the family, had examined Gennaro and immediately despatched him back to Messina, to the Margherita hospital, a decision taken much against the wishes of the boy's mother.

Now, Gennaro was dead and all that was left was guilt and misery.

The priest continues: "Grant that Gennaro, who is now reunited with your Son in death, may also be one with him in his Resurrection—"

Mira finds herself praying for Carlo, her husband who had died in the same wretched establishment some six years before: an iron bed in a ward crowded with feeble men; the sweet and sour odours of suffering; the discordant melodies of souls in pain; wives and mothers cleaning and feeding husbands and sons where they lay. Hoping, please God, let them live; and despairing, please God let them die.

"—when from the earth, he will raise up in the flesh those who have died and transform our lowly body after the pattern of his own glorious body."

Poor Carlo, it hadn't really been his fault that he had died, just as it wasn't Gennaro Ganci's fault either. The two of them had simply been where they shouldn't have been. After all, neither had planned to be where they were when God had called them.

Although to be fair, there was nothing wrong with being in Messina; that wasn't really the wrong place, was it?

No, for Carlo, the wrong place had been a town the name of which she found difficult to pronounce, a town in a country many moons away that some referred to as Abyssinia; a town where Carlo had been stupid enough to permit himself to be captured. And though he had returned to Messina, Carlo had returned incomplete: the fingers of his right hand and those most private of parts without which a man cannot father children having been removed by some crazed demon. As a result, his spirit had fled in terror and all that had been returned to Mira had been an infected carcass that might once, if her imagination could have stretched that far, have resembled her husband. For four weeks she had nursed him; for four weeks he had refused to look at her; and for four weeks he had slowly, so very slowly, died.

"To our departed brothers and sisters, too, and to all who were pleasing to you at their passing from this life, give kind admittance to your kingdom."

And Carlo and Gennaro had been, hadn't they? The shadows of young men admitted from beds of grey linen only to pass into a world of greyer shadows.

And now? For Mira?

Alone, but for the attentions of a gallant lieutenant from Bologna and the needs of a blind and strangely intriguing Englishman. One moment alone, unwanted; the next, besieged at all sides.

Ah, Aldo; she had seen him come into the church just before they had closed the doors. He was always on time. Always, but always only just.

On hearing his boots clip against the marble floor, she had turned around and he had smiled and raised his hand in acknowledgement.

Her father had noticed and poked her thigh, at which she had wriggled further away along the pew. They would never be good enough for her, would they? Neither Carlo, nor the Tenente, nor the Englishman. None of them.

"There we hope to enjoy for ever the fullness of your glory, when you will wipe away every tear from our eyes. For seeing you, our God, as you are, we shall be like you for all ages and praise you without end," the priest joins his hands, "through Christ our Lord, through whom you bestow on the world all that is good."

Oh, but now she surprises herself; for why is she viewing the Englishman in the same way that she views the lieutenant? And exactly how is she viewing them? As possibilities? As suitors? And how is it that she finds herself so easily drawn to the Englishman when she has only spoken to him as a nurse would to a patient? How is it that she shares such a sudden familiarity with him? Is it because she has only ever seen the Tenente in uniform, whereas she has seen Nicholas undressed and the only other person with whom she has ever shared such an intimacy was Carlo?

On her way back to her pew after taking Communion, she cannot help but lift her head to search for the lieutenant. He is there, seated at the back, smiling at her, albeit with his head a little bowed; and for the rest of mass she has the most peculiar feeling that he is watching her.

With hands joined, the priest faces the congregation and bids them, "Go in peace, glorifying the Lord by your life."

And the people answer, "Thanks be to God."

The priest then venerates the altar with his kiss, makes a profound bow and withdraws.

When the congregation file out, the light outside is bright and they hesitate and stumble as they shade their eyes. They mill about on the apron before the church, some clutching the white notices they have received from the Ministero della Guerra informing them that their sons are prisoners of war and therefore alive and accounted for; while others pause to offer the diminutive Signora Ganci their condolences. A few lift their faces in question: how can it be that they hear rumbles of thunder when the sky, though cloudy and the atmosphere only vaguely humid, holds no promise of storm?

"Signor Ruggeri," de la Grascia startles them and bows. "Signora Ruggeri, Signora Alberti."

They turn to find him waiting patiently for their recognition, his neatly pressed light green uniform in colourful contrast to the white shirts and black jackets of other men.

As he is the first addressed, Enzo responds: "Tenente de la Grascia, good evening," but offers nothing more.

"Tenente." Francesca smiles, politely.

Mira decides that is quite enough pretence and steps forward, offering her hand. "Aldo, good evening. How are you?"

"Thank you, Mira," he raises her hand to his lips and plays at kissing it, "I am as well as one can expect given the circumstances and the pressures of my post."

Enzo sucks his teeth a little too loudly.

"Aldo," Mira begins, "what is that thunder we have heard all through the day? Are the planes bombing where we cannot see?"

He ushers them to a bench and waits for them to sit down. "What you can hear is not bombing; it is the British warships shelling the Catania to Messina road. They are trying to interdict the lines of supply to the south."

"Interdict?" Enzo asks. "What is that, interdict?"

"Sorry, Signor Ruggeri. What I mean is they are trying to destroy the road so that reinforcements cannot be sent south to confront them."

"Well, why don't you say so instead of using military terminology that none of us understand?"

De la Grascia winces. "I am sorry, Signor Ruggeri, that my reliance on military speak confuses you."

"And talking of speaking in tongues," Enzo continues, "I hear that you speak German. How is that so, do you have Germans for ancestors?"

The Tenente glances at Mira, who frowns. "Papà?" Then she shakes her head, suggesting it wasn't her who has let on.

"No, Mira, your father is right to ask for an explanation. Signor Ruggeri, before I was posted to Sicily, I served with the 3rd Cavalry Division Amedeo Duca d'Aosta in Russia. I learnt some German in school, in Bologna, and during my time on the banks of the River Don, I found it helpful to communicate with German officers."

"Helpful to communicate?" Enzo presses.

"Yes, Signor Ruggeri. During my time there, I learnt that when it comes to intelligence, it is not always knowing what the opposing forces are planning that is important: knowing what our allies are up to is of equal use, particularly if one's men are not to be sacrificed on the altar of Teutonic arrogance."

"I see. You mean the Germans."

Mira rolls her eyes.

"And how goes the glorious battle?" Enzo's tone is undisguisedly cynical.

"Not well, sir. Not well for either side, that is. Today, I received a report that some of our troops near Enna, that's in the middle of the country—"

"Yes, Tenente, I know where Enna is. Please continue."

"I apologise, I did not mean to—"

"Stop apologising, man. You sound like a man who feels he needs to apologise for the sins of the world. Please, continue."

"Yes, of course." He coughs back his embarrassment. "Well, I have received a report that some of our troops near Enna mutinied. Apparently, they shot the German officer who was commanding them and then surrendered to the Americans."

"Can you blame them?"

"Papà?"

De la Grascia ponders for a moment. "Signor Ruggeri, how can I blame them when I was not present; I have no appreciation of their circumstances. However," he hurries to deny the fisherman another opportunity to interrupt him, "I think it only fair to warn you, all of you, that my battery is about to be placed under German control. In the future, I am to take my orders not from Generale Guzzoni, but directly from the Wehrmacht, who now control the coast from Messina to Capo Peloro and round to Mortelle. Most notably, and perhaps unfortunately, I am to take my orders from the same German captain I felt the need to introduce myself to yesterday."

"Oh, Aldo!"

"Yes, Mira. I have the most terrible apprehension that my good manners may be about to return to haunt me."

"And all at my expense."

"No, Mira. You must not blame yourself; the captain was in the wrong and that is all there is to it. And, if I might add, talking of men surrendering; increasing numbers of our soldiers are deserting. And by that, I mean in their hundreds. Now, whether or not you think these men justified in their actions," he stares at Enzo, yet not unpleasantly, "anyone found hiding them will be answerable to the Germans and we all know how… let us say unsympathetic they can be."

Enzo and Mira glance at each other; a look that does not escape de la Grascia's notice.

Before her father can volunteer his opinion, Mira says, "Thank you, Aldo, we will bear your warning in mind and we will tell anyone who might consider sheltering deserters to be careful."

"Good." He smiles, warmly. "By the way, I hope those medical supplies proved of good use to whoever it was that you needed them for."

His reference stuns all of them to silence.

"Now, if you will excuse me, and I suppose that counts as an apology, I have to return to the battery. Good evening." He bows, takes Francesca's hand and pretends to kiss it.

When he pretends the same to Mira, she whispers, "Can you wait for a minute, I'd like to talk."

"Of course."

Enzo stands and offers his hand; it may be only the second time he has met the lieutenant and yet it is the second time the man has won him over. "Thank you, Tenente. Thank you for taking the time to caution us."

And as if to lend gravity to his warning, the shrill blast of a whistle breaches the air.

They turn to look at the road.

The blast heralds the arrival of a motorised column. A stern–faced, steel–helmeted motorcyclist waves people to the side of the road, as shortly behind him follows a procession of tanks, halftracks and lorries loaded with troops. The column is long, perhaps forty vehicles or more; the expressions on the faces of the soldiers, humourless; the fog of vehicle exhaust, unpleasant.

When they have gone, only the slowly sinking clouds of dust attest to their brief presence.

Mira and de la Grascia walk down the steps before the church and stroll away towards his battered Fiat staff car. Once out of her father's sight, she takes his arm.

"Yes, Mira?"

"Aldo, I wanted to thank you for standing up to that German yesterday."

"You have no need to, my angel. If I had not pointed out to him the error of his ways, I would only be half the man I ought to be." He pauses and studies her eyes. "There is something else you want to say, isn't there?"

"Yes, Aldo, there is: and it is that when you were speaking to the German officer, Comune Simone had the strangest look to him. It was almost as though you were reprimanding him as well as the German officer. He looked like a man who had just witnessed his mother being insulted and he didn't know how to react; like he was amazed that you should do such a thing. His look frightened me."

De la Grascia pats her arm and smiles. "Oh, don't worry about him. I do believe he is a little jealous of our association. I will take care of him when the time comes."

Mira tenses. "When the time comes; what do you mean by that?"

"What I mean is, when the British and Americans arrive, I will ensure he cannot put any of us in danger, that is all. What did you think I meant?"

"Oh, I see. Well, nothing. I just wanted you to know that I don't trust him and that I want you to be careful."

"Don't worry, my angel, I will be careful. And it warms my heart to know that you are concerned for my safety, thank you." He takes her hand and kisses it, this time allowing his lips to make contact. "Oh, I almost forgot. Mira, I cannot guarantee any more supplies. I will try, but I cannot guarantee them. And you should know that the Germans are going to set up an artillery battery near the Chiesa Madonna della Lettera in Torre Faro, possibly even in the square outside your café. So, perhaps it is you who needs to be more careful from now on."

Chapter 12

"I am sorry to have to leave you for so long." She sits down beside him. "Here, Nicholas, drink."

He sucks on the tube and swallows, clumsily.

As she dabs, gently, at the dribble of solution from around his crusted lips, Mira asks, "Tell me, how do you feel?"

"Oh, not too bad. A little warm. A little frustrated at not being able to appreciate my surroundings, if I'm honest. How was mass?"

"Mass," she repeats, turning the word over as though he has spoken about an event that lacks any relevance. "I don't believe I really know how it was; it is in times like these that we question our faith." Mira stares at him, taking in his bandaged eyes and the wounds around his face that seem to be so slow in healing. "We mourned the death of a young boy, an innocent, the last of Signora Ganci's four sons. On such occasions it is difficult to believe that the Madonna is watching over us and that her son gave his life that others might live. Only they are not living, are they? At least, not poor young Gennaro."

"You knew him?"

"Yes, Nicholas, we all knew Gennaro. He was special to us, like all young boys and girls are special to us. Like you are special to your family. Do you have family?"

285

"A sister," he replies, and at her mention his throat tightens and he raises his hand to his mouth as he tries to cough.

Mira pushes his hands away and offers the tube up to his lips. "Thank you." He sucks and swallows. "Yes, a sister."

"What is she like?"

"Like?" Now, Nicholas quiets, summoning an image of her in his mind. "Like you, I think."

"Like me?" Mira asks, surprised. "How do you know what I look like? You have never seen me."

"I don't need to see you to know what you are like, Mira. I can hear my sister in your voice, in the way your father speaks to you and in the way Dottore Roselli addresses you. He knows you are strong. The tone he adopts with you, the way he asks you to do certain things: to clean my burns, change my bandages and give me an injection. He understands your confidence; he knows you are capable of looking after me; he doesn't doubt you. That's just how a doctor would talk to my sister."

"Is your sister a nurse?"

"Yes, in a hospital in London."

"Is she married?"

"No, not yet." He thinks for a moment. "Actually, she might be by now. I haven't had a letter from her in a while. Don't suppose I will for a bit, either. She does have a friend; a pilot. They're very sweet on each other."

"And you, Nicholas, do you have a friend, as you put it? Someone to go back to?"

"I don't know."

"You don't know? Surely, you must know. How can you not know when you are in love? Love occupies you; it consumes you. Either you are completely consumed or you are not. If you are not, then you are not in love; there is no in between."

"I mean, I don't know if she'll want to have anything more to do with me the way I look now. Or perhaps I should say, the way

I am not looking now. Mira, I may not be able to see myself, but my pain, the way Dottore Roselli talks without saying, the way you won't let me feel my face and the sympathy and compassion in the way you ask me how I'm feeling..."

She rests her hand on the upper part of his arm, a part of him the tongues of flame did not lick. "You should not think this way, Nicholas. Dottore Roselli is old and uncertain, and he would rather do no harm than make your condition worse. When your own doctors examine you, then you will know more."

"And how long will that be?" he groans. "A month? Two?"

"Two, at the most. Perhaps sooner."

"You seem to know more than the generals, Mira." What she has just said arouses his curiosity. "How is it that you seem so sure? How do you know? In fact, I have been lying here trying to work out where you got the morphine from; I can't imagine the stuff is readily available. I recall you said you got it from a friend. Is he the kind of friend you meant when you asked me if I had a friend? Is he a soldier?"

"Yes, he is."

"Do you love him?"

Mira lets go of his arm and clasping her hands together, she leans forward and rests her head.

Her silence bothers him. "I don't mean to be rude, Mira. I don't mean to pry, I just—"

"I don't know, Nicholas. I wish I did."

"But didn't you just tell me that we know when we are in love?"

She chuckles, a small, self-deprecating laugh, one filled both with an inevitable irony and an appreciation that he has so casually turned the tables on her. "Mm, I did, didn't I? I suppose that must mean I am not, otherwise I would be sure of it. Or," she hesitates, "perhaps it is that I would like to be, or that I am afraid of being in love when war seems so certain of stealing love from us before we have the chance to recognise it."

To distract herself from his cross—examination of her emotions, Mira busies herself with investigating the state of the bandages at his legs. "These dressings have stuck and Dottore Roselli warned me that I should be careful not to let them dry." From the collection of thick, fleshy grey–green leaves on the table beside the bed, she picks one and, holding it with the broken end close to his leg, she squeezes the translucent gel out onto the dried areas of bandage.

He shivers as it cools his hot skin. "I'm sorry, Mira. I didn't mean to remind of you of something that makes you sad. It must be the morphine talking."

She sighs. "It is no matter. You have no need to apologise, Nicholas. You ask questions that no one else has ever asked me; there is nothing wrong in that. If you must know, I was once married. And very happily so." Deftly and with great care and tenderness, Mira works the gel out over his bandage.

"However, like all the other widows, I lost my husband to a war none of us understood in a country none of us cared for. Carlo thought he was embarking on a grand adventure, a great enterprise, and yet all the time I knew he was being seduced by a charisma I could not compete with."

"Mussolini?"

"Yes, the great peddler of dreams. You know, I saw him once."

"You saw Mussolini?"

"Yes, when he came to Messina. It was six years ago, not long after my husband died. I wanted, no, that is not the right word… I needed to see this man in the same way that a wife needs to see what her husband's mistress looks like. I needed to see Il Duce to understand why I lost the battle to keep my husband; to understand why he found this man so irresistible; to understand what charms I did not possess."

Mira quiets, remembering. "It was a Tuesday in August, one of those days on which the sun appeared a deeper gold, the sea a deeper green and the sky a deeper blue. Mussolini arrived in the Strait escorted by a fleet of glorious warships. He was suntanned and dressed all in white, and standing on the prow of the torpedo boat Aurora. I remember watching him leap ashore and swagger around, like a god come home to his creations. And I was only one of many hundreds of thousands there to greet him, all waving flags and cheering as though we were for some reason made delirious by his presence. Well," she shrugs, "that's what they reported in La Domenica del Corriere and they were not far wrong; it was madness.

"Do you know, Nicholas, an old man told me Mussolini had come to Sicily to observe a war game, a rehearsal to repel invaders should they appear on the western shore; something our glorious leader had told us was impossible."

She scoffs, "Impossible? Then why play war games, eh? He even had the arrogance to tell us that Fascism had deleted the word impossible from the dictionary. Imagine that!

"He was driven through the city in an open car surrounded by Black Shirts with their uniform haircuts, their black shirts and their pretty white pants, all running around as if their great Duce was at every moment in danger of being assassinated."

"Mira?"

"Yes, Nicholas." She looks up, worried that she is hurting him.

"That's probably because people kept trying to assassinate him. If I recall correctly, an Irish woman shot him. Seventeen years ago. In the Piazza del Campidoglio in Rome. Pity she missed, really. Imagine the trouble she would have saved. Anyway, sorry to interrupt, please do go on."

"Don't worry, Nicholas, you can interrupt me all you like. For me the problem is that this memory is like a dream, a bad dream that I cannot get rid of. It is like a foul smell that follows me wherever I go."

Not knowing what else to say, he says, "Yes, of course. Now, try to remember for me."

"All right. I remember at the Municipio, they had built a stage: an enormous prow of a boat, which stuck out of the front as though the building had been halted in the course of giving birth to a great ship.

"Mussolini again assumed his proud stance on the prow and told us he had come to see what, after the earthquake of 1908, we had done to rebuild our city; what we were doing now; and, above all, what still remained to be done. He stated that all the residues of old Messina must disappear and he declared that He would build a great harbour and a grand station. Mussolini even bent his back to remove a few bricks from the roof of the old station. I remember he visited the Margherita Hospital and the poor district of Camaro, where the Americans had built many wooden houses for the survivors of the great earthquake and most of which had been destroyed by the fire of thirteen years ago. Mussolini promised Messina everything a city could ask for." Mira frowns and shakes her head. ""Is there anyone," he demanded, "who can doubt the unshakeable will of the regime? Anyone who can doubt that my promises will be strictly maintained?" The strange thing was that he said all these things would happen as though they had already happened, as though the new harbour and the station had already been built. And everyone believed him. We all believed him. We were like waves rippling in his wake. We were thrilled and enraptured and in love, and we forgot who we were, because we were his and he was ours." Mira shakes her head and sighs, as if by her exhalation she will expel Il Duce's foul odour. "And we were his. We were all his many mistresses, like Petacci and the Jewess Sarfatti.

"It wasn't until I began to walk home that I remembered who I was; that I remembered my husband and why I had gone to see this ridiculous saviour. And worse than the fact that I had allowed myself to be seduced, was that in all the excitement I had forgotten the future Mussolini had stolen from us and the future he was yet to steal from young boys like Gennaro Ganci."

Mira squeezes the last of the aloe gel from the leaf and, with her finger, spreads it softly and evenly over the dried bandage.

"Messina is once again reduced to rubble," she whispers, "and I fear there is worse to come."

Regaining her voice, she adds, "The Germans are setting up one of their artillery batteries in the piazza outside my café. I can no longer keep it open; it will be too dangerous and besides, I will be sure to run out of coffee. Even now, on a Sunday, they are patrolling the shore in front of this house. I tell you, Nicholas, if we are to survive, it can only be because the Madonna thinks us worthy of her protection."

CHAPTER 13

"If we run out of everything else, mama, at least we will always have this to be thankful for."

The two women sit, feasting their eyes in the pastel green slopes beyond the cool blue waters of the Strait. On another morning, their hands would be kept busy cleaning the catch; now though, as Enzo has decided that fishing, like many other necessary occupations, is too fraught with danger, they have little else to occupy their time with other than the view.

"Yes, Mira. Even if we have nothing, we will have this." Francesca pauses, a pause heavily pregnant with misgiving. Then she decides, "Mira?"

"Yes, mama."

"The Englishman."

"Yes, mama."

"I have seen the way you look at him and I have heard the way you talk to him."

"Yes, mama. In a house as modest as ours, how can one expect one's behaviour to go unnoticed?" Her behaviour brought to question, her ire provoked, Mira too decides, "So, now that you have both seen and heard, what do you think is wrong with the way I look at him and talk to him? And I suppose papà has put you up to this, which means he, too, does not like what he sees and hears."

Francesca groans and hangs her head in her hands. "Mira, why must you react so angrily whenever one of us tries to save you from hurting yourself? You are like a wilful child who blames her frustrations on her parents simply because she has no one else to blame."

Mira reaches out and strokes her mother's arm in much the same way she had stroked Nicholas's arm during the night, when the demons of war had returned to haunt him.

"I'm sorry, mama. I really am truly sorry. I know it is not easy for you and papà to have me here, especially when I should have left home so many years ago. And it's true, I could live in the back room of the café: but think of it, I would be the favoured topic of every wagging tongue in the village and that's why I prefer to live with you and papà, here at home. No one would dare tell lies about me when I live within my father's sight: they know they would have him to answer to. Maybe I hide behind him, who knows.

"If things had been different... If Carlo had not died, then we would have had our own place by now and I would have been out of your hair." Mira removes her hand and raises it to ward off her mother's pity. "No, mama, there is nothing wrong in speaking about Carlo in this manner. Is it six or seven years since he died? To me, now, it does not matter which because he has been gone so long it might as well be a thousand years. You must believe me, mama, when I tell you that however long it is, Carlo still lives in my heart and he will always live there; that is how it should be. Please, don't feel sorry for me, mama, just be patient."

German soldiers, their rifles slung casually over their shoulders, stroll towards them along the water's edge, kicking stones, chatting, laughing, and jostling each other like blithe adolescents.

"Is it that he is blinded?" Francesca asks. "Is it that he cannot see you that you find it so easy to discuss the way you feel? I know from years of living with your father that some conversations are best left to the dark. Is that what makes it easier for you to be so familiar with him?"

293

Mira smiles, though not in any lascivious fashion. Or perhaps, if she is honest with herself, when sitting alone with Nicholas irregular thoughts have come to her. "Until you had mentioned it, I had not thought so. But now that you do, mama, I think you may well be right. He is a nice man: polite and modest, and he seems to appreciate whatever it is I want to say. He makes me feel as though he wants to hear what I have to say."

"He is a captive audience."

"That is unkind of you, mama. I believe he would want to listen to me just as well as if we were out at passeggio. And the curious thing is, I enjoy listening to him too. He talks about his sister in the same way I hear myself talking about young Maria. In spite of the fact that he is lying in my bed all bloodied and bandaged, when I talk with him, I forget all about this terrible war."

The German soldiers walk idly, lingering only to strain their backs as they peer into the rowboats raised high on wooden blocks, or crouching down as they inspect the bowels of an upturned hull to satisfy themselves no one is lurking within.

Francesca fidgets. "You want to save this Englishman; that is only natural and I understand that. But are you trying to save this Englishman to make up for not being able to save Carlo? You must console yourself, Mira, some things in life are not ours to decide."

"You think this Englishman has replaced Carlo in my affections?" Mira's tone, though, suggests she is not offended by her mother's very personal observation. "I think you should ask papà this question. He seems to want to save this Englishman more than me. Papà just sits silently and watches him. He appears to communicate with Nicholas without saying anything, as though through his energy he is willing him to recover. And I shouldn't have to remind you, mama, it was papà who decided to keep Nicholas here in the first place. He could have sent him away to the hills or to the hospital in Messina where he would probably have been safer; but no, he wanted to keep him here, where he can watch over him. And now, with all these," she nods in the direction of the approaching patrol, "it is too late to send him away."

The German soldiers notice them and they turn away, pretending to look out over the Strait and discuss the splendour of the view.

"Mira, cover your legs," Francesca whispers.

She does so, pulling down her black skirt so that not even her ankles show. However, Mira then sits upright, squares her shoulders and makes no effort to veil the fullness of her breasts.

Her show of defiance is not lost on the soldiers, and a couple pause to stare unashamedly before being pulled away by their comrades. The men slope off, removing their helmets and wiping the sweat from their brows as they boast about what might have been.

"And the Tenente?" Francesca asks.

"What about the Tenente?" Mira replies, pulling her skirt back up above her knees, allowing the warmth of the breeze to play at her bare calves.

"Nothing, I just thought I detected a certain attraction. He is very charming and he possesses a certain refinement that one does not often see; his uniform fits him as well as any and his manners are, well, perfect."

"Aldo," Mira permits her mouth to toy with his name. "Yes, mama, he is both charming and refined, and perhaps too much of both. He thinks I am the same; at least he wants to think I can be the same. No, mama, Tenente de la Grascia would like me to be a person I cannot be and when he realises I am not, he will only try to make me into that person. And besides, I am too plainspoken and he is too fond of his food; the two do not go together."

"Try to be kind to him," Francesca says, as though Mira stands over the lieutenant with a sharpened axe.

"I will, mama. And I think that is all he asks for: a little kindness amongst all this cruelty."

They sit in contemplative silence and with the gleaming sun near its zenith, they cast their dreams upon the restless waters and bask in the tail end of the Sciroccu.

Before long, their silence is broken by a low droning noise from the south.

They shade their eyes.

"An aeroplane," Mira says.

Labouring up the Strait, not more than a tall mast's height above the water, comes a dull grey–green aircraft, trailing a thick line of black smoke from one of its three engines. Pitching up one moment, then hanging in the air for a few seconds before nosing down again, it is clearly struggling against the forces of gravity, the low droning noise of its effort interrupted every now and again by a crackling and popping.

Francesca and Mira watch as the aeroplane is drawn lower and lower, and as it passes them, they catch sight of a man standing in the rear door, looking down nervously at the blue waters.

The aeroplane groans and moans, like a cow knowing it is being dragged to slaughter. It lurches and stalls, and slips and slides, making its way clumsily up into and out of the neck of the Strait, before dipping to surrender the last of its lift.

The aeroplane, now one wing up and the other down, veers in a perfect arc away from them towards the unforgiving lump of rock, below which nestles the village of Scylla.

Deciding to take his chance to live rather than die in the collision that must now happen, the man hurls himself from the door, drops like a stone and makes a small white splash as he lands. A second later, one wingtip touches the surface and the aeroplane spins round, cartwheeling violently end over end before folding in half and breaking up as it crashes into the water.

Though a kilometre or so distant and the noise of the impact strangely muted, the shock of it causes both women to gasp.

Debris litters the water. Smoke plumes from the wreckage. Men, though only a few, bob about, their arms flailing as they try to stay afloat.

Within a very short time, the sea claims them: the only testament to their existence, to the lives they have left behind, evident in the smoke that palls as it would from a funeral pyre.

"Cruelty!" Mira whispers. "Such cruelty."

CHAPTER 14

Enzo joins them as they file between the tall columns, and when they take their customary seat, he leans first one way and then the other, as though he is searching for someone.

Francesca frowns and chides him for his fidgeting.

At the last moment, and as seems to be his custom since he has become a regular at Mira's church, Tenente de la Grascia enters.

From her pew, she loses her thoughts in the painting of Father Francesco welcoming his flock to the newly built Parrocchia San Nicolò di Bari. His gold robes and prescription glasses, a pair of which one of his altar boys also wears, appear strikingly out of place with the primeval simplicity of the bay behind him. But then, she notices the steamship making its way through the Strait in the background and the pall of smoke rising from its funnel, and she prays for the men who must have died when the aeroplane broke upon that same primeval simplicity.

A growing tide of whispers breathes through the congregation.

Mira looks up. The figurines of Jesus, the statue of the Madonna, the cherubs, they are murmuring, they are whispering. Words are being passed back and forth and along the pews. Looks are exchanged and glows of excitement spread like wildfire.

Something is going on. Something important. Something momentous.

A senior altar boy interrupts Father Antonio. He cups his ear and stands back in surprise, then hurries through the rest of communion as though he is late for supper.

The congregation file out promptly and swiftly, to be greeted on the steps by cheers of joy and jubilation.

"Fascism is dead!" one shouts.

"The war is over!" shouts another.

"Our boys are coming home!"

A woman screams and faints into the arms of an old man. Coppolas and other flat caps are thrown high in the air. Families embrace. Mothers cry and grandfathers lift up their grandchildren and hug and kiss them.

Mira looks questioningly at her father.

"Yes," he says, his expression radiant as that of a first–time father, "Mussolini has been dismissed by King Victor."

Leaving her mother and father to their celebrations, Mira seeks out de la Grascia, who is besieged by people eager for more detailed news.

The Tenente extricates himself from the crowd and walks away beyond the apron of the church.

"Is it true?" Mira asks, when she finally catches up. "Is the war really over?"

His expression, though, does not match the general euphoria. "No, the war is not over, not yet. This may be the start, but it is only the start. However, I do believe the end is now absolutely inevitable and at last the question is no longer how many months, but how many weeks?"

"But what is the situation? Are we about to be liberated by the British and Americans?"

De la Grascia removes his cap and mops his brow with a handkerchief. "The Americans have taken Palermo and Enna, and the British and Canadians occupy the southern slopes of Mount Etna. It is only a matter of time before the Germans realise they are losing the island."

"And what about our troops, will they continue to fight?"

"King Victor Emmanuel has appointed that sycophant Badoglio premier. Like Il Duce, Badoglio is a Fascist, so for the moment we will continue to resist even though our troops no longer have a stomach for the fight. The greater danger does not come from the British or Americans, though; it comes from the Germans. They will hate us for deserting them and before they leave, they will be sure to let us know it."

The promise in his tone frightens her and Mira reaches out and takes his arm. "And you, Aldo? Will you be safe? What can I do? Is there anything I can do to help you? To help you be safe?"

His previously grave expression wilts and he smiles and studies her face, perhaps wanting to gauge the depth of her concern. "No, my angel, there is nothing you can do. For now, there is nothing any of us can do except wait and see." Pausing to enjoy the tenderness with which she views him, de la Grascia moves closer to Mira and kisses her softly on her cheek. Then his grim countenance returns and his limbs stiffen beneath her touch.

"You recall last Sunday that I told you many of our troops are deserting?"

"Yes, Aldo, I remember. What of them?"

"Well, one of my men has gone missing. That in itself is not so much of a problem; I expect more of them to do the same before the end. The problem is that this man let slip to Comune Simone that he knows people in this village and that he expected them to hide him."

"That isn't good, is it, Aldo? What does Comune Simone expect you to do: you cannot keep all the men at the Battery?"

"What he cannot resist telling me is that it is my duty to conduct a house–to–house search of the village." He watches for her reaction.

Mira, though, is prepared for the test and adopts a face as straight as any she has assumed when playing cards with her father. "I see," is all she says.

A smile flickers in his face. "Now, normally I would accede to this demand: but, given Il Duce's dismissal and the fact that many of us expect the King to sue for peace in the coming weeks, I will ignore his persistence. This I can manage for a time, but only for a time. How long, I am not sure. If he squeals to the Germans, who as you have no doubt noticed are now here in abundance, they may insist on a search. And if that happens, I will no longer be the master of my destiny or, for that matter, that of anyone who might be hiding a deserter." He frowns to drive home the gravity of his point. "Again, Mira, as I cautioned you last week: if any of your neighbours need to attend to their laundry, now is the time for them to do so. Am I making myself clear?"

"Yes, Aldo, perfectly."

"Good," he states, in a manner she believes would not be too dissimilar from how he would congratulate a private on having all his buttons correctly fastened. "Now, I would like to see you tomorrow, if you can spare me the time."

Mira smiles to let him know she would like to, as opposed to the reason she is about to provide. "The café is closed: what else do I have to do?"

"Good," he repeats. "I will call for you at six."

"Aldo?"

"Yes, Signora Alberti, what can a humble Tenente do for his angel?"

"I need some sulfa pills; not the ointment that you very kindly supplied. Would it be possible for you to bring some of the pills? You remember the boy who received those burns? Well, he has an infection and the doctor says that if he is to save the boy, he needs a supply of sulfa pills."

Whereas before she had asked, his eyes were bright and lively, now they dim and his hesitation suggests he wishes she had not done so. He stares at her for longer than she would like and eventually the Tenente reaches a conclusion that quite clearly conflicts him.

"I will try. I cannot promise, but I will try. Tomorrow then." De la Grascia bows, kisses the back of her hand rather than her cheek as he had a minute or so before, and marches away towards the Fiat, where Comune Simone watches from the driver's seat.

Mira, too, walks away, aware that though she may have held her nerve, there is no doubt he has seen through her.

Chapter 15

"Mira?"

Silence.

"Mira?"

A rustling of cloth.

"Yes, Nicholas, I am here. Please, not so loud, you will wake papà. What is the matter?"

"You were talking in your sleep," he says.

"Oh, I'm sorry, I did not mean to wake you."

"You didn't; I was awake. I was listening to your breathing and you started talking."

Mira gets up and sits on the side of the bed. She lights a candle and holding it up, she looks him over: his forehead glistens and his bedclothes are soaked with his sweat. "I must change your sheets. How do you feel?"

"Cold."

"Come, sit up. I will give you mine; they are dry."

With her help, he obliges. "What about you? Won't you be cold?"

"No, Nicholas, the night is hot and it is certainly hot enough in here: it is this infection you have; it is raising your temperature and that is why you feel cold." Mira draws the wet sheet down. "Now, as before, lift your hips." She slides it out from beneath him and throws it in the corner. Mira wipes him down and as she folds her dry sheet in place, she asks, "And what was I saying... in my sleep?"

"You were calling out a name."

"And what name was that, Nicholas? Was I calling for Il Duce, the Pope, for the King or for Maria perhaps?"

"No. Carlo or perhaps Cola was what you kept saying. Over and over, you were calling for someone."

"Now, lift up once more. Yes. Good. Now sit up again. That's right. Now, lie back." She floats a second sheet into the air above him and allows it to settle gently against his skin.

"Nicholas," she says, dreamily.

"Yes."

"No. I meant that your name is Nicholas. In Italian this can be read as Nicola, the short form of which is Cola. Do you know our legend of Colapesce?"

"No. Please, tell me."

Returning to the edge of the bed, Mira sits again, though she is careful not to sit so close that her body heat adds to his. "Yes, I will. But afterwards you must promise me to sleep, eh?"

"You sound like my mother," he chuckles.

"Well, perhaps for the moment I am. Now be quiet." She pauses, thinking. "Nicola was the handsome son of a fisherman, a young boy who it was said could swim like a fish. He would dive deep into the waters of the Strait and on his return, he would so delight people with his stories of all the wonders he had seen that he became famous throughout the land. Soon enough, his tales drew the attention of the one–eyed King Frederic, who was... let us say, a little doubting of young Cola's abilities. So, the king decided to test Cola and threw his cup down into the waters of the Strait and bid the boy fetch it back, which he did very quickly. The king then threw his crown into the water and bid Cola fetch it back too, which again he did very quickly. For the final test, the king threw his gold ring into the deepest water and bid Cola recover it. But from this final test, the boy never returned. It is said young Cola dived so deep that he discovered our island was supported on three columns and that because one of the columns was damaged, our island was sinking. The legend says that Cola considered taking the ring and returning to the surface, but realised he couldn't leave Sicily to sink, so he replaced the column with his own form and even today he still stands beneath our island supporting it on his shoulders."

"Colapesce? Still down there?"

"Yes, our Nicola of the fish."

Nicholas giggles, just as he had when his mother had told him stories at bedtime. "Mira, do you think I am Cola returned from the deep?"

"No. No, I don't. Besides, Cola was beautiful and right now you are far from beautiful."

He winces. "Sorry to disappoint."

"No need to apologise, Nicholas; the way you look right now is certainly no fault of yours and I am not looking for another Cola in my life."

"Perhaps it was Carlo you said and not Cola. Who is Carlo?"

"You mean, who was he? Well, Carlo Alberti was my husband."

"Oh, yes. Signora Alberti, I remember now. You told me about him. You just didn't tell me his name."

Mira sighs and remains silent for a while.

"Sorry, I'm being nosey again," he says.

"Oh, don't worry, Nicholas. I realise it must be difficult for you to lie in this bed for so long with nothing to do. With good luck, you won't have to be here much longer."

"How so? How do you know?"

Mira relates all Tenente de la Grascia's news of Mussolini's dismissal and the allied advance, and she can feel through the bed the tension rising in his limbs as he listens.

"He is your friend, this lieutenant? He brings good news. For me at least."

"It is good news for all of us, Nicholas. The sooner this is all over, the sooner the Germans will leave and I can reopen the café and make enough money to find myself a place to live. Your being here has made me aware of many things and one of them is that I have outgrown my parents' patience."

They sit in silence for a while, each affording the other time to imagine what may be to come.

"What was he like, Carlo?"

Mira smiles at her memories. "What was Carlo like?" And recalling what her mother had said regarding how much easier it was to address certain issues from the sanctuary of seclusion, she blows out the candle and sets it on the table.

"What was he like? Oh, Carlo's eyes were unusual: they were the colour of olive bark and his hair was brown like a walnut. He was tall, taller than me, and for a girl from these parts I am taller than most. His limbs were long and slender and he moved with a grace one rarely sees in men, like his body had never grown used to manual work, even though he worked hard in the harbour in Messina. His skin was lighter than that of most, he was more likely of Norman blood, and his voice was always warm and comforting and he rarely raised his voice in anger. For a time, I thought perhaps he was a little feminine and I wondered if he might not be a man for women. However, it was not long before I found out he was." In the dark, she colours and Mira wonders whether, had Nicholas been able to see, he would notice.

"Where did you meet him?"

"At a dance to celebrate the end of Novena di San Giuseppe, the nine days of prayer. It is like knocking on the door of God's house for nine consecutive days, hoping he will answer. If you knock loud enough and for long enough, there is a better chance he will; so you knock as hard and as often as you can. It is no surprise that by the end one feels the need to enjoy oneself, eh? My mother was my chaperone at the dance, of course. I sometimes think that because Carlo was the first boy I met, he was always going to provide my mother and father with their first opportunity to reject whoever I wanted. That was so foolish of me, wasn't it, eh?"

"No, not foolish, Mira, so much as young. When we are young, we choose the easy way to understand life, otherwise it all becomes too confusing. Your father didn't take to Carlo right away?"

"Not just not right away, not ever. My father thought he was too immature, "too young for you" he would say. My father thought Carlo lacked even a fistful of common sense: he said Carlo was always talking, always dreaming, and that for Carlo the tomatoes would always grow quicker and rounder and redder in his neighbour's garden: he said Carlo would never be satisfied with life in Messina. Although my father did admit that he was just the same at that age."

"So, you ignored your father."

"Yes, naturally. I knew Carlo was a little childlike in his thinking, but I found his ambition, his hopes exciting. And things that concerned others, like the tide or the wind or the clouds or what saint's day or whose name day it was, didn't seem to affect him. That was one part of him that attracted me; that lightness and that he excited me in ways I had never imagined I might be excited."

"And because of the way he made you feel, you thought you could prove your father wrong."

"Yes, only I didn't, did I? Or perhaps it is that Carlo proved him right, I don't know. I had always trusted Carlo, that was my mistake. Trusted him not to look at other women. Trusted him to stand up for me. And trusted him never to leave me. And look what happened, eh? One smell of Mussolini's perfume and my husband was gone, not half a year after we were married. My God, how much we argued. My God, how much I cried. My God, how I hated having to return home with my tail between my legs. But that was how it was to be."

"I've done it again, haven't I, Mira? I've made you think of things that have brought you only sadness. I'm so sorry."

"Oh, I'm not so sad, Nicholas. Really I am not."

"Then why is my hand wet with your tears?"

CHAPTER 16

"But papà, we have to move him," she whispers, glancing towards the door to check it is shut. "I have told you what Aldo said. If the Germans come looking, how are we going to explain the presence of a wounded Englishman in my bed?"

"Mira, please think clearly. The risk of moving him is too great. How can we expect to move a man who is blind when around every corner walks a German patrol? We might as well turn him out on the street and leave his future to chance. We might as well shoot him ourselves."

"But if he is found here, they will shoot all of us. Are you willing to risk our lives? To risk me and mama and you, for this one man?"

He glowers at her. "I must say, I am surprised to hear you talk like this. Listening to the way you talk to him in the night, I would have expected you to be the one who wants to protect him, not me."

Francesca, fiddling nervously with her apron strings, stands mute; again, a spectator to their argument.

"I do want to protect him, papà, but surely there has to be a better way than keeping him here. Why don't I take him to the hills: there must be people we know who we can hide him with. What about the sottocapo; where did you take him?"

"I took him to Pipo's house. I told him he should send the sottocapo to the hills. He didn't. He should have done so when he had the chance and now, he has left it too long and the man is hidden in his loft. Even Pipo recognises that to try to move him is too dangerous."

"But papà, at least let me try."

Enzo stands up from the table and stares at her. "No, Mira. I will not permit it. And as long as there is a breath left in my body and I am master of this house, you will do as I say. That is the end of this discussion; the Englishman stays and I will hear no further talk of moving him."

She glares back at her father, not with hate or disrespect; rather with sadness that he does not trust her to spirit Nicholas away to safety. "You are as stubborn as Pipo's mule, do you know that? And I don't understand why you cannot see the sense in what I am saying."

"I am stubborn, eh? Well, let me tell you young lady, that were it not for my stubborn streak, you would never have been born. Now go, prepare yourself for your evening with your fancy Tenente de la Grascia. Perhaps he can talk some sense into you."

CHAPTER 17

As Mira expects, De la Grascia arrives punctually at six. Anxious to keep him away from the house, she waits at the top of the alley that leads up to the road.

The Tenente parks up and hurries round to open her door. "Good evening my angel. I was hoping to pay my respects to your father. No matter; now you are here, let us take a drive."

The Sciroccu of the previous day having blown through to the north, the evening air is less oppressive, though it fails to cool her temper. They drive in silence until their lack of ready conversation weighs too heavily on her.

"Is there any more news than yesterday?" she asks, gazing out the side window.

"The British and Americans bombed Milazzo yesterday and Marshal Badoglio has outlawed the Fascist party, which is ironic when one considers he was perfectly happy to do the Duce's bidding when it profited him. Caviglia would have been a better choice; he at least hated the Fascists."

"Politicians!" she scoffs. "They are like fish left too long in the sun: one smells just as bad as the other."

De la Grascia drives on, and the further he drives the darker, if he believes that it could be possible, falls Mira's black mood.

"What is it that bothers you, my angel? Have I called at a bad time?"

"No, Aldo, although I'm not sure that at the moment there is a good time."

"We have time together," he says, pleasantly, "is that not cause for some minor celebration? Can we not forget about the great disturbance to our lives and simply enjoy each other's company?"

"We can try," she replies, with an abruptness that implies the effort is unlikely to prove worth his reward.

He drives to the village of Pace, a distance of a mere four kilometres down the coast road, but a journey which seems to them to take an eternity.

At every turn, convoys of tanks, halftracks and trucks loaded with German troops head against them, forcing them time and again to pull over and wait, and roadblocks and checkpoints have sprung up like weeds, further truncating their journey.

They arrive at a café and order ice cream. The waiter appears honestly polite and a wizened pensioner serenades them with his accordion. However, that the café is open and busy serves only to deepen Mira's mood and she scowls at German officers when they pat their knees, inviting women.

De la Grascia is patient: he humours her, he flatters her and he agrees with her even when her observations are less than complimentary; and by the time Mira has finished her second ice cream, his patience is all but exhausted. Looking around to ensure he is not overheard, he whispers, "Mira, my angel, I must apologise for no longer being able to deliver you the supplies you need to open your café. I imagine this place keeps open only because it panders to the black market: that or it is owned by, well, let us call them marginal fellows and, judging by their prices, the black market is alive and thriving." He pauses, waiting or perhaps expecting his mention of how much her ice creams have cost him to provoke a change in her demeanour. When it doesn't, he plays his final card.

"And that medication you requested? I have managed to procure it for you. Not much, but the amount should suffice."

Mira's fortress walls, a moment ago seeming so high and impregnable, crumble. "Oh, Aldo, I am so sorry, so very sorry. I am being selfish. Here I am, being treated like a princess and all the while I am behaving like only the most spoilt princess would behave. That is unforgivable of me. All this talk of politics, all these uniforms – though not yours, I assure you – they remind me of so much that is unpleasant and I forget how much you do for me. Please," she reaches across the table and takes his hand, "please forgive me. And please, don't think it is because of the medicine that I agreed to come out with you; it was only that I find it so difficult to be cheerful just now."

"Here," Aldo says, handing her his perfectly pressed, white silk handkerchief.

She takes it and blows her nose. When she has finished, she goes to hand it back to him, but fortunately thinks better of it and pockets it. "I'm sorry. Thank you. It really is a welcome distraction to come here with you; you seem more suited to this café than you do to that dusty old battery up at Capo Peloro."

His eyes light up. "Yes, I must admit I do feel more at home here." He leans forward and fixes her with a conspiratorial glare. "Except for the foreigners, of course."

Now that Mira's guard is relaxed, if not dropped absolutely, and de la Grascia is reassured that she is properly listening to what he has to say, he talks freely of his family and his student days in Bologna. As the sun sets their conversation takes a more natural path and seeing that Mira is now relaxed, de la Grascia insists on more ice cream.

"That German officer at the table behind you keeps staring at you," she murmurs.

Aldo smiles. "And why wouldn't he? I must be the envy of every red–blooded, blond–haired, blue–eyed Aryan in Sicily. You have seen to that, my angel."

She colours. "If I did not know you were from the north, Aldo, I would think you'd studied at a charm school in Naples. That is the kind of ridiculous compliment a Napolitano would pay. All about how a girl makes him look; not about how beautiful the girl looks."

"I apologise."

"Now I know you are from the north: a Napolitano would never apologise for his compliments no matter how bad they were."

"Tell me, Mira, what is this officer like? The one who stares at me."

She leans to look past the Tenente. "He sits alone and he wears a uniform like all the others, except that he wears two crosses on one side of his jacket, one of which has swords and a small design above it and the other a swastika surrounded in gold. He has darker skin and could pass for Italian. Oh, and his left arm is…, well, he has lost his right arm below his elbow."

"You have good observation, Mira. Tell me, what colour are his eyes?"

"They are dark and set a little close together, a little bit like Comune Simone, but this man has the twinkle of humour about him: he is not all serious and stiff like the other officers."

De la Grascia turns in his chair and looks.

The officer, too, looks up and the light of recognition fires in his expression. "Aldo," he calls, "Is that you, you old rascal? I thought you were dead." For a man in German uniform, his Italian is near perfect.

"And I you, Franz. Ah, I see they have promoted you."

"It is true, Aldo, and now I am in command of a prison filled with unfortunate civilians and soldiers who either refuse to fight or cannot be trusted to. When they do that to you, you know you are as much a danger to your own men as you are to the enemy. I see you must be of greater use; they have demoted you."

De la Grascia winces and then remembers Mira is watching him. "With your permission?" he asks her.

"Why not," she replies, "this is as much your café as it is mine and soon, if what you tell me is correct, this man will be as much your enemy as he is mine."

He waves the German over to join them and introduces him.

The officer is tall and rangy. He clips his heels and bows, and before he sits, he turns to address Mira, "If you are sure I am not intruding?"

For a further hour the two officers sit, chat, laugh and drink a variety of liqueurs. They'd met in Russia, they'd fought, they'd suffered, they'd drunk themselves stupid and buried not only their men, but their emotions. And now, they mourn, they joke, they chuckle and they shoot each other knowing looks when either the Führer or the Duce wheedle their way into the conversation.

Mira finds their friendship a welcome distraction. Yet she finds it hard to come to terms with the fact that they are sitting in a café, eating ice cream and drinking liqueurs, while only a short day's train ride away other men are fighting and dying.

The German laughs, perhaps a little too loudly considering the sarcastic tone of his amusement. "Yes, young lady, you are correct; the world in which we find ourselves is truly bizarre. Why, I heard the other day that our glorious commander has taken a fancy to a villa in Taormina; a villa that used to belong to an Englishman. Casa Cuseni, they say it is called. And they also say that our dear Uncle Albert has had en suite bathrooms built for his three senior staff generals because he was fed up with sharing his own personal toilet with them. Fed up with sharing a toilet when his soldiers have to squat behind bushes. Bizarre, no?"

"So, what is the word from on high?" de la Grascia asks, sipping yet another glass of pear liqueur.

The officer leans forward: his good humour evaporates. "I'm sure a man of your intelligence already knows how all this," he sits back and spreads his arms wide, "is going to end. We have played out every possible scenario and every one of them leads to the same conclusion: we lose. And as soon as Kesselring has summoned the courage, he will report the same to the Führer. I am sure they are already planning the evacuation."

In the car on their way back to Ganzirri, Mira's mind floats. "He was very charming, your Franz."

"Yes. An Austrian. A mountaineer, a climber. From near the Brenner. Another few kilometres south and he would have been one of us, though we've never been able to work out whether that would have been a blessing or a curse."

"Aldo?" The liqueurs have loosened her tongue and her voice comes across as that of a girl engaged in idle chit–chat.

"Yes, my angel."

"If I ask you a question, will you be honest in your reply?"

"Of course. What is it that you think might trouble me to answer you dishonestly?"

"That German, or rather that Austrian, he said that you had been demoted: what rank were you before?"

He negotiates a bend in silence, then sighs. "I was a captain, like Franz when I first met him."

"Why were you demoted? What happened?"

"Oh, you don't want to hear the details, they are not relevant. Just take it that I pretty much demoted myself."

"Why?"

"Because."

"Because of what?"

"Really, Mira. Can you not just accept some things for what they are?"

She is quiet for a few seconds, before replying. "Oh yes, Aldo, there are many things that are all the better for being just how they are. I asked you a question though and I asked you to answer honestly which you told me you would."

"And that means I have to, I suppose."

She reaches across and pokes his arm, playfully. "Yes, Aldo, it does."

"Then," he sighs once more, "I will tell you, though you must understand that it is difficult for me to convey the context in which what I am about to tell you happened. And you must understand that military law does not allow for context; battles are either won or lost, they are never conveniently drawn."

"It was bad, was it?"

"Yes, Mira, it was bad. Do you remember at church the Sunday before last that I told your father I had served in Russia? Well, while I was there, my division was sent to the aid of a German regiment, the one Franz served in. The Russians tried to prevent us from crossing the River Don to relieve them and, against the odds and completely outnumbered, we managed to. It was during this battle that Franz lost his arm: I found him unconscious in a ditch, which is just one reason why we enjoy such a close friendship. Anyway, at one point, I had to send men to the rear to collect more ammunition and when they returned, one of them had gone missing: paralysed with fear, he had not come back. The Germans found him and brought him to us. As his commanding officer, it was up to me to punish him; to make an example of him. My senior officers demanded I had him shot and I refused. You must believe me, Mira, I tried every trick in my book to avoid this order being carried out but, in the end, they ignored my pleas and went ahead and executed him. For my sins of disobedience, I was demoted and banished to serve with this Coastal Division. In a curious way, my refusal to meet the obligations of my rank saved my life."

"Saved your life? How?"

"Because by December, the Duca d'Aosta Division was all but wiped out and very few of those I had commanded returned from Russia. Now, the division no longer exists; it has been disbanded. So, I lived and my demotion ensured I would at least never have to face such a situation again. Perhaps I am a coward, just like the man who was shot. Who knows? Only me, eh?"

"Oh Aldo," Mira slides across the seat and rests her head on his shoulder, "I am so sorry. So very sorry for asking you without thinking that my asking might bring a terrible memory to life, and so very sorry because that is exactly what I have done."

When they park up at the top of the alley which leads down to the house, the combination of her guilt at making him recall unpleasant events and his guilt at having survived, have elicited a sombre mood and not one suited to romantic parting. Nevertheless, Aldo puts his arm around her and with his other hand he encourages her face towards his. "Mira," he says, lightening and softening his tone, "one has no way of knowing what the immediate future holds, which is why it is important for me to make you aware of my feelings for you. So please, just listen to what I have to say."

She shrinks away from his embrace, chuckling. "Aldo, you are so very formal, I–"

He puts his fingers to her lips. "Ssh, Mira, just listen, please." Tenente Aldo de la Grascia assembles the ranks of his sentiment. "Mira, I have never met anyone quite like you: you are not only beautiful, but you are also clever and passionate and tender and headstrong and... and when I think of you I understand that you possess all the very wonderful attributes a man could ask for in a woman. The fact that you have been married only increases my love for you, for you have already loved and lost and so you know what love means: you know the value of love and you know how very transient and cursory love can be if one does not hold onto it with every fibre of one's being. Mira you stir in me emotions I have never felt before and for all of this, I love you and would very much like you to be by my side for however much time it is that we have left."

Though it is dark in the car and she cannot read the earnest intention in his expression, the weight of his affection is palpable;

it is like a smothering blanket which threatens to suffocate her. "Aldo, I—"

"Please, Mira, please let me kiss you. Let me show you how much I love you. Let me—"

She shrinks even further away from him, so much so that she presses up against the door. "No, Aldo. No, I can't. Please, don't think me mean or that I don't appreciate the way you feel and all you have done for me, and please, please believe me when I say I like being with you and that I have enjoyed our evening. If things were different, who knows, perhaps I would grow to love you. Now though, right at this moment, I find my own emotions confusing enough without you adding to them. Can we not just be friends? Can we not simply enjoy each other's company while we have the chance? Is that too much to ask in these dreadful times?"

In the same way that before she could feel the weight of his affection without seeing him, now she perceives him withdrawing from her. Aldo detaches and diminishes: his ardour, his fervour fading like a tide that laps at the shore only to find it tastes sour.

"No, Mira," he whispers, taking his time, "though it is not how I would like you to feel, this is not too much to ask. How can it be in the face of all this madness? But tell me, please, be honest with me, is it because there is someone else in your life? Is there another man who is more deserving of your affection than me, because if there is, he must love you very deeply? And if there is, please tell me and I will respect both you and this man, and leave you in peace. Sad though this would make me, it would at least provide me with reason and that would be of some small comfort to me."

Mira replaces her hand on his arm, which she strokes, tenderly. "No, Aldo, there is no other man in my life. I am sorry to disappoint you; there is no one, no one at all."

Chapter 18

"Your father," Nicholas murmurs, from up on the bed, "when he said that if it had not been for his stubborn streak, you would never have been born, what did he mean by that?"

First light is creeping into the room; not with sufficient strength to cast a shadow, but with enough promise for her to know that a bright sun will soon follow.

"You could hear us, eh, Nicholas," she replies, from down on the floor.

"Actually, at the time, I was thinking that it was impossible not to hear you. I guess I was paying more attention to your argument about what you thought best for me. It was only afterwards when you had come to your conclusion, that what he said stuck with me. Oh, and by the way, if you want to turf me out and leave me to the Germans, I won't hold it against you. I realise that my being here puts all of you at enormous risk. Last Sunday, when you were out at church, I very nearly got up and walked out."

"Why didn't you?" she asks, loading her tone with a barrel of humour.

"I didn't because when I lifted my legs off the bed, I didn't think I could trust them to get me as far as the door and I couldn't bear the thought of you coming back to find me like a beached whale on the floor of your bedroom. A bit selfish of me, maybe, but I thought I'd probably cause you more trouble than I might save."

"A whale, eh? More like an emaciated donkey, if you ask me. It's time for you to drink and take some more pills." Mira gets up and it is not until she is standing that she is aware of her nakedness. To have slept clothed in such temperature would have led her to perspire much as her patient perspires and because of his inability to see, there would be little point in enduring the heat only to preserve an unnecessary modesty. Nevertheless, she slips on a dress and taking the tin from the side–table and removing two pills, she places them in his hand. When he has put them in his mouth, she raises the glass and holds the tube to his mouth.

"Thank you," he mumbles as he swallows. "When this is all over, Mira, you must let me thank this friend of yours. He must be a regular fellow."

"He is. He is too much of a regular fellow. He is a gentleman and, in some ways, far too much of a gentleman." She pauses, reflecting, passing judgement, regretting a little. "He makes it too easy for me."

"Makes what too easy?"

Mira hesitates, then, "You asked me about my father's stubborn streak, Nicholas. Would you like me to tell you?"

"Please. Why do you think he is so stubborn?"

"You mean, so stubborn in wanting to save you or more so. Well, many years before I was born there came a great tragedy to Messina; a great earthquake that devastated the city and trapped my father in the cellar of his parent's house. He lay for many days in the ruins but, fortunately for him, in one of the aftershocks the beam pinning his legs moved and he was able to free himself. Because of the time he had been pinned beneath the beam, his legs would not work and, as a result, he had to drag himself for a long way over broken ground to seek help. It is why his hands are so scarred and why he walks awkwardly. You know, sometimes in the winter he finds it painful to get out of his bed and how he manages to go fishing, mama and I will never understand. He never complains though. Never. Not once have I heard him utter a word that suggests he is anything other than grateful for the good fortune he received in being spared."

"I believe," he says, "that many died. My mother kept newspaper cuttings of the period. I never understood her fascination with the earthquake and whenever I asked her why, she always changed the conversation. I have read some of the cuttings, it must have been terrible."

"It was, yes. So many died, thousands or perhaps tens of thousands, nobody really knows. Many people were never given the same chance as my father. So, when he says that if it was not for his stubborn streak I would not have been born, he is really saying that I should not question his judgement, because without his spirit, his belief and his will, he would not have lived to grant me the gift of life."

"And his parents died, in the earthquake?"

"Yes, and his brother and two sisters. All of them. His father was a wealthy man, or if not wealthy then well–to–do; they lived in a grand house in the Via dei Templari. It is not there now and, if it was, the air raids would probably have destroyed what was left of it just as they have destroyed much of Messina that was rebuilt after the earthquake. He may be a fisherman, my father, and most people think fishermen are simple because they take pleasure in simple things, but he is an educated man; it was my father who taught me to read and write, and not many daughters of fishermen are provided with such luxuries. And rather than allow my mother to teach me to sew pretty patterns on lace, he encouraged me to think and believe in myself, something I am sure he often regrets."

"Why? How could thinking for yourself be bad?"

"Because that is what lies at the heart of our arguments. In teaching me to think for myself, he showed me that it is better to question than simply to do what we are told. That, in the eyes of many, makes him look weak and makes me appear ungovernable. That goes against not just the Sicilian way, but the way of the world."

"The world is changing, Mira."

"You think so?"

"Yes, in many ways and I am sure it is only a matter of time before all women will be educated. Mira, if your father was from a wealthy family, why did he become a fisherman?"

"What else was there for him to do? The earthquake not only killed his family, it took away from him everything he had, everything he knew. In the time it takes to recite the mysteries of the rosary, the way of life for people in the city was altered beyond their recognition and to provide, many took to whatever work they could find. My father became a fisherman and besides, whenever I have asked him if he wishes his life was otherwise, he always says, "Why wish it was otherwise, when it is how it is. Be thankful.""

The light in the small room is sharper now. The imperfections of its crude yet substantial construction grinning through from behind the layers of white–washed plaster, reminding her of all that her father has worked so hard over so many years to build up.

"Your father is a strange man, Mira."

"What makes you say that, Nicholas? Strange, in what way?"

He lifts his arm and reaches up to find hers, then, gripping her forearm with an intensity born of his heightened temperature, he replies, his voice challenged, his pronunciation laboured as though an invisible force attempts to subdue him. "I don't mean to offend and I didn't mean he is strange in a poor way. What I meant was, he seems to want to sit beside my bed much of the time; he seems to want to talk. To me, a stranger."

"It is difficult if not dangerous for him to fish right now. He cannot venture far out into the Strait and so his catch is limited to the little fishes."

"No, it's not that. He asks me about my life, my upbringing and my parents, particularly about my mother. He keeps asking me why I speak Italian with such a Sicilian accent, why I understand words that he says only a Messinese would know."

"And what do you tell him?"

He thinks for a moment, clearly trying to find an answer that will satisfy her in the same way that he so evidently cannot find one with which to satisfy her father. Eventually, his effort and his patience are exhausted. "I don't know, Mira. I didn't know my Italian was so like yours until he explained the differences to me."

"It is true, Nicholas, you speak like we do. You must admit that is unusual."

"And my signet ring. He insists on examining it. It holds a kind of fascination for him and every time he sits with me, he asks to hold my hand so he can look at it. Why is that?"

Mira picks up a piece of cloth, dips it in the water of the jug beside the bed and wipes the sweat from his brow. "Perhaps it is time for you to cease talking. Perhaps you should rest and save your questions for when you have more strength."

"Sure, you're probably right, Mira. I'm sorry, I guess this fever makes my mind wander."

"Quiet, Nicholas. Listen."

"What can you hear?"

"Quiet," she insists. "There are men, shouting."

Mira stands, opens the door and steps into the front room.

Her father appears, hastily tucking his shirt into his trousers. "You can hear it, too, eh?"

"Yes, papà. What is going on?"

Together, they go outside and stand to look up and down the water's edge.

"It is coming from the village," he says. "Soldiers. Italian and German. Stay here, I will go and see." He walks away around the side of the house and it isn't long before he comes back. "They are searching the houses. They are looking for someone. Deserters, I think."

Sure enough, a patrol spills out from between the houses just a few doors down. Mira spots Aldo in the company of a German officer and several soldiers. They are knocking on the doors and walking inside in a manner that suggests they are not waiting to be invited.

Mira and her father watch and wait as they come back out and move to the next house, coming ever closer.

"What will we do, papà?"

"I don't know, Mira. What can we do?" Enzo briefly chews his knuckle. Then he turns to her, "It is too late to move Nicholas. Without his sight, he will never be able to run fast enough to get away from them and they probably have the area surrounded. Go inside. Think of something. I don't know what, but use your imagination. I will try to stop them."

"Papà?"

"Yes, Mira,

"Be careful of the one with eyes close together. His blood would pale obsidian."

Mira turns back into the house, past her mother, who stands fiddling with her apron, a look of abject fear written large in her expression. "Mama, put some water on to boil, find the last of the coffee. And for our sake, try not to look as though you've just stepped out of the confessional. Look anything, but don't look guilty."

In her room, her patient is agitated, he turns his head from side to side, straining to listen. "What's going on, Mira?"

"Exactly what we feared; they are conducting a search."

"Then help me up. I must get out of your house. If they find me here, they will shoot all of you."

"No, Nicholas. You will never make it to the end of the path. Stay still, I am thinking."

He tries to lever himself upright, but only makes it as far as his elbows. "Now look, Mira, I must get out. I must, you have no right to—"

"Lie back down," she orders. "Lie still. I know this will not be easy, but try to relax, I am going to get into bed with you." Mira shrugs off her dress and, pulling aside the sheet, lies down beside him. Trying her best in the narrow bed not to lean too heavily against his still broken skin, she drapes herself around him.

He winces.

"I'm sorry," she replies.

"Don't be," he whispers, grinning through his blindness, "that's a pain I'm quite happy to put up with."

"Be quiet, you fool. And remember, if anyone asks your name, it is Carlo. Remember. If you can only hold onto one thought, it is that your name is Carlo and you are my husband."

They hear voices at the front door.

"Ah, Tenente de la Grascia, what brings you to our house so early on a Wednesday morning? You would like to go fishing, perhaps?"

"No, Signor Ruggeri, I wish I had the time; however, we have a report that one of my men, a deserter, is being sheltered by a family and so we are searching all the houses in the village. Please stand aside."

"Now, Tenente. It may have slipped your memory, but have you not already enjoyed our hospitality. You are welcome to return, of course, but at a more social hour. My wife is not yet dressed to receive visitors and my daughter is not yet awake. Would it not be better for you to come back in, say, an hour or two?"

Francesca appears in the doorway to Mira's room and the contortions of her face reveal that the spectacle which greets her is quite possibly the last she had expected to see.

"Mama, get out," Mira hisses. "Go in the front room this instant."

Her mother closes the door.

The discussion outside the front door continues.

"Ah," they hear Enzo say, "if my nose is not mistaken, I believe my wife may have prepared coffee. Would you and this German officer like to share in a cup? I am sad to say it is not real coffee. After all, how could a poor fisherman like me afford a cup of real coffee? And even if I could afford it, where would I be able to buy it, eh?"

"No, no coffee, thank you. Please though, stand aside while we search the premises."

"Come now, Tenente, why would I be inclined to provide shelter to a man who absolves himself from his obligations? A soldier is a soldier and I am a fisherman. The duty of a fisherman is to go fishing. What would the hungry say if I did not provide them with fish simply because I thought the waters a little intimidating? Surely, one would say the same of a soldier who refused to pick up his gun simply because it makes a loud noise, if you see what I mean."

Reminded of what Aldo had told her the evening before about his refusal to shoot a soldier who deserted his post, Mira winces.

"Quite possibly, yes. Now, please? If you don't mind?"

A German voice and, judging by the tone, an order. A rifle is slowly cocked.

"Comune Simone," de la Grascia says, his tone impatient, "lower your weapon. If I need you to use it, I will order you to do so; and while I am your Tenente, you will take your orders from me and not any other officer, is that clear?"

"Ah," Enzo repeats, "I see our German comrade is a Captain, which I suppose means he outranks you, Tenente de la Grascia."

"Yes, Signor Ruggeri, he does. And while I would not order my men to shoot you, he, in all likelihood, will not hesitate to do so, so..."

"Then, by all means," Enzo replies.

Mira steels herself and whispers, "Lie still, Nicholas, and for both our sakes do not speak unless you are spoken to."

They lie and listen as the stamp of footsteps on the stone floor tells them Mira's parent's room is being inspected first.

"As I believe you have seen for yourself, Tenente, our house is modest in comparison to the airy villas of Bologna. One would need the competence of a magician to conceal much more than a goat in such a confined space." Enzo's humour falls on stony ground.

A chair is moved aside, a few more footsteps and a hand is placed firmly on the handle of the door.

The door swings open. Mira looks up from the bed.

Aldo de la Grascia stands watching her and behind him, craning his neck to see, stands a German officer; the same German officer with whom he had exchanged words outside her café only a week or so before.

They both stand and stare; the Italian officer looking for all the world as though whatever he may have held dear in life has just been ripped from his grasp; the German officer simply looking, part disinterested, part menacing.

Mira rubs her eyes and face, feigning a sleepy surprise. "Excuse me," she says, "can you not see we are sleeping?"

De la Grascia coughs, embarrassed. "Yes, why of course, we—"

"Who is this man?" the German barks in his native tongue.

"He is her husband," de la Grascia replies, his face deadpan if tinged with a shade of melancholy. "We have no interest in him."

"You, what is your name?" the German calls, shoving the lieutenant aside, filling the room with his grey uniform.

"Leave him," de la Grascia insists. "He is no danger to us. He is blind, perhaps like you?"

"What did you say to him?" Mira asks.

"I said, your husband is a danger to no one. He is blind and I asked the German officer if perhaps he was."

The German captain ignores the insult and asks again, "You, what is your name?"

"What does he want?" Mira asks.

De la Grascia exhales, loud enough for all in the small room to hear. "This German officer wants to know your husband's name. And frankly, I'd like to hear it too."

Mira, incensed, sits bolt upright, uncaring that she is both naked and that she exposes her breasts; breasts that no man since her husband has set eyes on. "Aldo, you know my husband's name, it's—"

"My name is Carlo," Nicholas interrupts. "Carlo Alberti." He fumbles for her shoulder. "This is my wife, Mira, and whoever you are, you have no manners. Call yourself officers? Believe me, if I could see to strike you, I would do so. But, as I cannot, perhaps you should show this injured former serviceman some respect and be good enough to leave us alone."

The German captain groans, "Damned Sicilians!" and he turns to barge his way out of the room.

De la Grascia, though, is not so swift in leaving. He stands, his expression glum, and watches. "Oh, Mira," he says in a voice that is barely audible.

She pulls the sheet up to her shoulders and stares back at him; and whereas his expression is wholly dispirited, hers is equally apologetic. "I will explain," she says.

"There is little point," he replies and turns on his heels to leave.

"Aldo," she calls.

He ignores her plea. "Thank you, Signor Ruggeri. I bid you a good day."

"Well, Tenente, my day will be whatever it brings. Yours, on the other hand, may require some lifting."

Mira appears barefoot at the door. She is clothed, though only in so far as she has put on her loose dress and is therefore no longer naked.

Enzo scowls at her and quickly turns back to the Lieutenant. "As far as your search goes, you will not find any deserters here. If there were any, thanks to your warning, they would be long gone. If I were you, I would go back to the battery. Why don't you take your German dogs with you and call it a day?"

De la Grascia fixes him with a hapless stare. "Believe me, Signor Ruggeri, I would prefer little else." He throws Mira a look that leaves her in no doubt he is disappointed with her. "Unfortunately, like the soldier you mentioned a few minutes ago I cannot absolve myself of my obligations, especially now that they are determined for me by our German allies. Of course, they may not be our allies for much longer, but until I receive orders stating otherwise, I'm afraid I will have, as it were, to play second fiddle. Signor Ruggeri." He turns and salutes. "Signora Alberti."

As the Tenente walks away up the water's edge, Comune Simone follows, turning around every couple of paces to throw Mira and Enzo glowers of unadulterated loathing.

"What's happening, Mira?" Nicholas asks when he hears her come back into the room.

"Nothing. Everything." She hurries to put on more clothes. "I must go; they are headed towards Pipo's house."

"What is at Pipo's house that makes you afraid for him, a deserter?"

"No, you remember the man you saved and who saved you?"

"Only vaguely."

"Well, my father thinks Sottocapo Falanga is still there. I must go and follow them." She slips on her shoes. "Nicholas?"

"Yes, Mira?"

"Your fever must be leaving you: that was very quick thinking."

"Mira?"

"Yes."

"It wasn't so much because you were in bed with me; it was more the way you talk of your husband, with such affection and such tenderness. I was just thinking I'd like someone to talk about me that way."

"Nicholas, you are a romantic and love conquers even the hardest of hearts; though judging by the expression on Comune Simone's face, I doubt he has ever looked love in the face. I will be back, later."

By the time she catches up with the patrol, they are threading their way through the alleys that will lead them to, amongst others, Pipo's house. The soldiers grow aware of her following them and the Germans grin and exchange what are self–evidently lewd remarks. The Italian soldiers, all apart from Comune Simone who thrusts his rifle out straight in the hope that a deserter will run around the corner and impale himself on it, dawdle and linger to pick flowers that grow through the cracks in the walls. The lieutenant notices her and nods his head, as though encouraging an inquisitive dog to return home.

As they approach the last corner, a figure comes belting around it towards them.

When he sees them, he skitters and skids to a halt, grabbing hold of the wall to help arrest his progress. No longer painted in black oil, Sottocapo Filippo Falanga is barely recognisable, for now he wears dark grey pants and a black waistcoat over a white shirt, and would pass for a local were it not for his look of fear.

He turns to look back and takes off the way he has come.

Scenting their prey, the soldiers run after him, some cocking their weapons.

Mira, too, hurries to the corner where, filled with a dreadful anticipation, she waits and watches.

Where the sun has not yet reached to dry the moisture from the smoothed stones, the surface is treacherous and Falanga slips and falls. He drags himself to his feet and starts off again, keeping to the wall, peering and rattling at locked doors.

Behind him, not thirty metres away, the Italian soldiers loiter and watch; they are not remotely interested in apprehending a man who, up until a few minutes ago, they would have changed places with. However, before them, Comune Simone leads the German patrol as they break step and start running.

"Halt!" Simone shouts. "Halt or I fire!"

Tenente de la Grascia, realising that he has lost control of his man, starts off in pursuit. His cap falls from his head. "No!" he screams. "Do not fire! Stand down!"

The pack, though, will not listen; they cannot listen, for they are consumed by their hunt and like a pack of hungry dogs they run, their ears closed to anyone who might want to hold them back from their chase.

"Halt!" Simone screams again, cocking his rifle and pausing in his step to raise it. "Halt or I fire!"

"No!" de la Grascia screams again.

Falanga runs, he slips, he gets to his feet and runs again.

"Halt!" shouts Simone. He stoops to kneel, aims his rifle and fires twice.

The sottocapo hunches his shoulders, spins as though twirled by invisible fingers and comes to rest half–leaning, half–falling down the white wall of a house. In his wake, he leaves a ghastly smear of blood.

The shots echo up and down the confines of the alley.

Sottocapo Filippo Falanga slides down the wall. He twists, he turns, he stares at the patrol, his fear now replaced by a need to comprehend the fullness of what has just happened. Why in God's name would one of my countrymen want to shoot me? Why would anyone want to shoot me? Why would... Why?

He slumps to the ground, his lifeblood pumping from his chest, his head resting at an unnatural angle.

CHAPTER 19

For the next three days, the village is submerged beneath a sea of trauma. Few, if any, are seen talking in public and people go about their business, such as circumstances permit, with their eyes unseeing and their spirits crushed. It as though a veil of silence has been drawn over the houses, forbidding the folk from either mentioning or discussing how it could be that one of their soldiers could be so callous as to shoot one of his own comrades.

The witnesses to the shooting had stood and stared until the German officer had marched up, inspected the body and, without the slightest sign of remorse, waved his men away to leave de la Grascia, his men and Mira all staring with unchecked hatred at Comune Simone.

The silence had eventually been broken by the opening of a door further up the alley. Out from the house had stepped Enzo and Pipo, and they had simply glanced at the stunned witnesses before turning to walk away in the direction of the village.

Tenente de la Grascia had watched them, then strolled over to Mira, put his arm around her and shepherded her away from the scene. "Go home, Mira. Please, go home. There is nothing more for you to see here."

And he had been right; there had been nothing more to see other than the sottocapo's lifeless form soiling the narrow lane, staining a previously chaste street where on a more normal day children would play with gay abandon, where wives would gossip while attending to their washing and where husbands would boast bright-eyed about the money their day's catch would bring. No one denied that death and destruction had already been brought to Messina, and Villa San Giovanni and Reggio di Calabria across the Strait, and they had watched with detached disquiet as the columns of armoured convoys had trundled through their village. Yet so far, death had come only to those who, like young Gennaro Ganci and his brothers, had ventured out beyond the boundaries of their security. So far, they and their families had been safe out of harm's way; now though, because of Comune Simone's despicable act, death had been brought into their midst.

On Thursday, Milazzo had suffered and ships waiting outside the harbour of Messina had been bombed and several of them sunk. On Friday, Milazzo had taken yet another pounding and small, fast, red-nosed aircraft had dived and swooped and poured hails of bullets into those ships still at anchor in the Strait. By the weekend, no one was left in any doubt that after the thirty-five years it had taken them to recover from the great earthquake, they were once again falling prey to death's insatiable hunger.

Mass on Sunday is a muted affair, even more solemn, if that is possible, than usual and de la Grascia arrives late. Many in the congregation turn at the sound of his boots clipping on the marble floor and whispers spread, shoulders shrug and heads shake in sorry bewilderment.

Afterwards, on the apron outside, the Tenente seeks out Mira, Enzo and Francesca.

"Signor, Signora Ruggeri, Mira, if you will permit me, I would like to greet you and the month of August with an apology on behalf of the Regio Esercito." He thins his eyes and lips in an appeasing smile.

335

"And what does his majesty's army feel the need to apologise for this time?" Enzo quips, playing along.

"Why, Signor Ruggeri, for the dreadful events of last Wednesday. I have since learned that the poor unfortunate who was shot was a naval rating. It appears he was a survivor from the sinking of one of our submarines on the night of 15th July, and rather than return to his duties he had decided to take his chances hiding out in the village until the end of hostilities."

Enzo is again quick to reply. "A survivor from a naval engagement, eh? And you had him shot? I must tell you, Tenente de la Grascia, that in my experience when an animal starts to feed on itself, that animal is lost."

"Yes, Signor Ruggeri, I believe you may be right. However, and if you recall, I tried to warn you that fugitives, and those harbouring them, were likely to suffer the consequences of their actions."

"It is just as well, then, that no one was found to be harbouring this poor unfortunate man."

"Exactly. Just as well," de la Grascia replies, leaving his words to hang in the air, while all the time avoiding eye contact with Mira.

"How goes the advance or the retreat or the progress of whichever side we are betting on today?" Enzo asks.

"The Germans have built a defensive line from Catania through Adrano and Troina to San Fratello near the northern coast. They will hold the British, Canadians and Americans back for as long as they need to."

"Need to?"

"Yes, need to. Signor Ruggeri, I believe I have more important news that concerns you and particularly those of your friends who live close to the water. And as the saying goes, you did not hear this from me, even though what I am about to tell you will become plainly obvious in the coming days."

"Yes, all right, Tenente, we heard it from the fish, now kindly get to the point."

"My news, Signor Ruggeri, is that the evacuation to Calabria has now been approved and this will be effected through several points. Our troops and artillery will leave from Mortelle on the northern coast, from Salvatore and from Messina itself. They will embark in landing craft and ferry steamers. That is, perhaps, good news."

His expression grows more serious. "The bad news is that our German allies," he rolls his eyes, "will leave from Pistunia, to the south of Messina, and from near our battery at Capo Peloro."

"That is bad news?" Enzo interrupts, mystified.

"Please, Signor Ruggeri, let me finish. The greater part of the danger lies in that most of the German troops, tanks and artillery have been designated to leave by Siebel ferry and barge from three other points; namely from Salvatore and Paradiso to the south, and from here in Ganzirri."

Not seeing any significance in what he is saying, Enzo interrupts once more. "But surely, Tenente, the quicker the Germans leave, the sooner we shall be left in peace?"

"That is true. Perfectly true. Unfortunately, though, that presents something of a paradox. And why? Because as soon as the British and Americans learn that German and Italian forces are escaping to the mainland, they will most certainly bomb all the embarkation points, and as the bulk of the German forces will be retreating from the central and western areas along the coast road in this direction, most of them will be leaving through here. I am sure I don't have to remind you that Ganzirri to Pezzo and Capo Peloro to Cannitello are the shortest routes across the Strait, which means that this area is likely to attract the most attention."

Enzo, Francesca and Mira all look at each other in horror.

"No one here will lend a hand to help them across the Strait," Enzo says. "Surely, they won't be bothered with us?"

"Please, Signor Ruggeri, mark my words well, as soon as they find out, the British will bomb by night and the Americans by day; so if you have the chance, I advise you to gather as much as you can carry and leave the village." He waits for a response; however, his audience is too tied up with their imaginings. "There, I have told you; what you decide to do is now up to you." At this, he gazes at Mira with the expression of a doctor who has just delivered his closest relative a damning prognosis.

Enzo is for once silent, overwhelmed by the shock, and Mira looks all at once both grateful and apologetic. Francesca, one usually inclined to stand mute while her husband speaks for her, is though moved to both tears and words.

"Tenente de la Grascia, you have been so kind to us. You have kept watch over us and proved our salvation several times over." She looks very directly and slowly at Mira, wanting the Italian officer to know she is very definitely and intentionally referring to the search of their house and the discovery of... "We cannot thank you enough. We are forever in your debt. In fact, I will return inside and say prayers for you."

"That, Signora Ruggeri, I would be very grateful for, though I feel that through the next few days we will need more than prayers if we are to survive."

"Yes, Aldo," Mira adds, crossing her arms to stop herself from hugging him and thereby sending him the wrong message, "we will all pray for you, won't we, papà?"

Enzo ceases his gazing at the ground and holds out his hand. "Yes, we will. Please try to keep yourself safe, Aldo. I will remember everything you have done for us, everything you have done and continue to do to ensure the safety of our village."

The unexpected and very personal use of his Christian name touches the lieutenant so deeply that his eyes water and his voice cracks. "Of course, Signor Ruggeri." He shakes the fisherman's hand, "Thank you. If only things had been other than they were."

Then he wipes at his eyes with the back of his hand and looks skyward in an effort to distract from his embarrassment. "Now, a word with Mira in private, if you will permit me?"

"Yes," Enzo replies, ushering them to leave.

They walk down the steps and stroll across the road to the small piazza overlooking the lagoon. The sky is clear, the atmosphere calm and balmy, and the flanks of Aspromonte away to the east obscured by the last of the day's haze.

Changing her mind about not wanting to send him confusing signals, Mira takes his arm. "Aldo, I am so sorry—"

"No," he says, his tone mellow, "love knows no apology, Mira. I will always hold you in great affection, please know that. And if all we can be is friends, then let us be close friends, at least that way I will have the honour of a place in your heart."

"Thank you, Aldo." Now, it is time for her eyes to water as his grace and his charm, and his ready acceptance of her decision to reject him, suddenly dismantles her defences. "I have never met anyone like you, Aldo. You would have been far too good for me; I could never have made you truly happy."

Gently, he swings her round to face him. "Yes, I know," he says, though his eyes betray his lie. "Now, before I go, I have some information that you must consider and this is far more important than my warning of air raids. Comune Simone—"

"That degenerate," Mira moans.

"Yes, listen to me. Like others who have visited your café, I know that the blind man you are protecting is most definitely not your husband. And the only reason the Germans don't as yet know this, is because they have only recently arrived and your café is no longer open. Your problem, our problem, lies in the fact that Comune Simone knows your husband died some years ago." Aldo pauses, allowing her time to take in the significance of what he is saying. "Comune Simone was, if not a regular at your café, then party to many of the conversations the men at the battery shared regarding your... circumstances."

"My circumstances?"

He sighs. "Mira, widows there may be in abundance; albeit that attractive and potentially available single women are few and far between. Please don't tell me you do not know the men talk about you. Why, most of them would throw themselves beneath the tracks of a tank if only you would promise them a date first."

"Aldo?"

"Yes."

"I know that he knows: I told him when I came to ask for the medical supplies. I did not think it important at the time." She searches the sky for some understanding and very quickly the importance of what he is suggesting dawns on her. "So, what you are saying is that because Comune Simone knows, we are still in danger."

"The gravest danger, Mira; for he has told me that if I do not act on this information, he will be sure to pass it to the German officer, the same man I upset at the café and the same man who accompanied me in the search on Wednesday. And as he is now the man from whom I take my orders, once he knows, I will be powerless to stop him returning to arrest you, your mother and your father, and this blind man, whoever he may be. Once that happens, I cannot guarantee your future. Your lives will be beyond my authority. Do I make myself clear? Do I, Mira? Answer me, please. Please tell me you understand the gravity of what I am telling you."

Chapter 20

There is no moon and the only light that penetrates the lanes and alleys of Capo Peloro is that provided by the ceiling of stars. The old Roman fort lies quiet; the gunners doze, the metal of their guns and the stone of their bastion cold like the air.

Comune Simone stands guard at the entrance to the battery, the smoke from his cigarette rising and curling out and upward from his sentry box.

A lone, spectral figure walks towards him out of the gloom and stands, waiting patiently a few paces beyond.

The old Sansepolcrista drags heavily on his cigarette and then, startled by the presence, grabs his rifle and dashes to the barrier.

"Halt and identify yourself."

When no reply is forthcoming, he repeats his demand, lifts the boom, cocks his weapon and walks, slowly, nervously, towards the figure, his rifle thrust out, threateningly.

The spectre waits until Comune Simone's shining bayonet is but an arm's length away and then turns towards him.

"Oh, it's you," Simone says, relieved, lowering his rifle. "What are you doing creeping up on me like this, you could get yourself killed."

Chapter 21

Mira wakes and asks the same question she has asked for so many mornings she cannot recall when last she woke alone in her bedroom. "How are you feeling?"

"Much better, thank you," Nicholas replies. "Apart from my face, which itches like hell, I no longer feel so cold."

The renewed confidence in his voice tells her that for the first time since he was dragged to the door of her family's small house, he is truly recovering. She untangles herself from her bedding on the floor, throws on her day dress, stands beside him and places her hand on his arm: his skin is warm to her touch, not chilled and clammy as it was before. "Good," she replies, "the sulfa pills have worked their magic. How did you sleep?"

"Same as I have since Sunday night, like a baby."

"You were not woken by the bombing in Messina? The last two nights have been ridiculous: there can't be a house left standing in the city."

"What time is it?"

"Early, an hour or so after dawn."

From the front room comes the sound of knocking at the front door.

As they listen, she grips his arm so hard it almost hurts.

The knocking is repeated, this time more insistent.

"All right, all right, I'm coming," her father calls.

The door creaks as it is swung open.

"Ah, Tenente, or rather I should say Aldo. What brings you to our door at a time when only fishermen are up and about?"

"Soldiers, too, rise at dawn: that is, if any of us have been permitted a minute's sleep. I must speak with you. A matter of some urgency, Enzo."

"What are those German soldiers doing? It seems they, too, don't sleep."

"General Hube's men are bringing all the barges and boats they can muster up to the beaches, to make ready their escape. Generale Guzzoni, our man in charge, or rather I should say our man who is supposed to be in charge, has told Hube he needs to wait for orders from the Supreme Command in Rome, but Hube is ignoring his protestations and doing what he wants, which probably tells us all we need to know about who really is in charge."

"Come in," Enzo says. "I'm afraid we don't have any coffee left, but..."

"Yes, thank you. I will come in, but only for as long as it takes me to tell you my news."

"Good news, I hope. Francesca," he calls, "the Tenente, sorry, Aldo is here. Please, some breakfast for the Tenente."

"What do you think I am," Francesca calls back, "a magician?"

"No, Enzo, there is no good news, only news."

Mira slips on her shoes and joins them in the front room.

"Good morning," Aldo says, tipping his cap.

"And to you," she replies, summoning a sleepy smile and running her fingers through her mop of morning hair.

As de la Grascia sits down at the table, he removes his cap and studies the brim. Without looking up to address them directly, he says, "I will come straight to the point of my calling by at such a... such an impolite hour." He coughs, clearly nervous, and seems reluctant to begin. "Yes, well..."

"Come now, Aldo," Enzo encourages, sitting down opposite him, "we are friends, there is nothing that you should not feel able to discuss with us."

"Friends, yes. Discuss, I don't think this will prove much of a subject for discussion." He pauses, still examining his cap. "All right, it is like this. During the night of Sunday, after I saw you at mass," he glances at Mira, "one of my men was murdered while on guard duty." He allows his news time to sink in, but does not make eye contact with any one of them as he waits.

"One of your men," Enzo repeats. "While on guard duty. Not much of a guard, then."

"No, Enzo, I agree, Comune Simone was not much of a guard."

"Simone," Enzo gasps, looking up at Mira who, in turn, mirrors his surprise. "You mean the man who shot the sottocapo last Wednesday?"

"The sottocapo?" de la Grascia asks.

Realising his error, Enzo reacts angrily. "Yes, the man you told us was hiding in the village."

"Mm, I don't recall mentioning this man's rank, but yes. The man Comune Simone shot, against my direct order."

"Well," Enzo mutters, "I am certain no commander accepts the murder of one of his men lightly, but I am bound to say Comune Simone was—"

"No, papà," Mira interrupts, "we do not speak ill of the dead: it will bring bad luck."

He holds up his hands in surrender. "No, I was not going to say anything bad about the recently departed Comune Simone: I was merely going to point out that—"

"Papà!"

"—that on the scales of justice, some men weigh heavily. Is that to speak ill of such a—"

"Enough!" Mira shouts so loudly it causes her father to flinch. "Your cynicism is inappropriate. Please, Aldo, when you say Comune Simone was murdered. Exactly when was he killed?"

"Is that really relevant, Mira?" her father snaps.

"Please, papà, allow Aldo to speak."

"Thank you, Mira. He was found when the guard changed at three o'clock and clearly, he had been dead for a couple of hours."

"So," Enzo says, bowing his lips, hunching his shoulders and splaying his hands as if to ask, didn't everyone know Comune Simone had shot Sottocapo Falanga and wasn't that sufficient justification for someone to kill him? "Comune Simone made many enemies and whoever it was that was good enough to rid us of the fellow deserves our gratitude."

"As you say," Aldo agrees, raising his eyebrow and inclining his head to suggest he agrees but that his agreement cannot go on record. "Nevertheless, he was about to report to the Germans that you are hiding a man who you pretend to be your husband, Mira. That betrayal, if one believes reporting a fact is tantamount to betrayal, would have provided his killer with added motivation."

He glances so briefly at Mira that she does not have time to meet his look with any particular reaction of her own.

"Yes, but," Enzo interrupts, "most of the village know we are sheltering this man, so most of the village would have been driven by the same motivation."

"Most of the village," Aldo repeats, as though counting them off in his mind. "Well, whoever is guilty, one of my men is dead and I have had to make a report. That, I hoped, would see an end to it but, unfortunately, my superiors have seen fit to share my report with their German counterparts and they have reacted... let us say poorly. Since some of our troops near Enna shot one of their German officers, you may recall I told you of this, they have been waiting for the right opportunity to demonstrate their... their dismay. That opportunity has now presented itself and, as

345

a result, they have decided to take fifty civilian hostages from the village; hostages they say they will execute if the murderer does not surrender himself before they evacuate across the Strait." He draws a piece of paper from his pocket. "I have the list of names."

The horror of the situation stuns them to silence until Enzo bangs the table with his fist. "No, Aldo, this is not justice. This is a crime in itself; a reprisal against those who are innocent. This is lunacy."

"Yes, Enzo, you are absolutely right; lunacy is exactly what this is. However, I am little more than a lieutenant and therefore powerless to stop it."

"What can we do?" Francesca pleads.

The two men sit and stare at each other, while the two women stand and watch the men, waiting for them to come upon a solution.

Mira grabs the paper and starts reading. "No," she shrieks, "they are taking all the older men. Pipo, Dottore Roselli and the Ganci uncle."

"Your name, Enzo," Aldo says, "was on the first list; this is the second. I asked for your name to be removed. They asked me why: I told them your daughter is my fiancée. No Mira, you have no need to look so pained; I could think of no other reason that carried enough weight or did not make me look somehow complicit."

"My name was on the list?" Enzo whispers. "You allowed my name to be taken from the list so that someone else's would be added?"

"Yes, I knew that might upset you, for you are a noble man, Enzo. Most others would be relieved. But you, no, you have no thought for yourself. That honours you. Now that you are off the list, though, there will be no way back for you. So, you will have to accept my gift, whether you want it or not."

Mira steps to the side of the table. "Aldo, this is all my fault."

Before he can reply, Enzo bangs his fist once more. "No, Mira, this is not your fault."

"No, it isn't," says a strained voice from the doorway into Mira's room. "If it is anybody's fault, it's mine."

They turn to find Nicholas clutching and leaning against the door jamb.

Enzo rises quickly and taking him by the arm, guides him to the table. "Sit, Nicholas. Please, sit down. Gently."

He lowers himself down and grasps the edge of the table. "Thank you."

Aldo de la Grascia studies the man opposite him. Lying in Mira's bed on the day of the search, Aldo had not bothered much with how his competitor for Mira's affections had looked. Yes, he had noticed the bandages at the man's eyes and the dark, scarred skin around the bandage. Yes, he had formed a kind of grudging respect for him in the way he had sat up and announced who he was pretending to be. Yet at the time, Aldo's primary concern had been to get the German officer and Comune Simone out of the Ruggeri house before he lost control of the situation, and he hadn't taken a proper look at him. "So, you are the man who isn't Mira's husband."

"Yes, Tenente. My name is Nicholas Lock. I am a Sub–Lieutenant in the British Navy. My boat was sunk in the same action as that of Sottocapo Falanga's submarine. The sottocapo helped me ashore. Without him, I would most probably have drowned."

"And now he lies dead at the hands of one of his comrades."

"As it would seem, Tenente. I am so very sorry for him: he was a brave man, a selfless individual."

Aldo chuckles, cynically. "Aren't we all, Sub–Lieutenant? Aren't we all? So, now I understand who all the first aid and pills were for." He turns to Enzo, who looks on, his expression part sheepish, part remorseful. "Ah now, Enzo, I have a question for you. And how you answer it will have some bearing on how I approach a situation that I do believe has now grown far beyond my comprehension."

"Ask away. Considering your many kindnesses, Aldo, you have every right to an explanation."

"Good. Thank you. Now my question is this: what has compelled you to keep this British officer safe at such an enormous risk to your family? And, I suppose I should point out, at the expense of the sottocapo. You evidently went to warn the people sheltering him that we were on our way and as a result, he had no alternative but to run. He sacrificed his life in order to protect them for if we had found him there, the family would have been shot. If it makes it easier for you, you must know that I too share in the responsibility for the sottocapo's death. If I had kept Comune Simone on a tighter leash, then..."

"It doesn't make it easier, Aldo. All the same, I thank you for saying so."

"So why, then?" the Lieutenant presses. "Why take this ridiculous risk? As I have just said, you are a noble man; but you are in no way a stupid man. Please, Enzo, please share with us why you have felt such a need to protect this Englishman?"

Enzo glances apologetically first at Francesca and second at Mira, and finally at the reclining figure of Nicholas, who sits and listens, his head bowed, his hands splayed on the surface of the table.

"I will try to explain," Enzo says, pointing. "You see this ring Nicholas wears?"

Aldo leans forward and inspects the silver band with the Templar cross engraved on its face. "This signet ring? Yes. What of it?"

"Well, this ring Nicholas wears... This ring..." He falters, as though the right words will not come to him: the right words, the adequate words, words he had hoped he would never have to speak, because with them they bring the hurt and sorrow he has buried deep in the cemetery of his past. Enzo grimaces. "This ring... It used to belong to me."

348

Francesca and Mira stare at each other in disbelief. Aldo takes another, closer look. Nicholas raises his head and inclines it as if he has just heard a shout from far away.

"I surrendered this signet ring to a criminal in the hours after the earthquake of thirty–five years ago. Yes, thirty–five years ago. Hard to believe, isn't it? Hard for you to believe and impossible for me to understand how, after all this time, this ring has found its way back to the city of its birth. But, it has."

"You surrendered the ring to a criminal?" Aldo asks. "This I find just as hard to believe. Why? How?"

"I was trapped in the cellar of my parent's house and the criminal said he would help to free me if I paid him. I had no money; only the ring. I gave it to him; he ran away. Sounds stupid, I know; but I was desperate. Messina was desperate. I will try to explain." He glances at Francesca, a sorrowful glance and one that begs her forgiveness.

"There was a young woman. No, perhaps to some she wasn't much more than a girl. We were very much in love," he glances at his wife once more, "and we had planned to leave Messina to seek a new life in America. Unfortunately, and I mean because of the greatest misfortune and sadness to befall so many thousands that night, we were separated by circumstances far beyond our control: the tumbling buildings, the wide fissures that broke in the streets, the tall wave and the great fires. With the help of an English lady, this young woman searched for me in the ruins for three days, though she did not find me. She did, however, find the ring; for when later the criminal was shot, she found it amongst many other rings in his possession. Finding the ring, led Lilla to believe I was dead."

At the speaking of her name, Nicholas sits bolt upright.

"With good fortune, I managed to free myself, crawl out and was found by a patrol and taken to an aid station in the Villa Mazzini; but in the meantime, this young woman was persuaded by the English lady to leave with her and take up a new life in England. Why wouldn't she? She had nothing left to stay for. As far as she was concerned, I was dead and so were her family." His throat tightens and grows hoarse with emotion.

"It's all right, papà," Mira says, moving to his side, comforting him.

He shrugs away from her; not so much an unkind rejection of her sympathy, more a movement that suggests he needs to sit alone while he recalls the memory. Enzo looks over at his wife. "I am sorry, Francesca, men should not speak of the women they loved before they met their wives."

"Except perhaps to other men and to themselves," Aldo says. "Please go on."

"Because of my paralysis, I learned too late that she was leaving. Pipo wheeled me in a cart down to the Corso, but we arrived as the boat was sailing." Enzo sniffs and Francesca hands him a cloth, with which he dabs at his eyes. "You see, the earthquake destroyed many lives, many thousands of lives, including those of my parents, my sisters and my brother. I had been spared and yet my hopes and my dreams, my..." again he glances at Francesca, "the woman I loved, had all been taken away from me. My guilt, that which weighs heavily on the survivors of such a catastrophe, was immense and without Pipo and Dottore Roselli's encouragement I would not have been able to bear it." He wipes the tears from his cheeks and continues.

"This young woman, her name was Lilla Lunapiena. And we had agreed that when we got to America and had set ourselves up, we would call our firstborn son Nicholas, after Colapesce."

The others all look to the Englishman sitting at the table.

"This man, this Nicholas, wears my signet ring. I would know it if I did not see it for a thousand years. You must understand, the ring was a gift from my mother and the ring would have been all Lilla was left with to remember me by, for as I said, as far as she knew I had not survived the earthquake. When Sottocapo Falanga brought Nicholas here and I was cleaning his hands, I saw the ring and recognised it. The sight of it brought back to me a part of my life that I had thought, like the hopes and dreams of so many others, long dead and buried beneath the ruins of the city."

Francesca and Mira watch him in wonder, not knowing quite how they should react to the tears of a man they have never once seen cry. Aldo looks on, quietly embarrassed that a man he had thought fashioned from stone should not only contain, but also show, such raw emotion. And Nicholas bows his head, out of respect for both those long passed away and the sottocapo, a man who first saved his life and then surrendered his own.

"This is why I have tried so hard to protect Nicholas." Enzo stares at the floor. "This is why I have been so selfish as to risk the safety of my beloved family. I can only ask you both for your forgiveness."

Chapter 22

It is Thursday evening and Mira and her father are sitting at the table. Nicholas lies in bed and worried about his loss of weight, Francesca is feeding him some of the dried fish and tomatoes she has been safeguarding.

"The Germans have taken those on the list to Messina," Enzo says. He has been morose most of the day, consumed by his own thoughts and, whenever she has pressed him, stubbornly reluctant to share them. "They came with trucks and herded them like goats."

"Did you manage to speak to any of them?"

"No, only Dottore Roselli's daughter. She blames me for what has happened. She said that if we had given Nicholas up when he first appeared, none of this would be happening."

"If. If. If, papà," she says, resigned. "None of us can know what might have been, just like none of us can know what is going to be. And this is no one's fault in just the same way it is everyone's fault. How many in the village will admit they were wrong to believe in the Duce? How many of those who waved flags and cheered that day in Messina, eh?"

"Yes, Mira, but I am now a pariah. I could see it in their faces, in the way they looked at me and the way they avoided looking at me. They hold me responsible and I know it."

"Papà, may I bring Nicholas to the table, I know he would like to talk to you?"

He nods and while she is gone, Enzo stares at the chair Aldo had sat in while he had completed his confession.

The Tenente had been gracious in his leaving, even going to the trouble of apologising for forcing the fisherman to recall the painful events of thirty–five years before. "I will set my mind to finding a solution to this wretched situation," he had said. "Perhaps, my new friend Enzo Ruggeri, you would try to do the same. My fear is that before they leave, the Germans will execute these hostages 'pour encourager les autres', a French saying that means they will want to set an example to others. Apart from that, they don't like to lose face and in losing the battle for Sicily they will be seen to. They can be spiteful; be warned."

"I doubted you, Aldo, and for that I apologise," he had replied, and the two men had embraced and kissed each other on both cheeks.

Once Nicholas is seated, Enzo says, "Now, no doubt you must have some questions for me."

Hearing the direction from which he is addressed, Nicholas turns his head. "Yes, Signor Ruggeri, I have."

"Nicholas, you have been our guest for three weeks, which makes you one of our family; I think it is time you addressed me less formally."

"Yes, Enzo, of course, thank you. If you will permit me?"

"Please. And I have questions for you, but later. So please…"

"My mother was always reluctant to talk about her life before she left Sicily, what were her parents like?"

"Like? They were like other fishing people: proud, honourable and with good intentions and always an eye for their own kind. I did not know your grandmother: I met her only once, on a day when I went hunting for swordfish with your grandfather and Pipo and the others of his crew. They were tough men, uncompromising, the sea had made them so; and they worked hard, long days in the sun rowing to first find the swordfish and then stalk them and harpoon them. At first, they did not take too kindly to me, but once I had proved I was willing to work, they accepted me and treated me as they did their own. It was perhaps their natural ways, their pragmatism and their humility that, in the months after the terrible earthquake, persuaded me to be one of them. They had no time for fools or pretentions."

"My grandfather was the captain of a fishing boat?"

Enzo quiets, thinking for a moment, no doubt searching for the best words with which he can describe Lilla's father. "Nino Lunapiena was more than that. He was the funcitta, the man who bears the greatest responsibility. If he harpoons the swordfish, the families eat and have something to sell from their stall beside the lagoon. If he misses, his family go hungry and they have nothing to sell. His men row, a man stands on top of the mast and spots, the funcitta harpoons. Even now, it is the same."

"A funcitta?"

"Yes," Enzo says, "but your grandfather was more than simply a funcitta. He was a king amongst fishermen: he was the father of the community. People looked to him for guidance, for leadership, for strength. His word was considered law. Unlike dons who control other men, your grandfather was looked up to; he was not one to line his pockets at the expense of others. I admired him and in many ways his spirit has stayed with me ever since."

"And my mother?"

"Your mother was very special to him. And to me. When I worked in the harbour of Messina, loading and unloading the boats, she would come by and watch: that was when I first saw her."

"What was she like?"

"Oh," Enzo casts his mind back, recalling the colourful vistas of his youth. "Oh, she was beautiful, she was spirited and questioning, always questioning. What was the cargo, where would the ship be going, where had the ship come from? She was, by her very nature, inquisitive. Of course, she had no schooling to speak of: her mother wanted her to stay at home, wash clothes, clean fish and sew lace, like the children of other fishermen. So, whenever we had the chance to spend time together, I taught her to read and write. She was, like Mira," he looks over at his daughter and smiles, warmly, proudly, "a good student, hungry to learn. You see, my father wanted me to be educated and to learn the business of the harbour: he sent me to school and organised a kind of apprenticeship, so that I would know everything there was to know about how he made his money. Above all, he desired to make me in his own image; it is not unusual; a mistake some fathers make. I rebelled, for like your mother I was headstrong and my father considered your mother beneath our standing. He forbade me to see her, which was why we planned to run away."

"And the earthquake? That put an end to it?"

"Ultimately, yes. But my father got wind of my intentions. Ha," he slaps his thigh, "keeping a secret when one worked in the port was like trying to find a place to hide in the Piazza del Duomo, it was unrealistic if not impossible. On the morning of the earthquake your mother and I planned to meet outside the Hotel Trinacria and board a boat that was leaving at dawn. Unfortunately, I had underestimated just how far the tentacles of my father's influence reached: the captain betrayed me and my father sent his men to take me home."

"And that was the last time you saw my mother?"

"Yes. I was lying in a cot in the aid station in the Villa Mazzini and your mother, she had an injury to her leg, was lying in the aid station in the Piazza Cairoli. I found out from Pipo, who had seen her, that she was leaving; although, I have a vague memory of hearing a lady talking about me to Dottore Roselli. This lady's name I cannot remember, but I found out later that this was the lady who took your mother to England."

"Mrs Robertson."

Enzo looks at Nicholas as if he has summoned a ghost. "Yes, Mrs Robertson. Incredible, that after all these years you should say her name. What happened to her?"

"She passed away some years back," Nicholas replies, raising his hand to scratch at his face.

Mira leans across the table and takes his hand, pushing it down.

"My mother cared for her through her last years in the same way Mrs Robertson had cared for my mother when she took her back to England. What I'm wondering, Enzo, is that if Mrs Robertson had not taken my mother away, you would have found each other sooner or later: surely, you would. Do you blame Mrs Robertson for doing what she did?"

"Blame her?" Enzo folds his arms across his chest and rests his head back, staring at the ceiling, considering, contemplating, calculating. Then he sits forward again. "Blame her? No. She did what she thought was right and there was no guarantee that your mother and I would have found each other. There were many unscrupulous men who came down from Naples and abducted young girls. There were many children who were taken into the church charity administered by the Sisters of the Poor. And there were some who died later in the ruins of the city as they scavenged for food. It was a bad time."

"Surely, it must be hard for you not to resent Mrs Robertson."

The fisherman sits quietly for a few minutes. That he has more to say is obvious to both Nicholas, who can perceive the intricacies of Enzo's thoughts weaving in the air, and Mira, who can see them taking shape in his face.

His conclusion reached, he says, "In my life, I have learned much: principally, to read the wind and the water, to appreciate the ways of the swordfish and to know who to trust and, perhaps more importantly, who not to trust. And, each day brings new and

356

different challenges and each of these challenges are, like people, constructed of minute pieces of material, of thoughts and of actions that are not always ours to control. When these materials, these thoughts and actions come together in a way that makes us happy, we think of the day as a good day and we are rewarded. When they come together in a way that makes us unhappy, we blame ourselves. Too often, we blame other people because it is easier to blame others than it is to accept responsibility for our actions. Yet one realises that whatever happens, we are far from in control of our destiny."

"Destiny," Nicholas repeats. "What the Gods have designed for us. Is that what you are saying?"

Enzo shrugs. "Yes, in a way. When I think of your mother, I understand that without my father's prejudice, without the great earthquake and without the intervention of Mrs Robertson, your mother and I might have shared our lives. It is the same now. If it had not been for this war, Sottocapo Falanga would not have brought you to our door and Comune Simone would not have shot him: these events were not for us to control, they are part of a destiny that has come to us."

Nicholas raises his head as though something Enzo has just said has given him an idea. "I hear what you say about destiny and I agree with much of it. But I do believe it is within our ability to alter events; events like those we find ourselves in the middle of. If I handed myself in to the Germans and owned up to killing Comune Simone, perhaps they would see my actions as those of a combatant, respect my status and release the hostages. If you were to let me, I would be happy to try. Best way, I get shipped off to a prison camp until this wretched war is over. Worst way they would stand me up against a wall, but I doubt they'd do that. What do you think?"

"What do I think?" Enzo chuckles.

Mira frowns and is about to speak when her father waves her quiet.

"What I think is that they are unlikely to believe a blind man is capable of killing an armed man. And whilst I admire your courage, Nicholas, it is your reasoning that is flawed. No, volunteering for such a noble mission would only make the situation worse, because they would want to know who has treated your wounds, who has supplied you with medicine and who has been hiding you. That would pose more questions than you could answer, but...," Enzo studies the ceiling for a few seconds, "but I do believe that without intending to, you have given me the answer to a question I have been asking myself."

CHAPTER 23

During the night, they are woken by the wailing of an air raid siren.

"Messina or across the Strait?" Nicholas murmurs.

Mira sits on the edge of his bed. "No, I have not heard this before, this is closer, much closer. I wonder if this is what Aldo told us about."

Soon enough, they hear the droning of aero engines and anti–aircraft fire, and very quickly the noise increases in volume and intensity.

"Those are our guns behind Sant Agata," she says, now having to raise her voice louder than a whisper. "And listen, those are the guns of the German battery beside the café. Now Aldo's at Capo Peloro. Please God, let him survive."

The thump of guns, the booming of engines, the shouts of panic and terror.

Mira reaches for his arm and grips it, tightly. "Nicholas, I am afraid."

"Yes," is all he says.

"Can I lie with you?"

"Yes. I'd like that."

She lifts up his sheet and slides into the narrow bed. Mira can feel his warmth, his security, and the anxiety of his beating heart. She holds him close, as close as she has held a man for far too long.

"It's all right," he says, stroking her hair. "It's all right. Close your eyes. Imagine we are somewhere else."

An explosion some way down the beach rattles the house.

Mira flinches and holds him tighter, burying her head in his neck, trying to bury her being in him.

"There, try not to worry, it'll soon pass." Nicholas pulls the sheet up over their heads. He can feel her breath against him, he can taste it, he can breathe it.

A succession of bombs burst, each one getting nearer, each one getting louder.

"I'm frightened," she repeats. "I don't think I've ever been so afraid. Are we going to die?"

"No," he whispers, and as he speaks there comes an explosion of such magnitude and so close to the house that its percussion compresses the air and pounds their ears. The house rocks violently and the small window above them shatters into tiny fragments, which smash against the wall and litter the bed.

"Nicholas!" she screams.

He raises his hand and putting it to the side of her head, he turns her face towards him. Now, he can feel her breathe against his lips. He can feel some of the fear ebb from her limbs and he can feel her breasts against him, her hips against his and her legs wrapped around his.

Another stick of bombs thump one by one, marching with giant's footsteps up the beach. The house shakes and trembles, and clouds of dust pour into the room as if blown by a devilish wind.

He cannot see her, but he knows that Mira also breathes his breath and he perceives a change in her. Her body suddenly feels less tense and less restrained; not as though she has completely overcome her fear, more as though she has found a wholly separate focus, a diversion which has overwhelmed her thoughts and pushed her fear aside.

Mira lingers for a few seconds, realising then knowing what is about to happen. She expects it to happen and revels in her anticipation. She glories in her excitement and savours a moment she knows all too well that once passed they can never relive. With every second she holds back, the sweet sensation of awareness heightens within her; and with every breath he breathes into her Mira knows, as surely as she has known since the first morning she dressed his wounds, she loves him.

CHAPTER 24

"Mama, where is papà?"

Francesca stands and stares into the crater outside the house, a crater as deep as their house is tall and considerably wider. Up and down the beach, barges lie upturned, some broken in two and others smashed to smithereens. German soldiers are working doggedly to clear the wreckage, shovelling, stacking, hauling. The house of their neighbours, the elderly couple Francesca had visited on Thursday evening, is now no more than an empty, smoking shell.

"He has gone to see the Tenente at Capo Peloro." And immediately she has told Mira, Francesca lifts her hand to her face and bites at her knuckles. "He was in the strangest of moods."

"In what way strange, mama?"

"Well, this morning before he left, he hugged me in a way he has not hugged me for some years. Do you think he is all right?"

"Mama, after a night like that, when none of us thought we would ever wake again, I am not surprised."

"Yes, Mira. Yet he also kissed me in a way he hasn't kissed me for a long, long time. There was an urgency to him and he looked at me the way your brother looked at me that morning he left on the ferry. And when I said I hoped he would come back and fill this hole up before someone came along and fell into it, he just

362

looked at me." She turns away from the crater. "Men can be so strange."

Mira gazes out across the Strait. Clouds of lamb's wool grace the peaks of Aspromonte, and Villa San Giovanni and Reggio appear calm and unmolested. A warm glow of satisfaction emanates from her stomach and quickens through her limbs.

Then it comes to her: her mother chewing at her knuckles. Something is wrong. She rushes over and grasping her mother's arm, Mira turns her round. "Mama, exactly what did papà say." She stares into her mother's eyes. "Exactly what, mama, come, tell me."

"Why, Mira, whatever is the matter?"

"What did he say, mama? Please, tell me, exactly."

"He said I was not to tell you he was going to see the Tenente. Oh, I am such a fool."

"No, mama, you are not a fool; you just hide your intelligence behind a mask of foolishness. What else did he say? Did he say why he was going?"

Francesca studies her feet, as though by not looking at her daughter she cannot be found guilty of repeating words she has been told not to. "He said I was to take care of you and Nicholas, and that he might be gone a while. He used to say this sort of thing to me whenever he took his boat out in rough waters. Oh, whatever is he up to now?"

Mira breathes deep and calms herself, softening her grip on her mother's shoulders. "Mama, I think I know what he is up to and I have to stop him. Stay here. Do not leave Nicholas alone. Please, mama, will you do this for me?"

Francesca's eyes begin to tear. "But that's what he said, that I was to stay here and take care of you and Nicholas. Well, who's going to take care of me?"

"Nicholas."

"A blind man?"

"Better a blind man who can see no wrong, mama." She kisses her mother's cheek and hurries back into the house.

"I am going out," she says to Nicholas, as she bends to kiss him on his lips.

"Where? For how long?"

"Oh, not you too," she mutters. "Nicholas... last night... it was..."

He smiles, and perhaps his smile is all the brighter, all the more natural and uninhibited because he cannot see the effect it has on her. "Yes, it was, wasn't it?"

"Look after mama," she says, kissing him again, just as she'd kissed him during the night. "Be a good man, Nicholas."

She strides out along the road beside the lagoon, like a woman dashing home to draw in the laundry before it rains, and every few yards she breaks into a run.

The nearer she comes to the Piazza di Chiesa and her café, the more numerous become the craters. Houses stand hauntingly vacant, gaping holes in roofs from which wisps of smoke drift in the morning air. Here and there, people wander aimlessly or stoop to right chairs and tables and pick through what is left of their possessions. On the far side of the lagoon, teams of labourers and soldiers fill in the craters on the main road as military ambulances wail and weave between them.

The road up to Torre Faro bends right, back towards the Strait and then up alongside the shore.

At the battery in the square, the German artillerymen are lying in the sun: most are stripped to their waists, some sleep, some lounge and others wander about chatting.

Mira picks out a tall, blond-haired, muscular soldier who sits separate from the others cleaning his rifle.

"Excuse me," she says, "is there an officer I can speak to?"

The gunner looks up, nonplussed.

"An officer," Mira says slowly and loudly. "Officer?"

He points over at her café.

She sees the door is open and, annoyed that her café has been requisitioned, walks over.

Inside, two men sit talking, their collars unbuttoned, their feet up on chairs.

"You are officers?"

They glance at each other.

"Officer, yes. I am Oberleutnant Becker," he replies in halting Italian. "What can I do for you, miss..."

"Your captain. The captain who was here last week."

"The captain? We have many captains." He grins, looking her up and down.

"The captain who conducted the search last Wednesday, I would like to speak to him."

Oberleutnant Becker plays dumb for a while, feasting his eyes.

Mira's impatience gets the better of her and she stamps her foot. "The captain. Your captain. Where is he? I demand to speak to him: I have information regarding the Italian soldier who was murdered. Information. Intelligence," she says, slowly.

Recognising the word, he mutters to the man next to him, nods in her direction and then towards the door. The second man gets to his feet and makes off at a gentle trot.

When Mira turns to go outside however, the Oberleutnant gets up and bars her way.

"You wait," he says in an uncompromising tone. "Sit."

Mira does as she is invited to, holding her back straight in an effort to impress on the officer that her visit is strictly business. She looks around her café. The gunners have brought their own fake coffee, and tins of processed meat lie open attracting flies. She scowls and rolls her eyes.

A minute or so later, the German captain enters and stands over her, expressionless. "What do you want?"

She stands, raises her head defiantly and looks him directly in the eye: "My name is Mira Alberti and I killed the Italian soldier at the battery."

———————

Mira is shoved into the back of a square–looking, open–top vehicle, the doors of which open against each other and the seats of which are hard, although probably not as hard as the square jaw of the soldier who climbs in beside her. Ignoring the view across the Strait, the captain sits erect in the front as they drive the short distance up through the village towards Capo Peloro.

Convoys of vehicles, similar to those they had watched from the church steps driving towards the fighting in the west, now queue in the warren of narrow lanes around the beach, waiting for their turn to be evacuated. The captain stands, holds onto the windscreen and waves troops to stand aside, which they do, if not quite as quickly as he would like.

At the battery, a soldier lazes outside his sentry box, smoking. He stands, he stretches and then ambles over to raise the boom, not bothering to salute.

Forgetting his manners, the captain barks at the soldier beside Mira, who then pushes her roughly towards her door. Ignoring him, she stays sitting and waits for the driver to run around and open it: as she gets out, she glares at her guard, who then cocks his machine pistol and levels it at her.

"Come," the captain orders, taking Mira by her arm and hustling her towards the door to the fort.

Before they can get there, though, Lieutenant de la Grascia appears. He seats his cap at an angle, squares his shoulders, pulls down on his jacket hem and shrugs his cuffs. Behind him Enzo stands, frowning.

"Good morning, Hauptmann." Aldo smiles, though not with any warmth. "How are you today?"

The German captain has no time for pleasantries. "This woman has confessed," he states.

"Ah, that is very interesting, Hauptmann, because this man has also confessed." Aldo shifts his attention to Mira, instantly dropping his light–hearted mien. "What the devil are you doing here? Didn't you know your father was coming here?"

Mira grins, mischievously. "No, Tenente de la Grascia, he didn't think to tell me or my mother; I wonder why."

"You'd better come inside, but watch what you say, eh: this fellow," he raises an eyebrow and inclines his head towards the German officer, "understands more than he lets on."

Inside the fort, the Tenente's command post, if one can call a room with a desk and chair a command post. The air is pleasingly cool and the light from the small windows pleasingly dim. He bids Mira sit down.

"Thank you, Tenente. How marvellous it is that Italian officers have managed to preserve their manners, while others..." She glares once again at her guard.

"Enough, Mira," Aldo snaps.

Enzo takes a step towards her, which provokes her guard to turn his gun away from her and point it at him. He stops. "The Tenente is right, Mira, what are you doing here?"

"Oh, I'm doing what is right, papà. Please, Tenente de la Grascia, you seem to have one too many martyrs than you need. If I remember correctly, you told me you used to study sociology, which means you are more qualified than most to understand human behaviour. So, tell us, how do you intend to find out which one of us is lying?"

"Mira, this is not a game, and if you remember correctly, I told you that this situation is now beyond my control. Whichever one of you did murder Comune Simone will be taken to the prison in Messina and likely as not be shot, so think carefully about what you say."

"Oh, but I have, Tenente. Rest assured, I have." She smiles at him, a sad, reluctant smile that suggests he should understand she cannot do other than answer him honestly, even if that means putting herself in danger. "So, why don't you first ask my father how he killed Comune Simone?"

The German officer looks on. "Yes, ask him."

Enzo very suddenly looks nervous. He glances at Aldo, who very subtly shakes his head.

"I don't think that would be the best way to play this, Mira. I would prefer to ask you."

"No," the officer interrupts. "Ask him." He points at Enzo, lest anyone be in any doubt who he means.

"Yes, Tenente de la Grascia," Mira says. "As much as it pains me to say it, for once I agree, kindly ask my father first."

Caught between the rock of the German's insistence and the hard place of Mira's refusal to cooperate, Aldo sighs. "All right." He turns to Enzo. "Please, Signor Ruggeri, please describe to us exactly how you murdered Comune Simone?"

Enzo gazes at his daughter, a look that reaches deep inside her and twists her stomach into a terrible knot.

"Go on, papà. I know you cannot know, so go on and tell them. How did Comune Simone die?"

Realising he has no alternative, he says, "With a knife to his heart."

Mira gasps and rocks back in her chair. Then a thought dawns on her and she fixes Aldo with a look of contempt. "You told him. You told him just now, before we arrived."

"No," Aldo states, vehemently shaking his head. "Your father arrived only a moment before you, Mira; we did not have the time to discuss it and there is no way he can have read the report."

"I don't believe you," she says. "He must have." Then she turns her attention back to her father. "But how, papà? How can you know?"

"Because that was how it was done. How else would one kill a man like Comune Simone other than quickly?" Enzo looks at her, his expression coldly triumphant.

"But you can't have, papà. You can't have. You didn't."

"Mira, I don't understand why you are so surprised and if you think you know better than me, then kindly tell us if a knife to the chest was his only wound."

She looks amazed, bemused, bewildered, and then frowns in thought. "You can't have, papà. You can't have."

Enzo pouts. "But Mira, as I have just asked, if you think you know better then please, why don't you tell us what other wound did Comune Simone suffer when the life bled out of him in the same manner it bled out of Sottocapo Falanga. Come on, Mira, tell us."

Like a child suspected of cheating at exams Mira looks from her father to the lieutenant, her eyes demanding their confidence, her hands outstretched in appeal. "What other wound? I don't know. What other wound would one inflict on a man who has already paid for his sins with his life? I don't know," she screams. "I don't know what you mean."

Enzo moves to her side and, bending to wrap his arms around her, he hugs her and kisses her tenderly on her cheek. "No, you don't know, Mira. The Tenente and the Hauptmann know because they saw Comune Simone's body, didn't you, gentlemen?"

"Yes, Signora Alberti," Aldo replies, "we both know what your father means and I for one am greatly relieved that you don't. That a woman could mutilate a corpse in such an abominable manner is unthinkable. So please, Signor Ruggeri, please tell us what further wound you inflicted on Comune Simone."

Covering his daughter's ears with his hands, Enzo Ruggeri turns to face Aldo and the German captain. "Why gentlemen, I cut out his tongue of course. What else does one do to a man who cannot keep his mouth shut?"

CHAPTER 25

"Where is your mother?" Aldo asks. They are standing in the piazza before the church.

"She is over there, talking with Signora Ganci."

"How is she?"

"As you would expect, beside herself with fear."

"Would it help if I spoke to her?"

Mira gazes up into the clear blue sky. "No, not right now. In fact, Aldo, I am surprised you have come to mass. Can you not tell by the way people look at you that if they were given the chance, they would probably put you up against a wall and shoot you?"

"If it is any consolation, I think they would be within their rights." He takes her by her arm and steers her away from the congregation who soon crowd around them, glaring at the Lieutenant with undisguised loathing."

"Look, Mira, please believe me that I will do everything within my power to see that your father is released. I have already sent a report to my senior officers explaining your father's motives."

"What was their reaction?"

"Oh, they told me in no uncertain terms that there could not be any mitigating factors that were worthy of consideration and that if I pressed them harder, I would be sent to Rome to face a disciplinary hearing."

As they linger beneath the tall palm tree, she says, "People are strange, aren't they? On Thursday, after they took the hostages to Messina, my father was their villain; and now that they have been released, he is their hero. Where has he been taken?"

"To the Carrubbara in Gazzi, in Messina."

"Did he get there all right?"

"Yes, I checked last night. They managed to get him there before the first of the three air raids. The American bombers gave the city quite a pounding yesterday but, thankfully, the prison was not damaged."

Mira quiets.

"I can understand that there is a great deal that bothers you, Mira. These are difficult times for everyone, but the situation your father has placed himself in is perilous to say the least."

"Aldo," she says, gazing out at the still waters of the lagoon, "I have a confession to make."

He lets go of her arm and steps back from her. "Mira, if it is a confession you need to make, you should have stayed behind in the church. Absolution is not mine to grant."

"Mother of God!" she groans. "Absolution does not wash away sin. What one has done stays with one, and no amount of contrition or any number of Hail Marys can atone for what I am about to tell you."

He looks deep into her eyes. "If it is that important, Mira, perhaps the priest should hear what you have to say."

"No, Aldo, I have to tell you and only you, and when I have told you, you will understand why."

"All right then, Mira, what is it that weighs so heavily on your conscience that you must tell a friend rather than God?"

She breathes deep. "Do you remember my surprise when my father admitted to murdering Comune Simone?"

"Mm, yes, I do. However, your father admitted only to mutilating the corpse of Comune Simone; at no time did he admit to killing him."

She looks back at him, a guilt, a misgiving stark in the tightness of her cheeks and the furrow of her thick, dark eyebrows. "Yes, Aldo, you are right, he didn't. And that's because I murdered the Comune, not him."

"Ah," he exclaims, the poisoned chalice of her confidence now passed to him. "So that was what brought such confusion into your eyes. I wondered what disturbed you so."

"You don't seem surprised."

"I am not," he replies. "Should I be?"

"In a way, yes. When we went out to the café that Tuesday evening, when we met your friend Franz, you said you thought you knew me well enough to want to spend the rest of your life with me: if you thought you knew me that well, Aldo, did that mean you always knew me capable of murder?"

"No, Mira, the thought had not crossed my mind at that time."

"So, why are you not surprised now?"

His expression softens. "Oh, I don't know. Perhaps it is that you appeal to my vanity. For us men, it is our weakest point, our Achilles heel."

"In what way? How? When did I do that?"

"When you allowed me to find you in bed with the Englishman. That was when my vanity spoke to me. "Aldo de la Grascia," it said, "you are not such a poor judge of character that you would allow yourself to love a woman who would behave in such a manner." You see, I knew you allowed yourself to be found 'in flagrante delicto' for the sole purpose of protecting this Englishman and the lives of your parents, and I know you feel enough for me not to have done that simply to upset me." He hunches his shoulders and splays his arm, a gesture of adjuration. "Mira, only the woman I have set my heart on would have the courage to do this, and a woman of such courage would not think twice about killing a man like Comune Simone, especially if she thought that by doing so she was protecting those closest to her, including me."

"But I had little choice," she pleads.

"Mira. My Mira," he says, his voice filled with tenderness. "Then if you need my blessing, why don't you explain to me how it happened that you were not intent upon killing him? You had more than sufficient motivation."

"I did not go with the intention of killing him: you must believe me. I thought that I might be able to persuade him not to give Nicholas away to the Germans. I thought I might... Oh, does it matter why?"

Briefly, Aldo closes his eyes in pain. "Yes, Mira, it matters to me."

Mira breathes deep. "I went to the entrance to the battery just after midnight. I wanted to talk to Comune Simone; to convince him of the error of his fascist ways; to drag him out from beneath the same clouds the Duce cast over my husband." She looks at Aldo, pleading with her eyes. "Unfortunately, you were right: he was a diehard... what was it? Ah, yes, a Sansepolcrista. He knew only one way and that was to obey his prophet; he told me I should do the same. He said that I should heed the words of the Duce and that if I did not, he would teach me a lesson I would never forget. He grabbed me. He tried to force me to do something a woman does not do unless she loves a man. What a fool he was to mess with a fisherman's daughter, eh?" Mira scoffs, then falls silent for a moment, remembering.

"I knew then that he needed to die and if not me, then who? So, I led him on and then stabbed him through his heart." Mira looks at Aldo, saddened that she has had to describe her act to him.

"And you did not mutilate him?"

"No, this morning I asked my mother if she had heard me leave the house last Sunday night. She said both she and my father heard me, and that soon after I left, my father left to follow me. He must have seen what happened, what I did, and then waited.

After that, he must have cut out the comune's tongue. He must have done it in the hope that no one, not even you, would believe I could have done such a terrible thing."

Aldo grimaces. "Oh, Mira. I knew it. I didn't want to believe it, but I knew it from the look on your face when your father... Oh, Mira."

"Do you see, Aldo? My father is innocent and now I have only made the whole situation worse. Please, Aldo, please think of what you can do to free him?"

Two old men approach them. The taller of the two looks tired and his fine features haggard and drawn, as though he has been dried out by the summer's heat. A shorter, older man clings to his arm. He wears black trousers and a black jacket, a white shirt buttoned but without collar and a grey waistcoat with a watch chain.

Mira shuts her eyes for a second and steels herself. "Tenente de la Grascia," she says, almost casually, as if she and Aldo have been discussing nothing more trivial than the weather, "I don't believe you have met Dottore Roselli. And this is Pipo Sorbello, my father's old friend."

Aldo straightens his back and bows. "Gentlemen, Signor Ruggeri has talked of you both."

Glancing very briefly at the Tenente, Pipo removes his cap and taking Mira's hand, he kisses it slowly, fondly, before raising his bald head and appraising her with rheumy eyes. "Mira, how is..."

"Pipo, I'm sure Dottore Roselli can give you a more accurate appraisal of his health. However, and taking into account the extent of his injuries when first he arrived, he is as well as can be expected."

Pipo affords the Tenente a second glance, this one longer and designed to let Mira know he is suspicious of the man in uniform.

She smiles, albeit politely. "It's all right, Pipo, Aldo knows our guest; my father has explained everything to the Tenente. Despite what people may think or whisper behind his back, Aldo is one of us. You can talk freely."

"Good, then I will try," he replies. "I gather it is uncertain whether or not this young man will regain his sight."

Dottore Roselli bridles his lips: the matter is obviously of some conjecture.

"I also gather this young man is the son of Lilla Lunapiena. Can it be true?"

Mira puts her hand on the old man's shoulder and bends to answer his question. "My father says it is him. His mother's name is Lilla and the young man wears the signet ring of the Templars that once belonged to my father. He also knows of the lady, Mrs Robertson, who took Lilla to England after the earthquake."

Pipo smiles, "So, her son has returned. Nino would have been so pleased to hear this news: he so loved his daughter. Now, before Dottore Roselli tells me I will exhaust myself if I keep talking; if you will permit me, I have a few questions. Mira, would it be in order if I came to see this young man?"

"Of course, Pipo," Mira replies, "I'm sure he would be both pleased and interested to meet his mother's godfather. But as I'm sure you have witnessed, the Americans are bombing the beaches and the Germans are busy loading and unloading the barges. They don't take kindly to people who get in their way and our house is far from safe. Perhaps it would be best if you came late afternoon."

"Good, I would like that." Then the pleasure falls from his expression and his face hardens to resemble the surface of the Strait when storm clouds lock out the light. He turns to Aldo, "Tenente de la Grascia, what news do you have for us? Now that Enzo is no longer here to relay what you have been telling him, perhaps you would inform us."

"Naturally, Signor Sorbello, with pleasure. As far as I know, Generale Guzzoni has accused General Hube of lying to him.

He says the Germans are already evacuating the island and as you can see," a convoy of German armoured vehicles roars by towards the beach, silencing him for a minute, "his accusations are well–founded. We therefore expect Generale Guzzoni to order the evacuation of all Italian forces to Calabria by the end of tomorrow. Catania, Troina and Adrano are now in enemy hands and it will not be long before the Americans find a way around the defensive line on the north coast. Once General Guzzoni departs for Calabria, what is left of the Livorno and Assieta divisions will follow."

Pipo sniffs. "You mean that once he has run across the Strait to save his own skin, he no longer gives a shit what happens here. What about you? What will happen to you?"

De la Grascia winces. "That, Signor Sorbello, is for my superiors to decide."

"Mm," the old man mumbles. "Superiors, eh? Superior fools, no less. Tenente, I have been told that you are a well–educated and principled man. If that is the case, how do you explain your part in bringing death and ruination into our midst? You may know that thirty–five years ago, our lives were turned upside down by the capricious forces of nature; a happening no man could either have foreseen or denied. But now, because of one man, a devil whose right hand you and many others became, we are faced with the same upheaval. Please, for the benefit of a simple and easily confused old fisherman, how do you have the temerity to wear this uniform?"

Dottore Roselli and Mira look on as Pipo stares and waits.

Aldo chews his lip in thought, then raises his left hand as if partially surrendering. "Signor Sorbello, I have asked myself the same question many times."

"That is not an answer," Pipo replies, his thunder summoned. "If I may be so rude as to point out, that is an abrogation of your responsibility, an excuse for your shortcomings. That is the answer of a man who has stood by while others commit crimes." He pauses, eyeing the lieutenant. "Mira tells me that you are also an intelligent man: if that is the case, surely you must have some grasp of what is right and what is wrong?"

"Oh yes, Signor Sorbello," the sharp blade of a scaling knife scratches at his skin, "I do have a considerable grasp of what is right and what is wrong." He frowns at Mira.

Pipo, though, is not finished. "Then I must appeal to your understanding and ask you what are you going to do about fetching Enzo back from the city? That is assuming there will be enough city left for him to be fetched from once the Americans have done their best to destroy it."

"As soon as I can, Signor Sorbello, I will see to it." He straightens, bows and adds, "Now though, for the moment, you must both trust me and excuse me."

"A tactical retreat, eh, Tenente?" Pipo grumbles. "Very well. Thank you, for your time. I hope the Madonna sees fit to keep you safe."

"Signor Sorbello. Dottore Roselli." Aldo tips his cap and turns to Mira. "You see, my angel, in one way or another we are all guilty: war makes us so."

Chapter 26

The relative calm of Sunday night is broken by the clanking of tracks and the screeching of wheels as vehicles arrive and queue for embarkation. Beams of ghostly light roam the waters, like all–seeing eyes in search of prey, and occasional bursts of tracer soar up through the dark.

Afraid for her husband, Francesca has taken to her bed and no amount of gentle sympathy or tempered cajoling will persuade her from it.

Monday, though, sees an eddy of activity as more and more troops, tanks, guns and vehicles are loaded onto barges and despatched across the Strait.

In the afternoon, Pipo is brought by his grandson, Beppe, to visit. The boy is fascinated by Nicholas and watches him with intense adoration, as though he is indeed Colapesce risen from the depths.

"So, Nicholas," Pipo asks, "tell me, how is your mother?"

"The last time I saw her, she was well, thank you."

Studying him, the older man says "You look like her, the same roundness to your features, although I can imagine you have lost weight in your face these last few weeks. If I close my eyes, I can see her as though it was yesterday. She was the most beautiful child and I should imagine she retains much of her youthful charm:

one knew, as one knows with certain people, that they will always be how they were when they were young. Please, indulge an old man: where did Lilla grow up? Where did she go to school? That woman, Mrs Robertson, she was strong; she must have seen right by your mother."

"She did. She sent my mother to a convent school, which was probably the most difficult period for her. Many of the other girls tried to take advantage of my mother and behaved unkindly towards her. As you remember, she spoke no English and she knew no real sophistication. However, and again as you remember her, she was nothing if not tenacious. She learned to speak English quickly and, after the convent, Mrs Robertson sent her to a secretarial school."

"Where did they live? Was it in the country or the city?"

"They lived near London, near the river."

"And your father? What is he like?"

Nicholas takes a moment to conjure the image of his father onto the screen in his mind. "By all accounts, my father was a good man."

"Was?" Pipo interrupts.

"Yes, was. He was a Royal Marines officer and, sadly, he died at Gallipoli in the first Great War, a month before I was born."

"Where did Lilla meet him?"

"In London. My mother took employment at the Lloyd's Register of Shipping; Mrs Robertson had a friend who worked there." He thinks for a while. "A Mr Gordon, I believe that was his name."

"Ah, yes, I know this name," Pipo says, his face lighting up as the doors to his memory are suddenly reopened. "This was the man who arranged your mother's passage back to England. Mira," he says, wresting his gaze from Nicholas, "your father and I met this man: a nice man, a very English gentleman, he spoke Italian and was something to do with the ships."

"Yes, that's him," Nicholas confirms. "Though I never met him, my mother often spoke of him. She said that without their chance meeting in the hours before the earthquake, she might never have gone to England. Mr Gordon also introduced my mother to my father, although it turned out that my mother had already met my father once before, here in Messina. He had helped her and Mrs Robertson look for Enzo in the ruins of the city. Small world, isn't it?"

"Your father was a wealthy man?"

"Pipo?" Mira interrupts. "To ask this kind of question..." She shakes her head and even young Beppe frowns.

The older man hunches his shoulders and raises an eyebrow.

Even though Nicholas cannot see the gesture, he recognises the silence. "Compared to some. He left us sufficient money for me to go to a good school and from there I went to university, to read languages. Listening to you talk, Pipo, I'm glad I did; there's more than a little Latin in your language. Of course, my mother speaks to me in her language whenever she doesn't want others to understand what we are talking about, but I mean no disrespect when I say that you hardly speak the kind of Tuscan Italian they teach in school."

"Does Lilla speak much of her family?" Pipo asks.

"To be honest, not so much. I think it brings too much sadness to her to be reminded of how they all passed away so suddenly. And I think that had a good deal to do with why she decided to leave Messina: that and believing Enzo, too, was dead."

"And now you are here with his daughter," the old man muses.

"Yes, Signor Sorbello: 'God moves in a mysterious way, his wonders to perform; he plants his footsteps in the sea and rides upon the storm.'"

"What is that, a poem?" Mira asks.

"A hymn we used to sing in the school chapel. It seems rather appropriate, doesn't it, what with me ending up here by the Strait, with my mother's first love and you, Mira."

Pipo grins at his use of the word love. "So, you followed in your father's footsteps, into the navy?"

"Sort of, I suppose. After university, I went to work in London and while I was there, I joined the Naval Reserve, a volunteer force; most of us are civilian yachtsmen."

"Volunteers, eh?" Pipo says. "We have volunteers, too. Most of the time they are volunteered at the point of a bayonet."

"Well, we are what they call hostilities only, which means that at the end of the war we don't have to stay on in the navy. Not that I'm going to be much use without my sight."

Pipo sniffs. "Dottore Roselli is not certain you have lost your sight."

"Thank you, Signor Sorbello. I appreciate your and the good doctor's confidence."

"Did you not like the big ships? Mira tells me your boat was small, like a Motoscafo."

"I prefer the small boats, though many in the regular navy think we only play at being sailors. They wouldn't think that if they'd seen the way we sent that submarine to the bottom."

"Mira tells me you saved a sottocapo's life and in return he saved you."

If young Beppe's look has until this moment laid bare his adoration for this brave young officer, this knight of the seas with his templar ring; now his expression escalates to one of veneration. War may be terrible; but without war, what would one do for heroes?

A knock at the door startles them.

"Maria?" Mira suggests.

"No," Pipo replies, frowning. "Beppe will walk me home."

Mira rises and pulls back the door. "Aldo, what are you doing here? Shouldn't you be at the Battery?"

"Yes, but may I come in for a minute?"

"Of course." She stands back to allow him into the room.

"Ah, Signor Sorbello, Nicholas." He musters a smile for Beppe. "Have I come at a bad time?"

"No," Mira replies, "please, sit down. I was about to say how unfair it was that Sottocapo Falanga should have died after he had saved Nicholas."

Aldo removes his cap, wipes his brow and sits.

"Yes, Tenente," Nicholas continues, "it all seems so unfair. You see, I've always believed one good turn deserves another and I don't think the sottocapo got the chance he deserved."

They sit in silent reverence for a while, each one alone with their thoughts of a man of immense dignity, a man who sacrificed himself in order not to betray those who sheltered him.

To break the silence, Mira offers Aldo a glass of her father's Amaro.

"No, if you don't mind. I cannot stop and my visit is only to give you some news. Some grave news, I'm afraid."

"If it is bad," Pipo offers, "then best deliver it quickly. What have you got to tell us, Tenente?"

"It is this: as expected, Generale Guzzoni has relocated—"

"Fled, you mean," Pipo interrupts.

Aldo widens his eyes in disapproval, shifts in his seat and begins again. "As I was saying, Generale Guzzoni has relocated to Calabria, leaving Admirals Barone and Parenti to oversee the evacuation of the Livorno and Assieta divisions."

Pipo sits more upright. "More fools in charge of fools. Yes, I am sorry for interrupting, Tenente, please go on."

Aldo shakes his head. "This is in some part good news, because it means that in these last few days there is unlikely to be any fighting in this area and, perhaps even better, it means the British and Americans will refocus their bombsights on the Calabrian side. Besides, soon there will be nothing left for them to bomb here and because of the many anti–aircraft guns, it would be suicide to try: the raids of last week cost them too many crews."

"Then where is the bad news, the grave news, as you put it?"

"I am getting to it, Signor Sorbello. Please, patience. The grave news is that Generale Guzzoni has passed control over what is left of the island to the German, General Hube. This changes everything because up until now, I have been only partially under German command, by which I mean that if I didn't agree with their orders, I could appeal to my senior officers; not that it would have done me any good. As of today, though, I have no recourse and I am theirs to control absolutely. They can order me to fight to the last man if they believe it helps to delay the enemy advance sufficiently for them to complete their evacuation, and why wouldn't they? Do we matter to them?" He hurries to answer his own question before Pipo can stick his oar in. "No. They would throw us beneath the tracks of the American tanks for all they care."

He glances at Pipo, daring him to speak. When he doesn't, he smiles briefly and carries on. "The worst part of it is that the prison is now under German command and I have heard that before they leave, rather than bother with transferring prisoners to the mainland, the Germans intend to execute all those guilty of capital offences."

CHAPTER 27

"Mama, please drink this."

"I'm not hungry, Mira. What is it?"

"It is a broth I have made from the last of the tenerumi, the dried tomatoes, onions and squash. I'm sure it won't taste as good as yours, I always add too much or not enough pepper. Tell me, what do you think?"

The photograph of Mussolini that once took pride of place above the stove now lies smashed among the greater wreckage beyond the front door.

Francesca sits up slowly in her bed.

Mira smiles at her mother; asking Francesca for her opinion has done the trick; for Mira knows that in the kitchen her mother holds sway and whatever Mira cooks for her, she is always, always going to find some fault.

The broth steams from the bowl: she dips the spoon and holds it up to Francesca's lips.

"Now, mama." Trying to exaggerate the supposed intimacy of their conversation, Mira speaks only a little louder than a soft whisper. "I know you are upset about papà, and that you are upset is perfectly normal and justified. But we have a guest and it doesn't do for you to ignore him, however much you feel he may be partly responsible for what has happened. Think of what papà would say if he was here."

Francesca wipes her mouth on the cloth her daughter has laid on top of the bedcover. "It could do with a little more salt," she says, craning her head forward in expectation of another spoonful.

Mira grins to herself. "Of course, mama, but we are running low and therefore I have been sparing. Remember what Aldo said?"

"No, what did he say? And the tenerumi should have been cooked for longer; the leaves are tender, I'll grant you that, but the rest is a little chewy."

"Yes, mama. The squash is dry, too, I should have allowed it to stew." Pleased that her mother's appetite has returned, Mira is happy to put up with the criticism.

"And more pepper, it needs more pepper. Otherwise, it's not bad."

"Aldo told us that we cannot expect to get our hands on everything we would normally expect to be able to, so we will have to be careful. The tomatoes, the lemons, the figs, the zucchini and all those peppers you have preserved in all those mason jars, they will have to see us through until things return to how we would like them. And salt particularly will be in short supply."

"And if your father doesn't come back and your brother does not return from Africa, who will look after us? We will starve."

"So that is what this is about, eh mama? It is not about whether or not our men will survive: you are more concerned that you will be left to fend for yourself. Well, have no fear of that; even if I have to sell my body to the Americans, I will never let you starve."

"You wouldn't! Mira! Please tell me you wouldn't. Why I would rather die than have you stoop to such degrading behaviour."

Mira lays the bowl on the bedside table and studies her mother. "We have known hard times before, mama, and I am sure we will know them again. And whatever happens to papà, I know we will make do. I cannot, though, face all of this with you lying here feeling sorry for yourself; your weight I will bear only when you no longer have two strong legs on which to stand. Do you understand me, mama?"

A scolded, apologetic and mournful expression assumes Francesca's face. "How long have I been here, Mira, I seem to have lost count of the days?"

"You have been here since Tuesday. Since Pipo and Aldo came."

"Pipo was here?"

"Yes, mama, I told you, yet you refused to come out of your room. How you will live down your poor manners is anybody's guess. And today is Sunday, so if you don't get out of bed, you will be absent from Mass and tongues will wag."

"No, you're right; people will ask questions and that I could not live with after all that has happened to the widow Ganci. What has been going on outside, Mira? All I have heard is men shouting, wheels turning, machinery grinding, bombs falling and that deathly rat–tat–tatting of guns. Have the Germans not gone yet?"

"No, mama, though I don't think it will be long now. The barges and ferries plough back and forth across the Strait: the aeroplanes come, they bomb the barges, the guns shoot the aeroplanes, the aeroplanes fall: it has been terrible. All those poor men lost to the waters: all those poor women who will never see their sons and husbands again."

"Yes, and Enzo? What will happen to him?"

"Nothing good if we do nothing, mama. I will bring hot water and you can do whatever it is you need to do with your hair; it looks like a handful of rat's tails. Get washed and dressed, please, I need you to come to mass with me."

Walking up over the rise and down to the lagoon, Mira hurries her mother with small talk. They have had no word of Enzo since he was arrested over a week before and because of the constant bombing and strafing in the Strait, and therefore the constant demands made on the anti–aircraft batteries, they have not seen Aldo since his visit five days before. As they walk, they can hear the not so distant rumbling and grumbling of cannon fire, and when they reach the lagoon, they stand for a moment watching the convoys of vehicles and battle–weary troops filing south.

The Tenente arrives just as the congregation floods out onto the steps. He no longer resembles the elegant dilletante in uniform, for now his boots are muddied and scuffed, his jacket is frayed and soiled, and the dark rings around his eyes tell a story of days and nights without sleep. People besiege him, desperate for news.

"Bronte and Maletto have fallen to the British and Americans," he states loudly so he will not have to repeat himself to those hard of hearing. "And yesterday, the ancient city of Randazzo was brought to its knees. As I speak, what remains of our forces are retreating north along Highway 116 to the north–coast road, and others east along Highway 120 to the east–coast road. Most of the large explosions you can hear are caused by the German engineers blowing bridges to the south of Tremestieri in order to buy themselves more time to complete the evacuation. However, the last to leave will be elements of the Hermann Göring Division and as we know, many of their soldiers are not well–mannered and it is likely that they will try to take with them anything they can carry. If you should come across them, I humbly suggest you let them take whatever they want; let your generosity be your salvation."

He waits while his news sinks in. More than a few succumb to their emotions, while others turn and jeer at the retreating troops.

"We expect..." Aldo searches out the faces of Pipo and Dottore Roselli, and once he sees them, he continues, aiming his words in their direction. "Please, if you can, try to refrain from making a bad situation worse. Do not vent your frustrations on these troops. Many of them will, like you, have lost friends and loved ones, and they are exhausted from days of fighting without water in this heat. Allow them to leave in peace. Please do not provoke them." He pauses to make his point.

"Now, the British and Americans will in all probability be here by tomorrow night or early Tuesday morning. So, for your own safety, please stay indoors. Do not leave your homes unless you cannot avoid doing so. That is all I have to say. May the Madonna look upon you these next few days! Thank you."

He grabs Mira by her arm and leads her away as they dodge through the convoy over to the piazza.

"You speak well," she says, attempting to flavour her compliment with a dash of humour. "Perhaps you missed your vocation, you should have been a politician."

"Mira, be serious. I have little time and I need you to listen. You want to save your father, yes?"

"Yes, of course, Aldo."

"And what would you risk to save him?"

She stares at him, her look hard and uncompromising, if a little questioning. "Why, everything. Everything. My life, if I have to."

"And what about the life of your Englishman? Will he risk his life for your father?"

Mira considers, but only for as long as it takes her to draw breath. "Yes, I am certain he will. You know what my father has done for him and you know the history that exists between them. But, Aldo, my father is in the prison, what can we do?"

"What you can do, Mira, is speak to Dottore Roselli. Ask him if he has some articles of clothing a nurse may have left with him: a Red Cross arm band, a white muslin cap, a cape with scarlet facings, an apron, anything that would make you look like a nurse."

She searches the thinning crowd. "Ah, yes. My mother is talking to him and if he does not have it, I am sure she can make it up. With a needle and thread, she is everything I am not."

"Good. Now, tomorrow morning, just after dawn, I will come by to collect you and your Englishman. I will bring him a uniform. Be ready."

CHAPTER 28

De la Grascia had knocked softly against the door not long after first light. "I am late," he had whispered. "I had to take fuel from other vehicles." And now, down at the beach, Germans troops are being issued with bright red lifejackets and crammed into barges before being despatched into the gently swirling brume.

"This uniform is a little on the large side," she says to Aldo as she helps Nicholas on with the shirt.

"I shouldn't worry," he replies, "show me a man who has not lost weight these past weeks and I will show you a man who has no uniform. Mira, you were right when you said your mother was a genius with a needle and thread; you could not possibly look more like a Red Cross nurse. Wherever did she get the material?"

"From Dottore Roselli and Pipo. The grey cape was a blanket, the white from a sheet and the red cross from curtain material. If the weather turns cold, the good doctor and the old fisherman will have to wear clothes in bed tonight; eye patches too, if last night's full moon is anything to go by."

"And the brooch at your neck looks most official."

"Dottore said it belonged to his aunt; apparently, it is an award she received from Queen Elena for her services to the orphans the Sisters of the Poor cared for in the years after the earthquake. It's pretty, isn't it?"

"Yes, Mira, it suits you." Aldo turns to Francesca. "You are a clever woman, Signora Ruggeri: these hands of yours," he grasps and kisses them, "have worked unimaginable magic."

"But why do Mira and Nicholas have to go with you?" she asks, her expression filled with anxiety.

"Because, Signora Ruggeri, if I try to go alone, there is every chance I would be taken for a deserter and shot. With Mira as nurse and Nicholas as patient, I believe I may be able to convince whoever stands in our way that we are hurrying to the hospital."

When he releases her hands, Francesca grabs at his and she pulls him towards her and embraces him. "Tenente, Aldo, please bring my Enzo back to me. Please keep Mira safe. And Nicholas. And please, come back to us; you have been so kind and you are so very dear to us."

"With your blessing, Francesca," he replies, lingering to stare into her teary eyes. "Now, Mira, Nicholas, are we ready?"

"As long as you don't want me to walk too far in these boots," Nicholas says, getting up and taking a few tentative steps.

The Tenente's Fiat rattles and jolts as they wind through the narrow alleys down to the lagoon, their passage interrupted only by the sea of German soldiers trudging the last two hundred metres to the beach. The men, their faces haggard and dirty, their uniforms unbuttoned, their rifles slung over their shoulders, stare listlessly at the car as it noses its way against the tide.

"They will be gone by the end of the day," Aldo says.

Beside him, in the front, Nicholas sits quietly, straining to listen, turning his head this way and that. "How has the evacuation gone for them?"

"I believe the Germans have sent nearly 40,000 troops across, though for every man they have rescued, one in ten of them has been wounded and will not see battle again. We have sent nearly twice that number, and nearly one hundred guns."

"And your battery?"

"They have taken our lighter guns, but the heavier cannons they have abandoned. My Coastal Division is spread over too great an area and many of the men are Sicilian and have gone home.

"Can they really have saved so many? Through all that bombing?"

"Yes," Aldo replies, sucking his teeth as he thinks. "Your air force could only bomb at night; they were inaccurate and they bombed many of the wrong beaches. Your small boats? They dared not come this far up the Strait."

"You men!" Mira scoffs, from the back seat. "Troops, boats, aeroplanes: they are nothing more than counters on a board. You make war sound like it is a game played by little boys."

"Yes, my angel," Aldo agrees, solemnly, "it is a game; a childish game played by pompous degenerates with fatal ambition."

Once out of the village and through Sant Agata, their passage south is made easier by fewer troops and vehicles. The small village of Paradiso is pockmarked with craters and they have to swerve left and right, and then wait while a broken-down truck is shunted aside by an enormous tank, which slews and jerks and rumbles off towards the beach in a dense fog of exhaust smoke.

The city begins at the Borgo del Ringo.

"Nicholas," Mira says, her tone void of emotion, "this used to be the fisherman's quarter. My father told me that just after the earthquake, a great wave came and because the houses were to the north of the harbour wall, there was nothing to stand in its way. The wave was as tall as the Duomo and it filled every house, drowning all those outside and inside. The same wave swept all the villagers from Ganzirri. They found fish in upstairs rooms; can you believe that?"

"The Borgo del Ringo. Yes," he says, once more feeling for the bandages at his eyes, "I heard my mother talk of it."

Mira leans forward and gently eases his hands down. "Perhaps it is best that you cannot see it. Now, there is nothing more than piles of bricks and mortar, and sad people who wander around hoping to find something of value in the ruins of their houses. The Borgo del Ringo probably looked exactly like this the last time your mother laid her eyes on it."

The car slows.

"There is a checkpoint ahead," Aldo says. "Nicholas, try your best to look as unwell as you can and speak only if it is unavoidable. Groaning would be better than talking."

A boom stretches across the road and four carabinieri stand waiting.

Aldo suddenly speeds up towards them and then brakes heavily at the last moment. He leans out of the window and shouts, "Get out of our way, I have an injured man here I need to get to hospital."

One of the carabinieri strolls up to the car, his rifle at hand, his bayonet fixed, his self–conceit evident. When he notices he is about to address an officer, he stiffens upright and salutes. "I beg your forgiveness, Tenente, but I will need to see your papers."

"Papers? What papers? Don't be ridiculous, man. If we do not get this fellow medical attention right away, he may lose his sight, or worse die."

"That may be so, sir, but my orders are not to allow anyone into the city unless they have the correct embarkation papers. There are many deserters who are trying to flee the island and we have received reports the Americans are already in the vicinity."

"And the Americans, are they trying to flee the island? When they pitch up here, will you be asking them for their papers too?"

"I'm sorry, Tenente, I have been given my orders."

"Oh, you are one of those, eh?" Aldo sneers. "One of those cornutos, one whose wife presses another man's trousers while he is out at work. Well, wear your own trousers for once and get out of our way: I have a wounded man, not papers."

Startled by the broadside, the carabiniere reels momentarily, and when his men snigger behind his back, he notices and draws himself up to his full height, a modest height that means he does not have to bend down to converse with Aldo, seated as he is in the Fiat. The carabiniere glances across at Nicholas.

Aldo nudges him with his knee.

Nicholas groans and holds his head. "Holy mother of God. Help me. Will someone please stop this pain."

The man frowns. "I am sorry, Tenente, I cannot let you pass without papers. If I do and later I am asked why, I am likely to lose my stripes."

Aldo glances at the man's sleeves, as though all has become clear, "Ah well, I have already survived demotion, sergente, and let me tell you it is a blessing. In the past few days I have realised that the greater the rank, the bigger the fool. Now, lift up that boom and let us pass. If you do not and this man dies, I will most certainly return and demote you myself."

The sergeant steps back and peers in through the back window to be confronted by Mira's most threatening scowl. He takes his time to look her over.

Mira softens; her uniform lending her a chaste almost virginal aspect. She smiles and with her forefinger curling like the harbour wall, she beckons him closer.

He leans in, uncertainly.

"Sergente," she mutters, "do you have children?"

He hesitates. "Er, no sister. Why?"

"Because if you don't let us pass this instant, you are unlikely ever to father them."

He glances back at his men then looks back at her, suitably confused. "Why is that, sister?"

In a flash, Mira reaches out through the open window, grabs him by his lapel and drags his head into the car so that it is only inches from hers. "Because when I get out of the car," she hisses, lightning flashing in her eyes, her brow lowering like a storm cloud and the blade of the filleting knife silver in her hand, "I am going to slice off your testicles and feed them to you. And not only will I slice off your testicles, I'm going to do this in the full view of your comrades, so if you know what's good for you, you'll be a smart boy and lift up the barrier."

The sergeant recoils, his face blanched, his jaw dropped. He fumbles with his rifle, which clatters impotently to the ground.

Amused at his state, his comrades laugh uproariously and one of them lifts the barrier and waves them through.

"Cornuto?" Nicholas asks, chuckling.

"Yes," Aldo replies. "I bet your mother didn't teach you that one. It means 'horned'. It is what my men call a man who cannot control his wife."

"You mean a cuckold"

"Exactly, Nicholas. A cuckold." He glances over his shoulder. "Mira, you should have been a sergeant major; you very definitely have the mouth of one. Or is that how all daughters of fishermen speak?"

In the back, Mira is quietly livid; upset that she has had to issue such a foul threat and annoyed with herself for having flown so comprehensively off the handle. "What else could I do, eh? He was a boy in a man's uniform and you were talking to him as if he was your favourite nephew. Now tell me, where are we going?" She gazes out of her window at the mountains of rubble and the derelict buildings. "Mother of God, is there nothing left of this city which is not smashed and broken?"

"I am taking you to your father," Aldo says, pulling on the steering wheel to avoid a crater.

"Then the prison is over in the Gazzi quarter," she says. "Take the Corso Cavour, to the right," Mira suggests. "That will take us away from the harbour. Then you should follow the Porta Imperiale through the Piazza del Popolo to the Via Catania; that will take us by the cemetery and straight to the prison."

"As you wish," Aldo replies.

Barely a soul out of uniform is to be seen, apart from a few children scavenging among the ruins. Hulks of burned—out houses and eviscerated churches line their route, and in the Piazza del Popolo a tented city has grown up like well—watered weeds between paving stones.

"Where is everyone?" he asks.

"If they have any sense," Mira scoffs, "they'll be with the great and the good in the air raid tunnels at the top of the Viale Boccetta. That's if there's enough room for them."

There is, though, life in the cemetery, where women ghost about the graves, praying and weeping.

The road ahead is blocked with a convoy of trucks, so Aldo pulls up and parks.

"Now, remember what I said. Mira, you walk beside Nicholas and I will be behind you." He draws his sidearm and ushers them forwards. "These Germans are amongst the last to leave, so with any luck they will be more concerned with making good their departure than bothering with us."

As they walk towards the entrance, a single volley of rifle shots echoes from within.

"I hope we are in time," Aldo says.

Barbed—wire tops the walls and two sentries stand either side of the gate, as other soldiers carry boxes of files back and forth.

Mira adopts a deferential manner, averting her eyes, standing out of their way and guiding Nicholas slowly forward.

"Halt!" One of the sentries bars their way, his rifle across his chest. "What is your business here?"

Aldo steps in front, his pistol plain for them to see. "My name is Tenente de la Grascia, I am here to see Oberstleutnant Moser. Please, take me to him."

Much to Aldo's surprise, the sentry simply nods at his colleague and stands aside to allow them to pass. He waves Mira and Nicholas before him through the gate and the sentry leads them towards a square grey building.

Before they can enter, they see not far down the way a solitary man standing against a wall, a firing squad lining up before him. The poor man's uniform is a ragged dirty grey and his eyes are downcast as though he is reading words chiselled into the ground at his feet.

Mira grips Nicholas's arm and she pauses to watch as an officer calls the soldiers to attention and bids them take aim.

They raise their rifles.

The man looks up, raises his arm in salute and shouts, "Viva Sicilia!"

The officer shouts.

The sudden and loud volley causes both Nicholas and Mira to flinch, and she cannot take her eyes from the man as his bloodied, inert form slumps to the ground.

Two soldiers step forward and drag the body away.

Guarded by four more soldiers, a small group of men stand awaiting a similar fate. Enzo is among them.

Mira is about to call to him when Aldo pulls her away. He frowns and inclines his head, encouraging her to move on.

They follow the soldier into the building and to a door, outside of which two more sentries stand at ease. He says something to one of the sentries who then knocks at the door, opens it and goes inside. When he returns, he nods at Aldo, ushers him in and Mira and Nicholas follow.

Lieutenant Colonel Franz Moser is standing by a desk, sifting through papers with his one and only hand. An aide sitting across the desk from him, hands him a piece of paper, which he glances at briefly before dropping it into a box at his feet. Moser looks up. "Ah, Aldo, to what do I owe this pleasure? Please, whatever it is you want, make it quick."

"Good morning, Franz." Aldo stands, his pistol still in his hand. "I'd like to speak to you in private for a moment."

"Well, say what you have to say. You can speak freely."

The aide sits back, waiting.

"In private," Aldo repeats, "if you don't mind?"

For a few seconds Moser is unmoved and Aldo has no alternative but to stand his ground.

"I see you have brought me a prisoner and a nurse; for what reason?"

Aldo frowns at the aide.

"Very well, then." The German officer nods and his aide rises to his feet and leaves. "Now, why all the secrecy? Are you here on official business or is this a social call to wish me luck with the rest of my war?"

Nicholas listens, turning his head as each one speaks, and though he stands upright, it is weeks since he has stood up for so long and his knees threaten to give way.

Mira puts her arm round him and guides him to the empty chair.

"Your nurse," Moser says, studying her. "This is the woman you were with at the café. I remember now; you always had an eye for nurses. That time you came to see me in the field hospital you found it hard to take your eyes off them. Well, you have good taste, my friend, you always did. Now, come on, out with it: obviously you want something from me."

"Yes, I do, Franz. Though it's not so much something as someone. You have a local man here, one Enzo Ruggeri. Right now, he is lined up outside with others waiting to be executed. I'd like you sign an order releasing him into my charge."

"You'd like me to do what?"

"I'd like you sign an order releasing him into my charge."

Moser smiles, clearly believing the request to be some form of joke. However, when he reads Aldo's perfectly serious expression, he realises it isn't. "My dear fellow, how can you possibly expect me to rescind an order that has been signed by my superiors? No, no, no," he shakes his head vigorously, "I may not like my orders, but…" He pauses and stares hard at the man who rescued him from a ditch in Russia. "Look, Aldo, I have already today had to carry out the unenviable task of executing eight of my own soldiers for various crimes ranging from desertion to rape. Believe me, to have to do this breaks my heart. Like you, I am a soldier and what sort of soldier would I be if I did not carry out the orders?" The German waits, not so much for a verbal response as a visible sign that his refusal is accepted. "Aldo, I owe you much, but—"

"Franz, you owe me your life. If, during our retreat, I had left you in that ditch, you would have bled to death; that's if the Russkies hadn't got to you first and carved your eyes out. So, I am calling in… No, let us say, I am asking you for a favour in return for the favour I did not hesitate to grant you."

"Aldo," he says, his tone hardening, "the army owns my life. You did the Wehrmacht a favour, not me."

"Then as a representative of the Wehrmacht, and unless you can present me to General Hube so that he can repay the favour, I suggest you find it within yourself to pick up that pen and sign the order."

As if to emphasize the need for a swift resolution to their squabble, another volley of shots echoes from outside.

"Aldo, I cannot."

"Franz, you can. Look, I have not fired my pistol since I found you in that ditch and if I hit the three Russians who were aiming to shoot you, then I am a better shot than I consider myself to be. If I didn't, then at least one of my men must have been, because all three fell heavily. In a room this small, Franz, I don't believe I could possibly miss whatever I was aiming at."

The German is very suddenly calm as he looks from Aldo, to Mira and then to the seated Nicholas. "Who is this man?"

"He is a British naval lieutenant. He has been hiding out since his boat was destroyed a few weeks ago. We found him and we thought you might like to take him in return for Enzo Ruggeri."

Nicholas looks up, his bandages not wholly concealing his look of surprise. Mira, meanwhile, moves to his side and hugs him, protectively.

"A British naval officer, indeed." Moser chuckles. "Wearing an Italian uniform. No identification papers. I said you were not to be ridiculous, Aldo, and now you are. For one thing, he is plainly blind and for another, out of his correct uniform I would be perfectly within my rights to shoot him for a spy. That's not a trade, that is merely exchanging one corpse for another."

"Lieutenant Colonel Moser," Nicholas says, sitting up and turning his head. "If it makes all that much of a difference to you, take me, stand me up against the wall outside and do your worst; as long as you permit Enzo Ruggeri to leave with the Tenente and this woman, I won't make a fuss and nobody besides us needs to know. You can tell whoever you need to tell that you've got the wrong man; that the man waiting in line outside is not Enzo Ruggeri, but that I am."

"Very gallant of you, Lieutenant..."

"Lock. And it's Sub–Lieutenant."

The German thinks for a second before stepping over to appraise Mira. "Right, now that I know who your prisoner is, let me ask who this lady is. Apart from being your... what shall we say, paramour. Is that acceptable? Well, this Enzo Ruggeri must mean a great deal to you, Aldo, if you are willing to risk this man's life for him." He looks her up and down, examining her the way a collector might examine his butterflies. "So, who are you, pretty lady? Mm? Tell me honestly and I might consider repaying my favour to Aldo here. Tell me who you are and what this man you want released means to you?"

Yet another volley of shots shatters the silence.

However, it does not distract Mira, who stares deep into Moser's eyes, a raw hostility burning in hers. "He is my father and he did not commit the murder of which he is accused."

"Oh," he says, evidently amused by her response. Moser looks at Mira, then shifts his gaze to Nicholas. "And if your father didn't commit the murder, who may I ask did?"

She glares at him, leaning towards him so that he can feel her hot, sweet breath against his face. "I did."

Dawn rises in the German's face. "Oh, of course, how stupid of me." He looks from Mira to Aldo and then from Aldo to Nicholas. "Now I realise what is going on here. Not only do I find myself caught in the act of running from this godforsaken island that hangs from the toe of Italy like a deflated football, but also I find myself caught between two men who love the same woman and both of whom would willingly sacrifice themselves for her father; for her father and for her love. Love in war; life in death. Oh, what dizzy heights!"

Moser lifts his one remaining hand to his chin and taps his lips while he considers. "In that case… Schneider?" he barks.

CHAPTER 29

As they walk back down the rubble–strewn Via Catania to the car, Mira takes her father's arm and rests her head on his shoulder.

Aldo guides Nicholas, their progress slowed by the uneven pavement.

"Tenente?" Nicholas asks.

"Yes."

"Would you have left me behind if Moser had requested you to?"

Aldo chuckles. "Yes, I was hoping you would not ask this question. But now that you have, I suppose my answer is I don't know. This morning, on our way here, I firmly believed I would. But when I suggested trading you for her father, I saw the way Mira looked at you and I perceived such a turmoil in her that I came to realise she loves you as much as she loves her father, and there can be no deeper love than that of a daughter for her father. It was in that moment that I realised I had quite clearly finished a distant third in the competition for her affections. Now, only a poor loser would permit himself to throw his competitor under the tracks of a German tank simply to win the affections of a woman, and my vanity would not have permitted me to behave in such a manner."

"Your vanity?"

"Yes, Nicholas, vanity. You see I also realised that in all this ugliness and through all this madness, it is important for a man to maintain a sense of pride in the way he both acts and looks. That his vanity appeals to him is fundamental in ensuring a man can maintain his pride. I recognised this in Franz Moser, for when I rescued him that time in Russia, he always maintained a certain pride in both the way he behaved and the way he looked; even covered in mud and as badly injured as he was, he would never let himself be carried as long as he had the ability to stand upright. Now, a man who believes this is either a fanatic or vain, and I got to know Franz well enough to know that he is not like others who wear the same uniform; he is no fanatic. So, I appealed to his vanity in the same way I rely on mine to police my actions."

"And if you'd misjudged him?"

Aldo pauses in his step. "Mind, there is a broken paving stone."

On the way back to Ganzirri, Mira and Enzo sit silently in the back. Enzo had been the next but one in line for the firing squad when Lieutenant Colonel Franz Moser had led them outside, and the relief of his timely reprieve has exhausted both if not all of them.

The checkpoint at which Mira had threatened the sergeant with a similar emasculation to that suffered by her husband, has been abandoned. The red and white boom lies broken and the sergeant lies very dead at the side of the road.

Rather than risk running into any traffic jams caused by the last of the troops queueing for embarkation on the coast road, Aldo takes the higher route through the upper reaches of Salvatore, Paradiso and Pace. The road is longer and narrower, and winds along the undulating contours of the lower slopes of the mountains.

Below them, a flotilla of barges and a salt and pepper smattering of smaller boats, plough dark furrows, their bow waves bursting brilliant white against the azure waters.

"What will you do now, Aldo?" Nicholas asks.

The Tenente hunches his shoulders, inclines his head a little, raises his eyebrows and purses his lips. And when his affectation garners no response, he remembers it is because his passenger cannot see him. "Oh, in the long term, I don't know. I suppose I'll have to wait in Sicily until either Badoglio negotiates an armistice or he decides to join the Americans and British in ridding our country of this Teutonic plague."

"I mean, in the short term."

"In the short term? Oh, I have to return to the battery and try to ensure no harm comes to my men from the Americans, for it is they who are closest to us."

"What were your orders regarding surrender?"

Aldo chuckles. "Orders? Fortunately, I received no orders dictating whether I should surrender or keep fighting. That is often the way it has been in the Regio Esercito. If you don't know which order to issue, rather than issue the wrong order and be culpable, issue no order and blame someone else for not issuing one. Our Coastal Division has been forgotten, not that there is enough of it left to remember, and I am told there are many men who have simply cast off their uniforms and gone home. I will probably give my men extended leave, but I must stay by the fort at Capo Peloro until someone tells me different." He quiets as he considers his future.

Out of the village of Pace, the road rises in a graceful curve before descending towards Principe, Sant Agata and home.

"What will happen to you, Nicholas? What will you do?"

"In the long term, I think that will depend on what the doctors say. For the immediate future, though, things will be pretty much the same for me as they are for you. I'll hand myself over to whichever unit gets here first and then it will be a case of hurry up and wait, as the pongos say."

"Pongos?"

"Yes, pongos. Our slang for the army. Though I suppose in my case it'll be the navy who'll decide. Malta first, probably, then Gibraltar and home. No doubt they'll ship me back whenever they can spare a boat; they'll need most of them for the invasion of the mainland."

"And I will build a boat and return to my fishing," Enzo says, from the back. "I have missed the tides of the Strait these past few weeks. I have missed the silence, the peace."

Mira, though, remains silent. Home, Nicholas had said. Ship me back, he had said.

The viaduct over the Torrente Guardia, a broad dry creek, is all that stands between them and Ganzirri, and as they approach, they see German soldiers hastening back and forth. Some carry boxes of explosives and coils of cabling, while others, many of them bloodied and bandaged and supported by their comrades, stumble across the bridge towards them.

"We are just in time," Aldo mutters, "they are preparing to blow the bridge."

They stop at the threshold and Aldo gets out to speak to the officer in charge. There is much head-shaking and pleading before the officer demurs and allows them to weave a path through the remnants of his army. The stragglers stare at the car as they pass; their faces gaunt, their complexions ashen, their gazes distant and their steps faltering; exhaustion, despair and death, the three comrades of defeat.

Aldo turns down a lane to join the lower coast road and as they reach the outskirts of the village, he slows the car.

"What is wrong?" Mira asks from the back.

"I don't know," he replies. "It is too quiet. Not even a dog. Nothing."

"Why are you surprised?" Enzo offers. "Were you not the man who told the people to stay indoors?"

"Yes, but—"

They turn a corner to be confronted by a vehicle some fifty metres or so down the road.

"That is not one of ours," he says, frowning, peering closer through the windscreen. "I believe that is an American jeep. I'll stop here and take a look."

Mira leans forward and touches his shoulder. "Aldo, be careful."

"Of course, my angel. Please, wait here in the car." He opens the car door and makes to get out. As he does so, four soldiers step out from behind the corner of a house and watch him.

"Those are not Italian soldiers," he says. "And judging by the shape of their helmets, they are not German either. They must be Americans. Stay here. Do not get out of the car until I have spoken with them."

"Oh, Aldo, please be careful," Mira whispers.

"What's going on?" Nicholas asks.

"Aldo is walking towards some American soldiers who are waiting by their car," she replies. "They are about fifty meters in front of him. They look nervous; one of them has raised his rifle and is pointing it at Aldo. Wait, he's stopped. They are shouting at him and he is talking to them. Aldo is taking his pistol out and he is placing it on the ground. Now he has raised his arms. They are walking towards him. They are watching the houses, the windows. Aldo is standing still, his—"

The silence is split by the blast of an almighty explosion and in the car, Enzo, Mira and Nicholas duck.

His head down, his arm around Mira's shoulders, Enzo says, "It's all right. It's just the bridge: the Germans have blown it."

And when they sit back up, the scene they had been watching is still the same: the sky is crystal blue, the walls of the houses white–washed and the road empty but for the four American soldiers who are walking slowly, tentatively towards them. The only difference is that Tenente de la Grascia kneels penitently and perfectly still in the middle of the road."

"Aldo!" Mira screams. She struggles to get out of the car as her father holds her back.

"No, Mira, no," Enzo shouts at her. "You cannot. It is too dangerous. They will shoot you, too. Wait. They are coming."

"Who is coming?" Nicholas asks, tilting his head to listen, wishing he could see."

Mira sobs uncontrollably. "Oh, no. Aldo. Not now. Not after all this."

"The American soldiers are coming," Enzo says. "Stay where you are, Nicholas. Do not get out of the car. Wait until they get here.

Mira continues to sob. She shrugs herself from her father's grip and buries her face in her hands. "Oh, Aldo. Aldo."

The soldiers surround the Fiat, their rifles levelled.

"Get out of the car," one of them shouts, his Sicilian perfect in its dialect. "Very slowly, all of you get out of the car."

Nicholas feels for the handle and gently eases open the door. He swings his legs out and stands up, holding on for support. "You can stand down," he says in English. "I am a British naval officer and these people mean you no harm."

"And I'm supposed to believe that, buddy?" one of the Americans carps.

"Yes, my name is Sub–Lieutenant Nicholas Lock and these good people have been looking after me since my boat was sunk just over a month ago. They have given me shelter and risked their lives for me. Now it is my turn to look after them. What happened to the Italian lieutenant? Is he all right?"

"Sorry, buddy, he's dead. I guess that explosion must have spooked one of my men and he shot him."

"But he was trying to surrender."

"Yes, bad luck I guess."

Mira gets out and runs away up the road.

Enzo, too, gets out. "You speak Sicilian?" he asks, the sergeant. "How is it that you speak Sicilian?"

The American shoulders his rifle, removes his helmet, and mops his brow with his forearm. "Not me," he says. "Him." He turns to one of his men. "Go on, tell him, Luigi."

"It's like this, sir, my grandparents are originally from Messina; they talk about the place all the time. Is the city still standing?"

Enzo waits, studying the man. "Standing? Standing after the beating it has endured these past weeks. No, young man, it is not standing; it is like the Tenente, it is on its knees." He looks up the road to where Mira sits beside Aldo de la Grascia, cradling his head, stroking his face.

As Enzo walks away towards her, he asks, "Luigi, do you know the difference between this Italian officer and Messina?"

The soldier thinks for a moment. "No, sir, I'm afraid I don't."

Enzo hesitates, turns and looks back. "Well, this man is dead; your comrade killed him. A city such as Messina... no man can kill."

BOOK 3

CATERINA
2019

Chapter I

The map lies; her walk up to Capo Peloro has taken longer than suggested and by the time she's arrived at the Piazza Chiesa in Torre Faro, just over halfway, perspiration has glued her blouse to the outline of her swimming costume.

Uncomfortable and more than a little self–conscious, she sits down at a table beneath the awning of a café and treats herself to a granita al limone. The water–ice both cools her body and freezes her brain, and as a result she relaxes a little, though not for quite as long as she would like. Men, only a few, but then again it only ever needs one, have begun to notice her; so she settles the bill and walks on, her flip–flops flapping to her stride.

Not that she is late, of course, for there is no time at which she needs to be anywhere other than where she is. However, the sun is now high and unrelenting, and even the traffic wardens have retired to smoke in the shade.

Their eyes follow her: a woman in her early fifties, or possibly younger when taking into account the energy in her gait; a good figure; neither tall nor short; nice, shapely legs, not too heavy; wisps of dark hair escaping from beneath the rim of her straw sunhat; a proud bearing, her nose slightly raised beneath the oval sunglasses which conceal much of her face; and finally, and most significantly, she wears a wedding ring.

Their interest wanes.

Their brazen appraisal, like that of the men in the café, bothers her; and if she is honest with herself, ever since she'd arrived a few days before, she's found herself all too often subjected to the subtle prejudices men harbour for single women of a certain age. "A table for the signora? Yes, of course. Here, we have one available at the back." "A room for the signora? Yes, we have one; it is not at the front and does not have a balcony, but the room is quiet." And, "A bottle of wine? Why not a glass, to see if it is to your liking?"

Her bother, her fatigue, the soaring temperature and her misjudgement of the time it has taken her to get to the beach: they are just a few of the reasons why she does not notice that no one is swimming. Yet the main reason why she walks directly onto the beach without noticing this one significant detail is the scene that confronts her; for in the same way a dish of tomatoes, avocado and mozzarella can discourage a diner from wanting to spoil such a perfect fusion of colours, she is suddenly taken with the notion that if she takes one more step, her presence will reduce the purity of the landscape.

It won't, of course: the narrow Strait that separates Sicily from the toe of Italy provokes a sense of awe within all those who see it for the first time, just as it did those Phoenicians who sailed through it nearly three thousand years ago. Even so, the notion causes her to linger and consume the view.

Across the narrow strip of turquoise–blue water, a red and white pylon stands tall and threatening, like a giant iron triffid rooted upon a green foothill. And, behind her, a second similarly red and white triffid looms over the golden beach, as if protective of its flock. She had noticed the pylons on her walk up, guiding her, hailing her, drawing her to Capo Peloro.

She walks to the water's edge, sets her bag down, lays out her towel and sits with her knees drawn up to her chin and her arms wrapped defensively around her legs.

Suntanned men in swimming–briefs strut and shout into their cell phones, they gesticulate and then caress their extended stomachs as if to inform anyone who cares to know that their wives are fine cooks. Mothers, modestly dressed, preen their children while they chat with friends, and teenagers play volleyball. It is a beach like any other, except perhaps for the view.

Noticing that the women seem reluctant to expose themselves to the sun's rays, she resists the temptation to remove her blouse and busies herself inflating the red plastic pillow she'd bought in the village the evening before. When she has finished, she coats her exposed flesh in sun cream, adjusts her drying blouse and lies back.

She is woken by a gentle nudge to her arm. A woman wearing a black swimsuit is talking to her.

"Mezzogiorno!" the woman says. "The wind at midday from the south. You don't feel the heat of the sun." Though her manner is brusque, her eyes speak kindly.

"Thank you. Yes. Thank you," she replies. "I understand. I'm sorry."

"No profit in being sorry; better to be careful." The woman makes to leave, then hesitates. "You speak Sicilian, but you are not from here?"

"No." She sits up, perhaps a little self–consciously, and draws her knees up as though she is drawing up a bridge. "I am English. I fell asleep. Stupid of me. Thank you for waking me."

"That explains it. Only English people are foolish enough to sit in the sun when they should be taking lunch." The woman appears to grimace and smile, all in one curious union of her facial muscles.

"Pranzo. Yes. Lunch. That's a good idea. Thank you very much."

Though she isn't hungry, she notices that many have left the beach, so she rolls up her towel, packs her inflated pillow under her arm and steps lightly through the hot sand after the woman.

A salad of tomatoes and anchovies lifts her spirits to the extent that she makes the unusual decision of forgoing a glass of rosé in favour of a chilled beer. The bar is lively with young mothers and children, and more than once a toddler approaches to stand and study her until mama appears, apologises and drags her infant away.

The raspberry ice cream is both cooling and delicious and provokes her to greater indulgence.

With her hand wrapped around a second bottle of local beer, she watches a vast tanker dwarf the Strait as it passes north into the Tyrrhenian. A blue and white boat, tiny by comparison, chases the larger vessel and once they clear the narrow strip of water and come level with a great rock that juts out from the mountains on the Calabrian side, the little boat darts in towards the tanker. A door not far from the water line opens, a man steps nimbly across and as soon as he is on board, the little blue and white boat turns and races back towards the security of the Strait.

The woman who had woken her sits at an adjacent table and notices her watching. "When the oil tankers make Scylla look small, you know we are using too much oil."

"Scylla?"

The woman arches an eyebrow and studies her, though whether hers is a critical assessment of a woman alone or simply a lazy observation, it is hard to tell. "Yes, that is Scylla, the great rock: if no longer as great as the boats which sail past," she says. "The legend tells us the rock is where the monster with many heads took the sailors from Ulyxes' ship. Now, it is the pilot who is taken from the boat; the boat that sails above the monster of the deep, Charybdis."

"Ulysses. Yes, my..." She was about to say it was her husband who had told her the story of Ulysses, but found she didn't want to grant him a voice in their conversation.

"You are here on holiday?" the woman asks.

"Er... Yes, that's right. A break."

Her hesitation is not lost on the woman. "Ah, I see. Left you, has he? Run off with another woman or man, perhaps?"

As was so often the case, she didn't need to grant him a voice for he simply assumed one. "No, it's not like that. Not like that at all, actually," she replies, very evidently put out by a stranger's impertinence; albeit a stranger with such a kindly, approachable bearing.

The woman is, though, not inclined to apologise for her assumption. "Well, you don't have the look of a woman who has run off with another man, so I'll ask no more."

"I don't have the look," she replies, now more irritated than put out. "So how does a woman who has run off with another man look?"

"Like my brother's wife. Like she doesn't care what others think of her. You don't look like that."

"So, how do I look then?" she asks, her anger flaring like a gas ring.

"Not like that, anyway. I am Angelica, pleased to meet you."

Unsure of how to react, she hears herself say, "And you. Are you from here, Angelica?" Catherine asks, shifting awkwardly in her chair.

"From Torre Faro? Yes and no. I live in Ganzirri, the next village down. Ganzirri is a fishing village and the lagoon is famous for its clams."

"Yes, I know that." A memory suspends, like a cloud; a cloud from another time, another place, a world where life was... "Sorry, what I meant was, I know it because that's where I'm staying, at the Hotel Donato; it's very nice. Quiet. The people are charming. Do you know it?"

"Of course. In a village like Ganzirri, everyone knows everyone." Angelica thinks for a few seconds, before adding, "And sometimes too much about everyone. But that is life in a fishing village, eh?"

Keen to keep steering the focus of their conversation away from herself, Catherine glances at the woman's hands and on seeing the gold band of her wedding ring, asks, "What does your husband do?"

"Alberto? Oh, he works at the Capitaneria di Porto in Messina." Then, as if she is mildly offended, she says, "I have my own business. It is important for a woman to have some independence. Men can be such dogs: if you don't give them enough food, they soon find someone who will feed them." Angelica winks, playfully.

"What do you do?"

"I am a seamstress, one of six in our shop. We make alterations and repairs. We take clothes in for the young and let them out for the old."

"Never out of work then."

"No, we are busy, except not so busy in the summer, which is why I am here today."

"I guess there's not enough material to let out in the swimming costumes most men wear."

Angelica laughs. "No, that is true: the smaller the briefs, the greater the vanity."

The cool beer, the food, the warmth, the shade and the meeting with a stranger kindly disposed and possessed of a sense of humour, relaxes Catherine. "I'm going to have another drink, can I get you something, Angelica?"

The woman smiles, her lips thinning, the lines at the corners of her eyes creasing in crow's feet. "Please, a coffee."

Later in the afternoon, back on the beach, the sun and alcohol join in unholy union and Catherine lies down, covers herself with her wrap and sleeps.

For how long she sleeps, she cannot know; for the demons of her dream—making grow impatient and soon enough they are up to no good, stealing through the bed of her subconscious, planting roses that will blossom with colour and vines whose grapes will surely taste sweet. And they do... And the roses bloom brighter than she can recall having seen before, and the wine tastes sweeter than as she has ever tasted. The good times... The good times... They are back.

She drifts, effortlessly, and a voice, soft and lilting, tells her she must not worry, for all will be well.

Only it isn't.

She wakes and all isn't well. All is the same as when she'd fallen asleep, except that now, her head thumps and her mouth is parched. Granules of sand itch between her toes and her stomach is tight, as though pressed down on by an enormous weight.

The side of her face, sheen with perspiration, slips against the red pillow. The pillow. It is part of why she is here. It is but one part of the reason she is running. Running to get away. Getting away to escape. Escaping in vain.

She sits up: the beach is still busy, though the sun is now low towards the mountains.

A swim to freshen her mind; to escape thought.

The water is cooler than expected, though not so cold that it catches her breath, and it swirls around her feet. She steps out further, unknowing that beneath her the seabed slips away sharply. Caught out and falling forward, she grasps the inflated pillow from under her arm and, like the young girl who once trained as a lifeguard, she swings it in one fluid movement under her shoulders to use as a float. Yes, a lifeguard. Catherine knows how to swim and she swims well: people used to tell her so, so the water holds no fear for her.

She paddles, splashing water on her face and, dipping her head back to wet her hair, she closes her eyes to the warmth of the sun.

A stream of cooler water tickles at her feet and then turns her round with all the ease of a cork spun in a bucket. A second surge of water pushes at the base of her hips, pushing her up and over her pillow.

She opens her eyes.

The beach is further away than it has a right to be. A man is standing, waving and shouting at her, but the water in her ears prevents her from hearing him. Perhaps he knows her.

She laughs. How could he know her? She knows no one here and no one knows her?

Small white–capped nymphs of waves dance about her and she finds herself swung round again: one moment she is facing the red and white pylon standing tall on the green slope of Aspromonte, the next she is facing the red and white pylon standing tall against the blue sky above Capo Peloro.

She stops laughing. How can that happen? She isn't kicking with her legs, so why is she turning circles.

The beach is further away now and the man has been joined by others. They are talking, waving and pointing her way. The woman is with them, the woman who knew more about almost everything, and they are all now waving frantically.

She kicks with her legs, but try as hard as she might, she is still floating away across the Strait. She drops one arm off her pillow and strikes out for the beach and yet her effort makes no difference.

The green water suddenly draws at her legs: a giant fish is trying to suck her into its mouth. The force of the sucking alarms her; it is as though the water is alive, part of a greater body whose muscle is determined to pull her in through a valve.

A glance at the beach: a gathering crowd, fear in their faces, the frenzy of waved arms.

Why do they wave? Waving won't help.

The woman: the woman who saved her from sunburn. Why did the woman not warn her about the water? Or did she? She talked about Scylla, the monster on the rock. She talked about Charybdis, the monster from the deep.

No one dares to enter the water. Why not? Is there really a monster lurking beneath the surface?

At least, she has the inflated pillow. At least she has that to hang onto. At least with that, she will be safe.

She rests her cheek against the pillow until a shocking, repellent, hideous memory reminds her why she should dislike the pillow. No, not dislike, more detest. How could she have bought it? Why didn't she think the red pillow would remind her of... "How stupid you are," she mutters. "How absolutely brain–dead, bloody stupid."

Staring at the pillow as if it has delivered her some disgusting insult, she lets it go and watches it slide swiftly away.

At first it floats, simply, quietly, then caught by the breeze it pirouettes and tumbles far beyond her reach. However, the recollection the pillow has goaded from the locker of her darker memories does not go with it: it does not leave her like the inflatable pillow is now leaving her. The image, now seared across the screen of her thought and which no amount of water will wash away, will never leave her.

He had asked her. He had asked. If only he hadn't. If only he hadn't asked her that.

Kicking, flailing her arms, she urges herself up out of the water. The beach. The people. The waving. The woman, Angelica, looks to be talking on her cellphone. Oh, why hadn't she warned her?

The monster has her firmly by her feet now. There is no hope, no chance she will escape the tow, the swell, the sucking of the monster's great mouth.

Her limbs grow heavy. She grows weary. She wants it all to stop. She wants it all to go away. If she stops fighting, if she gives in, surely that yawning chasm inside her, the chasm that has grown wider and deeper, and both noisier and yet more silent and which aches so hard there can surely be no greater pain of longing; surely, if she gives in, that yawning chasm will be filled.

"Please, God," she murmurs. "Please let me go. Please let it all stop."

A shadow passes over her: the glare of the sun is extinguished. Catherine breathes deep. She holds her breath. She lies back and looks up: an eye looks down at her, watching her. It resembles the eye of a pharaoh; perhaps it is God, perhaps he has been expecting her. And then it is gone and there is only water, soft and welcoming and salty water, and Catherine knows she no longer has the strength to fight the whirlpool of her emotions. She gives up her fight; she gives in to the monster and it sucks her down and down and down...

Chapter 2

A dorsal fin breaks the surface.

"Fish!" comes a shout from the crow's nest. "To port. Four hundred metres."

The four men on deck turn and, shading their eyes from the glare of the sun, they look hard, out across the silver mirror of sea.

The feluca's two engines burst from their slumber and the deck vibrates. From his perch high up on the metal tower Pasquale the skipper, the capobarca, wheels the helm to bring the bow round.

"Did you see it?" young Enzo asks.

"No," his father replies, "but get ready. See to the lines." As the boat heaves in its turn, Antonio steps round the winch–box and sets off up the long passarelle which extends from the prow. The planked walkway, though secured by the many cables supporting it from the central tower, is no wider than his broad shoulders and he hangs on, hand over hand, to the slender wire–roped rail as he makes his way.

When he gets to the end, he turns and looks back up at the top of the tower.

Giuseppe, the spotter, is still pointing and directing the capobarca. He glances down and nods in confirmation.

Antonio squares his hips and steadies himself against the iron rail that runs around his platform. He picks up his long lance, checks the sharp tips, flicking each hinged barb to ensure none of the five is stuck down, and lays it down horizontally on the rail at his hips. Keeping his left hand on the lance, with his right he slips off his cap, careful not to dislodge his sunglasses, and wipes the sweat from his brow with his forearm. He sets the cap back and, returning his concentration to the surface of the sea, scours it in long even sweeps, searching for any sign of disturbance.

Nothing. The Tyrrhenian rolls away west to the foot of the Italian mainland and east to the Aeolian islands, one of which, the cone–shaped volcano of Stromboli, just crowns the horizon. To the south the mountains of Sicily bake in the midday sun and in the distance, to the north, a hydrofoil speeds towards the neck of the Strait.

Away aft, on the deck of the feluca, the lads are inspecting the baskets of thin nylon rope; rope they have coiled neatly to ensure that when Antonio, the funcitta, strikes with his lance, and the fish runs and sounds, the line will pay out without obstruction.

Pasquale throttles back and the boat pitches forward into the trough of a large wave. The boat very suddenly slows and at the end of the passarelle Antonio holds onto the rail of his small platform as it dips down into the sea. No sooner has it dipped, it rises up, then falls again and rises and falls, before eventually settling to its original height.

Antonio's legs are now soaked. And whilst the cooling of his feet is a welcome relief, he cannot conceal his dismay at the capobarca's clumsiness.

He turns, looks up, shouts, "Mi–i–i–i–i," extending the i, so leaving his oath unfinished, and raising his hand to his mouth and touching his thumb with his fingers as if to pinch a kiss from his lips.

Up above, Pasquale shrugs his shoulders, as if to say, "I command the feluca, but the sea…"

The engines burble. The sun beats down. The men are hunting. They are watching and waiting and no one talks. Somewhere, either beneath the shallow bottom of the boat or deep about its flanks, a swordfish, glides elegantly, effortlessly, in search of smaller fish.

The crew of the feluca had risen before the sun, said their goodbyes to those sleeping and made their way down to the beach. Giuseppe's wife, Giulia, had made sandwiches and packed fruit, and Pasquale had dropped by the bakery to collect a bag of pizzetta, the palm–sized pizzas. Enzo had brought a six–pack of two–litre bottles of water and Karl had ensured he would not run out of cigarettes: the day would be long, the provisions would all be needed.

The Salvazione, the blue–painted feluca, measures fourteen metres from bow to stern and a tall square tower of tubed steel, no wider than a man's forearm and held in place by stays running down fore and aft, reaches up over twenty metres from the middle of the boat. On top of the tower sits a square platform, a crow's nest, accessed by a trapdoor and large enough to accommodate two, or at the outside three, people: Pasquale, the capobarca and driver, and Giuseppe, the avvistatore, the spotter. They will stay up on the platform from the moment they leave their mooring to the moment they return, not descending even for calls of nature. So high up and with no escape from the glare of the sun and its reflection from the sea, they wear shirts buttoned down to their wrists, long trousers and desert hats. At the foot of the tower stands a cabin and though the only available shade lies within, the noise from the engines beneath the floor deters the crew from lingering too long.

At first light, they had rowed out, boarded and motored north through the neck of the Strait, their conversations loud, confident and humorous. And when level with the vast container port at Gioia Tauro, they had turned and patrolled a boxed grid; first up along down and back; then further up, further along and further down and back.

A juvenile swordfish, leaping out of the water, dancing with a shoal of mackerel, is all they had seen to keep them occupied and so bored, tired and over–heated, Antonio had shouted up to Pasquale, pointed west and they had tried their luck over towards the Aeolian islands.

Young Enzo whistles from the deck.

Antonio turns and nods: the fish is gone and Pasquale, seeing his funcitta walk back down the passarelle, wheels the helm. He needs no instruction; it is time to head back to the Strait.

An hour later, as they round the low headland of Capo Peloro, Antonio's old Motorola cellphone chirps. He flips it open. "Pronto," he says.

Enzo and the other two lads watch him.

Antonio listens, his brow furrowed, his expression filling with concern. He looks up and over at the beach. A crowd has gathered; they are waving their arms, trying to attract his attention.

"Yes. Yes," he says. "Where? How far?"

The lads track his gaze and stare.

And just as he has passed the day scouring the water for any sign of swordfish, Antonio now returns his attention to the surface of the sea some hundred metres or so off the beach. Whatever he is searching for lies there, directly in the line of the sun.

The sea shimmers and sparkles white and silver, as if sprinkled with flecks of magnesium and specks of phosphorus. The brilliance dazzles, blinding him.

Enzo steps beside him. "Someone in the water?"

"Yes," Antonio replies, his tone dull and flat. "Tell Pasquale and Giuseppe. At this time, the tide flows fast out towards Calabria. Whoever the poor unfortunate is, they will not last long."

"No one survives Charybdis," Enzo mutters. He looks up and whistles again.

Giuseppe, the spotter, leans over, looks down and nods vigorously: they have seen the crowd and there can only be one reason for such an animated gathering.

"A float!" The high pitch of Pasquale's scream, alerts them.

Giuseppe is pointing.

They follow the direction of his outstretched arm.

"There. A hundred metres just to starboard of the bow. A red float," Enzo says.

"Go," Antonio shouts. "Go fast."

The engines roar, the deck shakes and the Salvazione pitches forward as it picks up speed.

"A head. In the water, beyond the float," Enzo says.

Although it is not so far, it seems to take the boat an age to cover the distance and they watch, helpless, as the person raises their arms in distress, in appeal, in vain hope. Whoever it is, he or she is sinking and sinking fast, losing the battle with the monster's unquenchable thirst.

"Get me the rope," Antonio orders. "The one we use for lifting."

Enzo scurries and returns with a long length of rope the thickness of a man's wrist. He helps wind it, quickly but deftly, twice around Antonio's chest and then ties it securely.

"Pay the line out as I jump," Antonio tells him. "If I go under, I will pull twice when I am ready to surface. Pull hard: don't worry about hurting me. Count to thirty, quickly, and if I have not come back up by then, bring me in anyway. Understand?"

"Yes. But why don't you let me; I am lighter."

"Do as I say, Enzo."

"If you are sure, papà?"

"I am sure."

They lift their heads: the figure in the water is sliding down beneath the choppy water as they close. Forty metres, thirty, twenty.

In the crow's nest, Pasquale eases the throttle back, disengages the gear, waits for a second, then jams the leaver backwards. Cogs grind and shafts clank, groan and whine in objection at being asked to reverse their rotation so suddenly.

The boat tips forwards and Enzo steadies his father from falling over.

They move to the side and without being asked, the other two lads take up the slack rope.

"A woman," Enzo says, as if, for some reason no one can fathom, he expected a man. "She is going under. Now, papà. Now!"

The funcitta breathes deep, filling his lungs with the warm afternoon air, and spreading his arms wide, he launches himself feet first over the side.

He lands in the sea with an almighty splash, disappears, surfaces, shakes the water from his head and looks around.

The woman is gone.

"There," Enzo shouts, pointing. "There, to your left. Down there."

Antonio breathes deep again, hunches his shoulders and dives under the surface, his arms dividing the water, his legs kicking out as they propel him down and down and down...

CHAPTER 3

The room is small and the walls white and bright, but for the gloomy corners of the high ceiling; gloomy, as though spun with misted spiderwebs.

The mask itches against the side of Caterina's nose, as does the cannula in the back of her hand. She turns her head: a young nurse, her face round and angelic, her hands in her lap, sits watching her.

The nurse goes out and returns accompanied by a doctor, his hair dark, neat and tidy, his trademark white coat hanging open.

He looms over her. "I am Dottore Roselli," he says in English, as he moves the mask up onto her forehead and peers into her eyes. "I understand you speak Italian if not Sicilian, or so the nurse informs me. How do you feel?"

"Not bad. A little thick, sort of tired, a bit heavy."

When he is satisfied with what he sees, the doctor replaces her mask and says, "Yes," a long, drawn out sigh that suggests he is not in the least surprised she feels so. He takes a clipboard from the rail at the end of her bed and studies it for a few seconds, "You will feel like this, heavy and weak, and it will be tiring to breathe for a while. This is, though, a small price to pay for one who came so close to drowning."

Her mask is connected by a tube to a machine on the table beside her, a machine which beeps rhythmically and which is in turn connected to a cylinder fixed to the wall.

"Can I take the mask off for a minute?" she asks, her voice both husky and muffled.

"Yes, but not for long. You are suffering from hypoxemia: this means you have a very low level of oxygen in your blood. You have been in the Intensive Care Unit overnight and though your oxygen level is gradually improving; I would like to see it return to normal. So please, replace the mask when you have said what you need to say." Gently, he lifts her mask and rests it back on her forehead.

"My throat is sore," she says, coughing.

The nurse wipes her lips with a tissue, then helps her sip water through a straw.

"This is also not a surprise," the doctor says. "We had to intubate you before we could remove fluid and prevent your lungs from collapsing. That danger has now passed and if you stay on the oxygen for the moment, I believe you will soon recover. Do you know where you are?"

"Yes, doctor; at least I think so."

"Where are you? Please, tell me." He frowns in concentration.

"I'm in a hospital." She coughs again; that dry hacking cough of someone who has swallowed a drink the wrong way.

He smiles at her answer. "Yes, of course: ICUs are more often than not situated in hospitals and you are in Papardo Hospital. Do you know what day it is?"

She thinks. "Saturday."

"No." He smiles, ruefully. "Today is Sunday. That you do not know is also not a surprise taking into account your condition when you were brought in." He flips back a page of the clipboard. "Now, I have to ask you a list of questions. They may appear a little ordinary, but we have to be sure you are not suffering from

430

any altered state; mentally, that is. Please, what is your full name and your date of birth?"

The list is long and she has to concentrate, particularly when asked the name of the British prime minister: a figure from another time and place and country, all of which for the moment hold little significance.

"Finally," he says, staring intently and inquisitively at her as though he is expecting her to reveal some profound secret, "I have to ask you if what happened to you was nothing more than an unfortunate mistake? Perhaps you did not see the signs warning you about the dangers of bathing? Perhaps you had consumed a little too much alcohol and were not thinking correctly? This is possible, eh, there was alcohol in your blood."

"Mm," she begins, evasively, "I do seem to remember I had some beer at lunch. But I'm not unused to alcohol, if that is what you mean?"

Dottore Roselli studies her, waiting.

Her expression suggests, if a shade unconvincingly, that she has no idea what he might be waiting for or what he might be expecting her to say.

He waits on, dragging the few seconds of his appraisal into a full minute.

"What I mean is, is there any reason why you should submit yourself to such danger? Is there any reason why you should have acted so carelessly? Any reason why you should not care about what happens to you?"

Now, it is her turn to make the good doctor wait. She fixes him with a vaguely aggressive look. "No, none at all. Why would you ask such a thing?"

Roselli arches an eyebrow, purses his lips and inclines his head. "Oh, some words you said, or tried to say, when we were assessing you: they weren't very positive, though naturally you were delirious. But you called out for someone: you kept saying over and over that you wanted to be with him."

"Well," she says, a hint of disdain in her tone, "I guess I was hoping someone was going to save me. And, as you said, quite naturally."

Though very obviously sceptical at her reply, he waits again, eventually nods and then closes his flip–board. "Bene. Okay. Now, I believe you have questions for me?"

"Yes, Dottore, you seem to know the answers to all the questions you've asked me, how is that? And where are my clothes and my bag from the beach? Lost I suppose."

He turns and opens the door of a white cupboard. Inside, hanging from the rail, is her beach–bag and on the shelf, her passport and wallet. "A lady… a kind lady," he repeats, "insisted on coming here with you in the ambulance. She brought your possessions."

"A lady? How? Who?"

"Angelica Lazzarotto. She told us she spoke with you. She was very concerned for you."

"Oh, I see. Yes. Angelica. That was her name."

"Angelica Lazzarotto," he confirms. "She came to ask how you were and I told her she would be better to come back tomorrow morning."

"Dottore Roselli, how long must I stay here? I mean, how long do you think…"

"I think it is best for you to remain with us under observation for another twenty–four hours. I will come and see you again tomorrow and if I am happy with the oxygen in your blood and you are strong enough, then you can be discharged." He leans his arms on the side of the bed and studies her face. "However, I think it would be best for the time being if you were to be released into the care of another person. You must remember, when you were brought in your condition was not… favourable. At first, we were not confident that we would be able to save you and there is little doubt that if the men who rescued you had not pumped as much water from your lungs as they did, then…"

"Is that why my chest aches?" She had meant to say breasts and stomach, but the idea that complete strangers had not only seen her in such a state but had also handled her intimately, unsettles her and she very quickly decides she doesn't want to dwell on the thought. "Is that why I feel so bruised?"

"Yes. You will be sore for a few days and you will cough, which will make you yet more uncomfortable: your lungs will also take a few days to clear completely, so if you feel faint or pass out, you will have to come back. This is very important, yes?" He closes the cupboard and checks his watch. "Now, there are people who need my attention, so…" He turns to leave.

"Dottore?"

He turns back to her. "Yes?"

"I'm grateful to you. I'm sorry if I was a bit… well… And I'm sorry to have taken up so much of your time when I am sure there are others who are more deserving. Especially after my being so stupidly careless."

He warms to her, his eyes surrendering their stern concentration. "No matter. Now, please keep the oxygen mask on until the nurse checks your blood in an hour's time."

"Before you go, Dottore, I have one more question."

"Yes, of course, what is it?"

"Who did rescue me?"

He replaces the mask over her mouth and nose: a medical necessity perhaps; a sign telling her she needs to stop talking, definitely. "I am not completely certain; La Signora Lazzarotto told me they were fishermen. You were, to say the least, very fortunate a feluca was so close by. Another minute, perhaps only another few seconds, and… Now, rest and if you can, try to sleep."

"A feluca. Yes. Thank you, Dottore."

"There is a lady to see you," the nurse says.

"A lady? To see me?"

"Yes, La Signora Lazzarotto. Dottore Roselli asked her to collect you. You can take off the mask now; I will remove your cannula."

When the nurse has left, there is a polite knock at the door.

"Come in, please."

The door opens into the room and a short, heavy–set woman, dark–brown hair tightly curled, enters. She carries a small leather holdall. "Signora, it is me Angelica, from the beach. How do you feel today? Better, I hope."

Though forced, due solely to her lack of energy, the smile she musters is genuine. "Yes, much better, thank you. Please, sit down for a minute."

"If I may." La Signora Lazzarotto's smile is warm if a little nervous, judging by the way she glances at the now silent machines that have been monitoring the patient's progress.

"Signora Lazzarotto, I—"

"Angelica, please."

"Yes. Thank you. I am Catherine. I don't think I told you my name when we met, or if I did, I can't remember."

"No, you didn't. I told you mine, but somehow… Anyway, what do names matter, eh?"

"Signora Lazzar— I mean, Angelica, the doctor told me you came to the hospital with me in the ambulance, that was very kind of you, you—"

"It was not kind," she interrupts, dismissing the compliment as if it was a bothersome insect, "it was necessary. Your bag, your belongings: I am sure someone would have picked them up, but as we had already spoken, I decided it was better that I should do it than someone less reliable."

In the two words, less reliable, it comes to Catherine that the woman has defined herself; for if one's physique can be shaped to formalise steadfastness, then Angelica Lazzarotto's bold chin, broad, rounded shoulders and thick, capable arms do so.

"Well, if not kind," Catherine replies, "then I am very grateful. Really, very grateful."

She waves again. "Nothing. It was nothing. You were in a certain difficulty, let us say, and I am sure had our circumstances been reversed that you would have done the same for me. You strike me as one who would: tell me I am wrong?"

Her brazenness, her willingness to talk in such a no–nonsense manner is neither impertinent nor impudent, it is pleasantly refreshing: it is as though someone has walked into the room and opened a window to allow in a cooling draft of fresh air.

"I'd like to think I would, Angelica. I'd like to think so."

"Of course, you would. I recognise the kindness in some as easily as I recognise the indifference in others. Now, what is more important than what I have done for you, is how you are in yourself. Do you think you are up to leaving? Do you have the strength to step beyond the portal of the Papardo and walk amongst the healthy? Though I must say, there are some in my village who look far from healthy. Pah! That is how it is these days, isn't it? People live the way they want to, not the way they should. Tell me, how do you feel? Are you ready?"

Catherine hopes her expression does not betray her misgivings in the face of such exhortation to confront the world outside, however... "Yes, thank you, I guess I'm as ready as I'll ever be. Though tell me, if you wouldn't mind, why does the doctor think I need a shepherd or chaperone? Or is nursemaid more appropriate?"

"Come, come," she waggles her finger, a thick, solid and insistent index finger that looks more suited to the cleaning of guts from a fish rather than the intricacies of needlework. "My dear Catherine, one does not question the advice of Dottore

Roselli: he is an intelligent man and a good doctor, as was his father, and in Ganzirri his grandfather is venerated before Saint Lucas the Evangelist: God rest their souls." She crosses herself and glances up at the ceiling. "You must be assured that Dottore Roselli always has one's better interests at heart; he remembers his oath and clearly he believes you need someone to keep an eye on you for a few days, isn't that enough?"

Whatever Catherine's misgivings, they are as chaff tossed in a gale. "Yes, you're right, Angelica, I'm sure you are. And he is very charming, too."

"Oh, yes: attractive, gentle with his hands and a very pleasing bedside manner." Her eyes sparkle with mischief. "What else can a woman ask for in a doctor? Now—"

"Angelica, please excuse my interrupting you..." Catherine, now formal and assertive, if only as assertive as her depleted reserves of energy will permit. "My clothes, they are at the hotel and I am booked in to stay for another week."

"Yes, you were, but now you are not: I have told them you have no further need of the room. And as for your clothes, I have already been and taken them to my house. I have brought you all you need to change into."

"You have taken my clothes?" Catherine asks, vaguely surprised, vaguely offended. "You have been to the hotel and picked up my things? Should they have let you? Didn't they object?"

"Yes, a little. But I know them well, very well, and I explained your situation and they understood. If you feel I have acted improperly, we can call by on the way home so that you can satisfy yourself all is in order."

"Angelica!" Catherine says, her frustration at being railroaded flaring in her tone. "I am not sure I should be your house guest just because Dottore Roselli has decreed I need a little watching. Surely, you could have kept an eye on me while I was at the hotel."

If Catherine had hoped to provoke some reaction from Angelica, her hopes are immediately dashed by the woman's disarming and sweetly mothering smile.

"No, that would not do. I promised Dottore Roselli that I would look after you for a few days. Tell me, and I know you can discharge yourself if you wish to, do you seriously believe you have the strength to care for yourself. Look at you: you don't look as though you have it in you to peel an orange. And... you could do with a good meal; you look far too thin for your own good. So, what harm is there in good food and resting under my watchful eye. Only for a few days, eh?"

Catherine struggles to drag herself upright in the hope that by doing so she will gain some authority. But when eventually she is sitting up, the room spins, slowly, irregularly, her eyes glaze over and she reaches out to hold onto the side of the bed. The effort causes her to cough and cough again until her throat and lungs ache and she clutches her ribs.

Angelica hands her a tissue.

When the spasm has passed and she has cleaned her mouth, Catherine asks, "You are married, aren't you? You told me your husband's name. Alberto, isn't it? You said he works in the port."

"Alberto, yes," she smiles, "at the Capitaneria. Your memory serves you well." Her expression darkens briefly. "What of him?"

"Well, won't he object? I mean, suddenly having a woman he does not know in the house?"

Angelica shrugs and grins. "No, he didn't object. I told him you would be coming to stay for a few days and besides, we have enough room and he likes his food. You know, Catherine... Or perhaps I should call you Caterina. Yes. Caterina; it sounds better, and with your dark eyes, your full lips and small nose, you could pass for one of us: your complexion is a bit pasty and you are a bit tall, but... Is your father tall?"

437

"Was. Yes. Taller than some, I suppose."

"Well, Caterina," she glances at the gold wedding band on Catherine's finger, "I am sure you know that all men are like dogs, eh? As long as you feed them, they will do what you want."

CHAPTER 4

Enough room, that was what Angelica had said.

Catherine looks around: a single bed, blue sheet and grey blanket folded square. The walls are rough–plastered, lime–washed and hung with paintings of fishing boats, folk congregating by the sea and, above the bed, an image of the Madonna della Lettera, clutching her child as she blesses the citizens of Messina. At least there is a window, even if it does look directly at the house not more than a few metres opposite.

"It's perfect," she says. "I still don't understand why you should show me such kindness. Wouldn't it be better if I—"

"The bathroom is next to your room," Angelica points to her right, "Alberto rises and leaves early, and he isn't always as quiet as one might wish. Please, make yourself comfortable."

Taken with an urge to flee and yet at the same time stay, Catherine sits on the bed, lowers her head into her hands and mutters, "What the hell are you doing, girl? How on earth did you come to this?"

For how long she remains so, she is not sure, until slowly Catherine becomes aware Angelica is still standing in the doorway.

"You will be fine now," she says. "Come, let me help you unpack. Even if you are with us for only a few days, it will make you feel better if you unpack: you will feel more... more at home."

The blessed tenderness of the woman fractures the dam of emotion Catherine has been shoring up ever since she'd woken to find the round–faced angel of mercy sitting silently, watching over her.

"I'm sorry. I'm so sorry. I don't know what's up with me." She searches in her pocket for a tissue, a handkerchief, a piece of cloth, anything with which she can dry her tears. But there is nothing: she did not choose her clothes, she is not prepared, she had not thought to...

"Caterina," Angelica whispers, handing her a tissue, "you have no need to apologise for your emotion. It is perfectly healthy for us to cry away our sadness and who knows, perhaps even our regret. You have had a shock: you are tired, I can see that. Why don't you lie down for a while, a little sleep, un pisolino? It won't hurt. And, when you wake, come downstairs, I will be in the kitchen." Gently, she shepherds Catherine to lie down and covers her with the blanket.

"I'm sorry, Angelica. I'm sorry and I'm so very grateful. Really I am."

———

"You look a little better," Angelica notes, as Catherine comes into the kitchen, adding, "There is colour in your cheeks."

"Yes, I feel rested, thank you. I feel like I'm still wearing the hospital though, I don't suppose—"

"Why don't you take a shower, eh? But please, be prudent: usually, we have water only from six in the morning until nine in the evening and though we have a tank, it does not hold much. Alberto, he gets irritable if I have used too much and there is not enough for him to shower when he comes home."

"Your water is rationed?" Catherine replies, surprised.

"Yes, Messina is always short of water. It is because we are squeezed between the mountains and the Strait. June, not so bad, but in August the tap runs dry at two in the afternoon."

When Catherine reappears, suitably refreshed, she stands by the door and watches her host busy herself with a recipe.

"Good," Angelica says, after a brief and overtly critical appraisal. "Earlier, you looked better: now, you look almost human. You dress well; those are nice trousers, a nice blue, a rich blue, like the sea in the evening. And that blouse, orange like the sun. Expensive, eh?"

"No," Catherine replies, a shade defensively, "not really."

"I did not mean to suggest you spend too much money on clothes," Angelica notes, cutting a chunk of cheese and setting it to a grater. "I mean that you dress well, that you pay attention to how you look. That is good for a woman, to look nice. Alberto will be home soon."

Catherine edges over, nearer Angelica and studies the various ingredients she has set out on the counter. "Looks... complex, what are you cooking?"

"Arancino. Do you know it?"

"Yes, but I haven't eaten arancino for years: I used to love it. That's pork mince, isn't it? And beef, too. Is that parmigiano you're grating?"

"No, this is pecorino; unlike parmigiano, it is sheep's milk and it has more salt." She stands back and points: "And this is arborio rice, risotto rice, we use it because it absorbs flavour better than ordinary rice. And here, we have crushed saffron, yellow onions because they are a little sulphurous, mozzarella, tomato paste, flour, eggs, vegetables, sea salt and black pepper. I use olive oil for cooking the filling and vegetable oil for cooking the rice balls. I guess you could say it is more complex than other dishes, but it is worth it and it is a personal favourite of Alberto's, so..."

"I'm sure it'll be delicious," Catherine says, her taste buds dancing at the thought.

Angelica pauses for a second, looking at her intently, perhaps gauging some potential in her. "Why don't you help me?"

"Oh no, I couldn't. Trusting me to come into your house is one thing; cooking a Sicilian dish for your Sicilian man might be stretching that trust a little too far."

However, in the short time she has got to know her host, Catherine understands that she is likely to turn a deaf ear to her protest.

"Cooking is good for the soul," Angelica states, nodding as if to lend her theory a degree or two of affirmation. "I have always found this to be so, particularly when Alberto and I have a difference of opinion and I am left to endure his silence until he sees the sense in what I have said." She winks, playfully. "Look, why don't we do this: you can help prepare and I will show you how to make the arancini. Then, if Alberto finds fault with it, I will say I am the cook; and if he doesn't, you can claim all the credit. It will be a game for us to play."

Catherine laughs, realising as she does so that it is the first time she has laughed in far too long. "Angelica, I bet your husband doesn't ever find fault with your cooking; something tells me he might go hungry if he did."

"Good. That is settled." She picks a knife out from the wooden block. "Here, you see to the celery and carrots, chop them finely, and I'll start with the meat and the rice."

As they attend to their allotted tasks, Angelica tells her how in the west of Sicily they call them arancine, because they are round, like an orange, una arancia; whereas here, in the east, they are known as arancini and they are rounded at the base and pointy at the top, like a cone, which makes them easier to eat. Then, of course, there is the matter of whether they are male or female, as in arancini or arancine, but then the men of the west are more feminine, so who cares what they think! No one, she says, really seems to know.

Angelica is content to talk while she stirs the grated pecorino, the butter, and the salt and pepper into the rice, tasting as she goes; and Catherine is happy to listen as she cleans, slices and chops.

Alberto, or so she would have Catherine believe, is an okay kind of husband. "He can't be too bad, can he? After all, he has kept me well and he has been a good father to our four sons, all of whom live in the north: the first near Milan, the second in Turin, the third in Rome and the fourth... Now, where was Ninolino when last we spoke?" And without any prompting, she manages to steer clear of subjects which might threaten to complicate or interfere with what seems so far to be a pleasing association.

While they wait for the rice to cool, Angelica grinds two varieties of coffee bean, before filling the group handle, tamping down the contents and inserting the handle into the espresso machine.

Thick, orange–brown liquid dribbles into small cups. "You like coffee?"

"Yes, of course, Angelica. I like the taste, but most of all I love the aroma. It makes me feel alive. I can't really get going in the morning without a proper sniff of coffee."

"I am the same, although I think I drink more than is good for me."

They sip and appreciate and relax, and during the silence the elephant of Catherine's circumstance steals into the room, all too soon growing too large for either of them to ignore.

Finishing her coffee and, perhaps, spurred by the hit of caffeine, Catherine sits upright and says, "Yes, you have a question for me. Several, I should imagine. Please, Angelica, you have been so good to me: please don't feel that you can't ask."

Unnerved by a stranger reading her thoughts, Angelica's dark eyes flash like black lightning in a sunlit room. Soon enough, though, she softens and puts down her cup.

"Whatever your situation, Caterina, this is no business of mine. Your silence is your silence, and it is not mine to break. God knows, it is not as though we women don't know how to suffer in silence." She arches her eyebrows, suggesting there have been far too many times when she has had to seek solace in her own counsel. "But, isn't there someone you should contact? Isn't there someone who you should call to tell what has happened to you or where you are? Unless I am mistaken, which is possible but not probable, you are a mother. I was watching your hands while you prepared the vegetables: like me, you are not a professional in the kitchen; yet like me, you prepare the food with love." She reaches out and grabs Catherine's hands, holding them up as if they are exhibits in a court case. "Look, you have the hands of a woman who cooks with love, and to cook with love means you have someone you love to cook for." Angelica lets go of Catherine's hands and leans forward as she speaks, pointing her finger to drive home her assertion. "You are a mother; I see this in you as much as I see it in myself when I look in the mirror. And as you are a mother, then there must be a child or children and, somewhere, a father. Is it not right for you to let them, one of them, know where you are? They may be worried; I know I would be."

Catherine's expression which had a moment before appeared relaxed and yielding, suddenly hardens and her posture assumes an aggressive rigidity. She stares, her eyes glazing over, seeing not the woman in front of her so much as the faces of others she needs either to address or to shoo away to some quiet corner of her mind, where they will have to wait for her to deal with them.

Angelica sees her withdraw and hurries to catch her before she runs so far away that she is out of reach. "Your phone: to my knowledge you haven't used it since you arrived here."

Her effort, though, is rewarded only with silence.

"If you cannot bring yourself to talk to someone, then what about a simple text message: that surely would be better than nothing?"

Catherine sits and looks at her without seeing.

"And your computer, your laptop. I know you have it with you because I brought it from the hotel. If you do not want to turn on your phone, if you are afraid of knowing that you have missed calls or that you have too many messages, then perhaps at least you could send an email."

Nothing; still nothing; no response, just the distant stare of a woman who cannot understand why something, some trauma, some injustice or some monumental misfortune, has been thrust upon her. The white noise of breaking waves floods her mind; the unbearable pressure of the deep crushes her skull; and the knowledge that her lungs must burst terrifies her. She raises her arms up towards the ceiling and follows them with her eyes. She tries to speak, but finds that instead of words coming out from her mouth, water rushes in. She is gagging, she dares not swallow, an eye watches her while she chokes: she—"

"Caterina?"

Someone is shouting.

"Caterina?"

She is still looking up, still searching for the arms that will pull her to safety.

"Caterina? Put your arms down. Look at me. Now. Look at me."

And she does, slowly. She looks down and lowers her arms, as if pretending to a languorous ballet, and her eyes begin to regain their focus. "Yes," she says, though she does not recognise the monosyllabic, monotone response as coming from her own mouth.

"Caterina? Look at me."

"Yes, Angelica. Sorry." Gently, she shakes her head, wishing the fog from her mind. "I don't feel so great. I'm cold and a little tired. If you don't mind, I'll go and lie down for a while?"

"No, my dear Caterina, I don't mind. You are exhausted. Go. Go and lie down. Rest your troubled heart." Though driven by her motherly instincts, Angelica does not get up and follow her; rather she sits and watches and whispers to herself, "Not such a fool that Dottore Roselli, eh?"

———————

Judging by the cooler temperature and the lack of shadow, Catherine has slept far beyond dinner. A plate of ciabatta and pata negra ham, a glass of water and a second smaller plate of little round sfingi carnival doughnuts sit on the chest of drawers. The idea appeals; the effort involved in fetching them less so.

She lays on the bed and, as the evening slips towards dusk, listens to the disparate harmonies of the narrow streets beyond her open window: the nasal whine of a scooter, the insistent hoot of a car's horn, the peal of church bells, the shrieking laughter of children, the plaintiff cry of herring gulls.

Angelica's imperative tones drift up the stairs. "No, Alberto, I will not have it. Whatever has happened to this woman, it is no fault of hers; this I sense very strongly."

A man, his voice a slow and steady basso profundo, replies, "Okay, okay, so this 'ngrisa; you seem to like her, but we don't know exactly what has happened to her. We don't know anything, apart from the fact that she nearly drowned. And I know that is not unusual, eh? There is always some idiot who doesn't know how dangerous the waters can be. But what if she has committed some crime, eh? What if it turns out she has; we could be in trouble for harbouring a criminal, have you thought of that?"

"My dear husband," she replies unafraid to conceal her patronising tone, "please don't refer to her as 'ngrisa. Yes, she is an

English woman, a lady, but she has a name, Caterina, and I would ask you to afford her the respect you would like to be afforded when you find yourself in someone else's country. Pah, you watch too many strangers getting off the ferry from Calabria; it makes you suspicious; it makes you prone to seeing the mystery in people. Why can't you see the light in them instead?"

"The light? Didn't you tell me Dottore Roselli was unsure as to whether or not she was trying to kill herself, that she is depressed and therefore a liability to anyone who should volunteer to care for her?" He pauses. "Ah, you and your lost causes!"

"No," Angelica says, the cold steel of her ire inserting itself into her denial, "that was not what the good Dottore said and, what's more, it is not what I said. Dottore Roselli believes she is troubled by something in her past and one doesn't need to be a doctor of medicine or psychology to realise that. As I said, she is welcome to stay here for a few days, at least until she has regained her confidence. Really, Alberto, there are times..."

"But you said she seems to show no remorse?"

"No, I said that even though she has said she is sorry several times, I don't believe she has done anything that merits an apology. I don't get the impression that if she had been intent upon taking her own life, she is sorry she failed, and that is a far cry from not showing remorse."

"Okay. Okay. I get it. Angelica, my darling wife, my love. Can you spare a drop of olive oil for my ears; I believe the wax–"

"Alberto!" she moans, spicing her menace with a pinch of sarcasm.

"Yes, yes. I apologise. I did not mean to be unsympathetic. You know as well as I do that this 'ngrisa is welcome to stay for as long as you desire. Besides, what with it being summer and many of the men demanding their right to go on holiday, you will probably see more of her than you will of me."

"Peace at work, eh?" she says.

Ignoring her gibe, Alberto carries on: "What intrigues me, though, is why, if she had been intending to take her own life, she should do so here and not somewhere else. Why would you leave your home country to do such a thing when you can do it much easier on your own doorstep? And how is it, as you tell me she can, that she speaks our language, eh? And I don't mean Italian; I mean Sicilian. That, you must agree, is most unusual."

Even though Catherine has not yet met Alberto, she can imagine him poking a stubby finger at Angelica as he speaks.

"Your risotto is getting cold."

"Yes, yes, I know. By the way, what happened to the arancini you promised? You know very well I would happily commit murder for your arancini and I have been looking forward to them all day."

"That is my fault," Angelica replies, meekly. "I ran out of pork mince. Yes, me, running out of pork mince. Can you imagine! But don't worry, I will finish them for tomorrow's dinner. Try not to be late, Antonio is coming."

"Me? Late? Ridiculous! And since when did your fisherman brother turn up on time, eh?"

CHAPTER 5

Since the evening before, she has lain in bed and closed both her eyes and ears to the world; and yet as hard as Catherine has tried, she has not managed to escape either the images in her thoughts or the noise from beyond her window.

Downstairs, she hears the rattle of a key in a lock, the creak of a handle and the screech of hinges long overdue a drop of oil, footsteps on tile. A minute or so later, a draught of disturbed air tells her the bedroom door is now open.

"Caterina," Angelica says, not loudly, but very definitely not quietly, "it is after midday, please, you should get up."

"And you sound exactly like my nonna," she replies, rolling onto her back to stare at the ceiling.

"Your nonna? She is your nonna or you call her Nonna?"

"Was. Perhaps is. I don't know. When I was in the hospital, I felt her presence; it was like she was in the next room, listening through the wall. I was her only grandchild and she was always just plain Nonna to me."

Angelica crosses the room, leans on the window sill and gazes down into the narrow street below. "If you were her only grandchild then you must have been close to her."

"There's no doubt I was precious to her; she used to spoil me rotten. But close? I was only eleven when she died: do you think you can know anyone when you are only eleven?"

"Oh yes. Children are very perceptive, much more so than adults. We complicate our appreciation of others with petty judgements and pointless jealousies: children know by instinct whether a soul is compassionate and affectionate. What do you remember of her?"

"Nonna," Catherine says, summoning her image. "I suppose my lasting memory of her was not long before she died. She was short and quite small, and she had these warm eyes and this way of smiling that melted your heart. She loved to cuddle and even when I was taller than her, she liked me to sit on her lap. I remember she always smelled of bergamot, a little like freshly–made Earl Grey tea."

"Yes, of course, L'essenza di Bergamotto," Angelica repeats, breathing deep as if inhaling the perfumes of citrus oil.

"Nonna always kept a tin of chocolates, but she would wait until tea–time before asking me to get the tin from the drawer and then reminding me I was only ever allowed to take three. I remember one time I asked her why tea–time and why only ever three, and she lowered her head to look at me over her glasses: "Caterina," she said, "the best things in life are always worth waiting for and if we were to eat all the chocolates today, there will be nothing left for us to look forward to tomorrow." For her, everything was always going to be better tomorrow."

"And she, too, called you Caterina," Angelica says to the window.

"Yes. Just like you insist on doing."

"And she died when you were eleven?"

"Yes. 1980, the same year and two months after my father died. I sometimes wonder if his dying didn't break her heart: you know, her only son."

"Eleven, eh," Angelica repeats.

"Yes."

"And I am now three years the wrong side of fifty and you are three years younger than me."

"If you like," Catherine replies, as though she could not care if she was a hundred years younger or older.

"Good!" Angelica bangs her palms against the window sill, as if she has come to a decision, steps over beside the bed, crosses her arms and looks down. "Good!" she repeats. "I do like. Yes. This means we both have time to achieve much."

"Much of what?"

"Much of many things. And first, I am going to take a leaf out of your nonna's book. From now on, you will know yourself as Caterina, I will know you as Caterina and I will introduce you as Caterina: the old Catherine is of no use to either of us for the next few days." Angelica waits for an objection and when none is forthcoming, she carries right on. "And second, you will, just as your nonna asked you, get out of bed: for if we have learned one lesson from our history, it is that however calamitous our misfortune, we must always rise again to rebuild our lives."

———————

"Now, look," Angelica says, encouraging her to the hob. "The vegetables are soft and the onions almost clear, so we are ready to add the pork and beef mince to the saucepan. Keep stirring until the meat is brown: take this, use this wooden spoon. Then, when you are satisfied with the colour, add some red wine from this bottle, and allow it to reduce. Don't look at me like that, Caterina, you do it."

"But I don't know how much wine," she replies, hesitating.

"Oh yes, I'm sure you can work it out. Add enough, but not too much. Use your imagination. Use your love."

"We seem to be cooking a considerable quantity: how many are you expecting for dinner?"

"Just the four of us."

"Four?"

"Yes, you and me, Alberto and Antonio."

"Antonio," Caterina repeats. "And who is Antonio?"

"He is my brother. Today is Wednesday and Antonio comes to eat with us every Wednesday evening. No, don't look surprised, I am not trying to match–make. First comes the day, then comes Antonio and now you are here. That is the way it works."

"This is your brother whose wife left him."

"Exactly."

"So he has no one to cook for him?"

"No, which is why he joins us on Wednesdays. Pay attention to the meat, Caterina, do not let it burn, eh?"

"Yes, sorry." She stirs and stirs again. "What is he like, your brother?"

"What is he like?" Angelica thinks for a moment. "Antonio is one of those men who once he has decided things are a certain way, he is unlikely to change his mind."

"Stubborn, you mean."

"No, not so much stubborn. You could say he is like an egg: he can appear a little hard–boiled, but he is not necessarily hard–hearted. He is a man for common sense, for logic and for patience. These are all qualities of a good fisherman."

"A fisherman?" Caterina says, surprised and at the same time curious.

"Yes, like our father and our grandfather. Unfortunately, our father was lost to the Strait when we were quite young, so we didn't really know him." She sighs, as she considers both her father's short life and the misfortune of children who grow up without the guidance of a father. "I sometimes wonder if that is not why Antonio took to being a fisherman too: perhaps he believes the sea will one day give our father back to us."

"That doesn't sound like common sense or logic."

"No," Angelica, says, slowly, reconsidering, "it doesn't, does it? Maybe that is just me reading signs that are not there. Or maybe

I have painted the wrong picture of him, I don't know; but it is important to understand that just because a man lives by what he sees, it does not mean he is not a spiritual person. Antonio is that and much more, although he keeps much of his spiritual side locked away."

"Is that because of what happened to him with his wife? Was he so hurt that he has buried his emotions? Once bitten, twice shy, that sort of thing."

"Now, Caterina, add the wine and when it has reduced, the tomato paste; then we will leave it for ten minutes before we add the peas. Yes, I think you may be right. He was very wounded by her leaving; it wasn't simply his loss of face, though he is no different from any man in that respect."

"Or any Sicilian man, you mean."

"Yes, perhaps," Angelica replies, standing to sniff the aroma rising from the saucepan. "Nearly; one more minute."

"What was she like, his wife? Why did she leave him?"

"What was she like? Oh, she possessed vanity the way some women possess small dogs: a plaything for her to lavish her attentions on, a focus for her love. So much so that Antonio could not compete with her vanity; there was not sufficient room in her life for both. Being married to a fisherman is not easy: the hours are long, the work is dangerous, and one would have to share one's husband with his mistress, the sea. For that, I don't blame her."

"Where does she live?"

"In the north. Milan, somewhere near there. Somewhere where she can feed her vanity the right diet of polenta and fashion. She remarried, that was her right, and she comes back to visit Enzo, Antonio's son, my nephew. But when she does, she always looks like she has come straight from a catwalk and that is not her right."

"How does Enzo feel about her?"

"Like most twenty–year olds who have been deserted by their mother; he resents the hurt she has caused his father."

"What age was he when she left?"

"Oh, ten, I think."

"That must have been tough for your brother, to bring up a young boy and have time for fishing."

"Naturally. Now," she says, as though she has talked enough of sadness, "the sauce has thickened, so put it in that bowl and we will let it cool. I prepared the rice before I went out this morning. It is over there, on that big plate. When you have done that, please cut the mozzarella into small cubes and we will have a coffee, which I will make."

"I see," Caterina replies, a hint of easy humour in her tone, "So you trust me to make your arancini, but not to make your coffee."

"No, that is not how it is. You make the arancini, the espresso machine makes the coffee and I make you smile, which I am pleased to see I have."

"Take a big spoonful of rice," Angelica, says, "and put it in your palm. Close your hand a little and press the rice into the shape of a cornet, like so."

Caterina copies her. "Like an ice cream cornet."

"Yes. Good. Now, take a small spoon of the sauce and fill the rice, leaving just enough at the top to add two or three cubes of the mozzarella and close it over. Be gentle, take your time; next to the preparation, this is the most important part." She watches her pupil and manages to resist the temptation to interfere. "Yes, exactly like that. Excellent. Try to make the thickness of the rice even and thick enough that the sauce will not leak through. When you have finished, put the arancino on the plate."

"I'm not sure that's good enough, Angelica. It's a bit thin in places."

"That was your first. Try another; the second will be better and the third better still. I will watch and if I am not happy, I will tell you. So, keep going until you have finished."

Caterina smiles, a resigned, good–natured and grateful smile. "Okay, but just remember, it's your head that's going to roll if I mess up."

"No, I don't think so. When cooks make a mess of their cooking, we do far worse than cut off their heads. Good, the second one is already looking more even."

Although as in the afternoon before, they sit in silence, this time Caterina's concentration provides a fence with which to keep the elephant of her circumstance at bay.

"How many arancini have you made so far, Caterina?"

She whispers to herself, counting: "two, three, four. Four."

"And how many children do you have?"

Caterina hesitates as she loads her palm with rice. "That's not fair."

"Life is not fair," Angelica states, solemnly. "How many?"

"One, my daughter Lucy." She carries on pressing out the cone shape, all the while not looking directly at her inquisitor.

"And how old is Lucy?"

"Twenty–five."

"What is she like?"

"She is tall, slim and very attractive: she has lovely hair, light–brown, not dark like mine. She's a bit of a fitness fanatic: goes to the gym, runs half–marathons, but then most of them seem to do that these days."

"Yes," Angelica replies, dreamily, "my sons are the same; well, not all four of them, but three of them anyway. I am sure she is very attractive, like her mother, but when I ask you what she is like, I mean what she is like as a person."

"Oh, she is a very positive soul: always the one to see opportunity in difficulty rather than the other way around. She's worked hard at her studies and so far, she's made the grades and earned the rewards, the accolades, the opportunities. That's what I mean about her, she never expects anything to come to her; she always makes the effort to go out and get what she wants. Wasn't quite like that when I was her age: mostly, we had it put in front of us and were told to eat it."

"When did you last contact her?"

Caterina puts the spoon down beside the bowl of sauce and stares at the cupboard. "Last week, before I..." She shakes her head, banishing the memory from her mind. "The day I met you at Capo Peloro."

"And we know today is Wednesday, because Antonio is coming; tomorrow is his Onomastico."

"His name day?"

"Yes. Usually, men do not work on their name day, but Antonio..." Angelica shrugs, pauses, stands and inspects the arancini. "You are getting through those very quickly; they look very good. Bravo! I will whisk the eggs, flour, salt and water; the breadcrumbs I have all ready, here. When you have finished, you can dip the cones and roll them in the crumbs: then, you can put them in the fridge to firm up." She taps the door; it is plastered over with photographs held in place by a variety of gaily–coloured fridge magnets.

"Angelica?"

"Yes, Caterina."

"Aren't you going to ask me about Lucy's father?"

"No, that is for another time; perhaps after you have spoken to your daughter or later, when you feel you are ready." She pauses, though not for long. "No, what I am more interested to know, is why you have come here, to Ganzirri. How long have you been here and did you come straight from the airport or from somewhere else in Sicily?"

"I came here from Taormina, last week."

Angelica waits, expecting.

456

"I'd been there for a few days."

Angelica is still waiting, still expecting.

"Seeing a few of the sights: you know, the amphitheatre, the Duomo, the Corso, Isola Bella."

"Yes, I know of these places; they attract many tourists. Where did you stay? Which hotel?"

"I didn't stay in a hotel, I stayed in a bed and breakfast; though I don't suppose Casa Cuseni is everyone's idea of a B&B."

Angelica frowns in thought for a moment. Then, her face lights up. "Ah yes, I have heard of this place. It is a national monument, a museum; it has much history. It was built by an Englishman, no?"

"A man called Kitson, in 1905. He left it to his niece after the war and she ran it as a meeting place for artists until she died in 2005."

"What is it like? It is very special, no?"

"It is, very special, very peaceful and the gardens are incredibly beautiful; citrus trees, olive and almond, bougainvillea, cineraria, stocks, white poppies. The gardens were designed by the futurists, Balla and Depero: I don't think I've ever seen such a profusion of colour or encountered such a perfume of flowers," she says, dreamily.

"Famous artists and writers," Angelica adds. "Yes, I remember now. Didn't Picasso, Hemingway and the philosopher Russell stay there? I think Greta Garbo, too."

"It's true, she did and for quite a long time. But the beauty of Casa Cuseni comes from within, not from the people who've stayed there. It comes more from the fresco on the walls of the locked room."

"The fresco? Of a locked room?"

"Mm, the painting tells the story of how Kitson and his partner, Carlo, rescued an orphaned infant from the ruins of Messina after the great earthquake. They took the baby back to Casa Cuseni and brought him up there. Imagine it, a same sex

457

couple adopting a baby in 1908. It's no wonder the room was kept under lock and key for a hundred years."

"You are right, Caterina; it is unimaginable. Think of the danger to both men and the baby if anyone had found out. To be homosexual in Taormina was not unknown: after all, the Greeks founded Giardini Naxos, so for a man to love another man was not perhaps so… so surprising. But for two men to bring up a child?"

"Yes, it's a remarkable story and it spoke to me in all sorts of ways."

Angelica watches her put the tray of arancini in the fridge. "So why did you come here from Taormina? Why here? Why to Ganzirri?"

"Why? Oh, I just remembered the name. I don't know why but it sounded familiar; like I'd heard it before, even if I couldn't recall exactly when or where."

CHAPTER 6

"Angelica tells me you are the captain of a fishing boat," Catherine says, to burst the ballooning silence.

Alberto had come home from the port around seven–thirty, changed into white chinos and a striped shirt, and sat down at the kitchen table to read la Gazzetta del Sud in peace. Antonio had appeared an hour later and half an hour late: his jeans torn and his dark blue short–sleeved shirt marked and sweat–stained. He had apologised: they had finished late, there had been not enough time for him to go by his house to change and if he had, he would have been even later.

"No, not the captain," Antonio replies, shaking his dark curls and helping himself to a generous serving of salad. "I am the funcitta; the capobarca is the captain. The capobarca drives the boat and the funcitta is the man who spears the fish."

"I see," she says.

"No, in all probability you don't," Angelica corrects her, clearly irked by her brother's economy of explanation. "Have you seen a feluca? Do you know what a feluca looks like?"

When she had come downstairs, Catherine had found Angelica in the kitchen, the table already laid. The woman had looked her up and down, before smiling broadly, sweetly, and nodding her approval of the plain blue pleated dress.

459

"I'm not sure, I think I may have seen one at a distance, across the Strait, before… Are they unusual–looking boats with a long gangplank at the front and a tall mast in the middle?"

"Yes," Antonio replies, and he looks very fleetingly at his sister, a glance Catherine interprets as a criticism of her own ignorance.

Angelica glares at him.

He flinches, drops his shoulder to rub his leg and frowns back in question. "I mean, yes, they are most unusual. There are only fourteen feluche in existence: nine on our side of the Strait and five on the Calabrian side." Antonio falls quiet.

Angelica leans her head across the table towards him and widens her eyes, bidding him to continue.

"Yes, of course." He clears his throat: an affectation which, Catherine decides, is precipitated more by his discomfort at having to engage a strange woman in conversation rather than from any choking shred of celery.

Angelica had introduced Catherine as Caterina, informing both Antonio and Alberto that as she spoke Sicilian, particularly the Messinese dialect, and even though she was christened Catherine, they had decided between them that Caterina sounded somehow less formal and therefore that was the name they should use when addressing her. Both men had smiled, much as if they were shy schoolboys, and again as though they were schoolboys, had proceeded to compete for her attention when time came to allocate seats at the table.

Caterina now sits beside Angelica, with Antonio opposite her: Angelica had decided.

"The feluca is a special fishing boat," Antonio continues, "designed specifically for the fishing of swordfish. She has a long passarelle, which extends from her prow and which provides the funcitta with the facility of hovering over the fish without the presence of the boat frightening the fish away. The tall mast, which we call 'ntinna, provides the capobarca, the captain, with the facility of observing the fish and directing the feluca to the fish from his elevated position." Antonio glances at Caterina and his hosts as if he is expecting and waiting for applause.

"That is most impressive, Antonio, did you write that yourself or did Enzo help you?" Angelica's sarcasm is a reprisal for his being late.

He shrugs in appeal, "It is not easy to describe a feluca to a person who hasn't seen one."

"No, I can imagine it isn't," Caterina says, leaping to his defence.

Alberto looks up at his wife in surprise; his attention at last engaged. "You should go and see a feluca," he says, finishing an arancino and wiping his mouth with his serviette. "They live inside the breakwater, down on the beach not two hundred meters from here. It is an impressive sight, six of them in a row, though at this time of year you will have to be up very early to catch them before they go hunting."

"Hunting?" Caterina asks.

Antonio sighs, though not in any exasperated or impatient manner; more his sigh is that of the man who has eaten well and is now more positively disposed to conversation.

"Yes, Caterina, hunting; for although we are humble fishermen, we hunt the fish. We do not simply cast a net or drop a baited hook in the water." He pauses waiting for his rationale to rest with her for a few seconds. "You see, the fish are cunning, the ocean is wide and deep, and the weather is either our best friend or our worst enemy." He scoffs, gently. "Ha, sometimes the wind can try to kill you and then rescue you in the same breath; this I have seen many times. But what is important to understand is that though some people are happy to call us fishermen purely and simply because we catch fish, I believe we have more in common with the hunters who stalk wild beasts in the jungle."

Alberto clasps his hands behind his head, leans back and turns his attention to the ceiling, whispering, "The old man and the sea? Dio, please, not again."

Antonio's face blackens, though before he can speak his sister intervenes.

"Now you know very well, Alberto, that the funcitta may only have one chance in a day, perhaps even in two or three days, to strike the fish. If he misses with his lance, his crew have no wages: if he hits his target, the crew go home happy. That is far more responsibility for a man to bear than for one who punches tickets on the ferry."

Alberto bristles. Antonio regains his composure.

"Is it just swordfish that you catch, or do you catch tuna, too?" Caterina asks by way of distraction.

Antonio smiles. "We are only permitted to catch swordfish. For tuna, we have no licence and there has been too much fishing of tuna in the Mediterranean, that is enough reason in itself."

Alberto scoffs, unkindly, disrespectfully and Antonio's face darkens once more.

"Oh, I apologise." Caterina says. "This is my fault, I seem to be pressing the wrong buttons, don't I?"

"No, you are not," Angelica says, "And it is not your fault. The men like to argue and when they do, they forget they are in the presence of a cook who has laboured hard to provide them with delicious arancini. They should be grateful... and more respectful."

Told off, both men sit up straighter and assume the deportment of children who have suddenly remembered their manners.

"You made the arancini?" Antonio volunteers, pleasantly surprised.

"Well, I..."

"Yes, Caterina made them," Angelica says. "Not bad for a first attempt, eh?"

"Better than not bad; they were everything a good arancino should be." Antonio hunches his shoulders and splays his hands. "If I had not known, I would have thought they were from Famulari's."

Alberto bridles. "He means the restaurant on the Via Cesare Battisti. Though personally, I believe your arancini are better: they are home–made and made with love." He beams.

Love. Made with love. It was what Angelica had said.

However, instead of the rash of compliments sparking another round of verbal jousting between the two men, they sit and smile at Caterina, and her heart melts, just like the cubes of mozzarella she has so carefully placed in the top of the rice cones.

"So," Antonio begins, his eyes twinkling with humour, "not only do you cook like a Messinese, you can talk like one, too. How is that so? Where did you learn?"

She colours. "I, er… Well, I studied languages at school and at university."

"University, eh?" he says. "An intelligent woman: it is a rare privilege to meet someone so… well, a rarity for one like me." There is a bitterness to his tone, but it is not aimed at her gender; rather, Antonio has reversed the insult to suggest he has not met many, if any, intelligent women and for that, he is to blame. "I do not include my sister in that sad exclusivity," he adds, bowing his head towards Angelica.

"I should hope not, Antonio."

"But, Caterina, it is unusual to hear a person who was not born here speak Sicilian. So, where did you learn? Who taught you?"

"I learnt Sicilian from my grandmother, my nonna; for though she lived most of her life in England, she was born here, in Messina, in the Borgo del Ringo."

"In the Borgo del Ringo?" Antonio sits back and studies her very openly and perhaps a little rudely. "You are sure?"

"Yes," Caterina replies, a little offended. "Why would I say she was born there if she had not told me? And why would she tell me she was if she wasn't."

"No," he says swiftly, his hands outstretched as if praying to her. "Forgive me, I did not mean to doubt your nonna; it is just unusual that any person should talk of the quarter of Messina that was once the province of fishermen. I apologise." Antonio looks from Angelica to Alberto and then back to Caterina. "How old was your nonna? When was she born? If, that is," he holds out his hands to her in appeal, "you don't mind talking about her."

"Why would I mind? I think Nonna Lilla would like to hear her name spoken so close to where her life began and was so very nearly ended."

"Lilla," Angelica repeats. "You say your nonna's name was Lilla?"

"Yes, that's right, why?"

"Oh, nothing, I just wanted to make sure I heard you right. I . . . I will make coffee," she adds, with all the controlled excitement of one who decides she must have an ice cream before the theatre curtain is raised. "Please, go on."

Caterina is curious as to why the mention of her grandmother's name has stirred such interest. "As I told Angelica, my nonna died when I was eleven and even though I don't recall that much about her, I do remember that when I went to stay with her, she used to tell me wonderful tales at bedtime. One in particular she used to tell me so often I never forgot it."

"Then, share it with us, please?" Antonio asks.

"Oh, it's only a child's fairy tale and I'm sure she made it up. I think we're a bit old for fairy tales, don't you?"

"Old?" he replies. "No, one is never too old for a good story. And besides, we Sicilians love fairy tales. Tell us, please. Take your time: try to tell the story just as your nonna would have told you."

She studies him for a moment, wondering if he isn't pulling her leg and then, because he looks at her so earnestly, so charmingly and so warmly, Caterina takes a deep breath. "All right," she says, "but if afterwards you laugh, I'll never live it down."

"We won't laugh. We promise. And if you tell stories half as well as you cook, then we won't be disappointed, we will be doubly grateful."

"Okay. Here we go. Naturally, the tale is about a beautiful young girl, the daughter of a fisherman, who falls in love with a handsome young prince. The king and queen do not approve of their love affair because the girl is from a poor family and her father cannot afford a dowry. So, the two young lovers hatch a plan to run away together: to sail from the island and live happily ever after in a land far away from the influence of his parents."

She stops for a moment and is confused as to why she should command their attention with nothing more than an old fairy tale.

Angelica serves the coffee. "Go on, please, Caterina, your nonna's story is fascinating." She glances at her brother, who acknowledges her look with the slight lift of his little finger.

"Are you sure?"

"Yes, yes, Caterina," Antonio says, "please continue. We are listening."

She looks at Alberto, and even he is rapt.

"Okay then. The way Nonna told it, the king's castle sits on the side of a mountain, inside of which there sleeps a great dragon. The king, desperate to thwart the two young lover's plans, locks the prince in a tall tower, and then climbs the mountain and asks the dragon if he will kidnap the girl, promising him halls of gold and silver in return. The dragon refuses, saying that though he is stronger than any ten, hundred or even a thousand men, it is not within his power to keep the two young lovers apart.

465

"In a fit of anger and frustration, the king drives his sword through the rocks of the mountain deep into the dragon's flesh. And the dragon, thus wounded, roars and howls; flames come from the wound in his side and he rolls over and over until the pain ceases. In his turmoil, in his irritation at being disturbed from his sleeping and because of the insult and injury the king has afforded him, the dragon breaks out of the mountain, breathes his fiery breath and shakes the castle until it falls down, killing both the king and queen and nearly all their subjects. By the time the dragon has finished, there is only one part of the castle left standing, the tall tower in which the king had locked the prince. And because the fisherman's family live beyond the castle walls, the young girl, too, is alive. She finds a ladder and together with some sailors who have come to help the survivors rebuild the castle, she frees her prince and they sail away to live..."

"Happily ever after," Angelica, finishes.

"Yes, of course." Caterina glances at her and for a split second she perceives tears welling at the corners of Angelica's eyes.

"Bravo!" Alberto calls, clapping enthusiastically. "Bravo. A good story. Like a fairy tale from Giuseppe Pitrè. You could not have told it better."

"Yes," Antonio agrees, smiling – no, beaming – at her. "Very well told, Caterina. Bravo!"

CHAPTER 7

Caterina had been woken by Alberto in the bathroom, and she'd lain in bed until a tide of restlessness had swept her outside and settled her beside by the lagoon. The stone bench is cool, pleasantly so, and she smiles to herself as her thoughts turn to the previous evening.

Before dinner, she had grasped the nettle and phoned Lucy.

"What about all my emails?" she'd groaned. "Didn't you read any of them?"

Caterina had offered a lame excuse about not being able to charge her laptop, as the socket on the wall of her room didn't take her plug and she'd mislaid the adaptor.

"And what about the texts I sent?"

"Couldn't charge my phone either, sorry. Never mind me, darling, how's everything with you?"

And the trick had worked, for there was nothing Lucy liked more than to talk about Lucy. Information had come thick and fast: people she'd met, facts she'd learned, a summer cold, prospects, obstacles, frustrations, her long–term partner, Rob, his annoying habits, his inability to...

"Oh, I'm sorry," Caterina had cut in, surprised to hear her daughter complain so. "Before I left, you both seemed happy. And you've been together quite a while now, I thought perhaps he might—"

"Well don't, mum. It's not going to happen."

When she'd finished the call, Caterina had stared at her phone and muttered, "So, that was what all the fuss was about. It wasn't about me; it was about you. You needed me. Well, fancy that!"

After dinner, the curtain of her evening had drawn to a gentle and unusually late close. Unusually late because Alberto had waxed long and lyrically about the art of the cuntisti, the troubadours, who in days of yore occupied street corners to earn their keep telling stories. Giuseppe Pitrè, he'd explained, was the father of Sicilian folklore, a senator and recorder of local customs, and her tale had reminded him of Pitrè's work. And Alberto, with the bit firmly between his teeth, had then gone on to introduce her to the long traditions of Sicilian puppeteering, to the knights of Charlemagne and his twelve Paladins, to Orlando, the hero, to Oliver, his rival, and to Ganelon, the traitor.

In fact, Alberto had proved a considerable surprise to her; for at first, she had thought him boorish to the point of being wholly uncommunicative, if not plain rude, when all along there lay concealed within his bald, round head a worldly refinement and, for a man who was no spring chicken, a good measure of youthful exuberance.

As far as Antonio was concerned, she'd found him peculiarly and unexpectedly urbane; peculiar in as much as the stains on his shirt and the scars on his large hands suggested he might lack sophistication which, judging by his knowledge of the history of Messina, he didn't. His shoulders seemed to her to be ridiculously broad and his head very square; or perhaps his head was made to look so by the way his wavy hair fell to frame his face. And although his face, thick neck and forearms were near mahogany in colour, when he reached across the table or stretched his arms up in one of his many theatrical gesticulations, Caterina could see that the skin beneath his sleeves was really quite pale. His eyes, though, were far from pale: they were blue, blue and a strangely vivid yet deep blue at that, and on the odd occasion he'd fixed his gaze upon her, Caterina had found the intensity of their colour more than a little unsettling.

The mirrored surface of the lagoon reflects fine wisps of high white cloud. To her left, traffic motors steadily, most of it heading south to the gradually waking city, and to her right, the sun has now crested Aspromonte, casting long, thin shadows from the lampposts of the promenade.

She leaves the bench and walks around the lagoon to the bakers, where she stops to buy almond biscuits, a brioche and a bottle of water, and then on into the warren of narrow lanes and alleyways that will, she hopes, lead her to the shore of the Strait. On a curved white–washed wall, a black witch, stovepipe hat, voluminous dress and stick legs, trails a thin line of black spray–paint from her can; on the line, a cat stalks a small bird and further on as the line disappears around the bend, a second cat stalks a second bird.

"Graffiti: from graffiare, to scribble," she says, standing back to admire the simplicity. "Can't really call that a scribble, now can we? It's just too affascinante; too enchanting,"

Caterina emerges from the stone maze onto the shorefront, where a terrace of low houses overlooks a shingle beach littered with all manner and colour of small wooden boats. She lingers, relaxed and yet pleasantly stimulated by the delicate air, gazing out across the waters of the Strait and the mountains beyond.

A row of large and irregular square blocks, tumbled like giant's dice, form a breakwater, in the quiet calm of which a feluca is moored. The tall metal tower of the blue fishing boat pierces the horizon, impaling the sky, and a man climbs up, hand over hand, steadily and carefully, until he reaches the crow's nest. Below him, the crew are making ready, untying and coiling lines.

Caterina steps onto the shingle beach and strolls down to the water's edge. She shades her eyes to the sun and watches.

The long passerelle bounces in rhythm as a man walks along it, pausing now and again to examine the lines.

Antonio: she would recognise those broad shoulders and that black wavy hair anywhere.

He turns, walks back and talks to a younger man: Enzo, his son, probably.

A second man begins the long climb up to the high platform and once through the trapdoor, he leans over and calls to one of the men on the deck, who ties a white plastic bag to a line and between them they run it up.

Engines rumble, oily smoke spews momentarily from the stern and the feluca is under way, nosing its long passerelle around the breakwater and out into the Strait.

Caterina lifts her arm up, but quickly lets it fall slack against her hip. "Stupid girl," she mutters, colouring with embarrassment. "What are you, the sailor's wife waving farewell?"

However, as she chides herself, it is as though Antonio has heard her and he turns to face the shore. That he has seen her, there is no doubt, for his body stiffens and straightens, and he steps his foot onto the raised lip at the outer edge of the deck, and holds onto a stay for support. He leans forward, watching her.

Again, Caterina lifts her arm and again she lets it drop.

Whatever the reservation that prevents her from completing her gesture, Antonio suffers no such restriction and he raises his hand, acknowledging her presence with a single, casual, lazy wave.

Behind him, one of the crew wolf-whistles and another barks. The lookout, up on the platform has also spotted her: he grins and digs the capobarca in the ribs. The capobarca, though, is not to be distracted: the slightest lapse in his concentration will see the passerelle crashing and crumbling into the breakwater; a day's fishing ended before it has begun.

Antonio ignores them. He simply smiles, waves once more and turns away as the feluca glides, popping and burbling out into the open water.

Caterina stays rooted to the pebbles and watches until the blue fishing boat has passed beyond the red and white pylon on the far slopes of Aspromonte.

"No matter how many times I see a feluca, they still amaze me." An old and shrunken fellow stands, or rather slouches, beside her. In her moment of... what, concentration, deliberation, distraction, she has not noticed him approach.

"They are like the huge metal aeroplanes that, for a reason I cannot comprehend, defy the laws of gravity." Like her, he shades his eyes and stares up towards the neck of the straight. His accent is thick, his every word running seamlessly into the next in a form of constant and continuous sing–song.

"Yes," she replies, "they look as though they're about to topple over or plunge down headfirst into the sea." She turns and looks down at him. "I am Caterina, pleased to meet you."

"Thank you, I am Beppe, though some still bother to call me by my full name, Giuseppe." His forehead is rippled rather than furrowed, his smile lines plentiful and deep, and his teeth few. Beppe smokes a roll–up cigarette so short it threatens to burn his fingers, which are long and slim, like those of the witch painted on the wall. "You know the feluca Salvazione? You know Antonio?"

She considers his question, realising she has met Angelica's brother just the once, across a kitchen table and only for... what, an hour or two. "No."

"You were waving to him," Beppe says, without turning his eyes to her. "People don't wave to boats unless they know the people on board. Either that or they don't expect to see them again for a long time: which is it?"

Caterina, unsure how to respond, stands back and studies him.

Beppe is short and bent and wizened, his chest a mat of thick white hairs and his shorts paint—splattered.

"I met Antonio last night, at dinner, at his sister Angelica's house," she says.

"Ah, okay, so you know him a little. He is the funcitta of what was once my boat. Now, it is his. He is a good funcitta; the best, he never misses."

"Superman, eh?" she giggles, before putting her hand to her mouth in apology.

"No," Beppe says, for the first time looking up at her, "Antonio is better." He grins, or at least he looks as though he is trying to.

A cruise ship, top—heavy with decks, turns in from the north. Beppe lifts his head and nods. "She is late."

"Is that what you do these days, Beppe; sit here and watch the ships go by?"

"No," he grins, "I used to. I used to sit here, watch the boys go out and wait until they came back. Then, one day I woke up and decided I was wishing my time away just when my time was wasting away. Now, I paint."

———————

Later, with the sun at its height, Beppe walks with her over to the lagoon and when they pass the wall with the witch, Caterina pauses and smiles. Hocus—pocus or quaint and therefore enchanting, she cannot make up her mind.

"Why should one make choices when one doesn't have to?" Beppe says, reading her thoughts.

He shows her the two old wooden feluche lying up on blocks beside the lagoon.

"This one we call a fulua."

A dozen or so metres in length and wide as a carthorse is long, a rope ladder runs up the wooden boat's tall mast. The hull is painted white with a green and red stripe below the gunwale, and an image of San Nicolo di Bari, Ganzirri's patron saint, at its bow. So solid and sturdy is the boat that Caterina imagines it must have taken a team of galley–slaves to row it.

The green hull of the second is shorter in length and sleeker, its mast shorter, too, and with room for only four oarsmen, a look–out and a funcitta. "This is what was called a luntro," he says, pointing at the smaller boat. "For thousands of years, this was how they used to hunt for swordfish. It was dangerous, eh? There are many tales of enormous swordfish towing boats away from the land only to drag them below the surface and leave the crew to drown. In those days, there was not the sound of engines to scare away the fish and the hull of the luntro was painted a dark colour so that the fish would not see the reflection in the water. In those days, men used to be afraid of sea monsters and whirlpools. Now," he shrugs, "we know Charybdis is nothing more than a pandemonium of tides, strong tides maybe, and Scylla nothing more than a product of Homero's fertile imagination. Think of it: think of how it must have felt way back before we educated ourselves in the ways of the sea."

"Educated," Caterina repeats, absent–mindedly, "in the ways of the sea. Yes, Beppe, you're so right. People think education is all about getting ahead in life: they forget that fishermen have to learn their craft."

"Yes, young lady, what do people remember once they are assured their food is available in the supermarket? Look," again he points, though this time at a small rowing–skiff out in the middle of the lagoon.

A man, a man of late years judging by his white hair and unhurried movement, stands waist–deep beside a boat in which a young boy sits. A triangular net is fastened to the serrated end of a rake, with which the old man is dragging clams from the bed of the lagoon. When he empties the net into a bucket, he sets down the rake and sorts through his catch, showing the young boy those that are too small to keep and saving those large enough to eat.

"This is the way the world has always been: we educate our young in the ways of the sea and our traditions. This area used to be the very home of boat building in Sicily: great boatyards, like those of Giuseppe Domenico Galbo, Giacomo Costa, 'Ntoni Mancuso and many others. In the next–door village of Pace, Peppe Federico and his son built beautiful boats and in Paradiso, in the yard of the Tringali family, they built the feluche. All along the coast, skills passed from father to son," he nods towards the skiff, "and from grandfather to grandson."

"Like Antonio to Enzo?"

"Yes, exactly like Antonio and Enzo. These are traditions we must fight to preserve." Beppe draws on his cigarette and peers at her, watching and waiting for her reaction to what he is about to say: "Remember, young lady, it was Jesus who called his disciples to become fishers of men; so, from Our Saviour we learn that to become a fisherman is to gain a nobility few can hope to acquire."

Caterina meets his stare. "Yes, Beppe, I am Catholic... or was. Even though I couldn't tell you when I last went to confession."

He draws again, winks through his fog of smoke and smiles. "You should try it, my dear. It helps one balance the soul." He studies the end of his cigarette, then looks up and studies her face. "Now, the morning is rushing by and I have painting to finish. Go and put your time to good use. Have you seen Guttuso's painting of Colapesce on the ceiling in the Teatro Vittorio Emanuele in Messina?" He pauses, waiting, then says, "I went to the city once, not so long ago; my nephew took me; he insisted. I tell you I have never seen anything to compare with Guttuso's work; not even the most beautiful sunrise."

"Thank you for leaving me your note," Angelica says, as she pours a glass of the Prosecco Caterina has brought home with her.

"That's all right. I didn't want you to worry. Thought you might be angry if I hadn't checked in."

"No. Perhaps concerned if you had not come back from wherever you were, but... So, where in Messina did you go?"

Caterina sighs. "Everywhere: the Teatro, Neptune's fountain, the Duomo, the Via dei Templari—"

"Did you see Guttuso's Colapesce on the ceiling of the theatre?"

"Yes," Caterina sighs again, "the theatre was closed for a dance rehearsal, but I persuaded a very kind man, the manager I think he must have been, to let me in and I sat in the stalls, leant my head back and lost myself in the painting. It's bold, isn't it? All those lithe bodies, the bare–breasted mermaids, the dolphins. And then there is the improbably perfect form of the naked young Colapesce diving into the waters of the Strait. I thought it quite sensuous in a way, quite surreal and very hypnotic."

"So it is," Angelica agrees. "And did you notice anything interesting about the colour of the water?"

Caterina grins, an eager, impish curl to her lips. "Yes, I think so; if what you're asking is what I think you're asking."

"That may be for you to know. Like the painting, art is a matter of personal appreciation. And the Via dei Templari? I don't know this street; where is it?"

"Well, the answer to that is I didn't know either. I was looking for it and stopped for a granita in a café, the Ritrovo Bellini, the café on the corner of Piazza Duomo: there was this old man sitting at a table; he was dozing, leaning against his walking stick and looked about to fall over until the kind lady of the house woke him up. I asked him if he knew the street and he mumbled something about the new Via Templari being up the steps, the Scalinata San Gregorio, whereas the old Via dei Templari used to be a street off the Via Oratorio San Francesco. He told me that after the great earthquake and then the war, they redesigned the city so that nearly all the roads were wider, which meant that some streets were moved and others simply disappeared."

"How did you know of it?"

"It was a street my nonna told me about: Via dei Templari. She said if I was ever in Messina, I was to visit it for her: there, Piazza Cairoli and Villa Mazzini. She never told me why though. I guess I'll never know now, will I?"

CHAPTER 8

As with the day before, Caterina wakes to a light frame of mind rather than one weighed down by the density of negative thought, and she knows it is early because Alberto has not yet occupied the bathroom.

The woman behind the counter of the bakery smiles when she asks for biscuits, brioche and water, and wandering through the lanes the village still sleeps but for the cats who flatten their ears, growl and eye each other warily from the bastions of their home steps.

She breathes deeply through her nose, filling her ribcage with the fresh morning air before exhaling smoothly and evenly through her mouth. Salt, the sea is not far.

"Good morning witch," she says, rounding the bend and smiling at the thought that she is talking to a wall.

Beppe stands at the waterline, deep in conversation with Antonio and the young man she believes to be Enzo.

Caterina hesitates.

A wolf–whistle from the feluca makes her look up: one of the crew is pointing at her.

Antonio, Enzo and Beppe turn, and while Antonio and Enzo stand their ground, the old man strolls up the beach towards her.

"Good morning signorina." He wears no protection against the cool air other than the thick matting of white hairs on his chest and his paint–spattered shorts; his legs are spindly thin, his knees knobbly and if he was any more stoop–shouldered and bow–legged he would pass for a junior spinning top.

"Good morning, Beppe."

"Did you see Guttuso's painting?"

"Yes, I did, thank you. More beautiful than one could have imagined."

He scratches at his ear. "The mermaids? Yes, very beautiful, though even with all my many years on the water I have never seen so much as a lock of hair. Oh well, one day, who knows?"

"And the colour of the water," Caterina adds. "How did Guttuso find such blue, eh?"

Beppe smiles, a conspirator's smirk, saying everything, saying nothing. He draws out the moment, then, "My friend, Antonio, there, he would like to invite you to pass the day on his feluca."

"He would like to, would he?" she replies. "Well, what has happened to his tongue? Have the cats stolen it?"

Beppe frowns. "No, it is pure self–interest on my part: I wanted to have the privilege of asking you, that is all." He grins, his teeth gapped, smoke–stained and worn. "Why should he have all the fun, eh?"

"Fun. Is that how you describe a day out fishing?"

"For you, yes. For them, no, it is work; it is how they make their living." He eyes her, a disconcerting appraisal. "It is no small honour to be invited. It will be an experience, a great experience; something I am sure you have never experienced before and may never have the opportunity to experience again." He shrugs his rounded shoulders, as if to suggest it would be foolish of her to pass up the chance.

"Oh, Beppe." Caterina frowns and shakes her head, though not in outright refusal; rather she shakes her head like a gambler shakes his dice, in the hope that when the dice come to rest, they will dictate what happens next. "Me? On a boat? Just me and what... six men. I can't imagine I... I mean not in my wildest dreams would I...

He cocks his head to one side and raises an eyebrow. "Then why?"

"Why what?"

"Why did you come down here so early this fine morning?"

"Oh, Beppe," she says again. "I don't know. I came down here because Antonio said I should see the feluche."

"You saw them yesterday, no?" He grins.

"Yes, but—"

"Come signorina, they are waiting."

She sighs, dithering and yet perhaps considering. "Look, Beppe, I'm not exactly dressed for fishing. I mean, I haven't even got shoes on."

He looks down. "Ah, la contessa scalza! Bogart, Ava Gardner."

"The barefoot countess?"

"Before your time, I believe." He grins again. "And Spain not Sicily, but who cares?"

Caterina shades her eyes to the dawn sun and studies first Antonio, then the feluca: the crew know, they are watching her, waiting to see her reaction.

Beppe sniffs the air and glances upward. "The skies will be clear today and the deck will be hot to touch, but... Antonio is not the kind to offer twice and I have always believed it is better to catch fish when you can, not when you have to."

"Is that Enzo... with Antonio?"

"Yes," he replies. "The son."

———————

Caterina sits in the stern and Antonio in the bow, as Enzo stands and rows them out to the feluca. The crew are waiting to welcome her. Welcome her, inspect her or appraise her: perhaps all three? And is a woman welcome on a boat crewed exclusively by men? A boat which looks not to possess the smallest of creature comforts.

"Enzo, I…"

"Do not worry, signorina: they might look as if they would eat you, but I can assure you they are all married. Except me, of course, I am single." His eyes light up with possibility: they are blue, like his father's, like the deep blue of the sea in Guttuso's painting on the ceiling of the Teatro.

Their arrival at the feluca triggers a melee of activity and as soon as their bow knocks against the blue hull, Antonio leaps up and keen hands reach down to lift Caterina, seemingly light as a feather, up onto the deck.

"I am Pasquale," a thick set fellow says. "Excuse me." He turns away and climbs up onto the roof of the cabin.

"Giuseppe," another, taller individual says.

And Enzo, because he has rowed her out to the feluca, believes he has the right to introduce the remaining two: "Ninolino," a darker–skinned, young man, "and Karl," a humour–filled, quirky face, a cigarette between his lips.

"Ninolino, Karl, pleased to meet you both."

"We are also pleased to meet you, too," they reply in perfect union.

"Thank you. And let's hope you are not just as pleased to see me leave at the end of the day."

Antonio, to whom she has not yet spoken and who, to her surprise, has not yet spoken to her, sits on the step up to the passerelle, poring over a three–pointed spear that looks remarkably similar to the trident from Montorsoli's giant marble statue of Neptune in Messina.

She turns and watches as the less than trim figure of Pasquale crosses himself and ascends the slender mast to his platform, twenty meters above. Once there, he unlatches a hatch, climbs up through it and as soon as he has disappeared, Giuseppe starts the climb up after him.

The engines rumble, the deck vibrates, lines are cast off and Enzo, who has clearly been assigned to watch over her and keep her out of the way, reaches up, pulls a white plastic chair from the roof of the cabin and wiping it with an oily–looking rag, plants it at the base of the mast.

Caterina sits down, the young man smiles and the feluca Salvazione noses her way out from behind the breakwater into the open waters of the Strait.

The air smells and tastes clean, perhaps just the faintest of salt, yet not as overwhelming as she had thought it might. Caterina studies the shore of Calabria as though it is a darkly foreign land, not simply a region of the same country little more than a kilometre or so away. Dappled sunlight caresses the terracotta roofs of Villa San Giovanni and behind the town, cotton wool clouds cast their shadows on the green carpet of mountainside.

Antonio busies himself and in doing so avoids her enquiring looks.

Caterina, irritated by his indifference, tries to provoke his attention by offering Enzo, Ninolino and Karl her biscuits, which they snap up. Antonio doesn't though rise to her bait, so she moves her chair into the sun, leans back and allows the breeze to ruffle her hair.

For the next hour and a half, they motor north through the neck of the Strait, past the great rock of Scylla and on through an even swell towards Capo Vaticano, a dull stain on an otherwise clean horizon.

Antonio remains seated on the step up to the passerelle, two buckets, one by either foot, a length of blue cloth across his lap and a square metal casing in his hands. He examines it this way and that, before taking a screwdriver, unscrewing the casing and dropping the various pieces into a bucket by his foot. He crouches by the winch—cover, hammers the sides of the casing flat against it and then picks out a pair of broad—bladed clippers with which he cuts the metal into small strips. Every now and then, he pauses in his cutting and hammering to reshape and examine the thickness of the strip, measuring and weighing each in his hand.

Enzo watches him studiously, glancing at Caterina to satisfy himself that she is doing the same.

When he is happy with the weight and size of his strips, Antonio selects a pointed angle iron and, with the hammer, punches holes in the top and bottom of the strips. He picks a couple of screws from the bucket, checks their length and nips the ends off using a smaller pair of pliers.

Caterina watches his hands: for although they are broad and thick, Antonio is dexterous and exacting. He chews his lips in concentration and does not allow the odd buffet of another ship's wake to distract him or knock him off balance.

From a second bucket, he picks out a small green wooden fish about as long as his forearm and half as thick. He weighs the fish in one hand while weighing a strip of lead in his other, and when he is content, he nods, takes the hammer and while Enzo holds the shortened nail in place using a pair of pliers, Antonio hammers the strip into the belly of the fish.

He speaks briefly to his son, who then removes a large coil of rope from a fourth bucket, ties its hooped handle to a line and slings it forward over the side to let it fill with water. As the boat moves, so the bucket draws level with Enzo and he hauls it up and places it beside his father.

Antonio nods his approval and tosses the wooden fish into the bucket: they both bend to watch it.

Caterina's curiosity gets the better of her and she, too, stands to look.

The fish bobs about, but touches the rim, so Antonio squeezes the sides of the bucket between his ample thighs and, by making the surface of the water broader, the fish floats freely.

"Good," he says, putting down the bucket, removing the first fish and repeating the whole process with a second.

Leaving his father to carry on, Enzo gets on with coiling and recoiling line, first dipping each arm's length of line in another water–filled bucket. When he sees Caterina watching, he says. "It makes the line easier to coil and makes it quicker and smoother to uncoil. Drink water, signorina, please, eh? Because of the breeze, one does not feel the sun."

She does so and, noticing her bottle is nearly empty, wonders what she is supposed to do if she needs the toilet. "It's easy for you guys," she mutters.

The engines slow: they have reached the boundary of their patrol.

Antonio looks up at the crow's nest, then out at the water: the even swell has waned, the sea is now flat and almost oily in appearance. To the east, large container ships loiter outside the port behind which storm clouds gather like angry conspirators.

The feluca runs a box course, extending its easterly and southerly legs by a hundred metres or so each time it turns to cover fresh water. The morning is long, the sun hot, burningly so, and shade at a premium.

Caterina stands and stretches her arms and legs. "Whoa!" she shrieks and hurriedly sits back down. "The deck, it's hot."

"Yes," Enzo agrees, "that's why we wear trainers." He quickly dips a bucket over the side, rinses her feet with the water and splashes the deck with the rest.

Antonio is watching her from the corner of his eye.

She smiles.

He looks away.

Enzo notices, grins and returns his attention to the sea.

"Would you like to sit inside in the cabin?"

Caterina looks up. "Thank you, Enzo, I'm fine. Really. Whenever we change course, I get some shade." She would happily sit in the deafening noise and the torrid heat of the cabin if it permitted her a moment's respite from the baking sun; however, there is absolutely no way she is going to give any of them the slightest inkling that she is finding the day at all challenging.

"You men must have the patience of Job," she says.

"It is true."

An hour or so earlier, Caterina had been staring out at the blur of the horizon, trying to determine where the sea ended and the sky began; and she had just decided it was impossible when, all of a sudden, she noticed a disturbance in the water some way to the rear on the landward side.

She'd blinked a few times, wiped the sweat from her eyes and looked again.

There. Again. Something rising out and splashing into the water.

"A fish!" she'd screamed, leaping up, pointing, an enormous wave of emotion flooding her body. She was to earn her stripes; she was, after months if not years of feeling completely useless, very suddenly of use.

Antonio had stood up from his perch on the step, followed the direction of her arm and hollered loud up to Pasquale, who'd instantly gunned the engines and heaved the helm over to starboard.

Enzo, Ninolino and Karl had begun to check the lines and holding on to the wire guides, Antonio had started his urgent walk up the long passerelle.

The wooden deck had vibrated as if the whole feluca was beside itself with excitement and as the propeller thrust her through the water, her bow had risen up, lifting Antonio like a trapeze artist high, high up in the air.

Then, as swiftly as the thrill of the hunt had infected the crew... it evaporated.

Pasquale had throttled back the engines, the feluca had bucked, the bow had dipped and the far end of the passerelle had dropped straight down into the sea, submerging Antonio up to his waist.

For a moment, all he had been able to do was hold on to the rail around him. But when the bow had risen again, he'd turned and delivered Pasquale such a mouthful that even the three men standing next to Caterina had turned away in shame.

"Enzo? Why have we stopped?" she'd asked.

"Look," he'd replied, just as a dolphin had leapt from the surface, twirled like a ballet dancer and slapped back down.

"Oh no, I'm so sorry. I thought..."

"Don't be sorry, signorina. If you are with us for long, you will soon learn the difference between dolphins playing and swordfish feeding. Anyway, it is better that my father shouts at Pasquale than he shouts at you." And they all, including Caterina, had gone back to whatever it was they were or weren't doing.

Now, drenched in sun cream, glowing with perspiration and yet out of drinking water, she needs the bathroom.

"Enzo?"

"Yes."

"I... Er, well, I..."

"Yes. Inside, please." He picks up one of the few empty buckets, points into the open door of the cabin and makes a gesture that she thinks means after you.

"Thank you, I think I can manage from here."

She waits until the feluca has turned down one of its longer legs and steps inside. When she comes out, Enzo's back is turned and not wanting him to think her naïve, or notice her embarrassment at having to ask him permission not only to use the crew's only shade for her toilet, but also then to ask him to empty the bucket for her, Caterina launches the contents over the side. The wind, much to her relief, is in her favour.

As she throws, Caterina looks up and sees again, some two hundred metres off the stern, a silver flash and a spray of water, followed by a larger splash.

Hearing her behind him, Enzo turns and takes the bucket from her. He, too, launches what he thinks will be the contents over the side and is baffled when he realises there are none. He then ties the bucket to a line, drops it over the side, hauls it back and empties it. He smiles, a rather cute, marginally coy appreciation that she had already emptied the bucket.

"Enzo?" Caterina raises her hand to point in the direction of where she had just seen the fish rise from the surface but, on looking back, she can see no trace of it. Nothing, just acres of shiny silvered water.

"Yes, signorina?"

"Thank you."

For the rest of the day, Pasquale steers the feluca up and down the peaceful waters of the Golfo di Gioia Tauro. So unbearably hot is it up in the crow's nest that Giuseppe climbs down the narrow tower to take a break. Even with his sweat–stained shirt buttoned to the cuffs, his legionnaire's cap with its long side–flaps shielding his neck and his oversize sunglasses dominating what little Caterina can see of his face, he looks fried to a crisp.

Antonio, having finished weighting his little wooden fishes, brings a litre bottle of water out from the cabin. He twists off the top, holds the plastic bottle up horizontally just above his open mouth and, without spilling a drop or permitting his lips to touch the rim, he pours the water.

Again, his dexterity, his agility, his poise, his composure and his grace, are, to Caterina, remarkable.

He offers her the bottle: she takes it, stands and in trying to emulate him, she manages to gag and pour water all down her front.

Antonio chuckles and takes the bottle.

"How do you do that?" she asks as she coughs.

"Oh, practice." Of all the multi–coloured caps sported by the crew, Antonio's has the longest bill, almost like that of a platypus, and he has taped small flaps of cardboard along each side to shut out the blinding reflection of the sun on the water.

"What are the little wooden fish for?" she asks, indicating the bucket.

"They are lures, although some might call them dead–bait." Antonio walks over, picks one out and hands it to her. The fish is painted in a luminescent green and even the head, eyes and the mouth are carefully defined. "It looks real, eh?"

"Yes," she examines it. "It's so light, too. How do you use them, on a line?"

He moves between Caterina and the sun, casting her into shadow. "No. When we know there is a swordfish close by, I take them to the end of the passerelle and throw them as far forward as I can. Thinking there is a small fish at his mercy, the swordfish race to the surface at which point I harpoon them."

She looks up, grateful that she doesn't have to squint into the sun. "And if that doesn't work, you lose the lures?"

"No. You see that long pole with the net on the end?" He points. "Well, that is one of Ninolino's tasks: as it floats past, he takes the lure from the sea with the net."

"But you've just added weights to them?"

"Because they were too light; I could not throw them far and we were on them too fast. Now I can throw them further forward and they will have more time on the water before Ninolino nets them."

"Ah," Caterina says, "okay, I get it. That's why you needed to be so specific with the weights you added: too much and they would go straight to the bottom, not enough and you wouldn't get any distance on them."

"Exactly."

Lesson over, they stand and look at each other until their silence grows awkward.

"I'm sorry, Antonio," she says, "it seems I may be a bit of a Jonah."

He frowns, "A Jonah?" He scratches his stubbly chin. "This is a person who brings bad luck to a boat, eh?"

"Or to anywhere or anyone. I don't think Jonah's are exclusive to boats."

He chuckles. "No, you're right, I don't believe they are. But you know, Caterina, not everything that goes wrong needs to be someone's fault; not everything is within our control or ours to influence. And if I thought someone was to blame for every day we didn't catch fish, then I would have run out of people to blame long ago."

"You're not superstitious, then?"

He scoffs, though not so dismissively that she might take offence. "Mm, I believe it is better to be a lucky fisherman than a good one. And believe me when I tell you, I have met some terrible fishermen who are often very lucky."

"Enzo is very charming," she says.

"Now," Antonio turns, "it is decision time," and he walks off back to the bow, leaving her in the dazzling sun.

Chapter 9

Her self–confidence revived by Antonio's insistence that she join them for a second day on the Salvazione, Caterina had woken to a sense of belonging. Now though, holding onto a wire stay in each hand and leaning over the side of the feluca, she is reminded of her stupidity that first day at Capo Peloro.

"It looks as though it is alive," she murmurs, gazing down at the swirling, churning eddies.

"Charybdis, the whirlpool, yes," Enzo says. "You have seen La Fontana del Nettuno in Messina?"

"Yes, Neptune, he's quite the God, isn't he? And with all those perfectly defined, larger than life muscles. Some presence."

"It is true. On one side of him sits Scylla and on the other Charybdis, the monsters he keeps in chains. You know, at one time he faced the city and now he faces the Strait."

"Why is that, Enzo?"

"Oh," he chuckles, "because he wanted to poke his buttocks at the Calabrese."

"Seriously?"

"No, not seriously. I don't know the reason: perhaps it is that he used to bless the people of the city and now he blesses the bounties of the Strait. I think it is strange, eh, how man can choose to make a god face whichever way suits him, don't you?"

"Yes, Enzo, I think I know what you mean: it's as though we mould our deities in whatever shape suits our purpose."

He glances at her, his expression that of a child who is trying to reconcile himself to learning that not all adults think alike. "Except for our Madonna," he says.

"Yes, of course, Enzo: except for our Madonna." Caterina, though, is still mesmerised by the whirling tide. "Well, she certainly kept me safe, didn't she?"

"No, signorina, it was not the Madonna who kept you safe, it was my father."

Caterina staggers back so suddenly she trips and falls. "Your father? I... You mean, he..."

Enzo helps her up. "Yes, you were fortunate we were close by. My father jumped into the sea and dived beneath the surface to find you. You didn't know?"

"I... No. No, I didn't." Standing on the deck in the middle of the Strait, the whirlpool all about them, the shore close yet too far away, there is nowhere for Caterina to hide. She could take shelter from her embarrassment in the cabin, but that would only provide her with some temporary haven; and she couldn't exactly shout up and ask Pasquale to take her to the shore or leap overboard and try to swim back, for the feluca had already rescued her once and twice would be—

"My aunt did not tell you?"

"No."

"Nor my father?"

"No. Although I'm not completely stupid, Enzo; I did suspect it. It's just that it seemed a strange question to have to ask."

"You don't remember anything?"

"Not much," she replies, frustration and irritation slinking past the guard of her tone. "All I remember is getting into difficulty and the water closing over my head. The next thing I knew, I was lying in the bloody hospital. Anyway, Enzo, what is this, twenty questions?"

"No, Signorina Caterina. I—"

"And stop calling me Signorina, will you? I am Signora Caterina, can't you see." She holds up her hand to his face, her palm towards him so that he cannot avoid noticing the gold band of her wedding ring.

The engines rumble and the deck shudders and heaves as she comes around through the glare of the sun to head west towards the mountains of the Sicilian shore.

They had been idling back and forth across the Strait; to the east, Calabria and the cloud–covered peaks of Aspromonte, to the south the widening Strait and to the north the twin pylons each side of the narrow channel that leads into the Tyrrhenian Sea.

Enzo, eventually deciding that Caterina had bitten a good enough chunk out of him that she was no longer likely to be hungry, had taken to explaining to her how before they had boats with motors, the men of Scylla would climb to the top of the cliffs on the Calabrian coast and spend the day keeping look out for swordfish; how when they spotted one, they would wave flags, directing the boat below to the right part of the sea; and how the four oarsmen would stand facing forward as they rowed so they could see the direction in which their spotter, the banniaturi, wanted them to row. The funcitta, who some called lanzaturi because of his lance, would stand in the bow and from there he would harpoon the fish."

Antonio, on the other hand, has passed much of the day, untying and retying rolling and clove–hitches to both the forked head and the shaft of his harpoons, ensuring that should they part company, neither would be lost.

"All the boats seem to fish the same stretch of water over and over again," Caterina mentions. "Is there some kind of patch for each boat?" She'd been watching the other feluche as they, like the Salvazione, patrolled back and forth and up and down what appeared to be a clearly defined, but unmarked box of water.

"Yes," he replies, chewing. "At the beginning of each year we are assigned our own section of the Strait and we must not fish in someone else's or there is big trouble. This season, we fish between the large buoy over there," he points up the coast to a round concrete block of cement on which sits a metal frame and light, "and down there, to that old Saracen tower."

"But you don't fish here every day," Caterina states. "I mean, yesterday we were north of the Strait out in the open water."

"Exactly. Yesterday the water was not good here: today it is better; we will catch fish before too long."

"You said season, Antonio, don't you fish all year round?"

"No. The swordfish migrate through the Strait in the months of May to August: we only have the four months to fish, so we work hard all through the summer."

"And the rest of the year?"

He shrugs. "We fish with other boats, other fish, find work, all different work. That is the way it is for us fishermen. In times before, in the winter when the weather was too bad to fish, the people of Messina would provide food for the fishermen. Not now though."

The engines surge and Antonio is very suddenly no longer standing beside her chair, munching his way through her brioche, he is leading Enzo along the long passerelle, the bucket of small wooden fish in his hands.

Ninolino looks around the deck, ensuring it is cleared of whatever might foul the coils of rope he will feed out from the baskets, and Karl picks up the long-handled net and stands ready.

Caterina slides her chair back to the base of the tower, hoping she is so far out of the way she cannot possibly get in theirs.

The feluca picks up speed once more, a gentle surge, a smooth acceleration, nothing urgent that might spook or alarm.

Antonio steps over the rail onto the small stage at the head of the passerelle and picks up his long lance. His cap is pulled forward and his dark, round, side—shielded sunglasses lend him a robotic aspect. Meticulously, he examines his three—pointed lance, squeezing and twisting each one of the barbs to satisfy himself they will not detach, and he checks the small threads attaching his lance to the line looped along the passerelle to the baskets at the bow. Antonio squares his shoulders and hips, his right hand at the raised end of his lance, his left nearer the tip pointing it down towards the surface.

"To starboard," Pasquale shouts, from above, his tone commanding, imperative.

Antonio searches.

The nose of the feluca swings round, the engines moan louder.

"Now, ten metres," Pasquale screams, the pitch of his voice rising.

Antonio tenses, raises the end of his lance higher and the tip lower.

"Five," Pasquale screams, "There are two. The larger one, she is there, before you. Straight ahead."

The feluca surges forward. It is as if the engines, the deck, the mast, the cabin, the stays and the crew are all part of one greater whole whose aim is to propel and support the funcitta to a position where he has clear sight of his prey.

"Now!" Pasquale shouts. "Now! You are on top of her."

Antonio tenses, his muscles seem to expand, his hips wriggle, his hands twitch. He raises himself up to his full height, drags his harpoon back and with all his might throws it down into the water.

The loops of line running along the starboard base of the passerelle are ripped from their ties. Antonio nods, turns and clambers out from his post; he knows he has found his mark.

Enzo knows, too; he is already halfway back down the passerelle. And Pasquale, high up in his crow's nest, has noticed them both retreating back to the bow and needs no more confirmation; he reverses the engines to stop the line dragging under the hull and then pulls them back to idle.

Ninolino and Karl are paying line out of the foremost basket. The swordfish is wounded, running, diving, sounding, flashing its tail, straining every fibre and sinew, swimming as fast, as desperately and as swiftly as it knows how to get away from the feluca.

Caterina watches and sits bolt upright, as shivers of excitement ripple up her spine, goosebumps rise along her forearms and the fine hairs at the nape of her neck quiver.

Enzo strides past her and climbs around the cabin onto the small aft deck. His father follows him and between them they wrestle the wooden dinghy over the raised lip of the deck into the water and pull it by its lead rope round to the side.

The boys need no second bidding and while Ninolino holds the line, Karl climbs down into the dinghy and Enzo picking up the basket, hands it to him. As soon as he has placed the basket securely, Ninolino passes him the line on the other end of which the swordfish is twisting and turning. Karl ties the line to a cleat at the stern, steadies the dinghy and Ninolino joins him. When they are set, Enzo throws them the lead rope, casting them off away from the feluca.

The routine is smooth and ordered and has taken no more than a few seconds.

Enzo hesitates and turns to Caterina. "There is another, the male."

Antonio picks a second lance from the deck and hurries back to his post, his progress slowed because he has only one free hand with which to steady himself. He ties the new lance to a second line which is, like the first, looped down the base of the passerelle.

The dinghy glides away across the ocean; no oars, no sail and no engine; just Ninolino standing in the rear, patiently holding onto a line connected to a wounded swordfish.

The engines groan, the deck reverberates, the feluca heaves away to starboard.

A shout from above: "Coming across the bow." This time it is Giuseppe who has seen the male.

Pasquale steers them back to port. "He will come by you," he shouts.

Antonio lifts his lance and waits. Enzo, too, waits by the bow, ready with the basket of line. Caterina stands and peers over the starboard rail into the green water.

A flash of silvery–grey, no more than a split–second streak of a ghostly shadow careening beneath the surface.

Antonio turns. He looks down. He raises his lance.

"Now!" Pasquale shouts again. "Now! He is there."

The funcitta searches the water, hesitates, looks again and then sets down his lance. He shakes his head, points towards the dinghy and shrugs his shoulders.

Caterina sits back down and tries to breathe; something, in all the excitement, she has neglected to do.

Pasquale steers in the direction of the dinghy, now some hundred metres away.

They wait, watching the water.

"There, dead ahead," Giuseppe shouts. "Between us and the dinghy."

"Yes, yes," Pasquale screams. "I will bring you to him."

The engines growl and moan. The feluca runs forward. Antonio waits studying the surface in front of his precarious perch; he turns to glance up at his capobarca as if to ask where, how far, which side?

"Now, twenty, to port. Soon. Very soon." With each word, the pitch of Pasquale's voice rises in urgency. "Now, now, in front. You must see him. In front."

But the funcitta doesn't. As the bow comes around, the sun is now behind Antonio and the water before him cast into his shadow.

Pasquale swings the helm to port; the shadow is removed and there beneath him, plain for Antonio to see, lies the swordfish.

He lifts the lance high; he thrusts it down and lets go.

The lance is gone, the loops of line are snatched from the base of the passerelle and Enzo feeds more line from the basket.

Antonio turns, clambers over the rail and sets off back down the walkway, all the time nodding his head.

Once back at the bow, both father and son pay out line. They wait patiently, chatting, smiling. Antonio waves the dinghy back and Karl stands up and begins rowing in their direction.

Enzo, his foot braced against the gunwale, keeps hold of the line; his father, standing immediately behind, has hold of the line too, but seems casually unconcerned that with one sudden jerk the swordfish might haul both of them overboard. And if they were, what should she do? Climb the mast and inform Pasquale and Giuseppe? Grab the line and save them, the catch, the day? Or sit and look spare and hope that someone else will rush to her rescue?

Caterina cranes her head and looks up at the base of the small platform that makes the crow's nest. Both mornings, she has watched first Pasquale, then Giuseppe, climb onto the cabin roof, cross themselves and then start the long ascent, hand over hand, foot over foot, neither looking up nor down, scaling steadily, smoothly, up and up and up, as though they are embarked on little more than their customary passeggio. Even from below, the mere prospect of climbing the twenty metres is dizzying.

She looks back at father and son and decides, in keeping with that of the capobarca and his spotter, their studied nonchalance is born out of years of experience rather than any desire to flaunt their machismo.

Antonio turns, sees her looking at them and calls. "Caterina?"

The bow swings round into the sun: she shades her eyes. "Yes, Antonio."

"Come help Enzo, eh?"

She does not need to reply; to be asked is enough, and she leaps up and strides purposefully to his side. "What can I do?"

He smiles, perhaps more to himself than her. "You can hold the line. You can help Enzo pull up the fish."

"Absolutely. Yes. Of course. Anything. Hold the line." Caterina sets her feet and pulls a little too hard.

Enzo stumbles backwards into her and Antonio ends up holding them both upright. "Whoa," he says, laughing, reining her in, "we are catching fish not horses. Be strong, be gentle and–"

"Sorry, I–"

He touches his lips to quieten her. "And don't be sorry. Now... Pull when he pulls."

Caterina looks down to where the line wears a crease in the lip of the deck; there are many such corrugations, all spread at irregular intervals, each one a testament to a swordfish brought up from the depths.

As his father steps back, Enzo pulls on the line and, like the measured pace with which the other men climb the tower, he hauls hand over hand, relying on Caterina to take up the slack and keep the line taut.

"There is a basket near your feet," he says, over his shoulder, "try to let the line drop into it; try not to let it fall on the deck, that way no one can trip over it."

"Sure. Okay. I'll do my best."

"Your best is all we ask for, Signora."

And together they haul the line and Caterina lets it fall, mostly if not exactly roundly, into the basket. At first, there is little resistance on the line except for the occasional tug, but as the swordfish nears the surface and realises that soon it will be lifted from the water, it begins to struggle frantically.

"Wait," Enzo says, his back straightening, his hips flexing as they compensate for the direction in which the fish is trying to drag him.

The line loses some of its argument, the weight at the end of it seeming dead.

"Pull again," he says, so they do, rhythmically, evenly, hand over hand over hand.

The line jerks and plays again.

"No, wait a moment," and then, when the line falls slack, "Now, up. Up, as quick as we can."

Antonio, meantime, has filled a bucket and brought a yellow towel from the cabin. He dunks the towel in the bucket and sloshes some water over the lip of the gunwale to cool the line furrow. Putting down the now empty bucket, he picks up a curiously medieval–looking instrument of torture; a stick about as wide as his wrist and as long as his leg. From the end of the stick a metal rod protrudes, curving in a u–bend and ending in a barbed spear.

He kneels down and leans over the side. "He is coming. Four perhaps three metres."

Caterina hauls, the continuous effort causing her to huff and puff a little. Her hands sting and blister as the salt–watered nylon line draws the skin of her fingers over and away from the flesh beneath. Beads of sweat break out on her forehead and drip into her eyes: if only she had a spare hand, she would wipe them away. If only, but... she cannot let go for fear of leaving Enzo to be dragged overboard.

He takes a step nearer the rail and glances over. "When he is on the water, my father will hook him with the gaff and we will bring him up onto the deck. It is best, Signora, if you stand away."

With one last heave, Enzo leans back and his father leans over the side and hooks the swordfish.

Antonio grunts as he lifts, rising first from one knee, then the other, and finally standing ready to pull the gaff upward.

The long rod of the harpoon appears, poking skyward towards Enzo. He takes a step to the side, out of its way.

Two more hands of line and Caterina is pulling for all she is worth, the nylon cutting hard into her palms.

Antonio grunts. Enzo groans. They lean back. The arcing dorsal and caudal fins of the fish are now visible just above the edge of the gunwale and... over, they stagger, half–falling backwards, dragging their catch with them.

The swordfish slithers up over the lip and slaps down onto the deck, its torso twisting and tightening, its tail flapping out, its head turning, its long, rapier of a bill slashing impotently this way and that.

Antonio immediately drops the gaff out of the way, picks up the soaking towel and spreads it across the head of the swordfish.

Caterina, standing behind the winch box, stares at a fish whose body, grey–blue to almost bronze on top and silver underside, is near as tall as her shoulder, but whose sword extends longer than her arm outstretched. The harpoon, the three prongs of which are buried deep in the flesh of the fish's back, sticks out from just behind the dorsal fin.

Enzo straddles the fish, holding it down and still, while his father unscrews the shaft from the head of the harpoon. Then, with the swordfish lying on his left side, flexing and twisting, its lower jaw opening and closing, desperate for the life–giving passage of water through its gills, he moves the wet towel forward, exposing its large gill cover, and he runs the nails of his right hand first laterally along and then vertically down the cover, leaving a lattice of diamond–shaped marks in the skin.

Caterina watches.

"A cardata ra cruci," Enzo says. "Our mark of respect to a noble fish that has given his life so that others will not starve. The funcitta must not do this or it is bad luck. And only on the right cheek. Call it a ritual, a tradition, a superstition; call it what you like, but it is important for us to respect the food our Strait supplies, don't you think?"

"Yes, Enzo, I do. Strange as it may sound to some, it makes perfect sense to me."

The dinghy bangs against the hull and Enzo is up on his feet, taking the line from Karl. Ninolino stands in the stern, wobbling as he keeps his balance in the swell, a half–filled basket of coils lying at his feet, the line to the fish in his hands. While Karl holds the dinghy steady, Ninolino steps nimbly to the bow and hands the line up to Enzo.

The boys leap aboard and stow the dinghy behind the cabin.

Now they are back, Caterina's help is not required for the second fish and even Enzo stands away and allows them to haul up together. She notices there is no tugging or opposition to their steady rhythm.

"The female fish will not fight," he says. "She is too tired from dragging the dinghy and once they tire, they die."

"You knew the male fish would be nearby? Is that how it works?" she asks.

"Not always, but we take the female first. She is the larger of the two and once we have her, the male will not desert her and he is then not so difficult to catch."

"Do you think he gives up? Do you think he surrenders because he can no longer be with his mate?"

He pouts his lips, considering. "Many people like to think so."

"Do you?" she asks.

"It is the way of things. If it wasn't, why would we catch so many males after we catch the female?"

With the help of Antonio, Karl and Ninolino land the female.

She is larger than the male, but only by a couple of hand's widths and she lies on her side as Enzo marks her right gill cover.

The swordfish is so perfectly formed that Caterina is moved to tears. Even lying prostrate, forlorn and defenceless on the deck, she is all at once majestic, angelic and statuesque: the composition and fusion of her contours and curves, her strong back, her sail–like dorsal fin, the half–moon of her caudal fin, the long spike of her tapered sword. She is beautiful, she is more than that, she is perhaps the most perfect creature Caterina has ever seen. She kneels and looks into the misty blue–black eye of the swordfish.

It is a mistake, as the moment she looks she knows plainly and absolutely that she shouldn't have done so. For what she sees is a soul dying; a soul once so very beautiful in life and now in death so very ugly. It is as though she is watching the very light of life fade slowly into the darkness of oblivion,

"Caterina?" Antonio says, standing beside her.

Her senses, though, are bewildered. She is deaf to all but her thoughts and all she can see is the light diminishing, dissolving, disappearing, and its withdrawal leaves her feeling so wretchedly, so utterly alone.

"Caterina," he says again, and this time he bends and very gently, so as not to startle her, lays his great paw of a hand on her shoulder.

She turns her head. "Yes, Antonio."

"Caterina, are you all right? Are you okay?"

"Oh, yes, I'm…" She tries to swallow, but not only is her mouth dry, the solution of her thought has dried too, and she says. "No, Antonio, no, I'm not." She looks up at him, tears streaming down her cheeks. "And I so thought I was."

CHAPTER 10

Angelica drives down the coast road. "Alberto says I am a fool to myself."

If Caterina had not seen on the previous Wednesday evening the way Angelica had looked so adoringly at her husband while he'd waxed lyrically about the troubadours and puppet story—tellers, she believes she might mistake her hostess for a committed misandrist. She isn't, though; Caterina is sure of that; it's just the way she has of implying that all people are fools, excepting of course that men happen to be bigger fools than women.

"He says I would get to Messina in half the time if I used the Strada." She takes her right hand off the steering wheel, raises it in appeal first to the road in front, then to herself and then to the road in front again, before finally, and much to Caterina's relief, replacing it on the steering wheel.

"But I like the Via Consolare: it is easy and there is more to see driving through the little villages than there is on that racetrack of a Strada. Hey," she lifts her hand, "Sant Agata, Pace, Paradiso. Beautiful, no?"

Even though the going is easy, Caterina has her own hands buried deep in her lap, her knuckles white with dreadful anticipation, the skin at her blisters stinging.

The evening before as they'd headed back to the breakwater, Enzo had asked Caterina to show him her hands. She had been reluctant, embarrassed that her soft skin should cut up so easily. But Enzo had insisted, then grabbed her hands and turned them over and inspected her palms: blisters, a couple of them broken open. He'd looked at her, a hint of sympathy in his expression, hauled her over to the side and pushed her hands down into a newly filled bucket. The salt water had stung and she had tried really, really hard not to flinch or wince. Enzo had not apologised.

"So," Angelica says, frowning: her hands are off, on and off the wheel again, "one has to deal with cars that jump out at you from side roads, young ruffians who believe their driving abilities exceed their looks and pedestrians who fail to so much as glance before they walk out into the road." Angelica leans on the horn. "Hey," she yells, leaning her head out the window, "watch where you're going. What am I? Invisible?"

The day had begun pretty much in the same vein as Caterina's evening had finished: with her wanting to hide and her hosts wanting responses and reactions from her. The couple had invited her to go into Messina with them."

"No, thank you. You have both been so good to me, I think it's about time you spent the evening together. Besides, I may have had a little too much sun and not enough water."

Angelica and Alberto had come in late, and Caterina had slept fitfully and was woken by their conversation in the kitchen.

In the morning, the two knocks at her bedroom door had suggested confident intention rather than impatience, but they had also suggested to her that sleep was not an acceptable excuse for her disregard.

"Yes," she had answered, disinterested, dispirited.

The door had opened wide enough to permit the words their entrance: "Caterina, Enzo is downstairs. He says you are to come immediately or not at all."

"Oh, Angelica," she'd moaned.

"Well?"

"Well, that will be not at all then."

The door had closed, softly. "She is not coming," Angelica had called down the stairs.

And Caterina had waited, resenting the rough–plastered walls, the paintings of fishing boats, the folk congregating by the shoreline and the Madonna with her child.

A half–hour later, Angelica had knocked again.

That second time, though, she had opened the door wide and walked right in. "Get up. It is time. I am going into the city and you are going to come with me."

At the Annunziata, the Via Consolare opens into three lanes, albeit three reduced to two by the random double and occasional triple–parking. "The Viale della Liberta," she says. "Before the earthquake, there used to be a tram that ran all the way from the port of Messina," she points forward, "to Villafranca," she points over her shoulder. "Fifty kilometres. Imagine. Over 100 years ago. There. Look. On the other side of the road: the great hospital of Queen Margherita. Empty for all these years. Criminal, eh?"

"Yes, I saw it the other day... when I came to the museum. It's quite lovely, isn't it? Such a grand building. More like a palace than a hospital."

"All of Messina was like this before the earthquake," Angelica says, a melancholy softening to her voice. "And this quarter, the Borgo del Ringo, was where the fishermen would have lived in the time of your nonna."

At the fountain of Neptune, Angelica turns into the Via Garibaldi and points: "Villa Mazzini: a place your nonna told you to visit."

"Yes," Caterina replies, dreamily. "A quiet place: that fig tree, the Australian tree. Never expected to see a Moreton Bay fig tree in Messina."

"Why not?" Angelica asks. "Once the Suez Canal was built, many ships came here directly from Australia. Someone brought a seed; a tree was planted, it's natural, eh? Look, here is the Teatro, where you saw Guttuso's painting."

"Yes."

"And here is where we will find a place to park. There are two places I want to show you, then we will have granita and brioche, okay?"

From the outside, the old red Fiat is tidy enough, but from inside Caterina is sure she can see the surface of the road through a hole in the floor.

Angelica pulls up. The drivers behind her honk their horns as if to shout, "Don't you know it is Sunday! Why are you making me late when there are plenty of places available around the corner?" She parks.

"This church," she says, leading Caterina across the pavement and pointing, "is the Chiesa della Santissima Annunziata dei Catalani. It is nearly 1,000 years old, perhaps older; nobody really knows. The legend says that first it was a temple of Neptune, then a church, then a mosque and now a church once more; it has seen many changes, but it is still a banquet for one's eyes, eh?"

"Yes, Angelica. It is very lovely. The colours of the stone, the star shapes, the arches, the columns, the curve of the apse, the galleried portals and the cupola: it is very Moorish and yet both Roman and Norman for a Catalan church."

"Ah, yes, at one time Peter of Aragon worshipped here and later the church became a hospital. But do you know why I wanted to show you this particular church?"

"Because it is so beautiful?"

"No, Caterina, because I want you to see that the floor of the church stands at least two metres below what is now the level of the streets."

She leans against the iron rail and peers down. "Yes, I see what you mean. Why is that?"

"Because one hundred years ago, after the great earthquake, they buried what remained of the old city beneath a sea of liquid concrete: the Chiesa dei Catalani stands at the old level, two metres below that of the new." She pauses, casting her eyes over the church as if it is an old and trusted friend. "Now, we go."

Angelica wears a sober black one–piece, knee–length dress with a round neck–line and three quarter length sleeves. Her dark brown hair is tightly curled and heavily lacquered, and her make–up generous. The click and clack of her heels betrays her impatience.

Caterina follows along like an obedient child.

They walk up the slope and arrive at a second church, completely alternative in appearance to the one they have just seen: the façade is plain and grand, and four immense rectangular columns topped with bundles of fruit frame two tall wooden doors below a windowed tympanum.

Thoughtfully, considerately, Caterina says, "Quite a contrast."

"Yes, a church rebuilt after the earthquake. So much more like a conventional church than the Chiesa dei Catalani, eh? We'll go inside."

The church is empty but for two men laying bouquets of white orchids, yellow roses and pink peonies along the marble nave. Their footsteps echo above the low murmur of their conversation and they nod respectfully and smile politely.

"Chiesa Santa Caterina," Angelica whispers. "Your church. I thought you would like to see it." At the central nave, she curtsies and crosses herself. Then she turns and motions towards a pew. "Why don't you sit for a while? I will be across the way in the Ritrovo Narciso; I will order for you. Don't hurry; take your time; talk with those you miss."

The granita al limone proves refreshing, the brioche filling and conversation hard to come by. Caterina stammers and stutters her way through an apology: something about feeling distracted, not concentrating, remembering too much and not all of it good.

Angelica says, "It is normal," and pays the bill.

The broad Viale San Martino rises gradually and a tramcar glides down the central carriageway towards the Piazza Cairoli and the harbour. A side road is arched with fairy–lights and lined with stalls not yet open.

"Where are you taking me now?" Caterina asks.

"Oh, now I am going to visit the graves of my family. I try to pay my respects once a month, if not more often. And because this Sunday is special and the weather is fine, not too hot, I thought it would be an opportunity. You remember last Thursday was Antonio's Onomastico, his name day?"

Caterina nods.

"Well, this weekend is the Festival of Saint Antony. You saw the lights in the Via Santa Cecilia? We passed it just now, on the right."

She nods again.

"So, tonight we will have a procession through the city: there are street fairs, folk dancing, live music, fireworks and many people from all around Messina come to celebrate. Last night was what we call our Notte Bianca. We call it our white night because there is no sleep from sunset to sunrise." She winks and grins, playfully. "Or perhaps until two in the morning; that is close to sunrise, is it not? People hold exhibitions and sporting competitions, there is more music, art and culture and faith meetings. I wanted you to come, but you were not in the right mood. Perhaps it was better you didn't," she adds, without any evident ill feeling.

507

"I'm sorry, Angelica."

"Yes, you were. But for yourself, not me. Tonight, you will have no excuse: you will come to see the procession and Antonio and Enzo will come too."

This time Angelica pulls up in a side road by a park, through which they stroll before arriving at the cemetery. Half–open black gates and railings decorated with gold–painted wreaths are flanked by two white angels, and to the right of the gates, a flower stall, from which Angelica buys two bunches of yellow and white chrysanthemums, one of which she hands to Caterina.

"No," Angelica says, when she objects, "these are for you to lay."

"But I don't know—"

"Where you feel it is appropriate. You will not find it difficult to lay flowers in a cemetery. Life," Angelica adds, as they walk slowly, respectfully, up the lane, "has been challenging for the people of our city; you can tell this by the size of our cemetery, our Gran Camposanto, the second largest cemetery in the whole of Italy." She scoffs, angrily, "Pah! It was not only fig trees sailors brought from Australia; in the middle of the nineteenth century, others brought cholera from India and that was when the cemetery was begun."

Caterina stops to read the plaques on the wall by the crematorium. "Enrichetta Cooper," she murmurs, "Cooper, such an English name."

"Yes, there are many British people buried here. You know, there is a stranger's quarter here: soldiers, sailors, wives, many young children and many sad stories. Your King George and Queen Mary paid their respects when they visited in 1925. There is a sign by the gate; I will show you, later."

"Are all your family interred here, Angelica?"

"All except those who went abroad and never returned."

"Do you and Antonio have brothers or sisters?"

"No. And this is unusual for a country that can breed children faster than rabbits. Remember, until the fifties, contraception was for prostitutes, not for wives."

"So how did your mother and father come to have only the two of you?"

Angelica pauses to greet other couples in passing: she nods her head, touches an arm, smiles in sympathy: "Good day, not too hot today. How is… well, I hope. Yes, I heard. Such a shame; a nice man…"

"In her later years, my mother was a quiet woman; although my grandfather once told me she was not so placid in her youth. She married our father late, in her forties, the same year Antonio was born." She glances; the slightest raise of an eyebrow, a subtle communication tinted with the inference of possibility rather than stained by the reality of fact. "My grandfather told me that my mother was married to a man before the war, but that he died in the service of his country. Of course, in those days for a widow, things were not so easy: they were considered untouchable back then. Why? Because for a widow to remarry was to insult the memory of the husband."

"I've seen that in men," Caterina says. "I know the look. They think that because your husband has died you should be consigned to some form of eternal mourning." She turns away and pretends to be fascinated by a tall, alabaster statue of a lean youth in tails, playing a violin. There is no noticeable date for his birth; however, the date of his death is noted as 28.12.1908.

Angelica studies her for a moment before realising that Caterina will not turn back until she has turned her attention elsewhere. So she does, and she continues walking slowly along the cypress–lined avenue as though nothing out of the ordinary has been said. "No, in those days it was nothing to do with the attitudes of the men, it was the women. They were in charge, they defined the moral code, they were the ones who were responsible for that tyrant Mussolini enjoying such power."

"I thought that was the mafia. Weren't they in league with the fascists?"

"Sometimes," she replies, a little ponderously. "But much of the time they were like the cats who stare at each other from across the street in our village. As far as social conventions were concerned, my mother told me it was the women who used to dictate how one should behave. She would say that before and for some years after the war, it was the hens who ruled the roost, not the cockerel. It is no longer the same now."

The lane winds its way up and along between the mausolea, some grand and flamboyant, others plain; some headed by intricately carved busts of cherubic children and others boasting fine images of upstanding, righteous, moustachioed patriarchs or stern–looking matriarchs.

"Your mother sounds like quite a lady. Were you close to her?"

She shrugs and holds out her free hand and waves it in small lazy circles. "I was very fortunate; my mother was always ready to discuss my affairs of the heart; and not all mothers are so welcoming with this type of talk." Angelica hesitates, obviously weighing up whether she should tell Caterina some long–held secret. Then, she decides. "There was a young man, the son of another fisherman, I was to marry him, I had agreed. At the time, I thought I loved him. And I did until I met Alberto, which was when I understood that I liked this other young man rather than loved him. My mother found out about Alberto; Beppe warned me; I was petrified. I thought she would lock me up in my room or worse. She didn't, though. She sat me down and told me a story: a story about how during the war she had fallen in love with a man who, for many reasons, it was not possible for her to marry. She told me she regretted not pursuing this man and that it took her many years to mend her broken heart; this was why she did not marry again until she was older and why she did not have more children. She told me I must follow my heart, and if my heart led me towards Alberto, then I should go to him and never look back. I remember she said to me, "Your past is already written; your future is yours to write.""

They stroll on through the city of tombs and vaults until they come to a modest, white–stone mausoleum with a pitched roof of ridged terracotta tiles and a padlocked wrought iron gate.

They pause before it and Angelica raises her right hand to touch her forehead, her stomach and both her shoulders, before kissing her thumb. She then lowers her head and, whispering, asks the Madonna to watch over all those departed.

Caterina hesitates, uncertain of whether to follow suit. She waits, her hand moves up, it falters: the living body says yes, her mind says no: she trembles in the face of a decision she does not want to make; her hand shakes, the clamour within, the violence, the wounding, the surrender, the ripples of the battle for her soul. She drops her hand.

Angelica glances at her, reaches out and squeezes it so very gently, a communion of tender compassion fused in the warmth of her eyes and the lines of her expression.

Letting go Caterina's hand, she steps forward to unlock the gate. Beyond it, in a room large enough for only the two of them, the back wall is graced with plaques noting the names and dates of the births and deaths of all those interred within.

"See, here," Angelica points up. "My grandfather, Enzo, born in 1891 and passed on in 1986, twenty years after I was born."

"And his family before him? Didn't you say the cemetery was set up in the middle of the nineteenth century?"

Angelica nods. "Yes, that's right. My grandfather's family, his parents his brother and sisters, God rest their souls, they were all killed in the great earthquake. He was the only one to survive. And here, as you see, my mother, born in 1915 and passed on in the millennium year."

"Mirella," Caterina reads. "Such a beautiful name, so bright, so positive. From what little you have told me of her, I feel like I know her already."

"Yes, I am sure you would have liked her and it is a nice name, Mirella. However, she was not known by her full name, she preferred to be known as Mira. Even to our children she was never Mirella, she was always Nonna Mira."

And yet Angelica's surname is different from the name chiselled into the lintel above the gate, Caterina is certain of it. She steps back outside and reads the name she had not properly read before she'd entered because she had at the time been so occupied by torments of her faith.

"Yes, of course. Alberto's surname, your husband's surname, is Lazzarotto. Your nome da nubile, your maiden name, your family name, it's Ruggeri."

Chapter II

"What do I wear?"

Angelica looks her up and down, shrugs and replies, "Similar. It is warm this evening and there will be many people, so... whatever you are happy to wear."

"May I have a shower?"

"Yes, of course. Just make sure there is enough left for Alberto. As I told you this morning, the cockerel likes an excuse to crow, so let's not give him one, eh?" She winks.

Alberto gets home early and changes into the clean white uniform of an officer of the port authority. Antonio, dressed down but suitably clean, arrives later but before he'd said he would which, Angelica observes dryly, really means he is not as late as he usually is. The stars, she adds winking aside to Caterina, must be in some form of serendipitous alignment.

As they drive into the city, the two men sit in the front of Alberto's clean and tidy Alfa Romeo, and traffic, as Angelica had predicted, is heavy. The driver and his front–seat passenger dispute the best place to park: the driver prefers to park further away from the centre and walk in and out; in the long run, it will take less time. The passenger, conversely, of course conversely, prefers to park nearer so there isn't as far to walk either in or out, that will surely take less time. And when they have exhausted their options,

Angelica decides they will park by the university, because it is not far to walk in from there and it is close to Rosticceria Famulari, where they are meeting Enzo for arancini.

"What do you think of Enzo's girlfriend?" Caterina asks Antonio afterwards, as they stroll up the Cesare Battisti.

"Paola? Oh, she is very nice. He has known her for a long time." Antonio pauses, considering. "My only concern is that she may find... What is the right word... Ah yes... that she may find her prospects a little limited. She is studying graphic design, whatever that is, so perhaps to live the rest of her life with a man who fishes in the manner of men who have fished for centuries, might make for a marriage of unequal minds. And that is not to mention that Enzo will make only a modest income in the summer and a good deal less in the winter."

"Do they have to share equal minds?"

He considers her question until they reach the broad Cannizzaro and are waiting for the lights to change before they cross. "These days, I don't know. The young seem to be so much more independent than we were. And I don't mean simply in their wanting to move out of their parents' house and set up on their own; I think they are more independent within their own relationship in the way that each accepts the other has different ambition." Antonio weaves his hands as though he is constructing thoughts. "Again, I say that when we were young," he turns to glance at her, "I apologise, I should say when I was young, it seemed important for couples to want exactly the same thing and to want the same things together."

Antonio takes her arm as they cross the road.

That she doesn't recoil at his touch surprises her but, when they have reached the front of the square monolith that is the stark, fascist–designed Tribunale, she makes sure to slip her arm away from his.

Negotiating their path through the crowds is time consuming; fathers carry children on their shoulders, grandmothers post sentries to protect their view of the road and people meander like zombies, as if controlled by some frequency emitted from their cell phones.

"What time does the procession start?"

Antonio checks his watch. "Soon, seven–thirty, from the Santuario Sant'Antonio. It is only two hundred metres further along, so if you find a place to stand, take it and I will go and tell Angelica and Alberto."

Every lamppost, phone–box, fence and railing is occupied by anyone old enough to assert their authority over it, and policemen, uniforms newly pressed, toecaps polished to match their mirrored sunglasses, dare anyone to stray from the pavement.

"Angelica and Alberto are behind us. Here. Stand here," he says. "Now, they are coming, look."

A brass band emerges from the corner, their cornets, horns and clarinets perfectly off–key. Priests in white cassocks and gold sashes precede cardinals in purple, their expressions thoughtful if not solemn. Policemen in traditional dark blue uniforms with white shoulder–straps and aiguillettes, and flat–topped bicorns sporting blue and red plumes; naval officers in dress whites and a general, his chest boasting an array of medals, lead city dignitaries, both men and women their faces fixed in grave appreciation of their importance.

On a float of white and orange orchids, an enormous globe of the world rests and at its base and around its equator young children, some Caucasian and many of south–east Asian descent, all dressed in identical nautical whites, sit and stare back bemused by the mass of devotees. In pride of place on top of the world, Saint Antonio of Padua stands, casting his blessings upon the congregation.

People applaud and cheer and Caterina is caught up in the rush of emotion that races through the crowd. Before she realises that the fervour has wrested control of her limbs, she too crosses herself and kisses her thumb. She glances quickly, self-consciously, at Antonio, but his attention is taken with the float, the flowers and the young children; and she can't be sure, because the light of early evening is fading and the glow from the arch of streetlights is beginning to assert its dominance, but his eyes seem to her to have taken on a moist glaze.

"The children," she says, raising her voice above the best efforts of the band following the float, "are they all from Messina?"

Without turning his attention from the procession, he replies, "Some, but not all. Our church maintains a strong connection with the churches of Sant'Antonio in the Philippines. As I am sure you know, Sant'Antonio is the Patron Saint of those who are lost and many of these children are orphans."

Soon, they are gone away down the broad avenue towards the centre of the city and many in the crowd pursue and join the procession. Antonio doesn't, though he does wipe his eyes with his handkerchief, and Catrina is left to bathe in an almost electric frisson of pride, joy and elation, as though an invisible hand has caressed her body with a cool, reinvigorating balm.

They walk for a while, together but each alone with their thoughts, and come upon a broad pedestrianised avenue. Crowds are milling about, gazing down at a collage that runs the length of the street; a carpet of vibrant yellow, gaudy red, purple, green and white.

"It's very beautiful, isn't it?" she says. "The pattern, it reminds me of the flower arrangements I saw in the cemetery this morning. How do they do it? What is it made of?"

"Coloured sawdust; they spray it with a fixative so that it will not blow away. They are clever, no?"

"Papà!" It is Enzo: he is standing with Paola; they are chatting to an old man and an old woman in a wheelchair.

The man looks up: it is Beppe. "Antonio, Alberto, Angelica, how are you? Come, Maria is here. Please, say hello, she will be happy to know you are with us this evening."

Caterina hangs back as the others walk over and bend to speak to the woman who, judging by the way she inclines her head, appears to be both blind and hard of hearing. She leans forward and Antonio pats her hand and whispers into her ear. The woman smiles, exposing the few irregular teeth she has held onto in her old age.

"Who is she?" Caterina asks Paola. "She looks to be very old."

"Sorbello, Maria Assunta. Beppe's sister. As to how old she is, Enzo says she was born before the second war and that she can remember so much about it that eminent historians sometimes come to ask her questions."

"She certainly seems to be lifted by whatever it is Antonio is saying to her."

"Yes, the Sorbello and the Ruggeri families have been as close as any for many years; Beppe's father and Antonio's father used to fish together. My Enzo told me that Beppe and Maria had three older brothers, all of whom were at one time fishermen, but none of whom returned from North Africa when the second war ended. By then, their father was too old to provide for Beppe and Maria, so Antonio's father looked after them. Now, Beppe is too old to fish and Maria... well, you can see. They don't have family to look after them, so Antonio is their main provider: he gives them money when they have need of it and he ensures they have enough food."

"That is very benevolent of him," Caterina says.

"Yes," Paola agrees, "and yet that is the way it is here. When families are close, there is no one closer."

"Paola, Enzo's mother..." she begins, but then loses her way for a minute. "Angelica doesn't like her."

"Yes, that is only natural. She is very protective of Antonio. Us women get this way when we see a man we love hurt. But Enzo's mother is not a bad person; she was young when she married – younger than Antonio – and he is not the kind of man to have second thoughts about wanting to live the way he wants. I sometimes wonder if it wasn't his will that seduced her as much as his good looks." She grins, sheepishly, even a little cheekily. "Many young women are drawn to strong, older men in the same way that some young men are drawn to strong, older women. I think that when Enzo's mother grew older, perhaps when she grew up, I don't know… but when she did, she realised that being married to a fisherman was not going to bring her the fine clothes, fine food and fine wine she wanted, so…"

"Does Enzo talk about her?"

"Not very often," Paola says, as though she wishes he would. "Men, eh? Who knows what they are thinking? And you would have more chance getting conversation out of a clam than asking his father how he feels. And you, Caterina? Are you and Antonio on a date?"

"A date?" she chuckles. "Strange isn't it? If you'd asked me that yesterday, I would have said you were barmy; I'd probably even have lost my temper and stormed off in a huff. But now, here, this evening, and I don't really understand why, but I don't find the idea of being on a date so completely ridiculous; a bit silly perhaps, but not completely ridiculous. Not that we are… on a date, that is."

Paola laughs, widening her eyes at the thought. "Why not? Antonio is an attractive man, eh?"

"Yes," she murmurs, allowing her gaze to settle on him. "Yes, I suppose he is in a strong sort of rugged kind of way."

And as she is thinking it, Antonio walks over and extends his right hand to her. "Caterina, please come and say hello to Maria. After spending all her time with people she knows well, she will be pleased to have someone new to talk to."

"Of course, I'd be happy to." She glances at Paola, who grins a little sheepishly.

He takes her by the hand and leads her to the old woman. "Maria," he says, "this is Caterina, a friend from England. This is her first time at the Festa Sant'Antonio; she is Angelica's guest."

Caterina squats and as though handling some rare and very delicate porcelain, she takes hold of Maria's hand. "Pleased to meet you."

The old woman turns her head in the direction of the voice and appraises her through beady eyes. "And to meet you, young lady. So, you are a guest of Angelica and yet Antonio presents you." She pauses, wrapping her free hand on top of Caterina's, allowing her fingertips to feel the texture of her skin. "These fools" she whispers, "they think I am blind simply because I cannot see much further than the end of my nose, but I see perfectly well when there is something to look at."

Lost for words, Caterina stutters.

"Ah," Maria says, softly, so that those standing around them cannot overhear, "you have not yet found your place in this world of ours. Don't worry, you will: everyone does given time."

"Thank you, Maria. I'm not sure I know what you mean. I'll think on it though."

"Good. You do that, young lady. And you have good hands; they speak well of you. Now, go. Go and enjoy your evening."

"Young lady," Caterina repeats, as they stroll away.

"What was that?" Antonio asks.

"I was just thinking: your friend, Beppe's sister, she called me young lady. I suppose I should be flattered."

"Flattered? No. When you are as old as Maria, everyone is young, except her brother of course."

She chuckles. "Yes, Paola said something like that. I gather no one knows how old she really is, not even Beppe."

Antonio bridles his lips, arches an eyebrow and sticks his chin out. "I remember my mother saying that during the second war

Maria used to help out in her café at Torre Faro. She was very attractive, as was my mother, the soldiers used to flirt with them and my mother would drive them away with her broom."

In the round of the Piazza del Popolo, a raised stage is alive to the sights and sounds of a folk–dancing troupe.

"Peloritani," he says. "From the mountains."

The women, their hair plaited, their white blouses billowing, their skirts and waistcoats hand–stitched and patterned in rich greens, reds and yellows, whirl and twirl and stamp their feet. The men, black knee–length pants and waistcoats, white shirts and socks and red sash belts, dance and whoop in time to the accordion, the drums and the zampugnaru pipes. The audience is swept along with the tempo and many link arms and form circles in which to perform their own imitations and interpretations.

They pass a stall.

"Would you like an ice cream?" he asks.

She nods. "Lovely. Yes. Strawberry, please. Where are Alberto and Angelica?"

Antonio smiles. "As is their way, they are discussing which fridge magnets to buy. You've seen their fridge?"

"Yes, quite a collection. There must be one for every fruit and vegetable."

"It's true; they buy another every Festa Sant'Antonio and soon they will have no more space. Either that or the door will fall off because of all the extra weight."

"I'll be over there." She points towards the stage.

"I'll find you," he says, turning back to the stall.

Now that it is dark, the mood of the people is both happy and benign: elders chat, husbands debate, mothers agree, and teenage girls crowd round prams to fuss over their new nephew or niece, just as older nephews and nieces play hide and seek behind forests of legs.

Caterina finds a spot from which she can see the stage.

The speed with which the women pirouette between partners and the precision and intricacy of the choreography is mesmerising: they smile as they skip, their arms raised, and their poise and the joy with which they bring to life the traditional dances of their village is infectious and soon enough Caterina is once more lost to the moment.

A man moves in front of her, blocking her view, so she in turn steps to the side. Her view now, though, is not clear to the stage, so she has to stand on tiptoe and peer over a sea of heads. She steps again to the side and somehow, she finds herself on the periphery of the crowd and much further away than before.

"Signorina?" A man is standing next to her; a short man, late–middle–aged, his hair sparse and untidy, his heavily–lidded eyes those of a lizard. "You are far too beautiful to be alone, permit me to–"

"I'm not alone," she states flatly, granting him only a flash of eye contact.

He makes the kind of play of looking round that one might expect from a mime artist. "Forgive me for my foolish intrusion, but a woman of such beauty should not remain unattended on an evening such as this, may I–"

"No," she says, this time very directly ignoring him.

"But, signorina, surely I–"

Now, she does turn; and she fixes him with a stare into which she pours all the hate and pain she has stored and locked away over the previous years.

"Now, signor, I'm not going to tell you again, so–"

"Is everything all right, Caterina? Here," Antonio says, "strawberry, isn't that what you asked for?"

However, she is so riled that she cannot at once alter the direction in which the heat of her anger is focussed.

Antonio is slow to catch on but when he does, he steps forward and the look on his face suggests he is not about to make a gift of either of his ice cream cones.

"You have me at a disadvantage, signor," he says, his tone half mocking, half threatening, "we have not been introduced." He turns and glances at Caterina, just to be certain that she does not know the man and he isn't, therefore, making some terrible mistake.

The lack of movement in her expression provides him with the answer.

He turns back to the man. "And please don't think me ungenerous, but it is not in my nature to buy strangers ice creams, so please leave us in peace to enjoy them."

The manner and measure of Antonio's politeness are not replicated or extended in the hardness of his look, for his eyes are wild with the promise of violence, so much so that even Caterina is intimidated.

"Big man, eh?" the little man hisses. "Big man in front of the woman." Slowly, he looks Antonio up and down. "I see you have bought her only a small ice cream cone, what's the matter, couldn't you afford a second scoop?"

Antonio turns and hands both the ice creams to Caterina.

People around them have taken notice of the change in the body language of the two men and they stand back to allow them room.

"Now, you listen to me," Antonio begins, balling his fists, "you know you can only fuck a cat once."

The little man glowers at him.

"Such language!" a new voice says. "And in front of women. Is there a problem here?"

Alberto has arrived, his whites still pin clean, and at his side, a member of the Policia Local so tall that it is not simply his uniform that lends him authority.

Outnumbered, the little man blanches and does not answer. He simply snarls, turns and disappears into the crowd.

"Antonio," the policeman says, his white teeth shining beneath his cap, his tone sprinkled with a mischievous levity, "causing trouble again?"

Before he can open his mouth, though, Caterina jumps in ahead of him.

"No, it wasn't Antonio's fault. It was that man: he wouldn't leave me alone."

"So," the policeman replies, "your prince charming came to your rescue. Good choice: that man would have been a fool to make anything more of it." He turns from her. "He must have come in from Catania, otherwise he would have known who he was dealing with, eh Antonio?" He turns back and looms over Caterina, "Oh, and by the way signora, I should hurry up and eat your ice cream before it melts."

———————

Their evening had finished on a pleasant, promising note. Once the unfortunate incident had been allowed time to disperse like a cloud that had on appearance promised rain, they had wandered casually amongst the festival revellers. In a side street, firecrackers had exploded in sporadic and sharp strings of percussion, street—sellers had lofted curiously fluorescent whirlybirds up into the night sky, magicians had picked coins from children's ears and in a small piazza a band playing live rock music had provoked the young and old to gyrate and swing. And when the smell of roasting almonds and caramel had drawn her to a stall, Antonio had insisted he buy her a cornet of torrente, warning her, as he probably must have warned Enzo when he was younger, to suck them until they had softened, lest she break her teeth.

In the car on the way home, Caterina and Antonio had sat in the back, and crammed as they were, with thigh touching thigh and shoulder pressed against shoulder, he had taken her hand and held it in his.

Caterina had not known quite how to react, for no one, absolutely no one, had held her hand for a very long time. And although his show of affection was a comfort; his proximity and his familiarity had represented a threshold that Caterina was aware she needed either to cross or stand back from. To leave her hand where it was, to squeeze his hand in return or just to look at him, would mean stepping over that threshold; an affirmation it would be difficult later to reverse, should she want to.

And Antonio had, through the hesitancy of her fingers and the tension in her knuckles and the tightness of her palm, sensed her confusion. So, in the slow stroboscope of the streetlights, he had smiled apologetically, let go of her hand and whispered that she might like to eat with him the next evening.

"Yes," she had heard herself reply, "I'd like that."

They'd dropped Antonio off at his place, a modest, middle-of-terrace house on the front near the breakwater in which the feluca is moored, and Alberto, moaning about how tired he was because he was no longer young enough to contend with two late nights in a row, had gone to bed.

"What did that policeman mean when he said the man must have come from out of town or he would have known who he was dealing with?" Caterina asks Angelica as, later, they sit in the kitchen drinking coffee.

"Nothing much. It is a figure of speech. Everything bad comes from either Catania or Palermo or any place that isn't Messina."

"A figure of speech," Caterina says, turning the clear and obvious deflection of an answer over in her mind. "No, I think he meant Antonio has something of a reputation. Does he?"

Angelica raises her hands, imploring. "Many of the fishermen have reputations for being tough; it is a tough business and not only because of the weather; they have to stand up to others who want a part or all of their business. The market is not a world for the timid, eh? And with Antonio? He has had his fair share of fools to deal with and many of the fishermen come to him for advice and help; he is good to people and for that reason some try to take advantage of him."

"Yes, so I gather. Paola told me he looks after Beppe and his sister. What a lovely lady Maria is."

"It is true: she knew our mother very well. The Sorbello family are our family through good times and bad."

"Angelica, what did Antonio mean when he said you can only fuck a cat once?"

She bursts out laughing, a long unrestricted and giggly laugh that infects Caterina and causes her to join in.

"Ah yes, a strange expression and one that should only be used as a last resort. It means that you can only make me look foolish once and after that, you will go where I send you."

"Send you?"

"Yes, most probably to your grave or, if you are lucky, to the hospital." She chuckles, then begins to laugh again, as though some second thought has occurred to her. "Your prince charming, wasn't that what the policeman called Antonio? Your prince charming." And they both split their sides and cover their mouths, concerned that they might wake the cockerel snoring upstairs.

CHAPTER 12

"What do you mean, where am I? I'm in Sicily, you know that." Caterina had woken and called Lucy.

"Yes, mum, I knew that. But where, where exactly in Sicily?" Her tone is that of a daughter exasperated.

The question, though, stops Caterina in her tracks; for the last time she'd spoken to Lucy, she'd avoided mentioning where she was. Then, she'd had no plans; now... "Well, I'm no longer in Taormina, if that's what you mean. I left. Felt I'd done the place. Loved it. Really, very beautiful. Just needed to move on, that was all."

"So I gather."

"What do you mean, so you gather?"

"Mum?" A daughter now offended.

"Yes, darling?" Caterina adopts an ignorance carefully positioned halfway between hauteur and plain deaf.

"I gather, because your phone has been off and I had to ring the hotel."

A lightly pregnant silence ensues until: "Casa Cuseni is not a hotel, darling; it's a B&B. And not only a B&B, a National Monument and museum, too."

"Mother?" Lucy's annoyance is rapidly developing into full–blown indignation.

"Thought you ought to know, that's all. Wouldn't want your friends thinking I was on the Grand Tour like some dowager duchess. Just saying, as you used to say."

"If only," Lucy scoffs. "Getting you to spend money on yourself, now that would be a first. No, what I meant was, when I phoned the B&B," she emphasizes both Bs, "they said you'd checked out and it would've been nice if you'd let me know when and where you were going. And another thing, mother—"

Caterina steels herself.

"—when we spoke last week, it would've been only fair for you to tell me you were no longer in Taormina. Strange as it may seem, mum, I do worry about you." She pauses for a second. "Or would it sound better to you, if I said I love you and care about you and that's why I worry."

The winds of anger having spilled from Lucy's sail; her raw emotion, her acute articulation of her emotions, catches Caterina off balance.

"Just as I worry about you. And I do care about you and love you; it's just that... Look, what have you been up to? Plenty of summer parties at home while you've had the house to yourself? It's been very hot here, though I understand you've had a fair bit of rain. Still, the garden must be looking wonderful. The cosmos should be out by now and—"

"Don't change the subject, mum; we were talking about you not me. Why do you always have to do that? The moment anyone asks about you, you flip the conversation on its head and start talking about them." Her tone is now soft, worn down, a shade pleading, as though Lucy is no longer content to engage in her mother's preferred ping–pong dialogue. "So please, mum, where are you? And I don't care if you're staying in the most expensive or, come to think of it, the cheapest B&B in Sicily but, for my sake, for my peace of mind, please mum, please tell me where the bloody hell you've got to?"

Another silence, one more heavily pregnant.

Caterina clears her throat and assumes her most reasoning tone. "Lucy, what I am going to say, it's not easy for me but I've thought about it a lot. Actually, I've thought about it, strange as it may sound, very deeply and... I don't want you to jump at what I'm going to say, so... please hear me through, that's all. Listen until I've finished and then you can tell me I'm being stupid, or that I'm still trapped in one of those stages of grief all my friends seem to be so keen on telling me about, but...

"Look, I found I'd had enough of being on my own in Taormina. I was beginning to find my own company rather boring, and everywhere I went, in the reflection from every shop window, in the bathroom mirror, in every empty chair in every restaurant and café I sat down in, I saw your father. Even though I'd gone there to remember our wonderful holiday together, you know, that last wonderful holiday before he was... was diagnosed... Well, instead of helping, I found it all rather depressing."

She pauses, expecting Lucy to interrupt. When she doesn't, she asks, "Are you there, darling?"

"Yes, mum." She replies, her voice brittle.

"I know this is hard, darling. Believe me, I'm sorry, I know it's hard; I've had plenty of time to think about it, perhaps too long, I don't know."

"It's okay, mum, go on."

"Do you remember that chum of your father's... Oh, what was his name? Saul or Simon or something. The one who became an alcoholic... about eight or nine years ago... your father helped get him into that clinic, do you remember?"

"Stephen," Lucy corrects, then sniffs.

"Yes, quite right, it was Stephen. Anyway, after he came out of the clinic, Stephen came to dinner with us and he talked about all he'd been through. I remember he said to us that an alcoholic on his own is an alcoholic in the worst possible company. At the time,

528

it struck me as the strangest thing to say, as I'd always assumed that the worst place for an alcoholic to be was in the company of another alcoholic. But he was right, he'd learned what we all learn and that is that when you are on your own, your problem – alcohol or drugs or depression, or whatever – becomes your only companion and the two of you become co–dependent and before you know it, inseparable."

Lucy blows her nose. Her mother waits.

"You see, that's what coming here has made me realise," she continues. "It wasn't the fault of my being in Taormina and yet in a curious way, it was. I thought by going there I might understand why I've been so depressed, when all along it was, in some part, that last holiday with your father which was making me feel so… so… so perfectly wretched. I thought I wanted to remember the good times, when all the time it was the memories that were making me miss what I have lost… what we have lost. I hope I'm making sense, Lucy, am I? Please tell me I am?"

A sniff, a half–stifled or at least a barely–concealed snivel. "Yes, mum. Yes, you are making complete sense. In fact, that's the most sense you have made in a very long time. Trouble is, I don't like to think you've been through all that on your own: it seems like an awful lot of pain for you to endure all by yourself."

"Yes, darling, it was; except I wasn't on my own, was I? I had you and your father with me all the time. Just because you're not here, doesn't mean to say I don't carry you with me wherever I go. Same thing with your father: he may be gone and I miss him so much it hurts like hell, but I haven't forgotten him, I never will."

"Mum," Lucy says, a note of both query and gentle empathy in her tone, "you sound different."

"In what way different, darling?"

"I don't know, just different. You sound like you're in a good place, like you've found something." She pauses, clearly trying to place what or where that something is. "You haven't gone and joined some happy–clappy cult, have you?" She laughs, nervous of her mother's response.

"No, darling. I've simply met some very nice people who would appear to be happy to have me as their houseguest. I can't stay forever, naturally, so I'll be back soon."

"When though, mum? When will you be back?"

"Oh, I'm not sure. I haven't thought about when. I guess I'll know in the next couple of days. And I mustn't outstay my welcome; fish and houseguests and all that."

"Fish and what?"

"Yes, darling, fish: they're like houseguests; if you have them in the house too long, they go off – and it is pretty hot here. So, as I said, I won't be outstaying my welcome."

"Mum?"

"Yes, darling."

"This is the most I can ever remember you using the word I; it's like you've woken up and remembered that you do really exist. Are you sure you're not at some kind of funny farm?"

"Yes, darling Lucy, perfectly sure. By the way, I meant to ask how Rob is; last time you sounded a bit down about him. You said he might come and stay while I was away. Don't worry, I don't mind him being with you in the house; as I said, you two have been together for quite a while now."

"Three years last weekend."

"That long? Congratulations, darling. Do give him my best."

"Your best," she repeats as though her best is not by any means adequate and her love would have been more appropriate. "One last thing, mum."

"Go on, what have or haven't I done now?"

"It's not you, mum; it's me. I've got some news."

"News? Well, good news, I hope. House in one piece, is it?"

"Of course."

"You're not—"

"Mum!"

"Sorry. Silly of me. Go on then."

Lucy huffs down the phone. "No, mother. I'd rather tell you in person. It'll wait until you get back."

"Oh, don't be a spoilsport. What is it, please, darling? What news?"

Whatever the carrot she dangled; Lucy quickly removes it. "Mum, these people you're staying with, what's their name?"

Now it is Caterina's turn to huff. "You're not going to tell me your news, are you? Oh, you are so like your father." She looks at her free hand, noticing that without thinking she is gesticulating with it, waving it around in appeal in exactly the same manner as those she'd seen on their phones last night at the festival and before that on the beach and in the cafés. Caterina grins, blushes and drops her hand to her lap. "Still, no reason why you shouldn't be like him and in the long run no bad thing.

"So, if you must know, Lucy, I'm staying with Signor and Signora Lazzarotto in a small village just to the north of Messina called Ganzirri. I haven't committed myself to some ultra–religious, navel–gazing, colonic irrigation glorying, twenty–four–seven chanting, idol–worshipping sect; I'm simply spending a few days with a couple of charmingly generous people, who would appear to enjoy, or more accurately suffer, my company. Is that so hard to believe?"

Angelica smiles. "Good morning, Caterina, I hope you slept well."

"I did, thank you. I had hoped to go for the day on the feluca, but I overslept. First time I've done that in ages."

"Oh, I wouldn't worry. The sleep has done you good and I doubt they will be out for long. Here, a coffee. And I have made bread." She nods at the counter. "Mafalda with sesame seeds. I hoped the smell would tempt you from your room."

"It did, and I'd have been down sooner, only I was speaking to my daughter. Why won't they be out for long?"

Angelica purses her lips and frowns a little disconsolately. "Oh, today we will have rain and for the fish, the noise of rain on the surface is like the banging of a drum; it frightens them and they go to the bottom. How was your daughter?"

"Lucy?" she asks, as though she has a bagful of daughters one of whom happens to be called by that name. "Oh, she was okay. I woke her up; clean forgot there's an hour's time difference and that she's twenty–five and home alone." Caterina pauses in lifting the small cup to her lips. "Or probably not, as it happens."

"A boyfriend?"

"Yes. Do you know, I can't work out whether he's highly intelligent or not all there."

Angelica hesitates. "Not all there?"

"Yes. You know, one olive short of a pizza."

"Ah, yes, I understand. Perhaps it is better for her if he isn't so smart."

Caterina chuckles. "No, I was being facetious; he's very bright really. And very nice. It's more that I was wondering what he sees in Lucy."

"Mothers and daughters! Now you know why I had sons, eh." Angelica grins. "Their women can only be more intelligent than they are and it helps to understand the beast in them. So, how is she, your daughter? Is she missing her mother?"

The coffee is strong; her senses blossom. "Mm, judging by the number of times she says she's tried to call me, the novelty of having the house to herself is wearing off and as she hadn't heard from me, she was concerned I might have gone off and joined the Hare Krishna. I can't say I haven't thought about it once or twice; they always seem so blissfully happy."

"If it looks too good to be true…" Angelica begins.

"It usually is. Yes, I know." Caterina finishes her coffee, leans her elbow on the table and plants her chin on the edge of her palm. Her eyes glaze over and thoughtfully, and with a certain reluctant and yet inevitable tone, she says, "That was one of my…"

"What was his name, your husband?"

"Charles, though he hated being called that: I suppose that's a bit like Lucy calling me mother rather than mum. When she uses mother, it means I'm bound to have done something she doesn't like. That was the way I was with Charlie. Always Charlie: only Charles when he'd done something to annoy me — which he rarely did." She glances at Angelica.

"Yes, I am listening. Please, go on."

"What was he like? That's what you want to know, isn't it?"

Angelica smiles. "Yes, good. Now you are beginning to think for yourself; I am pleased. So, what was your Charlie like?"

Caterina smiles in return and the look on her face tells a plain and pleasant story, that of a soul who, for the first time in a very long time, is remembering how to smile.

"Oh, he was as good a husband as a woman could ask for, Angelica. He was that and so much more."

Chapter 13

"It is very good of you to come and collect me, Enzo."

"This is my very great pleasure, Signora Caterina. My father said you would know where he lives, but the rain..." He raises his hand at the grey, drizzling sky as if it is to blame for all the ills inflicted on the village over the last three thousand years.

"Well, thank you. I don't suppose your father would have appreciated it if I'd turned up looking like a drowned rat."

He glances at her hair and shrugs. "The weather shows no respect, eh, and your hair looks very nice."

She had been to a hairdresser in the village. Angelica had suggested it and Caterina had told her in no uncertain terms that she felt more than a little silly having her hair done when all she was doing was going to Antonio's house for something to eat. "And don't tell me you and Alberto wouldn't like an evening to yourself?" she had suggested.

Angelica, however, had ignored her and insisted. "It is about time you spent some money on yourself."

Had Lucy not said something similar only a few hours before?

"You will feel good, too." And because Angelica had gone with her and sat in the background and dictated the styling, Caterina did feel good about herself. Good if not better than good; for although her hair was now longer than it had been for a few years, she could never have imagined that it would cascade around her shoulders in such languid, lengthy curls.

"Thank you, Enzo, that is very charming of you."

"It is true, eh?"

"You are eating with us, aren't you?" she asks.

"No, I am going out with Paola; we are going to see friends in Milazzo. My father said I could have the car if I came to pick you up."

"Ah, I see," she says, vaguely offended.

He glances at her once more as he spins the steering wheel first left and then right. "No, you don't." He grins. "That was simply my humour."

When he parks outside the house, Enzo asks her to wait while he retrieves his umbrella from the back seat and rushes round to open her door.

"Quite the gentleman," she notes.

"Quite the lady. Enjoy your evening."

She expects him to wink or leave her with some knowing look, but he doesn't; he simply knocks on the door, waits until his father opens it and then jumps back in the car and speeds off.

"He really is a credit to you. You've taught him well."

"Not me. And not his mother. Paola perhaps. Come in." Antonio stands back and cannot hide his surprise at how she looks. "You look... different."

"According to my daughter, I sound different, too. Anyway, I'll take the fact that you think I look different as a compliment; though I guess that means I must have looked something less than that last night."

"No, that was not what I meant. Last night you looked–"

"Thank you, Antonio. Go easy on me, please. Compliments from both father and son and I might not know which to choose."

"Oh, I see." His face darkens in a frown.

"No, you don't. That is simply my humour. Come on, let's not stand on ceremony."

"No, of course." Yet he fails to move.

"Well, I don't have a coat or a handbag, so I can't give you either of those." She looks him up and down, and waits. "Antonio, why don't we have a drink, then you can tell me about your day and I'll tell you about mine?"

His stupor, her thrall over him or possibly the novelty of introducing someone completely new, and a woman at that, to his house, eventually wears off. "Yes, I have some almond wine, Il Blandanino, Riserva Speciale. Have you tried it before? It is from Castelmola."

"No, I don't believe I have. Sounds lovely."

The living room is not exactly expansive: another three of Antonio's build, either seated or standing, and there would be no space left for either Enzo or the tortoiseshell cat, which studiously ignores her. However, there is a distinct lack of clutter such as she would expect to see in a modest house lived in by two men; a house which some might label a bachelor pad. There are none of yesterday's papers, no casually–tossed clothes or shoes, and nothing that one might expect to see in the home of a fisherman either; no coils of line, no netting, no boxes of hooks or harpoons, and no sea shells decorating the walls. Instead, and much to her surprise, the room is painted a light pastel cream and the floors carpeted in a similar shade; a deep–red sofa and two fabric easy chairs dominate, a music system and a rack of cds stands in one corner, and the most glaringly obvious, and to her mind fabulous, omission is that of a television.

Caterina slips off her shoes.

"There's no need to…"

"Oh, but there is," she says.

The almond wine is both rich and bitter, suffused with herbs and yet sharp with citrus.

"What are we eating?" she asks, sipping, following him into the kitchen.

"I will give you three guesses, though I think you will only need one."

"Fish of the day?"

"Exactly."

"Angelica thought you might not catch anything today. She said the rain would drive the fish to the bottom."

Antonio unwraps a parcel of brown wax paper. "And she is right: when the rains come, the fish go. This one we caught before the rain."

In the now unfolded paper lie two thick swordfish steaks.

"And you kept some for yourself."

"Of course . As you saw on Saturday, when we have caught the swordfish a man comes to meet us with his dinghy and he takes it ashore. From there it goes either to the market or directly to the fishmonger; which one depends on the price offered. Also as you saw, because I am up above the fish when I throw, the lance drives into the back of the fish and this part is always removed and given back to us. It is another of our old traditions, a measure of respect and one that ensures the fisherman does not go hungry for his effort."

"Ah, I wondered about that when I was walking by the lake with Beppe. In one of the fishmongers, I noticed the swordfish on his counter had a neat section cut out of its back. Also, I couldn't see where the harpoon had struck the fish; there didn't seem to be any mark or wound. Now, it all makes sense."

"I hope you are hungry. Would you like to make the salad?"

"Sure, whatever I can do to help."

"Good. There you have tomatoes, cucumber, red onions, olives, celery. Here is the knife; a sharp knife, eh? And over there is the oil and vinegar, salt and pepper."

Caterina smiles. "How are you going to cook the swordfish, Antonio? A recipe handed down from generation to generation; one kept secret on pain of death?"

He laughs, generously. "No, it is no secret. Only a complete idiot could make swordfish inedible. Enzo and me, we like to keep our cooking simple: a sauce of parsley, garlic sliced thin, salt, pepper, lemon juice and white wine. Grill the fish for five minutes, add the sauce and grill for another five. See what I mean? Only a complete idiot..."

"No such thing as a bad cook, Antonio, only bad ingredients." Caterina sets to slicing the vegetables. "When I was watching the fishmonger, I noticed he was butterflying small fish to order. Sauri negri I think they were called."

He nods. "Sauri negri: silver with blue and green on the top, like a small mackerel you would say."

"Yes. Only he was dropping the guts and the spine of the fish into a bucket, which I assumed he was going to throw away until an old man came in and bought them. Were the bones for his cat?"

Antonio shakes his head. "No, not for his cat, for him. You see, it doesn't matter how precise the fishmonger is in cleaning the sauri, there is always some meat left on the bones. The old man would have taken them home and boiled them with garlic, vinegar and mint: boiling them makes the meat that is left fall away from the bone, so it is easier to pick out and eat, and with what is left he makes a soup. We use every part of the fish, even the parts of the fish many people would throw away."

They sit at his kitchen table and the swordfish tastes so very different from the swordfish she buys in her local supermarket back in... in England; for though the steak is thick, firm and fleshy, it is so much lighter and more succulent.

"It is fresh, eh?" Antonio says, as he notices her eyes close in appreciation.

"Isn't it just. I had no idea."

And when he nods in approval of her salad, Caterina cannot hold the colour of her pleasure from rising to her cheeks.

They talk, what about she does not remember later, and there are no uncomfortable pauses or silences while they wander from one topic of conversation to the next; they seem to flow with each other in easy and all directions, like the changing tides of the Strait, except without their negative influence.

She watches him as he explains about how, in the days of his grandfather when their boats were without engines, the fishermen would tow the fulue, the larger of the two boats Beppe had shown her by the lagoon, out to their posts in the Strait, where they would station them: i terra those near the Sicilian shore, i fora those near the Calabrian and i menzu those in between. The lookouts, the avvistatore, would then climb the tall masts, much as Giuseppe and Pasquale do every day, and spot the swordfish, directing the smaller boats, the luntri, towards them.

Antonio is patient with his explanation and Caterina is a ready and perhaps, given her days on the feluca, attentive listener.

"How do they manage to spend all day perched so high up on that tiny platform?" she asks.

Except for his chin, which is a little angular in its curve, Antonio's face is quite square and very evenly proportioned; for while his cheekbones are prominent, they are no more prominent than his nose or his forehead. He has shaved the stubble from his chin, a small detail, yet a detail that earlier in the day she had caught herself wondering about; wondering whether he would, for her. And she is glad he has, because his skin is coloured the deep brown of mahogany and his complexion is smooth as if polished by one of the cotton wool clouds that float above Aspromonte. Yet it is his eyes that draw hers: the blue is remarkable, mesmerising, spellbinding and at times Caterina has to look away because she knows she is staring.

539

"If I am honest, I don't know," he replies. "Only a brave man or a fool would pass his days up there in all the heat. There are days it is so hot that when Pasquale comes down, I think he will have shrunk and be half the man he was when he climbed up in the morning. Imagine, six o'clock in the morning until nine o'clock at night: fifteen hours." He shakes his head in disbelief. "All I know for certain is that I could not do this. Sure, the pressure on me to hit my mark is great, but to take the risks that Pasquale takes day in day out is beyond reason. Perhaps we are lucky he is so mad. Perhaps one day I will see his body fly from the top of the tower and crash into the sea. I don't know: he is mad, quite mad."

"Has a woman ever climbed to the top?"

"A woman? Why would she? In fact, why would anyone, doesn't matter if they are a woman or a man... why would anyone if they didn't have to?"

"Beats me, Antonio. You wouldn't catch me up there if the many–headed monster was chasing me. Can I do the dishes?"

He looks at her, quizzically. "Why? Do you have to go so soon?"

Caterina laughs but, as she sweeps the hair from her face, she is careful not to let him think she is laughing at him. "No, I just thought you might like me to do the clearing up seeing as you went to the trouble of catching and cooking the fish. Why don't you put some music on; music you like."

"Oh, the music is mostly Enzo's."

"Mostly," she says, smiling playfully, "means not all." The cat follows her into the kitchen and is rewarded for its patience with the morsel of swordfish she has kept aside expressly for the purpose. "What is your cat's name?" she calls.

"Aida," he replies.

"As in the opera?"

"Exactly. Not my choice, Enzo's."

"Why Aida?"

"We had a tomcat. He appeared on the doorstep and laid claim to us; quite the warrior, he was. At the time, Enzo was dating a girl who liked opera; she named him Radames. Well, we didn't know what his name was, did we? Then one day, Radames brought his girlfriend home with him, so it was only natural we named her Aida."

"What happened to Radames?"

"Oh, a big fight one night. I think he took a beating and his ego never recovered. You know, old lions and young lions. Besides, we had no way of knowing how old he was when he adopted us."

A delicate and curiously lilting medieval folk tune, a variation of a slow Tarantella played on a lazy mandolin, floats like the vapours of a soothing drug.

As she dries her hands, Aida stares up at her. "So," her eyes say, "you've finished the dishes. What are you waiting for? Go and join him on the sofa."

"That's easy for you to say," Caterina mutters.

She settles a little awkwardly beside Antonio, but not too close. "I... Well, I... Thank you for dinner," she says, her words strung together in a flat, rather formal manner.

"I make you nervous?" he asks, half statement, half question.

His candour catches her unprepared and she sits up, leans her elbows on her knees and looks sideways, slightly over her shoulder, at him. "Yes."

Caterina pauses, buying time by studying the glass of wine in her hand. "And no. No, Antonio, you don't make me nervous; I think I manage that all on my own." She pauses again and turns back to look very directly at him. "And yet, in a curious way, you do. Or maybe it's not you, maybe it's us, you and me sitting here. Maybe it's simply the idea of me sitting alone with you, a man, any man... Please don't take that the wrong way; I don't mean any man, I mean... It's just the whole idea of it, of you, of us. I haven't been out to dinner or sat like this talking with a man who isn't a family friend since... well, since my husband died. You must have felt this way after your wife deserted you and Enzo, so I guess you know how I feel."

"Yes." And that is all he says as he sits and watches her; a hunter once wounded by his own harpoon; a man unwilling to reveal the extent of the pain the wound caused him.

"Yes?" she repeats. "Just yes, nothing else?"

"Yes, it is no surprise and no, you should not be nervous. Did you not look in the mirror before you came out this evening? Did you not see the new Caterina, your hair, what the sun has done for you, how your eyes shine? If I did not know you came from England, I would think you were Messinese."

She delivers Antonio a knowing look, not cynical, not unforgiving, just knowing that if he does not want to talk about himself, then she is not inclined to talk about herself, either. "Perhaps I am, who knows?"

Her glass is empty: he refills it, returns to sit down and waits, expecting.

"Two years before my husband died, not long before he was diagnosed..." A thought creeps up and startles her. "Or maybe he already knew he was ill, I don't know. Anyway, we went to stay in Taormina; a holiday, a short break. God knows, there was never such a thing as a long holiday, not with Charlie. He'd get fidgety after a day by a pool; he bored easily; always wanted to be out and about, seeing this, playing that; never sat down. I sometimes wondered whether he revolved more relentlessly than the planet." She sips her wine and stares into the distance. "We were in Taormina and I went to one of the churches, the Santa Caterina. Well, I would, wouldn't I?

"We stayed at Casa Cuseni, did all the things tourists do; you know, strolled up and down the corso, saw the amphitheatre, dined al fresco. But two things stuck with me: one, we went down to the beach by Isola Bella and two, I went on the tour and learned all about Robert Kitson and Carlo and how they'd adopted a child from the ruins of the Messina. But both of them reminded me of my nonna's story: you see, after the earthquake, my grandmother, who was only fifteen at the time, was found in an aid station by a woman who had been nursing an English lady at Isola Bella. My nonna's family had all been killed, so this woman took my nonna back to England with her, which is where she grew up and married." Caterina silences, thinks for a moment and then turns back to him. "So, when you say I could be mistaken for a Messinese I'm not surprised, because not only am I one quarter Sicilian, when I learnt all about Casa Cuseni and remembered my nonna, I felt as though in some way I'd come back to a beginning."

"And that," Antonio says, taking what she has told him one step further, "is why you speak Sicilian like a Messinese."

"Yes, although I learnt as much from my father as I did from Nonna Lilla."

"Nonna Lilla," he repeats, frowning in thought, "and your father."

"Yes. He spoke Sicilian, too. He told me Nonna Lilla always spoke to him in Sicilian whenever she didn't want others to know what she was saying."

"Tell me about him, your father. Is he still alive?"

"No. As I told you, my father died the same year as Nonna Lilla, when I was only eleven. He was blinded during the war and I'm not sure he ever truly recovered. He met my mother while he was in hospital; she was his nurse. I'm not sure that I was planned, if you know what I mean by that."

His expression suggests he doesn't.

"Well, my mother was a fair bit younger than him and he was in his fifties by the time I came along. I sometimes wonder whether it was my mother who wanted me perhaps more than my father. She told me that it was while he was serving in Sicily that he lost his sight; he was badly burned about his face and his lungs were damaged. I remember him as a slightly sad figure."

"He was here in Sicily?"

"Yes, so she told me. He was in the navy and his boat was sunk, though I never remember him talking about it. I was probably too young to understand and you know what that generation was like; getting them to talk about their experiences was like trying to open a tin with your bare hands."

"What was his name?"

"Nicholas, Nicholas Vincent Lock."

Antonio looks up at the ceiling and rubs his lip with his fingers.

Caterina waits, patiently. "Why do you ask?"

He lowers his head and rubs his hands lightly together. "Oh, no reason. It was only that my mother told me that one night not long before the British and Americans came to Messina, she and her father and mother watched a ship sink out in the Strait. She said a British naval officer was rescued by an Italian sailor and that they cared for the man until the Germans had gone back to Calabria." Antonio returns his attention to remembering.

"I doubt that was anything to do with my father: with his wounds, he must have required considerable medical care. And besides, I would imagine there were many ships lost to the waters of the Strait during the war."

"Yes, many ships and many lives. You should ask Beppe; he may remember such things. He was only a boy at the time, but the old man has an encyclopaedic knowledge and, when it comes to the Strait, the most extraordinary memory. I sometimes wonder if he doesn't remember exactly where the pebbles were fifty years ago."

Aida sits at her feet, watching her, asking in that way polite cats ask, if she can sit on the sofa or perhaps on her lap.

Caterina smiles, pats her thigh and Aida pauses, decides, climbs stealthily, turns about, settles and purrs.

Antonio smiles. "A fisherman's cat knows who to love, eh?" He pauses; his half–taken breath, his hesitation, the way he dips his head slightly before returning his gaze to her, suggests he is steeling himself to ask an awkward question.

In turn, she rounds her shoulders and looks away as though she knows perfectly what he is about to ask and would prefer he didn't.

"Caterina, you said you went to Taormina before your husband was... was diagnosed: please tell me, what happened to him? Tell me about him. You don't speak of him and if I am to know you, it is better that you tell me rather than allow his memory to come between us."

She opens her mouth to reply, but finds she has not yet thought how to answer such a question. Blood surges to her face like a red fountain gushing up through thick fog, a jet of thick and powerful liquid that blasts aside her every effort to suppress it. Her breath comes in rapid, short, sharp bursts as though she is about to hyperventilate and the heat in her cheeks is hot to her touch when she puts her hands up to hide her face.

"And what about your wife?" she asks, through her hands. "You never use her name when you speak of her; you always refer to her as Enzo's mother. Is she a ghost? Doesn't she have a name? Or is it that you cannot bring yourself to say it?"

Antonio, though, is calm in the face of her storm; in fact so calm is he that it seems he has predicted the sudden gathering of her clouds and has reefed his sail in preparation for her tempest.

"Vanaria," he says. "That is her name. You would have thought I should have known things were not going to work out with her. After all, she is as her name suggests, Vana, vain through and through. Or perhaps that was what drew me towards her, her vanity." He scoffs, casually, as if he has consigned a distasteful fruit to a hedgerow. "I should have seen it; she was always dressed in a fashion that spoke to the lion in men. And me, a fisherman! Oh, don't worry; many people warned me, people like Beppe and

Angelica and some of my friends, even those who could never shift their eyes from her." He pauses, a half–smile, resigned, possibly a little self–pitying or critical of his own naïvety.

"Vanaria," he says her name again, so that she will be certain he has no issue with saying it, "was my wife; I sent her away or she left me, it makes little difference–" Antonio stops in mid–sentence. "No, I am wrong; it makes all the difference: it was a decision we made, together, and she is no longer my wife. Your husband was taken from you and so he will always be your husband. He will always be with you."

Aida, growing aware of the hardening in the supple contours of her lap, raises her head, concerned.

Caterina stares back at Antonio and though to some small degree they are tinted with regret, her eyes now blaze with the sun of her anger. "Yes, Antonio, you are so right. You are so perfectly, so bloody absolutely and so terribly righteously right."

Realising that Caterina has not finished or is perhaps only just getting started, Aida rises, stretches and leaps down, only to stand and stare at her.

"And that's the problem, isn't it, Antonio. That's the problem. For whatever I do or wherever I go, I can never get away from him, my husband, Charlie: get away from him or from the memory of how he died, how he was taken from me and how I failed him. I guess," she says, looking down at the gold band of her wedding ring, "I'll just have to put up with the burden of that knowledge until God decides to relieve me of it, in just the same way he woke up one morning and decided to ruin my life by taking Charlie away from me."

Chapter 14

She leans against the upturned hull of a dinghy and gazes at the line of feluche and their tall towers reaching up to the powder–blue sky. The bakers had been open and the woman behind the counter had smiled and without asking had handed her a brioche, a bag of almond biscuits and a bottle of water.

Waiting, plagued by doubts, chased by her fears and humbled by her outburst, Caterina gazes out across the calm of the sea.

Pasquale is first. He greets her, though it is perhaps too early to smile. Then Giuseppe appears and not far behind him the young Ninolino and Karl. And even though she looks to have brought her provisions for the day, they know better than to ask her if she is coming with them, for that decision is not theirs to make. "Good morning, signora. Good morning. A nice morning. I hope you slept well."

"Thank you, I did," she lies.

The rain has moved on north to the coast of Amalfi, leaving in its wake cooler, clearer air.

The door to Antonio's house, opens and father and son emerge. They are respectfully quiet in closing it behind them. Why wouldn't they be? Just because their day is beginning, they see no need to wake their neighbours.

Caterina watches them, traces of guilt lingering in her expression.

When, at last, the evening before, her shoulders had ceased to heave with her sobbing and she had all too gracelessly blown her nose and dried her eyes, she had of course apologised.

"You have no need to apologise to me," Antonio had said, so softly, so comfortingly, so touchingly that she had burst once more into a flood of tears. He had waited patiently for her to regain her composure, before taking her in his arms and gently but firmly resting her head on his shoulder. "You have only yourself to apologise to."

"To blame, you mean."

"No." And he had squeezed her tenderly. "There is no one to blame. Not you, not God and certainly not those who have been taken. Our life is ours to live, not ours to regret."

When she had calmed, Antonio had insisted on walking her home. The rain had stopped and even though she was no more than ten minutes from Angelica's house, he would not hear of her walking alone at night. "You could stay," he'd added, casually, as if it was an afterthought rather than an invitation he'd been working towards.

"Oh, Antonio," she'd replied, mustering a weak and rather watery smile. "Please believe me when I say I so wanted to; I was so ready to. Really, I was. But I feel so perfectly bloody useless, which is ridiculous, because I've been feeling so much better about myself, about everything and about you." She'd blown her nose again and he'd waited patiently, again; and Caterina had realised that his patience was as much a fundamental part of his nature as was his son, the boat and the Strait. "I mean that, Antonio: I was feeling so much better. But the thought that spending the night with you might end in disaster – not because of you, because of me – frightens the hell out of me."

"Yes," he'd said. "Me, also."

She'd sat back from him and gazed at him in astonishment. "Really? Seriously? But you're so... so confident all the time. You always know what to do; how can anything frighten you?"

He'd breathed deep and sighed. "Oh, one is forever frightened of the unknown. It doesn't matter if one is a child or an adult."

And he had walked her back through the narrow lanes and alleys, past the cats goading each other from the security of their steps, and she had clung to his muscular arm. At the door, she had offered her lips for him to kiss, but he hadn't; he'd simply kissed her forehead, then turned and walked back down the cobbled lane.

Now, both Antonio and Enzo notice her and the son makes an aside to which the father nods in reply.

The crew busy themselves with the dinghy, which they then drag across the wooden blocks down to the water's edge.

Caterina stands up.

"Are you sure you want to come?" Antonio asks her. "Today will be hot. You may not think so now, but later..." he shakes his hand as if drying it.

"Are you sure you want me to?" And she waits for his eyes to answer her question.

"Good," he confirms. "Today we will catch fish."

———

The crew seem pleased to have her company and Ninolino and Karl make a particular fuss of her, wiping down her chair with a clean cloth and positioning it at the base of the tower before inviting her to sit.

Pasquale climbs up onto the roof of the cabin, crosses himself and begins the dizzying climb, hand over hand, foot over foot, smoothly and steadily up to the platform. When he has unlatched the access hatch, he disappears and Giuseppe follows him up.

Caterina cranes her head and watches them, in awe of their courage.

"A long way, eh?" Enzo says as he ties to the line the plastic bags filled with hats, sunglasses, food and water, and runs them up.

"Have you been up there?" she asks.

"Yes, of course. One has to."

The engines rumble, the lines are cast off and the Salvazione motors from behind the safety of the breakwater out into the Strait.

One by one the other feluche slip their moorings and head out, each one peeling off either south or north to patrol their allotted stations.

"My father thinks we will do better out in the open water beyond Scylla. Perhaps we will come back here this afternoon."

The moisture in the air is soon evaporated by the sun climbing above the heights of Aspromonte; however, the breeze born of their progress serves to temper the heat.

By the time the sun has reached its zenith, Giuseppe has spotted, Pasquale has driven, Antonio has harpooned and Enzo, Ninolino and Karl have landed five swordfish. They are not large, but they are mature; their dorsal fins, as Enzo explains to her, being high and short, not long and slender like the sails of immature fish. And judging by the way the boys smile at her, offer her water, ask if she's not too hot and tell her that if she is, they can rig up a sheet to provide her with shade, they are coming to view her as a good luck charm.

The five fish, covered by a breathable sheet and blankets which Enzo keeps saturated with regular douses of water, lie side by side on a pallet at the base of the tower, so they have placed her white chair out of the way on the roof of the cabin.

"You don't gut the fish?" she asks.

He shakes his head. "No, they go to the market whole. I understand that in America, they clean the fish as soon as they have taken it out of the water, but this would be to disrespect the fish and it is not our way."

"Is that a good catch, five fish?"

"It is, though some days we catch ten or perhaps twelve and then on others nothing. When the Sciroccu blows we catch fish, and today the wind begins to blow."

The feluca has turned onto a heading towards Capo Peloro, the mountains of Nebrodi rising off to their right.

"We are going back?"

"Yes," Enzo replies, his leg bent at the knee, his foot resting on the gunwale. "We will unload them and they will be in the market ready for this evening. It is not just the timing; in this heat it is better they don't stay too long in the sun and on the boat. As you have learned, there is no shade. Do you have enough sun cream Signora Caterina? It is good you have brought a hat."

"Thank you, Enzo, I do; though as far as my hat goes, it does the job even if I feel a little ridiculous having to tie it on. Is it all right if I sit up on the roof of the cabin?"

He shrugs. "Oh yes. My father will come up and talk with you; there is no point in him being at the far end of the passerelle when the feluca is making this speed. Here, I will help you."

Caterina, with a helping hand, makes it up onto the roof and sits in her chair, and soon enough, Antonio has made his way aft and climbed up to relax beside her.

"A good day," she says. But the wind catches her words and bears them away.

Antonio looks up at her, arching an eyebrow in question.

"I said, you seem to be having a good day," she repeats, raising her voice just shy of a shout.

"Yes. We will stay in the Strait this afternoon; there will be more."

They watch Ninolino and Karl re-coiling the ropes and washing down the deck. They glance up at the two on the roof of the cabin and exchange knowing looks before laughing, though not unkindly.

551

"The boys," Antonio says, nodding his head in their direction, "they think this is some kind of date."

She waits, before replying, "Isn't it? I get the feeling you don't take too many women passengers on your feluca."

He nods his head from side to side: he cannot use his hands to show her that he is considering his response, as he is sitting back, his weight on his arms. "On occasion. We have tourists, mostly Americans, they pay well to come for a day with us and once they have understood that this is not America and that we do not have a bathroom or a medical facility on board, they usually have a good time."

"Do they ever ask to climb the 'ntinna?"

"A few."

"What about health and safety?"

"I told you already," he says, chuckling, "I tell them we have no toilet and no hospital on board, and that if they fall down into the sea, there is no point in coming back to the surface, for we will not be able to bring them back to life."

"Antonio?"

Because she is sitting up in her chair with the sun above and to the side of her, he has to turn his head and look up at her. Closing one eye he winks with the other.

"You're joking. Yes. Of course, I–"

"No. I don't want to hear any more of your apologies."

The essence of what he has just said and the way he has assembled his words, could so easily be misconstrued. However, his tone suggests it isn't that he is fed up with her seemingly constant need to apologise; rather it is that he thinks it would be better for her, as opposed to him, if she didn't.

"And I wasn't going to. No, what I wanted to say was how much I enjoyed last night and I wanted to thank you for your understanding and for allowing me back on the Salvazione, that's all, nothing more."

He looks up again. "That's all? Minchia!" he says. "I believe that is enough, eh?"

"Minchia," she repeats. "I remember my father saying that once when he touched a hot mug of tea. What does it mean?"

Antonio chuckles again. "It is a statement, a frustration, an expression, a way of swearing, like cock or prick; only neither of those things and yet both of them. It is not a polite term for a woman to use."

"Oh, okay. I'll try not to."

He smiles. "Good. Now, you must be careful of the heat; up here you will not notice your sunburn because you feel cool. I will get you some water."

"Antonio?"

"Yes."

"I have decided something."

"Yes, and what is that?"

"I'm not going to feel guilty ever again. It's time for me to change. I've realised I'm not useless and I want to thank you for—"

A noise from above distracts them and Antonio gets down off the roof.

Giuseppe has opened the trapdoor in the base of the platform and is making his way down the tower.

Caterina watches, counting his steps, learning that he never allows himself to be attached to the metal frame by less than either both of his feet and one hand or both of his hands and one foot. He is not tied to any safety rope and if he slips and falls, there is nothing to keep him from plummeting to the deck or, if he is lucky, into the sea. There are also the pairs of wire stays to negotiate, all of which are attached to the tower above halfway: six running forward down to the long passerelle, four to the gunwale either side of the cabin and another four to the stern.

By the time he sets foot on the roof of the cabin, Caterina has counted to forty–eight. Forty–eight steps!

As soon as Giuseppe sets foot on the roof, he crosses himself, glances back up and then smiles at her as if to say he knows he is a little bit crazy, but…

He gets down off the roof leaving her to stare up at the platform.

"Crazy," she murmurs to herself. "Crazy, eh? Well, perhaps not as crazy as me." Caterina takes off her hat and ties it to the chair. She looks up, she looks down and then in one fluid movement she stands up and places her hands on the metal tubes of the tower.

Ninolino, Karl and Enzo are swapping stories, kidding each other and laughing, and Antonio and Giuseppe are inside the cabin, talking.

She lifts her hands up and steps onto a rung. "Now remember," she says to herself, "don't look down, just concentrate," and she begins to climb.

"Twenty metres," she says. "Come on, count." She lifts her right leg and feels for the foothold, and once she has set it square on the rung, she lifts her left hand up, gains hold and lifts her leg. Slowly, as though in a dream, she ascends, hand over hand, foot over foot.

One, two, three, on and up in as smooth a rhythm as her limbs will allow. "Four, five, six," she whispers.

She slows. "No, don't stop, keep moving. Keep moving."

The wind ruffles her hair, she can feel it cool against her cheek.

"Twelve, thirteen, fourteen." She slows again, leaning in to the tower, holding on tight. "Relax, Caterina," she murmurs. "Just keep going." Urging her legs and arms to resume their motion, she climbs. "Fifteen, sixteen, seventeen."

A voice from below.

"Papà," Enzo calls. "Come quick!"

He steps out from the shadow of the cabin.

Enzo points.

He looks up. "Caterina," he shouts, the urgency plain for the others to hear, "Stay where you are. Don't go any higher."

At the sound of his voice, her muscles stiffen and her legs very suddenly feel heavy. She stops, but refuses to look down. "No, I'm okay. Leave me. I'm fine."

"No," he shouts. "Please, wait, I am coming."

"Papà?" Enzo asking, no, imploring. "Two of you? The tower is not strong enough; it will not take it."

"Tell Pasquale," he shouts, climbing onto the roof of the cabin. "Bring the feluca into wind, slowly. Tell him to keep her steady."

A wolf–whistle. "Hey, Pasquale."

The capobarca peers down from his platform. "No, signora. No, please go back down. You must not."

Caterina looks up. She can see Pasquale's head, see his lips move, but she cannot, or perhaps will not, hear whatever it is he is saying. She looks out at the coastline: it is beautiful, a bright yellow rim of sand, a road cut into the hillside, the hills rising to mountains, the sun beating down.

"Eighteen, nineteen, twenty."

The metal between her hands and beneath her feet trembles and the tower begins to sway ever so gently from side to side.

"Antonio, leave me. I'm fine, don't follow me, I'm okay." She climbs again. "Twenty–one, twenty–two–"

He is coming up after her; she can feel the disturbance in the metal.

"Don't, please," she pleads. "Go back."

She feels the tower still; he has paused.

"Caterina, this is madness. Please come down before you get any higher. Please. Think of your daughter. Think of me. Think of yourself," he pleads.

"Three, four, five, six." Hand over hand, foot above foot. "God," she asks, "how many more can there be?"

"You are over halfway," he calls. "Don't, whatever you do–"

"Look down? No, I won't. I have no intention of looking anywhere but where I'm putting my hands; my feet will follow; they must."

The mast sways, the wind blows and the air is warm and salty.

"Twenty–seven." She urges herself up, one rung at a time; one reach, one grab at a time. "Twenty–eight." She groans, she grunts, she breathes deep through her nose and exhales through her mouth. "Twenty–nine."

Caterina is slowing, becoming aware that her limbs now feel heavy and if not heavy, then leaden. "Thirty." Her arms ache and her fingers flutter and quiver as they feel for the next rung. She shivers. Even in the heat, she shivers.

"Thirty–one." And slowly, inevitably, like cogs drying, in need of some life–giving lubrication, in need of oiling, in need of something, she grinds to a halt. "Thirty… two."

"No," Antonio shouts. "Now you must keep going, you are too high to turn back."

"Too high," she whispers. "Too high. Well how high am I? I must be nearly at the top." Caterina glances up. "Oh no, where was I? Now I've lost count."

Pasquale has the trapdoor open; he is looking down on her. Like Charlie, somewhere above, high up in the heavens, he is looking down on her.

"Oh, Charlie! What am I doing? I let you down. I'm so sorry. The one thing you asked of me and I couldn't do it. Forgive me, please. I am so tired of running."

The tower wobbles.

"You are not running, Caterina. Up here, there is nowhere for you to run." It is Antonio; he has climbed up and is now just below her. She can feel his presence.

"And Charlie is not here," he says, tenderly and firmly, as if he is soothing a distressed child. "You are here and I am here. No, do not look down."

"Oh, but I'm not. I don't know what I was thinking. This isn't me; this is someone I thought I could be; someone I wanted to be. Oh, I can't; I'm too tired. Just leave me alone, please." She closes her eyes, leans back and breathes deep, tasting the salt on her tongue, smelling the freedom of the air, letting it in and holding it in until her lungs threaten to burst.

"No, Caterina, don't lean back." Antonio climbs and swings round the tower so that his head is level with hers. "Open your eyes, Caterina. Look at me. Know that I am here."

And she does open her eyes, and they are white with fear and frozen like ice and she does not see him. "I can't do this, Antonio. I can't."

"Yes, you can. You must listen to me, Caterina. When my wife left me, I became blind to the world; I could only see the storm raging inside me. This storm, this turmoil, it threatened to overwhelm me, it took away my desire to live and without Enzo and Angelica's love, the storm in my heart would have destroyed me." Antonio does not shout; he does not need to; his face is but a hand's width from hers. And yet he projects his voice from deep down in his chest, as though it is his soul speaking to her. "Look at me, Caterina. No, don't look down. You have to go on. If you do not, you will remain forever lost to the storm in your heart."

She stares at his blue eyes as the tears stream from hers. There is nothing she can do to stem them, for if she takes her hand off the tower, she will fall. "Does it ever stop, this storm?"

"Yes, yes. The storm comes to its own end, but you cannot always wait for the winds to blow themselves out. We must go on, otherwise we stay caught in our storm and none of us are strong enough to weather such sadness. You blame yourself for Charlie's death, why? What happened?"

She shakes her head so violently that the tower trembles and when she has finished, her eyes are wild with terror. "No, you don't understand. I don't blame myself for his death, I blame myself for not having the courage to do the one thing he asked of me: the one thing, the only thing, the one wretched bloody thing I could not bring myself to do."

Antonio hesitates, uncertain of the wisdom in reaching out his hand to her in case his touch frightens her. "And why was this request of his so hard to honour, Caterina? What was it that Charlie asked you to do that you could not?"

Her eyes are glazed with tears and her face pale as dawn. "No, I can't," she says. "Don't you understand, I can't. I just can't."

"No, Caterina, it is not that you cannot; it is that you could not and it is now time for you put down the burden of your failing. Tell me, what was it Charlie asked you to do?"

She blinks, to clear her tears and whispers into the wind: "He asked me to end his life, Antonio. He asked me to kill him and I couldn't bring myself to do it."

Chapter 15

At first, the significance of what she has just said does not register with him and he looks simply back at her. But then slowly, perhaps like the swordfish harpooned, he comes to understand the gravity and the hopelessness of her situation. Antonio frowns and repeats very slowly, "Your husband asked you to kill him, why?"

"Because," she begins, but then her voice fails her as she tries to recall the words she has worked so hard to forget; words she had banished to the furthest corners of her mind where, since Charlie's death, they have lain and festered and multiplied and infected her entire being. "Because he was dying. Because he was dying, slowly and horribly and there was nothing anyone could do to free him from the captivity of his prison. Nothing anyone could do, except me."

They stand, clinging to the tower; two people alone but for each other and the wind and the sea and the never–ending sky.

Now, he does lay his hand on hers and as he'd feared, her arms very quickly surrender their strength.

"Caterina, you must breathe, you must hold on and you must carry on. I want you to climb. Come on, I know you have it within you to do this. Move your leg up, take a step. Slowly, do it. If you cannot do it for yourself, then do it for me. For me, for your daughter and for Enzo who is watching us. Lift your foot. Do it now."

Her legs, too, surrender their rigour and turn to jelly. Caterina pauses and looks through him. "I have to, don't I?" she states, dreamily.

"Yes, you have to. You must go on. Now, lift your leg." His voice is all at once intense and yet calm, comforting like a balm that takes the heat out of a burn. "There is only one way now and that is for you to go on. Come, move your leg."

And slowly, she does; tentatively at first, feeling for and finding the next rung, easing her foot forward and settling onto it.

"Good. Now your other leg. Push. Stand up."

And she does.

"Now your hand. Lift it. Reach up. Hold."

And she does, gradually. And she starts to move as before, slower than before but with purpose and renewed strength and now, without faltering, Caterina climbs up and up.

"Ten more," he says, rising beside her. "That is good, keep going. Count out loud. Speak. Lift your voice as you are lifting your arms and legs."

"One," she says. The temptation to wipe the tears from her eyes is difficult to resist; if only she could lift her hand to them. "Two. And three. Four."

"Mind the stay," he says. "Lift your arm inside it. Good. And again. Five, say it."

"Five... Six... Seven... Eight."

"Nine," he says. "Just a few more."

"Antonio, you said ten and we are not there yet."

"Yes, but it is only a few more. Come on, Caterina, keep going. Pasquale, are you ready?"

"I am." His voice is gravelled and raw. "Keep coming, signora. Keep coming. Now stop. Reach up with your right hand."

She does so, feeling for his. He is there; their fingertips brush. And before she has the time to realise what is going on, Caterina feels the warm reassurance of his hand about her wrist.

"Be careful, Pasqua," Antonio says.

"Careful?" the capobarca repeats, dismissively. "How can a man be careful in the face of such madness? Let go, signora. Let go of the tower, I have you."

And she feels herself hauled upwards through the hatch as though she is a cork drawn from a bottle. In an instant, she is through the trapdoor and up onto the platform.

"Now," he orders, "hold on to the rail. No, you cannot sit down; your legs must work first. Stand up, breathe and when you are ready, open your eyes, but do not to look down."

Caterina feels Antonio's hands at her waist, steadying her.

He encourages her to a small seat and when she can feel the lip of the seat against the back of her thigh, he eases her down. "Caterina," he says, "you have been brave and you have made it. Thank the Madonna and all the saints. Now, as Pasquale says, open your eyes."

And when she does and the wind has dried her tears and her eyes have found their focus, Caterina is met by the cerulean sky, a brilliant white disc of cloud perched above the green, green slopes of Aspromonte, the tall red and white pylon astride the yellow sands of Capo Peloro and an azure sea that glistens and sparkles as though Neptune has sprinkled the surface with diamonds.

"Oh Antonio. Oh Pasquale, I don't think I have ever seen anything so beautiful. Can it be real? Am I on top of the world?"

———

Beppe is waiting on the beach inside the breakwater. He pats her arm, grins and scratches his head. "Women, eh? Like the sea, a mystery."

"Yes, Beppe, and like the sea, eternal."

The journey home to Ganzirri had remained fairly uneventful after the drama of La Signora's ascent to the crow's nest. The boys had wandered about below, looking up every now and again and shaking their heads in disbelief.

As far as Caterina was concerned, and once she'd grown used to the giddying elevation of her position, she had exalted in her freedom from the constraints of the secret by which she had been bound.

She had watched wide–eyed as dolphins had raced beneath the waves, leaping gracefully to spiral in the air before slapping back down in frothy explosions of white water. They had seemed to sense the joy of her abandonment; they had made her laugh and delight in their apparent immunity from the pressures of human existence; they had seemed to her carefree and she had shared in their lightness of being.

After a while, Antonio had left her and descended to oversee the offloading of their catch, and Pasquale, when he wasn't concentrating on the feluca's course, had eyed her warily.

At one point, just before he'd pulled back the levers controlling the engines and wheeled the helm to bring her head to wind, he had glanced at her and said, "You are crazy, you know that."

And Caterina had looked back at him and smiled and replied, "Yes, Pasquale, I am. Perfectly crazy."

Getting her down had proved a protracted affair. Giuseppe had scaled back up the tower and Enzo had run a rope up to him, which he had then fed through the trapdoor, secured through a shackle and looped around her shoulders. He'd pulled a face at her, a curious gurning with which he wanted her to understand that he was about to pull her leg. "Now, you don't need to be afraid; I will hold you."

In the end, he needn't have worried, for Caterina had climbed back down without so much as a pause or slip – the boys had applauded, though this was perhaps more with relief than any desire to show their appreciation of her ridiculous gymnastics – and when, finally, she'd set her feet on the deck, Caterina had found her balance removed and she'd staggered about like a Friday–night drunk.

"Perhaps it is better for you to spend the rest of the day on terra firma," Antonio had said.

"Beppe?"

"Signora?"

"Antonio tells me that you remember a great deal about the war years."

He eyes her, beadily, then shrugs. "Some would say."

She waits and watches as the Salvazione motors back out into the Strait. The afternoon is baking hot, too hot for even a mad woman to be standing in the full glare of the sun.

Beppe grins; his odd collection of teeth seeming to Caterina to change place, as if in some bizarre game of musical chairs. "Why? What is it that you want to know?"

"There is something I want to show you," she replies. "I don't have it with me right now. I'll bring it with me tomorrow. Will you be here in the morning?"

He rolls a cigarette between his gnarled, arthritic fingers, licks the paper, picks a few strands of tobacco from the ends and deposits them in his pouch. Beppe lights up, puffs and decides. "With the sun, I will be here."

Caterina leaves Beppe to paint an odd assortment of oars, and strolls back up the beach to the lane. She stops by Antonio's door; Aida sits preening herself in the shade of the step.

She bends and strokes her head, and the cat presses against Caterina's hand in appreciation of her affection.

"You see it all, don't you, Aida?" she murmurs, before turning and walking off in the direction of the lagoon and Angelica's house.

"Good afternoon," she says to the witch on the wall. "Must be hot in black."

The Pasticceria is closed; it is siesta time; Ganzirri is dozing.

Barely able to contain the excitement born of her ascent on the feluca, Caterina floats on a tide of euphoria through the lanes and soon enough arrives at the front door.

"What do you think our Angelica will be up to, eh?" she asks herself. "Feet up? Resting?"

The little cobbled street is quiet, quiet and deserted and cool in shadow. The handle gives as she presses and Caterina enters slowly, trying not to make a sound that might disturb her host.

Someone is in the kitchen. Someone? No; two people are talking and judging by the halting conversation one of them is definitely not Sicilian.

"Caterina, is that you?" Angelica calls.

"Yes, it is me," she replies, her foot on the first step of the stairs. "You have company, I'll leave you."

"No, come in, there is someone here to see you."

She pauses, frowning in thought, and turns into the living room. "To see me? Who earth would be here to see me?" Caterina glances at Angelica, then at her guest.

"Lucy!"

"Hello, mum."

CHAPTER 16

Caterina plays the guilty schoolgirl. "I know it's late, I'm sorry."

"Late?" Antonio smiles. "I think I have told you once already that you are never too late. Besides, I was expecting you, come in." He stands back for her.

The cat looks up and mews in welcome.

"Aida, you're still up." Caterina bends and strokes. "Talking of which, is Enzo…"

"No, he is in Messina. Would you like coffee or a glass of wine?"

She grins, mischievously. "Both?"

They sit on the sofa, together and closer to each other than the evening before. His coffee is thick and on the sweet side; the Blandanino dry. And relieved of the hindrance of observers, they sip and revel in the flavours as though they are elements fundamental to the chemistry of their attraction.

"Your daughter is here," he says.

"Yes," Caterina arches an eyebrow. "Word travels fast."

"Angelica called me. She said you were surprised to see her. You didn't know she was coming?"

"No, a complete surprise."

"Angelica, too, was surprised: by you, by your enthusiasm and by how pleased you were to see your daughter."

"I was pleased to see her." Caterina frowns at him. "Why wouldn't I be?"

"Ten days ago you would not have been so pleased."

She considers this for a moment. "Mm, you may have a point there."

"Angelica said you looked like a woman who had been delivered from sin. Redemption, I believe that was the word she used."

Caterina hides behind her glass, as she searches for her own words to describe her moment of madness on the tower. "Or perhaps a conversion. Perhaps I won't feel the need to persecute myself any longer. Maybe I have rediscovered my faith: my belief in myself." She gazes at him, remembering. "You showed me that light, Antonio; without you I would still be stumbling down the road to Damascus."

"Where is your daughter staying?" he asks, batting her compliment, her acknowledgement, aside. "At Angelica's with you?"

"No, Angelica managed to get her a room at the Donato and I took her for dinner in a restaurant by the lagoon. Actually, no, come to think of it I should say she took me for dinner and she talked; I listened."

"What did she have to say?" If he is steeling himself to hear news he would rather not, Antonio shows no sign of it.

"As you can imagine, quite a lot."

"She thinks you are behaving in a childish manner and that you should return to England with her."

"Of course, though she stopped short of looking down her nose at me and calling me an idiot; that was some small consolation, I suppose. Antonio, there's not much point in me repeating her monologue, except to say that the more important news is that she is getting married. Her boyfriend, or fiancé I should now say, wanted to come down here and ask my permission; that's why she's been so desperate to get in touch." Caterina pushes the hair back from her face and glances across at Aida, sleeping soundly in the armchair. "Silly me, eh? And there I was thinking she was worried about where her mother had got to. No, that's not fair of me, she was concerned, it's just that... Oh, I don't know. She seems to have made everything that bit more complicated. It's like the moment I thought I'd at last found some direction, I suddenly find myself pulled in another."

Antonio lowers his head, the schoolteacher about to ask his pupil to own up to a misdemeanour. "Did you tell her about what happened at Capo Peloro? Or perhaps I should ask how much have you told her about what happened?"

She smiles, though not so mischievously as when she'd met him at the door, but... "Yes, I told her. I told her I had gone swimming in the wrong place at the wrong time and that a charming man had appeared out of nowhere and rescued me."

"Did you tell her you were some time in intensive care?"

"Mm." Caterina glances at the ceiling, her tone suggesting she cannot remember the detail.

"Did you tell her you were in the hospital?"

"I, er..." Surely, the answer to that one is written somewhere on the ceiling.

"And did you tell her that the doctor was under the impression that you may have been trying to take your own life and that the only way he would agree to signing your discharge was if you were released into someone else's care?"

She sits up straight, her legs crossed, her expression sincere. "Look, Antonio, there's no profit in my scaring the hell out of her. Knowing Lucy, she'd return with a court order and half a dozen men in white coats to drag me onto a private jet and deposit me in some nuthouse."

"Can she be that bad, your daughter?"

"No, of course not, I'm exaggerating. But there's nothing to be gained by frightening her; particularly when she's feeling so rosy about her own future."

"And you did not tell her about your ascent today?"

"No. Even I think that was a bit crazy. Look at it this way, Antonio, if she thinks I'm happy here, there's half a chance she won't worry when I tell her I'm coming back here."

"Coming back." His surprise is muted, controlled, understated. "That means you are going. Good. I think this is the right decision for you; I think this is best for you."

If ever a man has said one thing while meaning another, it is the man who sits in front of her with his arms folded and a resolute yet resigned look on his face.

"Best for me? Best for you? Or best for us?" Caterina leans towards him and places her hand on his knee, his broad, thick, dependable, reliable knee.

He drops his arms and very gently places his hand over hers. "If you go, you will not return, you know that."

She gazes deep into the blue pools of his eyes; eyes the same colour as the sea in which she'd nearly drowned and in which she'd watched the dolphins play.

"I've thought about it and yes, it's possible." Caterina smiles through her frown. "It's possible, but not probable, because the thought of not seeing you again tears me in two." She sweeps her hair from her face and winces at the ceiling, embarrassed by her openness and amazed by the ease with which she has said exactly what she feels. That she does not feel inclined to apologise for her honesty encourages her. "I suppose I could tell Lucy to get on with her life in the same way I suddenly find myself wanting to get on with mine, but that wouldn't be very... generous, very loyal, very... motherly of me. Not when she's already lost her father."

Although Caterina is now looking at Antonio, she is talking to herself as much as to him, for she is remembering her first day on the feluca, sitting in her white plastic chair beside the 'ntinna, the sun on her face, the breeze at her cheeks and the salt on her lips; watching him shape the metal into small strips, watching him meticulously and delicately attach the strips to the small wooden fish, watching him weigh the lures in his hands, no scales, no machine, no technology, simply his hands and a greater sense of knowing when something is right.

"The trouble is," she whispers, "I feel like the one who's learning to take her first steps."

Antonio turns her hand over so that her palm is against his; his touch is gentle, reassuring and wonderfully intimate. "You took your first steps when you climbed the tower today, Caterina. You will find your feet; I am certain of it."

"Certain of it? Yes, certain; that's what I said about you last night, isn't it? You are always certain, always so confident. Without having to think, you always know exactly what to do." And as last night, the colour rises in her cheeks, though this time the blood coursing through her form is driven by an entirely different pressure. "Well, now for once I know what you need to do, Antonio, and that is kiss me. For your sake and for mine, for our sake, please kiss me."

———————

They lie in his bed, both looking up beyond the ceiling and the stars, and both drifting alone and yet together in their sea of shared intimacy.

They had heard Enzo come in, his whispers to Aida, his footsteps on the stair, the closing of his bedroom door. If he was aware of her presence, he had not reacted other than to show his respect by keeping silent.

"Antonio?" she whispers.

"Yes, my love."

"What if I decided to stay?"

He leans up on his elbow and kisses her, at first long and deeply, then slowly and gradually as though he is withdrawing from her, breaking the bond that had not a few minutes before tied them together.

"And what if you did stay? What is there for you here?" He pauses in thought. "Caterina, I am a fisherman and I have only that which a fisherman can offer. Your life, the life you have been used to living, is not one that you can easily walk away from. Your family is your home and you cannot simply ignore the person you were and become someone new; that would be too much to expect. I have no money to speak of and I am not sophisticated. In the summer, all we have is heat and not enough water; in winter all we have is cold and too much rain. I have often thought that if we did not have the compassion of our Madonna, then…"

She looks up into his eyes, searching for what she isn't sure. Then she smiles. "If you're trying to sell me life in Ganzirri, you're not making a very good job of it."

"No, that's not what I'm trying to do. What I mean is, Vanaria was used to nothing and she wanted more: you have more, so how could you, why would you, want less? And then there is your daughter: she is your family and you are hers. Lucy has no father to guide her: she has only you."

"Me? Guide Lucy?" she replies, casually amused. "I only have her to guide me, you mean."

Antonio does not answer her though. He reaches out and caresses her breasts, her hips and the intimate contentment between her legs, as if he is tracing the contours of her body so that in the future, on cold nights or perhaps warm mornings, he will be able to recall the texture of her skin, the shape of her, the feel of her. He kisses her shoulder, breathes in her perfume and again withdraws.

"She has booked your flight?"

"Yes," Caterina whispers, her voice fracturing with emotion. "She has my future all mapped out for me: what I am going to do when I get home, sell the house, buy a flat, find a job, rebuild my life, everything."

"Home," he repeats. "You see, you said it, home." He sighs and smiles the resigned smile of a man who knows what's best, even if it is not what is best for him. "So, what time are you leaving for home?"

"Early afternoon flight, via Rome. Angelica has offered to drive us to the bus in Messina. I owe her so much; I don't know how I'll ever repay her for all her kindness." Her eyes fill with tears. "And I don't know how I'll ever be able to repay you, Antonio, I—"

"You know the real meaning of our word ciao, Caterina?"

"Yes, it means goodbye."

"No, Caterina," he frowns, for he knows she speaks Italian well enough. "Arrivederci means goodbye: we say ciao for both goodbye and hello, but we also use ciao when we tell someone we will see them again."

"Antonio, are you fishing tomorrow?"

He grins, playfully. "Of course, did I not just say I am a fisherman?"

"What time though? I mean what time is the Salvazione leaving in the morning?"

He raises an eyebrow. "You need to ask? If my memory serves me well, there was this English woman, a strange and unusual woman and one curiously attractive to sailors. She would call to the sailors as their feluca passed by Capo Peloro; it seems she liked to go fishing with them..."

"Very funny," she replies, though her response is in no way meant as a reproof. "Antonio, seriously, what time are you leaving in the morning?"

He shrugs. "Six–thirty, as normal. We will fish up in the bay of Gioia Tauro and then return to the Strait in the afternoon, why?"

"Because if you are leaving at six–thirty, we still have four hours before we have to say ciao."

CHAPTER 17

Caterina had strolled back through the village alone, greeting the witch on the wall and the cats on their steps, and lingering on the bench by the lagoon to watch the early morning mist disperse.

Closing the front door behind her, she hears Alberto in the bathroom upstairs and it is not long before he appears in the kitchen, resplendent if not dazzling in his whites.

"You are going? Today?" he asks.

She nods and looks away. "Alberto," she says, "thank you. Thank you for allowing me to be a part of your family, for allowing me into your home. I feel I may have stayed too long and I am truly grateful for your kindness."

He puts his hand on her shoulder and squeezes, affectionately. "It is not kindness, Caterina; it is our pleasure. Be strong." And with that he is gone, off to the port to shepherd the hundreds of folk and kilos of commerce coming and going across the busy Strait.

Angelica comes down just as Caterina is making her first cup of coffee. "Yes, I will have one, too," she says, and then, "You have been crying?"

"Yes, I guess I'm still a little sensitive when it comes to goodbyes."

"Antonio?"

572

"And Alberto. He has been so patient. You know, some of my friends find it hard enough to have their adult children home for a few days, never mind a crazy fifty–year–old woman."

"Crazy," Angelica repeats, as though she cannot decide whether the word describes someone wild or lunatic, or perhaps both.

They close their eyes and revel in the aromas of the coffee.

Angelica nods her approval and then chuckles. "If it was not Antonio who had told me you climbed the 'ntinna, I would not believe it. To the top! Right to the top! Surely, Caterina, you are crazy." She hunches her shoulders and cups her hands to her chest. "Eh, I should have known this when we met that morning on the beach. Or perhaps I did? Perhaps I saw the madness living in you. Perhaps I could see it was trying to get out."

"Yes, I think madness might be about right and for that I believe I owe you an explanation. Remember a week ago, you said I should tell you about Lucy's father when I felt I was ready. Well, now I am." She finishes her coffee and sits up straighter, as if preparing to deliver a eulogy.

"Charlie, Lucy's father… my late husband, died four years ago. We'd been married for nearly twenty–five years and for most of that time our life together had been… well, pretty wonderful really. That was, until Charlie was diagnosed with Motor Neurone Disease. I'll never forget the term the neurologist used, Amyotrophic Lateral Sclerosis; there, you see, it's burned in my brain like a brand on a cow's hide and, like a brand, it has owned me for the last six years. I won't bore you with the ghastly symptoms, except to say that he began to trip over a lot and he became extremely clumsy. He took to drinking a lot too, which was unusual for him, and he ignored his exercise, which he had always been fanatical about. However, I really only began to realise something was wrong when I noticed he was finding it increasingly difficult to pay attention. His mind began to wander, which was not what we were used to from a man who was always so clear of thought." Caterina pauses to draw breath, realising that on the rare occasions she has spoken of Charlie, breathing is something she forgets to do.

"I know of this disease: it is terrible." Angelica scowls. "It shows no respect; no mercy."

"No, you're quite right, it doesn't: not for the patient and not for his family or friends either. And, if you know about it, then you will know he became increasingly paralysed: first his hands, then his legs, then... well, pretty much everywhere. That paralysis, that gradual removal of his being, was hard enough to bear in itself; but you know how it is these days, the doctor diagnoses, you hit Google and by the end of the day, you're totally confused and you've frightened the hell out of yourself."

Caterina pauses to make another coffee and, possibly, to give herself time to think of what she needs to say. "Sorry, Angelica, it's just that by talking to you about it, I can now see how and why I got into such a state. I really didn't have much of a chance in the first place, did I? You see, before Charlie became completely incapacitated, before he couldn't speak or move his arms, he made me promise I would never allow him to become the person we both knew he was going to become. He said that when the time came, and he said I'd know that it was time by the look in his eyes, he wanted me to put a pillow over his face and suffocate him."

Although she does not cry as she is speaking, she has to wipe her eyes and blow her nose continually, and her voice, though definitely hers because she can feel her lips move and her throat vibrate, sounds as though it belongs to a distant news reader. "Sorry."

"Enough with the apologies, Caterina. Please, go on."

"I asked him if he wanted to go to Switzerland, to that euthanasia clinic, but he said he didn't, absolutely didn't. He said he wanted to be at home and he wanted my face to be... well, to be the last thing he saw." She glances at the ceiling and then at Angelica, searching and hoping, if not pleading, for some absolution. "I think, right at that moment, I felt every imaginable emotion: surprise, joy, anger, fear, disgust, sadness, love, loathing, hate, abandonment, resignation and in the strangest way trust. You see, Charlie put his life in my hands. His life! In my hands! And all because his life would no longer be in his own hands." She glances down at her palms; just as every morning when she washes her face, she glances down at them, wishing it was their fault and not hers.

"And I agreed, didn't I? Looking back, I've no idea why I did, but I suppose I was numb; all those emotions at once, it was like one enormous psychological concussion that anaesthetized my thinking."

Angelica passes her another tissue and says, "Then it is true what Antonio told me: your husband really did ask you to kill him?"

"Yes. And when the time came, when he could no longer move even the smallest muscle, he gave me that sad, pathetic look, that hollow stare from his hollow face; that expression which said, "Now, you promised. Don't wait. Don't let me down." And I couldn't bring myself to do it. I couldn't; it was just never going to happen. Well, after that, and for the last four months, I couldn't bring myself to look at him again; I just avoided his eyes, because every time I looked at him his eyes told me I had not done the one thing he'd asked; the one thing only I could do to prevent his suffering."

And now she cries; blowing her nose, wiping her wet cheeks and thumping the table in frustration. And she cries for a full five minutes before Angelica whispers, "Life is not ours to destroy, my dear Caterina. Life may be ours to give, but we do not have the right to take it away. Only God can decide."

"Yes, you are so right, so very, very right." She fixes Angelica with an uncompromising stare, adding, "And because you are so right, I will never, ever forgive him."

The avenue, like the lagoon beside it, is deserted. "You didn't want your Lucy to come with you?" Angelica asks.

"Are you kidding? I didn't even want you to come but, as you so sensibly pointed out, I'd never make it in time if I had to walk." Caterina turns to look at her driver. "And I know what you're thinking: I could have gone down to the beach and seen them off, it would have saved you the trouble of having to run me up to Capo Peloro. But I'd never have been able to hold it all together and I'd prefer them to remember me as the crazy 'ngrisa who climbed the mast rather than that blubbering wreck they left on the beach."

They pull up in the shade of an olive tree that stands, like a weary sentry, beside the stone walls of the old Roman fort.

"My mother told me that during the war this fort was occupied by Italian troops; an artillery battery. Think of it: a war in the middle of all this beauty." Angelica locks the car and they start walking up the sandy lane towards the beach. "Not long before she died, my mother confessed to me that during the war she killed a soldier."

"Your mother?"

"Yes, my mother, Mira, and in this very lane. She killed a fascist corporal, a man who could not keep his mouth shut. I don't know if I believe her; it is possible, I suppose: they were very desperate times. I asked Beppe and he said something bad happened, but he will never talk about it." Angelica chuckles to herself. "I'll say this for my mother, she was a tough one; whatever she asked me to do, I never waited for her to ask a second time.

"Only God can decide," Caterina states.

"Yes," Angelica replies. "Only God and my mother, eh?"

They walk through the cool, clean air and come to a raised path of duckboards, which lead down to the beach. The sand, too, is cool beneath their feet and the dew of morning sparkles before them.

"I'll wait here," Angelica says. "You go down to the water's edge. They will be along soon."

Here and there, a handful of men are casting their lines out into the Strait, and across the way, below the soaring flanks of Aspromonte, the curiously alien red and white pylon looks ready to leap from its perch to join its brother soaring behind her.

The sun is clear above the ridge now and Caterina raises her hand to shade her eyes, gazing south in search of the feluca.

"Where are you, Antonio?" she murmurs.

And sure enough, on a flat shimmering sea the Salvazione is making her way up towards the neck of the Strait; the feluca's impossibly tall metal mast, her 'ntinna, rising up to pierce the sky, her passarelle extending forward from her bow like a long arrow. Antonio stands out front on the platform, his hands holding the rail to keep himself steady, and Pasquale and Giuseppe sit up top in the crow's nest, gesturing, gesticulating, probably arguing. On the deck, she can see the boys, Enzo, Ninolino and Karl talking and joking and slapping each other on the back: the day will be good, the sea will be clear, the catch will pay their wages.

Caterina waits, patiently. And when the feluca clears the turbulent, tidal waters of the approach to the neck of the Strait, it is the avvistatore who spots her standing on the beach.

Giuseppe points, he waves, he leans over and shouts to those below.

The boys turn and Antonio pauses and looks towards her.

Caterina raises her arms and waves. And no longer does she feel like the sailor's wife waving in farewell; for now, she is no longer sad; now, her happiness outweighs her sadness and she wishes them well and hopes the sea and sky will look kindly on the hunters in the same way the sea and the sky has looked kindly on her.

The crew of the Salvazione wave back: the two up high from the crow's nest, the three below from their deck and the funcitta from his passarelle.

She can see their smiles; she can hear their voices and she can feel them just as if they had their arms around her.

The blue feluca motors steadily away in the direction of the great rock, Scylla, and the capobarca and avvistatore return their attention to the sea. The cabin masks the crew from her view and the funcitta is still waving as the Salvazione passes beyond her sight.

"Good luck, Antonio," she murmurs. "Be safe."

"The café," Angelica says, taking her hand off the steering wheel and pointing as they enter the square. "We will stop and take a coffee. They are open now and I thought you would like a mezza con panna e brioche."

"Mezza con panna?"

"Yes, half coffee and half cream. It is a good flavour, a strong taste for you to remember."

They take a table beneath the awning and gaze out across the Strait to the terracotta roofs of Villa San Giovanni. A long and low vessel glides up through the Strait.

"The Chiesa Madonna della Lettera." Angelica nods at the church to their right and as she does so, bells chime and clang in glorious union. "You see where the statues should be? The niches are empty. You see where the beautiful stained–glass windows should be? They are no more. Damaged during the war and never replaced. This square: this is where my mother had her café."

Beside the piazza, a white framed plaque commemorates Largo, Giovanni Cavallaro, Lieutenant of the Carabinieri, fallen at Nassiriya (Irak) 12th November 2003.

Reading it quietly to herself, Angelica murmurs, "The wars, they never cease, eh?" She looks for the waiter. "Yes, my mother was the proprietor."

"I remember, Antonio told me about her. How old was she at the time?"

"Oh, twenty–seven or twenty–eight; something like that."

The waiter asks: Angelica orders.

"Wasn't that unusual for a single woman to run a café in those days?" Caterina asks.

"Yes, but my grandfather, Enzo, in some ways like Antonio, was a very big man back then. A king among fishermen they called him and my mother was safe as long as he was there to watch over her."

Caterina frowns. "Didn't they have rationing. I mean, how did she keep the café open, I remember reading somewhere that during the war many people starved?"

"Oh yes. For many, it was easier to find tomatoes than water. My mother told me there was an officer in charge of the guns at Capo Peloro – you recall I showed you the fort where we parked this morning. He was from Emilia Romana, in the north, and he was very sweet on her; very kind to her and her parents. He would give them food in return for the fish my grandfather supplied him; he also gave my mother coffee so she could keep her café open."

"Your mother had protection from the officer, too, then."

Angelica sits up. "Yes, I think that was right. Days of protection and provision, she used to call them. She told me, also, that she and her father had been hiding a foreign sailor and that this officer found out, but refused to give them away because he was so fond of my mother. You should have asked Beppe; he knows about such things."

"Beppe, yes. I'd almost forgotten about Beppe; there's something I meant to show him."

The mezza con panna and brioche are brought to their table and Caterina stares in wonder at the cream and coffee. "This does look too good to be true." She sits back to savour. "Oh, it is delicious. Angelica, are you trying to bribe me to stay?"

"No," she replies. "You have stayed with us long enough."

"Yes, long enough but not too long, I hope. I don't know how to begin to thank you. Both you and Alberto; you've been so patient with me. And I don't know how or where I would be if it wasn't for your kindness." She reaches across the table, takes Angelica's hand and hopes the depth of her feeling is plain in her expression.

"Your thanks are welcome, Caterina," she replies, smiling warmly. "We are friends now; perhaps more than friends, perhaps even sisters."

"Angelica? I—" But the words catch in her throat and though she'd told herself she was done with crying, her eyes water once more.

"Yes... Antonio, you want to talk about him. You can. Talk to me now as if I was your sister."

Caterina takes another sip of the mezza, hoping the lively flavours of the coffee and cream will inspire her to choose the right words. "Antonio, yes, well. As you know, the day we met he risked his life when he leapt into the sea to save me from drowning and yesterday, he risked his life again when he climbed the tower to save me from falling. But more than that, much more than that, by helping me to get to the top he made me realise there is so much more I'm capable of. He showed me that there's nothing wrong in wanting to feel joy and love again — and yes, very probably fear and anger and pain and sorrow. All those emotions that I thought could only harm me, he made me realise I need to feel them, because that's why we live, to feel, to feel alive."

She smiles, as the tears that had been coming are now dammed by her understanding of just how alive he has made her feel. "So that's three times he's given me my life back. I want him to know that and I want him to understand that I recognise all he has done for me; I'd like you to tell him."

Angelica, in much the same way as Antonio, turns her hand and holds Caterina's, their palms together, each sensing the depth of feeling in the others affection. "I will, Caterina. Of course, I will."

A small grey Fiat sporting political posters and a large speaker on its roof rolls into the piazza. "Remember to vote," a tinny voice urges them. "Take control of your lives. Make decisions. Make a difference, if not for yourselves, then for your children. Remember it is your right to care about your future."

Angelica urges her little Fiat forwards and it seems as though she is in a desperate hurry, as opposed to the casual hurry with which she normally drives.

"What time are we meeting your daughter?"

"Not until midday. Are you sure you don't mind taking us into Messina? I'm sure we can get a taxi."

Angelica checks her watch and in so doing forgets the curve where the large fulua and the little luntro are hauled up by the side of the lagoon. The Fiat veers across the road and a car coming the other way swerves and hoots.

"Have you packed your things?"

Caterina shakes her head. "No, but that won't take me long."

"You said you wanted to see Beppe, eh?"

"Oh yes, I did, didn't I?"

She cannot see him, but when she calls, Beppe suddenly pops up from the middle of a large wooden rowboat, a brush in his hands, blue paint dribbling from it. He wears a loin cloth, several daubs of blue and a cigarette. He waves, sets down his brush and commences the protracted process of climbing out of the boat, down a stepladder and onto the beach.

By the time Beppe has hitched his bandy legs over the side and onto the stepladder, Caterina is holding it firm so that it no longer wobbles.

"La Signora Caterina!" He smiles, his few and separated teeth once more having assumed in his gums alternative perches to those of the day before. "I am told you are leaving us. Tell me, what have we done to deserve your inflicting such sadness upon us?" He takes the roll—up cigarette from between his thin lips, examines it and looks more than a little offended that he now needs to relight it.

"You have done nothing, Beppe," she replies, returning his smile, "I can assure you it grieves my heart just as much to leave you. Family calls."

"Family. Yes. Families are important. Without family, the world falls apart. So, goodbye or as we say ciao and please don't let the sun rise too many times before you return: beauty such as yours should know sunlight."

Caterina is driven to kiss the old man and hug his spindly frame, though whether she might break him in two or never manage to remove the paint from her clothes, she isn't sure.

"Beppe, before I go, there's something I'd like you to look at for me." She hands him the silver signet ring.

He gives it only a cursory glance and then looks back at her. "You expect me to look at this?"

She is only a little offended by his reaction — after all, who could possibly be more than only a little offended by a charming old man such as Beppe, so she says, "Yes."

He grins. "Then I will need my glasses. They are in my hut."

They walk up between the upturned boats to the wooden shack in which Beppe spends his afternoons resting and in which he maintains his treasure–trove of nautical paraphernalia.

"There," he says, pointing.

Caterina picks up a pair of scratched and worn half–moon glasses, and decides they will require cleaning before they are of any use.

A paraffin–soaked rag and a good deal of spitting and polishing later, they are ready and she plonks them on his small nose.

"Ah! These are not mine: I can see with them. Now, this ring, please." He turns it over and examines it. "A templar ring: a simple design, no hallmark or Sterling mark either. However, I think it is solid silver, not electroplate." He weighs it in his hand, picks up a magnifying glass and subjects the ring to further scrutiny.

Preferring the intense glare of the sun to the heavy, pungent aromas of chemicals one associates with paint, Caterina decides to step outside while the old man takes his time.

She gazes out across the water and beyond the breakwater, the feluche – feluche other than the Salvazione – are out patrolling the Strait and she fixes the image in her mind.

"Signora?" He startles her.

"Yes. Sorry, Beppe, I was miles away."

"How did you come by this ring?"

"My father left it to me when he died. Why?"

He eyes her with the same scrutiny he had just a moment before been applying to the ring and says, "Then your father's name was Nicolas and he was blind. And not only that, his mother's name was Lilla and she was from Messina."

Caterina is wide–eyed with disbelief; a heady giddiness affects her and she feels as she did when looking down from near the top of the 'ntinna. "From Messina? But how on earth can you tell all that by looking at the ring?"

"Because I saw this ring on your father's hand."

"My father was here, in Ganzirri?"

"Yes, to be exact, he was right there," he lifts a gnarled finger and points at the front door of Antonio's house, "seventy–six years ago. Mira, Antonio's mother, and her father, Enzo, looked after him in that house. He had been blinded by an explosion out in the Strait and he was brought ashore by an Italian sailor; a sailor who for his trouble was then killed by a Fascist corporal. Old Dottore Roselli and Mira cared for him; without their medical knowledge, there is no doubt he would have died."

"Dottore Roselli?"

"Yes, Dottore Roselli. His grandson is now a doctor at the Azienda Ospedaliera Papardo. This is perhaps why he placed you in the care of Angelica. Our families, the Ruggeris, the Sorbellos and the Rosellis, we go back many years."

"Hold on a moment for me please, Beppe. This is all a bit much to take in in one go. We are talking about my father, Nicholas Lock?"

"Oh, I did not know his surname, I only knew him as Nicolas: it was what Mira called him." Beppe grins. "He was Colapesce, come back to us from the sea. You know, Nicola the fishboy; the legend, the boy who keeps Sicily afloat."

"Yes, the subject of Guttuso's painting on the ceiling of the Teatro?"

"Exactly, yes, I told you to see it. Well, Mira had a romantic notion that this Englishman had been given up to her by the sea; she fell in love with him and when he had to go back to England after the hostilities finished, her heart was broken. Of course, there was no way he could have stayed." He shrugs and spays his palms. "First, he was in the navy and second, he was blind. It was not until many years after the war that she remarried."

"Remarried? She was married to my father?"

"No. She was married first to a local man. He died before the war; a tragedy of Mussolini's hubris; I have only a vague recollection of her first husband. It was their café in Torre Faro where Mira worked with Maria, my sister." Beppe fetches a couple of old wooden chairs and wipes the seat of one. "Antonio and Angelica's father was also a local man, a fisherman: Mira married him after the war but, sadly, the Strait claimed him."

Caterina sits. "So, Antonio and Angelica's mother knew my father."

"Yes, signora, Mira. And her father, too. Did I not say your nonna's name was Lilla and that she came from Messina?"

"Yes, Beppe, you did. How do you know that?"

"Because the ring originally belonged to Enzo, Mira's father. He told me the story of how Lilla came by the ring in the days after the great earthquake, of how she went to England and he became a fisherman, just like her father."

"Enzo?" she asks, repeating the name as much to buy herself time in which to absorb all the extraordinary information.

"Yes," he confirms. "And to think of it: all those years ago, they were separated by events far beyond their control: Enzo and Lilla by the capricious energies of nature, and your father and Mira by man's inhumanity to his brother."

"You are sure about this, Beppe?"

"Yes, that's why I needed the magnifying glass: the shape, the design, the Templar cross. I have no doubt it is this ring that brought you to Messina, to us."

Chapter 18

The day has been long, just as whenever they are out fishing all the days are long, and the sun is now falling towards the cradle of the Peloritan Mountains.

"Enough," Antonio shouts up to Pasquale.

The capobarca does not need to acknowledge his instruction, he simply flicks the silver helm over and the nose of the feluca comes around, edging towards the Sicilian coast.

"A good day," Enzo says.

"Yes," his father agrees. "A good day."

"Although perhaps not so good for you, papà."

"What makes you say that?"

"Oh, La Signora Caterina. Come on, papà, there is no profit in playing games, I know you too well. You are sad. Why else would you spend most of the day out alone in the sun on the passarelle?"

Antonio does not scoff as Enzo expects him to, he simply shrugs his broad shoulders and says, "Yes, to you I would not deny it. She was... There was... No, I am wrong, there is something in her way, something about her. It was as though she reminded me of someone I have always known; as though I had once loved her even though we had never met. I don't think I have felt such peace since the day you were born." He ruffles his son's hair and smiles.

"Then you have every reason to feel both happy and sad."

"How so?"

"Papà, I am learning love is like that; it is a sea of conflicting emotions. You are at the same time happy that you spent time with her and yet sad that she is gone. Do you think she will come back?"

"Oh, all things are possible. At least I have always believed so."

A few minutes later, the feluca Salvazione noses her way round the breakwater: the engines reduce their moaning, the deck surrenders its trembling and the boys make ready with boathooks to catch the mooring lines.

The shadows on the beach are long now and Beppe waits patiently to greet them. He is smiling, though it is impossible for those on the feluca to judge the true sense of his expression.

Leaning, one foot on the gunwale, his hand holding a wire stay, Antonio raises his hand and waves, and it is then that he notices a figure sitting in the long shadow thrown by the hull of an upturned dinghy.

Enzo, studying his father, feeling his loss as intensely as if it was his own, follows his line of sight and he, too, notices the figure. He rubs the salt from his eyes, looks again, and his face adopts a broad, relieved, joyous smile.

"Yes, son," Antonio says, "Caterina! You were right, it is a good day. A very good day."

ACKNOWLEDGEMENTS

Constant Tides would not have been written without the assistance of many people, first and foremost Tony Freno and Christine Merel, who introduced me to Messina, arranged interviews with historians and journalists, and regaled me with spellbinding stories; their inspiration and patience was fundamental to my learning about the great city, the coastline of the Strait and the character of its communities. I owe them a significant debt.

Francesco Libro, a font of knowledge who has very generously permitted me to use his beautiful photograph for the cover of this novel, kept me honest when indolence tempted me to err and made it possible for me to spend time on a *feluca*, a swordfish fishing boat.

Nino and the crew of the feluca *Antonio Padre* welcomed me on board and ensured I neither dehydrated nor fried to a crisp. Through fifteen-hour days of relentless sun we gained each other's respect and confidence; they have left their mark upon me.

Angelica Nuccio and Francesca Quatarone provided me with a wealth of information, put up with my feeble attempts to converse in Italian and allowed me a deeper insight into the people, the architecture and the cuisine of the region.

Leading historian Dottore Franz Riccobono gave me his time and in so doing pulled back the curtains to the stage that was the catastrophe of Il Terremoto dei Terromoti, the Earthquake of Earthquakes in December 1908; his depth of knowledge is profound and his book on the subject is the most consummate narrative and photo record of those dramatic events.

Direttore Responsabile Geri Villaroel of the cultural journal of Messina, *Moleskine*, answered my queries and subsequently furnished me with copies of his articles from the newspaper Gazetta del Sud; his contribution, particularly in my understanding of feminine attitudes to Mussolini, proved invaluable.

In Taormina, Il Direttore Francesco and Signora Mimma Spadaro, Maria Puglio and Magdalena Polewska opened the doors and my eyes to what is perhaps the most culturally significant European home of the last century. Having read Daphne Phelps' *A House in Sicily*, I thought I knew all there was to know about Casa Cuseni; I was wrong but, fortunately for me, Maria and Francesco decided a presumptuous English writer worthy of their education.

Dr Tina Grayson leant me books, produced articles, answered questions and provided vital insight into relevant medical conditions.

H.F. (Bert) Cooper RNVR, my uncle and co-author of *MTBs At War* (Sutton Publishing in association with The Imperial War Museum), served in the Mediterranean theatre during the Second World War. His memoir and manuscript *Dusk To Dawn* is a frank and vivid account of operations in the Mediterranean and the Strait of Messina, and I am grateful to his daughter, Carol Scoble, for her permissions.

Roger Perkins and John Wilson's book *Angels In Blue Jackets* (Picton Publishing) contains a detailed account of the extraordinary international relief effort in the days following the great earthquake; The Times newspaper of the period reported many eyewitness accounts, both of the earthquake and later the Allied invasion of Sicily; and the works of authors too numerous to mention helped ensure the accuracy of this historical novel. If there are mistakes, they are mine and mine alone.

Finally, I must thank the people of Messina who have welcomed me into their homes and their hearts, and encouraged me to tell their story.

One afternoon in the Piazza Cairoli, I asked Christine and Tony the species of the trees shading us from the glare of the June sun. Christine suggested they were a variety of fig tree; however, not being one hundred per cent certain, Tony approached a gentleman strolling by and asked him if he knew. He replied that he didn't and apologised for his lack of knowledge. We stood for a few minutes examining the leaves, before retiring to a table outside the Bar Santoro where, after several coffees and much debate, we were still none the wiser. Then, to my surprise, the gentleman reappeared to inform us they were Ficus benjamina, weeping fig trees: his brother was something of an authority and the man had gone to the trouble of calling him to gain the answer to our query. This, I came to understand, is how the citizens of Messina are: they are charmingly polite, invariably interested and only too happy to invest their time in helping others learn about their city. The people of Messina are also incredibly enduring and rightfully proud of their heritage. I thank them.

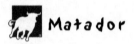